Tell Anna She's Safe

A NOVEL

BRENDA MISSEN

Inanna poetry & fiction series

INANNA PUBLICATIONS AND EDUCATION INC.
TORONTO, CANADA

We gratefully acknowledge the support of the Canada Council for the Arts and the Ontario Arts Council for our publishing program.

We are also grateful for the support received from an Anonymous Fund at The Calgary Foundation.

Excerpts from #s 3, 16, 19, 62 from *Tao Te Ching by Lao Tzu, A New English Version, with foreword and notes,* by Stephen Mitchell. Translation copyright © 1988 by Stephen Mitchell. Reprinted by permission of HarperCollins Publishers. UK and BC rights: Macmillan Publishers Ltd., 25 Eccelston Place, London SW1W 9NF, United Kingdom.

Cover/interior design: Luciana Ricciutelli

Library and Archives Canada Cataloguing in Publication

Missen, Brenda, 1961-
	Tell Anna she's safe / Brenda Missen.

(Inanna poetry and fiction series)
ISBN 978-1-926708-20-1

		I. Title. II. Series: Inanna poetry and fiction series

PS8626.I825T45 2011		C813'.6		C2011-900730-4

Printed and bound in Canada

Inanna Publications and Education Inc.
210 Founders College, York University
4700 Keele Street, Toronto, Ontario, Canada M3J 1P3
Telephone: (416) 736-5356 Fax: (416) 736-5765
Email: inanna@yorku.ca Website: www.yorku.ca/inanna

This book is for Louise
and her indomitable spirit.

Throw away holiness and wisdom,
and people will be a hundred times happier.
Throw away morality and justice,
and people will do the right thing.
Throw away industry and profit,
and there won't be any thieves.

If these three aren't enough,
just stay at the centre of the circle
and let all things take their course.

—Tao Te Ching

PART I: SEARCHING

*[The Master] helps people lose everything
they know*
                        —Tao Te Ching

1.

I WOULD NEVER HAVE GIVEN the yellow Sidekick a second glance if it hadn't been parked in the middle of a construction zone. Or if a temporary traffic light hadn't stopped me close by.

I was on River Road, on my way home from my twice-weekly visit to the chiropractor. I didn't mind the half hour drive to Wakefield at the end of the workday. The bottleneck on the interprovincial bridge had always thinned out by the time I made it up the long slope of highway, past our place in Chelsea, Marc's and mine, and deeper into the Gatineau Hills. And I knew I would have this old rough road to myself afterward.

Except, today, I was stopped at a traffic light in the middle of nowhere. I would have taken the main highway if I'd known about the construction. But I wasn't sorry. The delay gave me a chance to drink in the view. The road, aptly named, ran like a second river beside the Gatineau. Straight out of the opposite shore rose high, ancient, enduring fortresses of Shield. The craggy grey rock was most visible at this time of year: the snows were sloughed off; the spring greens hadn't yet replaced them.

But today I barely glanced at the hills. My eyes were drawn to the open water. It was a welcome sight. Our bay was still locked in ice. The river up here was narrower, with a stronger current, though it was still unnaturally wide. The entire lower Gatineau had been dammed and flooded in the 1920s. I always wondered about the lands and cottage remains submerged in its depths.

The construction zone was located right at the point where the road curved up and away from the river. The reason for that was clear now that I was stopped. Here was where the railway tracks crossed the road and ran parallel to the river the rest of the way down to the city. The steep drop separating the rise of the road from the tracks and the river below was being reinforced with cages of rock. The work was blocking the northbound lane.

The light turned green, and I took my turn in the single lane. That was when I noticed the Sidekick. It was parked on the narrow shoulder, facing south. There was barely room to squeeze by. I wondered at the construction worker who had parked it there. But it didn't look like a construction worker's car.

That was my first thought.

It looked more like a woman's car.

That was my second thought.

It looked, in fact, like Lucy's car. I made a mental note to ask her if her Sidekick had a white geometrical design painted on the side. Maybe she had come up here to go for a walk on the tracks. Many people did. The trains no longer ran.

And that was my only thought about Lucy Stockman the rest of my drive home.

I had other preoccupations. I had two dogs who had been cooped up all day. I had sciatic pain that the chiropractor assured me was going to be gone in time for spring cycling and running. And I had an absent boyfriend working on a construction project fourteen-hundred kilometres away, who said he wasn't coming back to me at the end of the summer.

Marc's absence was the reason the dogs were cooped up. For most of the year, he was on a job site nearby and could check on them. I hated leaving them tied up or in the house, but Beau was a wanderer and Belle tended to follow.

I came to the junction at Highway 105, where the Tulip Valley Restaurant sat, and turned south on the highway to our turn-off at Chemin Cameron. I hoped the dogs' bladders were holding out.

Like many Chelsea roads, Cameron sloped down to the river from the old highway and branched off into several dead-ends. Our house was at the end of one of those dead-ends, the only house on the road. Marc had built it from hand-hewn logs salvaged from a pioneer homestead. It was tucked into the side of the hill, above the tracks, high enough for a clear view of the river.

I limped my way up the stairs. It was a long climb, leading to a wraparound deck and the front door. Two golden retrievers sat looking out through the glass. At the sight of me, they stood up in unison, bumping into each other in a mutual tail-wagging wriggle. Once the door was open, they ran circles around me, then raced down the stairs to relieve themselves.

I was about to head down after them when a familiar sound, like soft wind chimes, brought me over to the deck railing.

The spring winds had finally done their work. They had whipped up the water at the edge of the frozen bay. The waves had been working at the ice all day, breaking it into tiny pieces. They tinkled in the undulating water, working closer and closer to shore. I smiled wryly. Just the day before, I had hosted our annual ice-breaking-up party (on my own) to herald the arrival of spring. It had been a day too early.

Marc would have liked to have seen this. Every morning in April he waited for the day he could put one of his boats in the water. They sat, a good half-dozen in all, on a multi-tiered rack below me, a fleet of white-water, flat-water, and racing canoes in various designs and colours. The canoes mocked me from below: *you misled him.*

That was the bomb Marc had dropped on me the previous week.

A bomb set off by a fight about Lucy.

Looking out over the river, listening to the icy chimes, I choked on a laugh. Marc's stand on Lucy seemed eminently understandable now that he wasn't here to impress it on me.

I had been living with Marc for two years when I met Lucy. I was working, then as now, for a small company called Roots Research that did contract work, mostly for the museums. The National Gallery was also a client, and that year I was putting together a research package for a retrospective on Emily Carr.

Lucy was the contractor who had been hired to write the panels and the guide for the retrospective. Our first meeting was at the glass-cathedral Gallery with our client on a cold, damp November day.

Her grin and the grip of her hand immediately set her apart from the other writers I had worked with. Where the others seemed to channel their personalities into their writing, Lucy's seemed to explode out of her tiny, wiry frame. She emanated intensity, sexuality, and an enviable self-possession. There was no other word for it: Lucy Stockman was *alive*.

Standing beside her, I felt big and gawky. My freckles and strawberry blonde hair were no match for her smooth tanned skin and long, glossy dark hair. I wondered what she did to keep so trim and fit. It was hard to judge her age. It turned out she had more than a decade on me—she was in her early forties.

She talked very fast, as if being paid by the word. "I hear you live up in the Gatineaus. Are you right on the water? Lucky you. I've always wanted to live in the country. One day I'll get up there. It's in the five-year plan." She grinned, as if at a private joke. There was a faint aroma about her—not quite perfume, not quite musk. Distinctive. But I couldn't place it.

While the client went over the details of the project, Lucy produced from a thermos, and drank, mug after mug of steaming black coffee. With each mug, her sentences and ideas spilled out faster. They were good ones.

At the end of the meeting, she gripped my hand again. "I look forward to working with you, Ellen McGinn. Maybe you'll invite me up to your place. I think I could commune with Emily Carr up there."

"We aim to provide the complete experience at Roots Research," I joked back.

Lucy beamed at me. "I'm sure we could commune with Emily Carr over a glass of wine at my place, too. I'm in Ottawa South. Drop in any time."

"I'll even hand deliver the research package."

"Deal," she said.

She turned to our client and alternated her cheeks for his kiss. I was struck again by her self-confidence.

Preparing me for the meeting, our Gallery client had mentioned a half-Hungarian background, a hyper-intensity, and a quick temper. He hadn't mentioned the intelligent gleam in her eye. Or her quick wit and generosity. He hadn't mentioned her passion for justice. Or her fear of being far from home. Or her propensity for panic attacks when she found herself in big spaces or anonymous institutions. He hadn't mentioned that she was on a conscious spiritual journey, hell-bent, she once put it, on healing the traumas of her past. But over the next year I got to know all these things about Lucy Stockman—all these things and more.

More than I bargained for.

The dogs shot ahead of me into the house and straight into the kitchen to wolf down the food they'd left untouched all day. I limped upstairs to change. The tidiness of the house unsettled me. I complained about the clutter of Marc's paddling gear, but without it the house seemed big and empty. As it did every summer when he was off on a construction project.

I promised myself again I would start looking for my own place. But I had until the end of August. Marc wouldn't be back before then. If we had to break up, it was good timing. That was what I told myself. There was really no shock to the system: I was used to his summer absences. He chose his construction jobs for their proximity to the rivers he wanted to run. Not their proximity to me. By the time he came back, I would be ready. Maybe I *was* ready.

The ringing of the phone brought me out of my thoughts and into my office.

I glanced at the familiar Ottawa exchange on the call display, picked up the receiver and spoke with a smile in my voice. "I've just been thinking about you."

There was a pause, and then a male voice. "It's not who you think it is. It's Tim Brennan."

It wasn't logical, my shock at hearing Tim Brennan's voice phoning from Lucy Stockman's house. Lucy and I had kept our conversations focused on work these last five months. The only thing I remembered her volunteering during that time was that Tim had moved out at

Christmas. She needed her space, she'd said. He needed to learn to be more independent. I hadn't pressed for details. The shutting down of our budding friendship a few months ago had been my choice. It had also been my choice, only a week ago, to open it up again. But there hadn't been any opportunity yet for catching up. So there was no reason her common-law partner couldn't have moved back in without my knowing. No reason at all.

Lucy did not immediately tell me about the man in her life. We had started with the things we knew we had in common. Obvious things, like our love for what she called "the country" and our interest in staying fit and healthy. She wasn't a runner or a long-distance cyclist, but she had a touring bike she rode along the canal and to the stores. And she kept herself in shape with yoga and dance. "I've been dancing ever since I can remember," she told me in one phone conversation. "When I was a kid I danced so much I wore out the kilim carpet in our living room." Her tone turned wry, almost bitter. "My father wasn't too happy about that."

From there she managed to segue the conversation to astrology, meditation, psychic phenomena, reiki, dream analysis, Zen Buddhism—all the other things that interested her. I had no experience of such things. My world was the physical, tangible terrain I could take a hike or ride a bike in. I couldn't prove or disprove the validity of those other kinds of things, so I didn't spend much time thinking about them. But Lucy brought a thoughtful intelligence to it all—and a passion—that drew me in, in spite of myself. She made it all sound so normal. She talked about meditation and her spiritual journey in the same matter-of-fact way she expounded on a subject she was working on for Correctional Services or the Justice Department, or the kind of soil her garden needed. There was no separation: a vision was as real to her as a vegetable. I listened in amazement—and a secret curiosity.

Her independence, I think, drew me to her the most. She was self-employed; she owned her house. She seemed very much in control of her life, not having to answer to a boss, or to a partner who wanted her to do things she didn't want to (or simply couldn't) do. It occurred to me that maybe the metaphysical things she was into played a key role in that. That maybe I should keep listening.

One topic we avoided: relationships. Surprising for two women. But I had my own reasons, and I thought I knew Lucy's. I might have been envying her independence, but when I'd told her I was living with someone, she'd sounded wistful. I assumed she didn't want to hear about someone else's happy relationship when she was on her own. And if she assumed Marc and I were happy, I wasn't ready to set her straight.

It wasn't until my second visit to her house, after many long phone conversations, that she told me about Tim. It took a half-consumed bottle of red wine between us on the table and a warm May breeze filtering in through the kitchen window.

She had been to my house just the weekend before for that spring's ice-breaking-up party. She had met my keen, competent canoe-head boyfriend. She had raved about our log house and its location near the water. I had invited her to come up and use the dock any time. It felt as if we were moving to new ground, from personal chats in the midst of work phone calls to social invitations and visits.

She waited until I was into my second glass of wine. Her own she topped up with water. She trained her eyes on me. "There's someone I want to tell you about. His name is Tim. Tim Brennan." She paused. "I've known him a couple of years."

I felt a sudden unease. I was used to Lucy's intensity but there was something different here.

Lucy paused again, then continued in a rush. "He was a witness at the Supreme Court hearings for Colin Fajber, two years ago. D'you know the case?"

I nodded. I did. A little. It had received national media attention.

"I went to the hearings," said Lucy. "I saw Colin Fajber on TV. There was no way he was capable of raping and stabbing a girl. And I saw his mother. The way she stood by him. I had to go. To show my support. That's where I met Tim. He testified against another convict."

Another convict besides whom? Colin Fajber?

Fajber had been convicted of murder two decades before, when he'd been just sixteen. The victim had been a young nurse. She'd been stabbed and slashed more than two dozen times. And brutally raped. It had been an unusual case to reach the Supreme Court. It was Fajber's mother who had got it there. She had even pleaded with the Prime Minister. That much I knew.

"I don't know how familiar you are with the case," Lucy was saying, "but Fajber's defence was that a guy named Archie Crowe actually committed the murder. By that time Crowe was doing time for something else, and he bragged to some other inmates that he'd got away with it by pinning it on Fajber. That's what Tim was testifying about. I ran down the hall after him when they were taking him away. I had to thank him for speaking up for Colin. He risked his life doing that. There's no worse crime in prison than being a rat."

In prison? *Tim* was the other convict. What had he been in for? Was he still inside? I didn't want to ask.

"I wrote to him. Then we started phoning, and then we arranged visiting privileges for me. I never meant it to go beyond friendship. I never *dreamed* we'd have enough in common for it to become a relationship. But," she smiled, "it did."

She leaned forward then and looked at me intently. "Tim is serving ten years for manslaughter."

I took in a quick breath, released it. Made sure my shock didn't show on my face.

"It was an accident." She was still looking at me intently. "He was being threatened. He tried to subdue the guy by pinching a nerve in his neck. He didn't mean to kill him. It was an accident."

I nodded, still trying to keep my expression neutral. My God, she was involved with a man who had killed someone. With all her fears. How had she even been able to enter the Supreme Court building without having a panic attack? Let alone visit a prison.

"They screwed up his sentence calculation," she was saying. "He should have been released by now, but it keeps getting delayed. I've been trying for almost two years now to get him out. I even hired a lawyer. It looks like he's going to be out soon. Finally. It's been a long haul." She let out a sigh. "A *really* long haul."

She showed me photos from a prison yard. He was a powerfully built man. He obviously worked out. He would have had time to work out. His features were too boyish for me, but others might have called him attractive. His hair, cut short and receding, was almost as dark as Lucy's but greying at the temples. His skin was fairer and he looked younger by a few years. In one photograph Lucy sat on his lap. Glowing. In another he stood in a pair of loose-fitting sweat pants. They were knotted low on his hips, displaying an impressive washboard stomach.

But it was the eyes that held me. I had been expecting the vacant stare of a criminal in a mug shot. But these eyes were warm and smiling, crinkled at the corners. They were a relief, these eyes. His eyes and his infectious grin. They matched Lucy's in the photograph.

"He has nice eyes," I said, to say something.

"Yes!" said Lucy, as if I had made a particularly astute observation. "He's a gentle soul."

I cringed at the term. I wasn't into souls. Not then. But if a "gentle soul" was someone with warm smiling eyes and an infectious grin, then I could agree with her. There was a child-like innocence about him. Innocent men did go to prison. Accidents did happen. I decided I should keep an open mind.

Lucy was warming to me, revealing more. "We have so much in common—music, he meditates, he's into Buddhism. I've looked *so long* for someone like him. I can't believe I found him in *prison*."

It was good to laugh with her. To share disbelief at the situation.

Over our dwindling glasses of wine, she talked in animation about Tim. What it was about the Fajber case, and in their childhoods, that connected them so strongly. How they'd declared themselves common law and got conjugal rights. There had been a recent pregnancy scare. And now he had proposed. He was giving her two years to decide. To match the time she had given him. No one, said Lucy, had ever said they'd wait for her. That meant more to her than anything.

By the time we had drained the bottle, my brain was reeling from the onslaught of information, but my apprehension had mellowed into tentative acceptance. She seemed to know what she was doing. Lucy wasn't someone who would get taken in. She was smart and shrewd and self-aware, and she didn't put up with bullshit. She was, she said, usually the one who broke up her relationships. So she wouldn't be abandoned. Again.

That fall had been a time of rare and lovely harmony for Marc and me. I couldn't help waxing on about it whenever Lucy asked how we were doing. By that time, Tim had been living with her for six months. I had seen them a couple of times in the summer. She had appeared happy. But now, every time we talked, she seemed to be having a bad day. Still, I didn't realize how my cheerfulness was affecting her until I got snapped at one day on the phone: "Everyone I know is going through *something* right now. I don't know how *you've* managed to avoid it."

I was used to Lucy's flashes of temper. They weren't usually directed at me. Or at least I was good at deflecting the arrows. But this arrow was clearly aimed at me. And one thing I didn't need was a friend who got mad at me for being happy. And so, for the past five months, I had kept our conversations professional.

So there was no reason Tim Brennan should not be calling from her house.

"I'm calling," he said, "'cuz I'm wondering if you've seen Lucy. She was up in the Gatineaus on the weekend. She hasn't come home yet."

"I haven't seen Lucy," I heard myself say, "but I think I might have seen her car."

⸺⸙⸺

SHE TOOK A DEEP BREATH and then she was diving across the cavernous marble hall, a swimmer cutting across the current of a raging river. On the inlaid mosaic in the centre of the floor, she was compelled to stop, as if she had run out of air under water. She swivelled her head up and around. She took in the double set of rotund marble columns at either end of the hall, the twin set of massive staircases, the ceiling several storeys high above her. The vastness of the hall made her dizzy. She looked down before she got sucked into its colourless expanse. She took another swimmer's breath, and set her course again for the nearest flight of stairs.

On the landing, halfway up, she paused again for air. A small crowd was already gathered at the top, waiting for the doors to open. She steeled herself to be swallowed into the immensity of the room that must lie behind the imposing wooden doors. The courtroom for the final arbiter of legal disputes and the last judicial resort for all litigants in the nation would be at least a continuation, and more likely an exaltation, of this immense marble entrance hall. It would be suitably styled to follow through on the marble staircases and those colossal wooden doors that exceeded by a ludicrous number of feet the height of the tallest person who would ever enter them. Behind those doors waited a cold, uncaring cathedral to Truth and Justice.

What was she doing here? How had she even had a moment's illusion of thinking she could spend a minute in such a room, let alone a day, or a week or more?

She tried to hang back from the crowd, but others were pushing in from behind. The physical pressure sounded the jangly warning in her veins that panic was about to issue the order to run for home. Today, she was determined her body would obey her. Today, she would be in charge. Today, her fears would do the running—for this one day (at least), for this one cause. If Mrs. Fajber could stand by her son, beating her head against the thick walls of the prison system for twenty years before anyone paid attention, she could sit for an hour or a week in her own version of prison.

Suddenly, the doors were opening with smooth silent splendour, and just as smoothly and silently, the crowd was forming into a line, offering its bags for a second X-ray inspection.

Passing through the massive doors, she stopped short. Someone bumped into her from behind and shoved past. She could not move. She stared, awe-struck, at the room around her.

This was no cold cavernous cathedral. This was an intimate chapel of walnut walls and red carpeting, of warm furnishings of wood and crimson leather. Natural light streamed in through floor-to-ceiling lattice-work windows, three on either side. Light? Windows? How could there be windows in a room situated in the very heart of the Supreme Court building? They must look out onto some kind of inner courtyard.

Maybe the architect had anticipated that the wisdom of future judges might need to be illuminated by natural (if filtered) light.

Something in her throat opened up, something relaxed. The modest size of the room, the warmth of the colours, the friendliness somehow created by the surrounding courtyard, the windows and their light all made it possible to breathe. She would not have to do battle to stay in this room. She could stay, and possibly the dominant feeling that would stay with her would be wonderment—that such an intimate room could be in any way the "supreme" court of the nation.

An impromptu chair and microphone had been placed facing the judges' chairs. Witnesses did not usually testify in the Supreme Court. This was an unusual case, in more ways than one. The chair sat empty, waiting for the first witness to be called.

She found a seat, watched the judges file in, black-robed, nine in all. After the preliminaries, the lawyer for Colin Fajber stood up and addressed the judges. She opened her notebook and began taking notes as if she were a university student. She wasn't planning to do anything with the notes. The notes were rather something to do. Writing—where she was, what was happening around her, how she was feeling—sometimes helped forestall a panic attack.

In the first week she filled nearly an entire notebook. She attended every day she could spare from work. She was there on a blizzarding Monday morning in early March, having given herself so much extra time to navigate through the snow that she was one of the first through the doors. From her seat she had an unimpeded view of Mrs. Fajber sitting at the front of the courtroom with her son's lawyer. That she had never given up on her son, ever pushing for a retrial, was nothing short of a miracle. The miracle of mothers. Not her own. Her own mother had never done anything remotely like stand by her or try to free her from prison. Her mother had, in fact, played an instrumental role in her incarceration.

2.

I DID NOT WANT TO drive back up River Road. I drove with the hope that the car would be gone. Or that it would not have the plate number Tim had given me over the phone. Or that if Lucy *was* missing, her car would be found somewhere else. That I wasn't going to be the one to find it. Most of all I wanted to believe that Lucy had gone for an extended walk and was now driving the Suzuki, and herself, safely home.

But I knew before I arrived on River Road that it was a hopeless wish.

Lucy, Tim had told me on the phone, had had a recurring dream. I was startled. Lucy had often talked about her dreams, but she'd never mentioned a recurring one.

"She dreams she's being choked."

He seemed not to hear my sharp intake of breath. He was already embarking on his story. "It was Friday night she had this dream. She screamed so loud she woke our tenant, and she's two floors above us. It took a long time to calm her down. We were both a little shell-shocked, but she was better by morning. Saturday she was in good spirits. She told me she loved me. She said she was going to see friends in the Gatineaus. I expected her back last night—this morning at the latest. She's got work she's gotta do. I been phoning her friends all day. I just saw your name on the calendar for one o'clock yesterday."

I started again. He was referring to the Sunday afternoon ice-breaking-up party. I felt a sudden pang of guilt. I had never given Lucy a thought. Which was ironic, given how my invitation to her had precipitated my break-up.

"She didn't show up," I told Tim.

"Maybe I got it wrong where she was going. Maybe it wasn't the Gatineaus. I left a message for another friend of hers. There's some retreat she knows about. I haven't heard back."

"Do you know Lucy's licence plate number?"

"No, but I can find out. It should be here somewhere." I heard the sound of rustling paper.

"I've never been in her papers before," he said.

Yes, you have. It was an irrational thought. I dismissed it.

There was more shuffling. "Here it is."

I wrote down the number, even as I was wondering what papers would have Lucy's licence plate number written on them. I didn't think mine was recorded anywhere in the house.

"I'll call you back in twenty minutes," I told Tim. We hung up.

The invitation to my party had been extended during a phone conversation. I had called because I'd forgotten if I'd faxed a fact sheet that Lucy had requested. We were working on another exhibit for the National Gallery. When she answered she sounded terrible—weak and hoarse. She apologized and said she couldn't talk, she'd call me back.

The next day I found the fax transmittal sheet and called to tell her, and to see how she was doing. She came on the line, the first part of her "hello" cut off. Could she call me back? She was on the other line with her bank manager, and it had taken her ages to get through.

"It's okay," I said. "I solved the problem; I don't need you." I let her go back to the other call.

She returned my call anyway, sounding surprisingly cheerful. "You may not need me," she said, "but I need you."

She needed me to look in the local paper for a cottage rental. I felt a twinge of guilt; it wasn't the first time she had asked. While I hunted through the *Low Down to Hull and Back News*, she chattered on. She felt much better for the massage she'd just received. She wanted a cottage for the whole season, and it had to have electricity; she wanted to bring her computer. She sounded refreshingly upbeat. She also spoke in the singular. It sounded like she and Tim were still apart—that maybe they'd broken up for good. I found a notice for a cottage just down the river and gave her the number.

The invitation to the party came out naturally, when she mentioned she was going to be in the Gatineaus on the weekend. "Well, if you're in the area, drop in. Any time after three."

I was hanging up the phone when a voice startled me from behind. "What are you doing?"

I swivelled my chair around, knocking into Belle, lying at my feet. I put an apologetic hand on her back as she got up and moved out of the way.

Marc was standing in the entrance to my office, arms crossed, legs apart. He was still dressed in his work coveralls. His shaggy hair, already streaked light and dark blond, had additional streaks of cream paint in it. There had been no noticeable anger in his voice, but I could see it in his stance, usually so relaxed. And in the chiselled angles of his face, usually softened by his easy smile and boundless enthusiasm. The anger, the dirt on his face, made him look older than thirty. He had obviously been listening.

His tone brought out my sarcasm before I could censor it. "I've been arranging to go for a nice paddle with Lucy on Sunday afternoon while you entertain the other guests."

"I will not have a murderer in my house."

"I wasn't aware Lucy had murdered anyone."

He levelled his gaze at me and said nothing.

"She didn't say anything about bringing him."

"But you do not know for sure that she will not." His francophone accent was more pronounced than usual. And he wasn't using contractions. Signs of his increasing agitation.

"So? What if she does?"

"I told you before, I do not want you to have anything to do with this murderer. I do not want you to bring him here. I do not want him to know where we live."

It always got my back up when he dictated to me this way. I crossed my own arms. "Get it right: he's a manslaughterer, not a murderer. Read:

accident. Read: give the man a second chance. Read: open your mind."
Like I'm trying to do.

Marc was silent.

I relented. "Marc, I really don't think she's going to bring him, but I can call back and check if you like."

"*Comme tu veux.*" His voice was a hard monotone.

For a moment I looked at him. Then I took a breath. "I *do comme je veux* but somehow it's never good enough for you."

Marc was staring at me as if he had lost all comprehension of English. I rushed on. "You claim it's okay that I don't paddle with you, but there's this—I don't know, this underlying *reproach* or something. It's always there, in my head. Even when you're gone for a month at a time, I feel it. I did try you know. It's not as if I didn't try."

"You misled me."

"Mis*led* you? What are you talking about?"

"I thought you were a different person. I thought we had more in common."

"We have lots in common. You knew I wasn't a paddler."

"You led me on. I thought you were into it."

"I *was*. I tried. You know I tried. It's not my fault."

"It's not good enough. It's my life," he added flatly. "And you never come with me. Anywhere."

I crossed my arms. "So you're just looking for a paddling partner? Is that it?"

"I want to *be* with you."

"So stop running off every summer and weekend and *be* with me. You always expect me to come with *you*." We were far into the tape of an old argument by now.

There was a small humourless smile from Marc. He made a circle in the air with his forefinger: "And around we go." He hesitated. "Maybe it's time to admit it."

Something clamped around my heart. "Admit what?"

Marc avoided my eyes. He crossed over to the window and spoke to the river. "That it is over between us."

"*Over?* You want to break *up?*"

Marc half turned, made a gesture with his hand. "What is holding us together?"

My frustration came bursting to the surface again. "I thought it was *love* holding us together." God, I was sounding like a clichéd pop song. "Are you saying you don't love me anymore?" What had happened to us? The short winter days seemed to have shortened our tempers and erased all the acceptance and understanding we had worked so hard at in the fall.

Marc made that futile gesture with his hand again. He didn't speak.

I watched the back of his head. The head I knew so well. I memorized the patterns of streaking in his hair. The white paint, the shades of blond. My own head felt numb. As if someone had whacked me on the ear with a two-by-four.

Marc's voice came as if at a great distance. "It will be better this way. I will be away anyway. It will not be so…."

I was shocked. This wasn't the way people broke up, in one fell swoop. I pulled myself together. Tried for a joking tone. "Not before a party. Maybe after. If we don't have a good time."

Marc kept his back to me. My feet wanted to walk over to him, my arms wanted to turn him back to me. Neither were working. My voice could only come up with a lame response. "Marc, you can't go. We have a party to host."

Marc turned around then. His face was full of emotion. Exasperation. Defeat. "*You* have a party to host," he said and his voice cracked.

I couldn't meet his eyes. I fought my own tears. "And where are *you* going to be?"

Marc seemed to straighten up, to pull his emotions back inside himself. "By Sunday afternoon? Thunder Bay."

I stared at him. "But you're not starting that job for another two weeks."

"Am I not?" he asked and walked out of the room.

I watched him pack. He was trying to scare me. He was packing to be ready to leave on May sixth, as planned. He was going to stay for the party. For me. Of course.

But early Friday morning, he loaded up the truck. And I retreated to my office and looked out to the grey April sky and porous ice on the river. Unable to say, "Stay."

The construction site was deserted. Except for the yellow Suzuki Sidekick parked on the side of the road. It was facing toward the city, as before. I did a U-turn and pulled in behind it. I didn't need to read the licence number in front of me to know it was Lucy's.

The shoulder was bordered by a scruffy row of bushes, and beyond the bushes was a cottage, and a man in the yard.

I got out of the car, cut through the bushes and crossed the lawn. "Excuse me," I said to the man. "I'm wondering if you know anything about that car parked over there."

He turned slowly, with the help of a cane. He was slightly built, with thick greying hair and a topographical map of a face.

"It belongs to a friend of mine," I said. "I'm wondering if you've seen her."

"No, I 'ave not seen her." He spoke each word slowly, with a strong Québecois accent. "That car 'as been parked 'ere since Saturday afternoon. My wife and I, we 'ave just come back from town tonight—we live in Hull. This is our cottage. We are renovating. We were going to call the police. We thought it might be stolen and abandoned."

"Do you have a phone I could use?" I seemed to be speaking from a script, knowing both my lines and his.

"Yes, in the house. *Ma femme,* she is there. Go ahead," he added. He waved his cane.

This was in the script too—that I should go ahead and let him make his way behind me. That I should feel I was being rude, but know that under the circumstances it was necessary.

I stepped around the construction materials on the porch. The woman who answered the door spoke little English, but she understood the word "phone" and my agitation. She guided me through a half-finished hall to the living room.

I sat in a chair and dialled Lucy's number on an old black rotary-dial phone. My hand shook. Tim answered on the first ring.

"It's her car," I said.

"Should we call the police?" His voice was as shaky as mine. This was also part of the script—the line and the delivery.

"Yes, but I don't know if it should be Ottawa or Quebec." I leaned my head in my hand, trying to think. "Quebec, I think, since it was found in Quebec."

I wanted to hang up and leave it to Tim. But he would have no idea how to call the *Sûreté du Québec*, or how to communicate, if necessary, in French. I could feel his helplessness. I couldn't block it out. I couldn't change the script.

"I'll call them," I said.

His relief came across so strongly the feeling of scripted roles faded. The melodrama of the evening stayed.

"Where are you?" he asked. "How do I get up there? I'm no good with directions or finding my way at night."

I remembered Lucy telling me the same thing the previous summer, explaining an idiosyncrasy I couldn't have cared less about at the time.

She had been ecstatic to have finally gotten him out. The battle was over. But it had been an adjustment. Tim had been completely dependent. He had little idea how to live in the outside world. She'd had to drive him everywhere, show him how to do the simplest things, the grocery shopping, getting a library card. She'd bought him a mountain bike. Shown him the bike paths along the canal. Finally, he got his driver's licence. That had made a huge difference. Except, I now remembered her telling me, he had a lousy sense of direction. He kept getting lost and calling her from phone booths to come and get him. "He doesn't go by street signs," she explained. "He goes by landmarks, which you can't see at night, so he doesn't drive at night."

It was one of those useless things you retain in your head that suddenly become relevant. How was I going to explain where I was? It was getting darker by the minute.

"Do you know where Tulip Valley is?" I asked him.

"No, I never been up there before. Is it near Kingsmere? I've been to Kingsmere."

"No, that won't help." Kingsmere was at the other end of Gatineau Park, closer to the city.

I couldn't deal with him right now. I had to get the police here. "I'll call the police, and call you back when they get here."

I sat opposite the couple in their living room—the Rivests. I sipped water from a glass. Each tick of the clock pushed the sun farther behind the hills. Each sound of a passing car brought me to the window.

Every time I sat down I smiled an apology to the Rivests. They had better things to do than wait in their living room with a strange woman for the police to come and investigate the disappearance of another strange woman. It wasn't their fault she'd parked her car in front of their house. They hadn't asked to be in this drama. Neither had I.

Sitting intensified the pain in my leg. I stood up. "I'm just going to go outside." I gestured out the window. Mr. Rivest nodded. From behind me, I heard him speaking in French to his wife.

The temperature had dropped with the sun. I pulled my jacket tight around me and walked with crossed arms over to Lucy's car. Walking relaxed the sciatic nerve a little.

I cupped my face against the passenger window. I was expecting the car to be empty.

It wasn't. A pair of sunglasses lay on the dashboard. There was a dark bag on the passenger-side floor, and another, bigger bag in the back. Would she have gone for a walk without her sunglasses? Would she have left her purse in full view on the floor? Both seemed unlikely.

I avoided touching the door handles, but I could see the locks were pushed down.

I looked up and down the road. No cars. No police.

Back in the house, the Rivests were still sitting in the living room. As if frozen there until their part in the next scene began.

I dialled Lucy's number again on the old rotary phone. "The police still haven't got here," I told Tim. "I looked in the car. Her purse is there and her sunglasses. The car's locked. Do you have a spare set of keys?"

"Yes, there should be one here."

"Could you bring them? I'm going to try to give you instructions to get you up here. The police are taking so long."

"Okay," he said. He sounded as if he were bracing himself.

I braced myself too. Lucy had said he didn't go by street names. I tried to think of obvious landmarks. "Do you know the bridge from Ottawa that takes you onto the big highway that cuts right through Hull?"

"Is that the one from King Ed-ward?" He said the name hesitantly, as though pronouncing a word in an unfamiliar language.

Relief. It was like trying to ask someone a question in their language and having the response come back, haltingly, in your own. "Stay in the left lane," I continued. "There will be a sign pointing to Hull."

"Is that the sign that says Hull left, Sussex right?"

"Yes, that's the one." More relief. It was so much easier than I had expected. He would be here soon.

I had met Tim only twice. The first time had been just a few weeks after his release, almost a year before. The same day Lucy had explained his idiosyncrasies with directions. I had ridden my bike down from Chelsea for an early supper. I was nervous about meeting him, though Lucy hadn't mentioned whether he would be joining us. And she hadn't made it a foursome. Which was just as well, given Marc's reaction when I'd told him where I was going. He didn't want me socializing with Lucy at all, now that Tim was out of prison. But he hadn't been home when I'd left for Lucy's. He was conducting a paddling workshop on the Ottawa River.

Wheeling my bike around behind the house, I spotted Lucy working in the garden at the bottom of the yard. She came over to greet me. She was wearing an oversized shirt thrown over a white tank top and black cotton leggings. I was shocked at how tightly her skin was stretched across her collarbones. I saw fragility and aging, toughness and sensuality.

She tugged off her gardening gloves and invited me inside. There were steps from the backyard to a small porch, presumably leading to the kitchen, but she took me in through a sliding door on the same level as the yard.

Walking through this door was like a small revelation. Technically it was the basement. In reality it was the rest of her living space—her bedroom. Now hers and Tim's.

It was a large room with partial walls separating off other rooms. Her office. A laundry room. Even though it was above ground at the back, my impression was one of darkness, of partial walls leading into dark corners.

We climbed a set of stairs and we were in the bright kitchen. Then Lucy revealed another room I hadn't noticed on my previous visits: a sitting room off the kitchen. It was a tiny cozy space, with a window overlooking the yard. Just big enough to hold a love seat, a bookshelf and a TV in a corner cabinet.

Ensconced on the small couch with a glass of wine, I relaxed. There was no sign of Tim. There was no sign of his presence, either, though he'd been living there for a few weeks already. He would have had few belongings. Still, there was nothing to indicate someone else was living in the house.

"How's the new tenant working out?" I asked. I was referring to the woman renting the top floor. The previous tenant had apparently been a disaster.

"Which one?" Lucy grinned.

I made an apologetic gesture. I should, of course, have been asking about Tim. But Lucy didn't seem concerned.

"So far, so good," she said. "Her name is Lakshmi. Goddess of prosperity. How can I go wrong?"

She went on to talk about her other new "tenant." They'd started a handyman business—Brockman Repairs—a combination of their last names. Tim was out at the moment, she said, seeing a woman about a painting job. He was good at carpentry too. "Maybe Marc could hire him."

I made excuses. I didn't do them very well, and she wasn't fooled.

"Well, just ask him. He must need an extra worker *some*times."

I lied and said I would.

We were in the kitchen eating a delicious homemade vegetable stew when we heard sounds from down below. There was a steady thud on the stairs. The door opened and the man from the photos on the refrigerator stepped into the room.

Lucy introduced us, and Tim shook my hand. He looked almost solemn, as if he understood how I might be feeling. I was touched by his sensitivity.

He turned to Lucy, and his face transformed into smiles. He'd got the painting contract.

Lucy beamed back at him.

The *Sûreté* had only just arrived when a green pick-up pulled into the driveway. The man I hadn't seen in over half a year got out of the truck. He looked different from what I remembered. Not the attractive confident man from the photos who had been working out. Not the solemn sensitive man shaking my hand in Lucy's kitchen. Just an ordinary guy in a loose-fitting windbreaker, jeans, and a baseball cap. No one I would have partnered Lucy with.

Tim looked me in the eye. "I was okay until I got to River Road. Then I stopped at that restaurant there, to make sure this was the right road."

I felt mildly irritated. He had to be pretty dense to stop there. It was the one place I had given him an obvious landmark—the restaurant itself.

I explained the situation to the two *Sûreté* officers. At least I assumed I did. My dealings with the *Sûreté* stayed in my mind afterward as a series of blocked scenes. A tableau followed by a plunge into darkness before the next is illuminated.

In the first tableau, Tim and one of the *Sûreté* officers and I were rushing to the car. The spare key was in Tim's hand. Tim was unlocking the driver-side door, opening it, reaching over to unlock the passenger door for the officer.

I stood behind Tim. I watched him reach up to the dome light on the ceiling. I watched him lean in and put his hands on the steering wheel. I watched him insert the key in the ignition and heard him say, "Maybe this is how you turn on the interior light."

You don't need the key in the ignition to turn on an interior light.

In the second tableau, the *Sûreté* officer was reaching across the inside of the car, handing Lucy's handbag to Tim and me. Our hands were inside it. Two books were suddenly in my hand. The titles didn't register. Lucy's wallet was open in Tim's hand. Licence, money, credit cards: everything was there. I didn't want everything to be there. I wanted signs of theft. Ordinary theft.

Tim pulled out a white plastic bag. Her lunch, he said, feeling it. We didn't look inside.

Why are we touching everything? We shouldn't be touching anything.

In the third tableau, Tim was reaching into the back seat, pointing out Lucy's overnight bag. He lifted up the bag. "See," he said, "it's heavy. I carried it to the car for her because it was so heavy. She packed her pyjamas, a bottle of wine, hot water bottle."

Why are you lifting her bag? How come you know what's in it?

We were sitting in the back seat of the cruiser. The officer in the driver's seat was asking questions. What did Lucy look like? How old was she? What was she wearing when she left the house Saturday morning? He was checking things off on a clipboard, as if he were doing a consumer survey.

Beside me, Tim was describing what Lucy was wearing. "She had on a navy blue coat. I don't know what you call it—it comes down to the knees." He looked at me, as if I might know.

I did. I could see it in my mind's eye, from our very first meeting at the National Gallery. "A pea coat," I said. I spelled the word for the francophone officer.

"A pea coat," repeated Tim, nodding, "with a thin red stripe down the sleeves. And dark blue or black leggings." I was impressed by his powers of observation.

"What kind of shoe was she wearing?" the officer asked in accented English.

"I know she was taking three pairs of shoes," Tim said. He counted them off on his fingers: "Her runners, her loafers, and her slippers."

"'Er loafer were in 'er overnight bag," said the second officer. At some point he had got into the car and now sat in the passenger seat. "And 'er slipper were on the front seat floor on the passenger side."

"Then she must have been wearing her runners," said Tim. "Nikes, I think. Yes, she was wearing her Nikes."

"How would you describe 'er mental state?"

Tim and I looked at each other. "Nervous," he said. "High strung."

I was surprised to hear him admitting this about his loved one.

"Was she on any medication?" the officer asked.

I expected Tim to say no. Instead he said, "She had a prescription for Valium. She would get eight from her doctor and they'd last her a couple of months."

"Would you describe her as suicidal?"

"No. Definitely not." Tim was adamant. I thought about the Lucy I knew. *I'm hell-bent on healing the traumas of my past.* Those were not the words of someone who is suicidal. I echoed Tim's answer.

The light from a set of headlights suddenly swung through the inside of the car from the rear. A vehicle passed us. Red tail lights intensified. A tow truck. I watched it back up into place in front of Lucy's car. The second officer got out of the cruiser.

I wanted to jump out of the car after him and stop them. *You can't take the car away. It's our only link to Lucy. It has to stay here until she's found.* I didn't speak these irrational thoughts.

The officers and Tim and I were standing beside the cruiser. The interview was over. There was nothing more they could do tonight.

"They will send 'elicopter, dog, in the morning," said the first officer. "We will now search the track before we go."

"We should go and thank the Rivests," I told Tim.

We walked up the drive to the house.

Tim was holding a tissue offered by Mrs. Rivest.

"I know she knew how to swim," he said, through tears. "But the water is so cold."

He wiped his eyes. Mrs. Rivest offered him another tissue.

"She was—is—just a tiny person; I've got a hundred pounds on her. I know how easily she can be hurt—when we play-wrestle on the living room floor."

I didn't want him to have play-wrestled with Lucy on the living room floor. I didn't want him to be speaking about her in the past tense.

We were back outside. The police were gone. Their search had been too short. Tim agreed that we should do a search ourselves. He fished a flashlight out from his truck.

Lucy was at the end of the beam of Tim's flashlight. Everywhere. She was lying on the tracks just ahead of us, disguised as one of the dark railway ties. She was lying in the black ponds between the tracks and the rock face, among the rocks and stumps. She was lying in the river, her hair waving gracefully in the water beside a dock....

I nearly stumbled on the steps down to the rickety dock beside the floating hair.

Tim was right behind me.

He shone his light into the water. Under the prolonged beam, what I had thought was Lucy's hair revealed itself to be the fraying end of a rope floating on the surface. I breathed again. And then realized where I was, close to water on a rotting dock. I stood stock still, terrified the dock was going to give way under my weight. Terrified I would fall in the water. Had Lucy fallen through from here?

Tim shifted the beam to the dock to illuminate the broken boards. I stepped back to the relative safety of the stairs.

Out of the light, the unravelled rope ends in the water beside us transformed themselves back into Lucy's hair.

Tim stood before me, a black shadow on the rotting dock. I couldn't stop staring at the dark mass in the water. "She could have come down here to write in her journal," he was saying. "Do you remember seeing her journal in her bag? She took it everywhere with her."

I tried to remember what books I had held in my hand. I was sure I would have noticed if one of them had been her journal.

Tim shone his flashlight into the water again, beyond the rope. "It's so shallow here."

Could she have fallen in and not got out? I shuddered. It was my own worst nightmare. She could swim, Tim had said in the house. But how long would she last in the frigid water?

We climbed back up the steps to the tracks.

On the way back to the car, Tim swept the beam of light over the brush beside the shore and at the water's edge.

"It's so shallow," he said again.

Beside his truck, he began to cry. I held him.

Then I invited him to my house for tea.

It hit me on the highway heading home, with his headlights blinding me in my rearview mirror. Who this man was. Where he had spent the last ten years of his life. Why.

———— ∞∞∞ ————

SHE WAS IMMERSED IN HER thoughts and missed the arrival of the first witness of the day. Vaguely, she heard the clerk reciting her usual litany: "Do you swear to tell the truth…." But the answer came with the clarity of someone speaking directly in her ear: "I do."

She started and opened her eyes. She sat forward in her seat and tried to peer around the heads in front. She could barely see the back of the man sitting in the chair before the judges. But she could hear him, clearly, even before the lawyer asked him to speak up. It was the voice of someone she knew, someone she was, or had once been, intimately familiar with. She hadn't caught his name. She knew she wouldn't recognize it anyway.

She sat back as if she were the court stenographer, recording the conversations the witness related to the court that he had had with the inmate Archie Crowe while he had been appealing his own sentence.

"What prompted you to come forward?" Colin Fajber's lawyer asked when the witness had finished. "Obviously it's against the code to come forward. What prompted you?"

"I was sitting in my cell one day just after supper," the witness responded. "I had watched the local news, and I saw Mrs. Fajber speaking with the Prime Minister. The way she was talking to him—she was begging him to help her son and help her.

"I thought to myself, well, inside it just made me feel a lot of empathy toward her. And sympathy. I thought to myself: if this lady has been hanging in there … that is what struck me. I thought to myself: If what I know is relevant to the situation, I would like to offer it up to help her."

Her pen stopped mid-page. She sat open-mouthed. Out of this stranger's mouth had just come an exact echo of her own heart's reasons for being here.

The witness continued. "I thought about it for two or three months before I ever made a decision to do anything after that. But definitely the reason I got into it was because of how I felt about what she had been doing with it."

"Mr. Brennan, have you ever in your life met Colin Fajber?" the lawyer asked.

"No, I don't know the man. I never met him."

"Have you been offered anything whatsoever for coming forward? Is there anything in this for you?"

"No. In fact, by doing this my life is about to change as of tonight. I've got two years left, and my life is going to seriously change from what it was yesterday by being here. I have given up a lot by being here. I am not asking for anything."

Again, his words hit home. It had taken courage for her to come here, too. But overcoming her own fears was nothing, she knew, compared with this man's courage to sit where he was sitting and say the things he was saying, and as a result put his safety, maybe his very life, in jeopardy. Would she have been able to do what he was doing? The answer was painful, but not difficult. Sometimes, she could barely drive or walk down her own street without having to race back home, scurrying like a squirrel back to some illusory notion of safety. Yet, here was this man, who had spent most of his adult life in cloistered walls, who had had, it seemed, little access to the outside world all those years, and he had set aside his fears of the world and the people in it and, even more, his fears of those inside the prison walls who might threaten his life.

The lawyer for Colin Fajber finished his friendly questioning, and then the inquisition began—first from the lawyer for Archie Crowe and then from the Counsel for the Manitoba Attorney General. Through it all—the insinuations, the attempts to discredit him—the witness kept his cool. Answering difficult questions about his past with devastating forthrightness and calm. She would never have been able to do that.

She didn't care what he had done in his past. What came through—shining through—was that his intentions for being here today were good. "In the life of the Spirit," she quoted in her head, "you are always at the beginning." One of her favourite lines from *The Book of Runes.*

The Counsel for the Manitoba Attorney General finished his questions. There was a brief re-examination by the lawyer for Colin Fajber, and then the Chief Justice addressed Mr. Brennan: "You may go."

He made it sound so simple. As if the witness could just stand up and leave the room.

Instead, the witness waited for a police guard to come and escort him down the main aisle. She craned her neck as he passed by her row. He looked straight ahead. He wasn't handcuffed, but he was wearing prison greens. He wasn't a tall man but there was a breadth to him. He walked with his shoulders set back. He walked with the presence of a man who knew he had done the right thing, the act of his doing it made greater by the risk to his safety that he had taken to come here, and the fact that few were going to thank him for it.

She didn't stop to think. She found herself on her feet, pushing past the bony knees and blank faces in her row, walking as fast as decorum would allow, down the aisle, through the anteroom, and out into the cold marble hall.

She ran down a corridor she was not supposed to go down, away from the main staircase. No one stopped her. There, at a set of elevator doors, stood Mr. Brennan with his police guard, and Mrs. Fajber.

She waited until Mrs. Fajber had finished thanking him and then she approached, out of breath. "Excuse me."

He was holding out his hands to be cuffed. He didn't immediately turn around.

"Excuse me," she said again.

The guard gave her a stern look. "What are you doing down here?"

"I wanted to speak to Mr. Brennan."

At her words, the prisoner started and turned. He looked younger than his voice had sounded, and his mouth turned down naturally at the corners, giving him an even younger look. But it was the eyes that held hers. They were the eyes of an ancient friend and lover, in the face of a stranger.

His eyes gave her courage.

But then he glanced at the notebook in her hand, and his receptivity changed to a stranger's hostile stare.

She almost lost her nerve. And then she realized: he thought she was a journalist, here to expose him.

She spoke quickly, still out of breath. "I think what you did today was very brave."

His mouth turned up at the corners. "Thank you."

"I was wondering…." She started again. "My name is Lucy Stockman. I'd like to write to you. To thank you for what you've done for Colin Fajber." She barely knew what she was saying. She only knew she couldn't let him disappear without making a connection. She could only look at him, willing him to look in her eyes and see her. She wanted him to recognize her, the way she recognized him.

The guards were leading Brennan through the elevator doors. She was an annoying fly they were trying to brush away.

Inside the elevator, Brennan turned and faced her. "I'm at Collins Bay," he said. He punctuated his words with a smile that reached into his eyes.

The doors closed between them. Brennan went back to prison. And, with a new lightness of heart, she went back to hers.

3.

I HAD MET TIM ONLY twice before, but I knew a lot more about him than two brief meetings would reveal. Not just because Lucy had talked about him, but because she had also shared his letters with me. Letters he had written from prison before they'd graduated to phone calls and visits. She'd wanted me to understand who he was. The letters, she'd said, during one of my visits, would explain him better than she could. I could take them home, read them at my leisure.

I didn't want to take the letters home. It seemed like taking Tim home. But I looked up from my end of her small couch to see Lucy looking at me. There was a shy pleading in her eyes. I relented. "Sure," I smiled. "I could read them."

I waited until Marc was out of the house. I didn't want to jeopardize our recent return to harmony. It felt too fragile. We had called a truce. He had stopped expecting me to paddle with him. I had stopped asking him to come for a bike ride or listen to CBC. We were affectionate with each other again. That was what I had been missing the most. It was heaven to wake up to find his warm, ropey, paddler's arms around me. I didn't know how he did it, but when I was in Marc's arms, I felt I'd come home. It was worth curbing my tongue to be at "home" again.

I took the letters to the couch with a cup of tea. They were written on lined foolscap, three-hole punched. The finest in prison stationery. I unfolded the first.

He thanked Lucy for writing. He was sorry he hadn't replied to her first letter. There were a lot of kooks out there....

I could imagine Lucy enjoying the fact that he had a sense of humour.

Seriously, he said, he didn't trust too many people. He guessed she'd heard that in court.

I am writing to you from Warkworth Institution, where I was transferred. In testifying they promised not to use my name. But what do I hear on the radio on the way back, but my full name. I was pretty upset about that. I lodged a formal complaint, but my life has pretty well been in jepardy since then. They took me out of the general population. Then they transferred me here. Warkworth is a lot more civilized than Collins Bay. Your treated with more respect here. But I'm waiting for the threats on my life to begin here also which it will when word gets out. I have no regrets whatsoever about testafying on behalf of an innocent man. I did it for his mother too, the way she stood by him. I understand you share that personal view from the things you said in your letter.

I didn't grow up in a fancy home like you. We lived on a farm past Renfrew area. A place called Brudenell. You probably never heard of it. Its not worth knowing. Our fields were full of rocks, hard to grow stuff. I hardly remember my old man. My mom managed the farm and the lot of us. She didn't treat me good. Like yours didn't. You used some big words in your letter: tyranny. There was tyranny in my home too. You wouldn't want to hear the things done to me. I probably deserved them. I ran away when I was 15. What else do you do on the street but lie and steal? A person has to eat.

His letters were an odd combination of an unnatural formality and poor spelling and grammar. I turned the page over.

He'd ended up arrested and sent to reform school a year later, an experience he didn't really want to talk about, he said, except that it did have the surprising result of getting him to finish high school and into university on a bursary. He'd completed first year.

I would have been all right. I was even married at the time. It was my misfortune that some of my old friends located me. And it wasn't affordable living on my own. I was in need of money. And I guess you heard the rest in court.

I don't have excuses for the things I done. Only that there in my past now. I'm looking forward to getting out of here and into therapy. I am aware that I need therapy. Like what you talked about. What they give you here is micky mouse. Its nothing like what you talked about. What you said about wounds that need healing, I never heard anyone talk in words like that before. Here they talk about behaviour that needs fixing. But it strikes me, one don't come without the other.

Lucy, I thought, would have completely identified with this. It would have been a magnetic draw—communicating with someone who "got" it—or at least wanted to get it.

He was, he wrote, overdue for release. The system had screwed up its calculations. But why would anyone listen to him? He wanted more than anything to have a normal life, a steady job, a wife to share a home with. His marriage had been a disaster, he'd been too young, hadn't understood women's needs.

But I'm scared too. I am not too ashamed to admit it. I'm scared of what's out there. I don't have much experience out of this joint. It was never my expectation that anyone would write from outside. I'm sorry I didn't answer your first letter. I figured you must want something from me. I don't know what. I don't have a thing anyone would want. But everyone has always tried to screw me around. Besides, do you know how intimadating it is to write to a writer when you know your spelling is bad? (I'd say atroshus, but I don't know how to spell it.) I hope that you will overlook all the errors you find in this letter. And I hope you will write again, if you would care to I would very much look forward to hearing from you again. Maybe yu cood help me with mi speling.

I couldn't help smiling at the last line. Clearly, the year he'd spent at university had done little for his spelling and grammar. I was sure they would have bothered Lucy. But his own awareness (and humour) about them would have helped her to look past them. She had obviously been able to look past his non-intellectual exterior to the similar interior life they seemed to share. I almost admired her for that.

Letter by letter, Tim revealed the past that had shaped him. I couldn't believe he had grown up in this century, let alone in my own province. He had been raised on a farm with no running water, no television, no phone. He was the oldest of six children, the only son. His father had left after fathering five children, returned long enough to impregnate his mother with the sixth, and left again, for good. His mother had relied on Tim to be the "man of the house."

At that point, the topic of his letters abruptly changed from his relationship to his mother to things he'd done outdoors. He wrote of hunting and fishing with an uncle, helping to build a hunt cabin from logs they'd cut in the bush, of sleeping on a camp bed in the cold cabin, listening to wolves howl on the next ridge.

> *We lived off the land when I was a kid. We were always selfsuficient. The opposite of what I am here. You know what I mean?*

I imagined Lucy did. She had spoken to me of wanting to live off the land. And she had told me often how lucky I was to have a capable carpenter boyfriend. She would have been excited by Tim's skills—wood cutting, hunting, fishing, house-building, farming. Here was someone not only voicing her own dream but entirely capable of making it a reality.

But he wasn't just a practical male. He obviously shared her esoteric interests. He, too, he wrote, was into astrology and dream analysis. In one note, he thanked her for the Miles Davis tape she'd sent. How had she known Davis was his favourite jazz artist?

After April his letters became more sporadic. They would have been interspersed with phone calls and visits by then. But they also became more intimate. In July he wrote:

Its only right you should be getting more from Curtis than he is giving you. Its not selfish, like you say. If its not being presumptive, I would give anything to be in his shoes, in your house, your world. If I could I would give you everything. I would never hurt you or yell at you or abandon you like Curtis. If we got mad at each other we would hang on to each other. We would work it out. I can't do much from this joint, but if its worth anything I offer you my love, no strings attached, it is here for you. (And me too.)

That was the last letter. I folded it up, secured the elastic around the packet and put it back in my knapsack to return to Lucy. Love with no strings attached. What was that? I will love you even if you keep taking off to go paddling and can't talk about anything else? Was that unconditional love? Or denial? And who was Curtis? He was mentioned in the present tense. It sounded like Lucy had been seeing someone else when she'd met Tim. There was a lot she hadn't told me. But she had given me these. She wanted me to understand the connection she felt. I could, I thought, give her the benefit of the doubt. As long as I didn't have to actually deal with Tim. Marc really didn't have to worry on that score.

Tim's headlights lit up the interior of my car as he pulled into the drive behind me. I wished Marc were home. And was glad he wasn't. I could rebuke myself without his help. Anyway I had the dogs.

Beau and Belle wagged their tails and made a fuss over Tim—the way I was doing—without fear. If he were dangerous, wouldn't our ears be laid back? Wouldn't we be growling in our throats, pacing in our uneasiness?

We weren't uneasy, not about Tim. Not yet. I made a pot of mint tea. I hoped it would stop us both from shaking.

"I have this hungry feeling inside," said Tim. He put his hand on his stomach. "I've felt it all day. It's like an emptiness inside. I eat, but it doesn't go away. I miss Lucy. I missed her as soon as she left the house. I never been alone without her for so long."

It bothered me, that gnawing emptiness even though he'd eaten. He was equating an empty, lonely feeling with hunger. He asked if he could use the phone. "I need to call my psychologist. I talked to him earlier today. He told me to call if I heard anything."

He sat on the kitchen stool at the counter beside the phone. I stood beside him. The dogs lay at our feet. I handed Tim a tissue for his tears. I listened to him explain the evening's events. I squeezed his shoulder in comfort.

"I should phone Marnie too," he said when he had finished the brief conversation. "She's a friend of ours. She's the one I left the message for asking about the retreat. She'll be worried about why I been trying to get hold of her."

He dialled a number and his first words were a surprise. Not the explanation I was expecting of why he was calling but, in a low voice, "We found the car."

Then he was silent. Marnie seemed to be doing most of the talking.

Finally he asked, "Can I call you later if I need to talk to someone?"

I listened to him repeat the question three more times before he hung up.

"What about a missing person's report?" I asked.

Tim reached into his pocket for the business card the *Sûreté* had given him and picked up the phone again.

"They said I have to do that in Ottawa," he said when he hung up. "'Cuz that's the last place she was seen. I'll stop in at the police station on my way home."

He began to cry again. "She had her lunch with her and everything. There was an apple, and some peanuts—some kind of nuts."

I handed him another tissue.

"I'm going to have to pay the bills at the end of the month. I never had to do that before. I got no idea how to do that. God, I'm going to have to call my parole officer. That's an ordeal I'm not looking forward to. I guess I better get going. But I have no idea where I am. How do I get back to the main highway?"

I handed him his jacket. "I'll lead you back out in my car."

Once more he broke down.

I was suddenly impatient with his tears. I wanted him to go. It took me aback, how strong the feeling was of wanting him out of my house.

And how unkind that was to someone in his situation.

I let him follow me out to the main highway, and then turned the car for home. My brain was spinning as fast as my tires.

Mary Frances answered with a sleepy hello, but her voice became sharp and alert when she heard it was me. I never called after eleven. "Ellen, what is it? Are you alright?"

"Yes. No."

"Hang on a minute, love. I'm going to go downstairs. Jack is snoring like a log. I can barely hear you." Her words, spoken in her Yorkshire accent, were oddly comforting. She was my closest friend.

A moment later, her voice came on the line again. Sympathetic. "Is it Marc?"

I appreciated her concern. She had never approved of Marc—he was a "labourer"—but she'd tried to set aside her feelings to be supportive. And she only had herself to blame for our meeting: she had hired him to renovate her Chelsea farmhouse.

"No, it's not about Marc. I haven't heard from him." I took a deep breath and plunged into my story.

There was a silence when I was done. Then the unmistakable sound of inhaling. I imagined her high cheek bones becoming even more prominent as she dragged on her cigarette.

"Do you think he did it?" Her voice was tight from holding the smoke in her lungs.

"I don't know. I didn't even remember his past until I was on my way home. And Marc away, oh, you know. I was so stupid, Mary Frances, inviting him here."

I heard her exhale. "You mean because now he knows where you live?"

"Oh, God. I was thinking about my safety *tonight*. Anyway, he didn't seem to know where he was. I don't think he could find his way back. God. I don't know what to think. I just walked down the railway tracks with a man who has served time for killing someone. He might have killed again. But he didn't behave like a murderer." I laughed a shaky laugh. "What do I know about what a murderer behaves like? But nothing about his behaviour seemed suspicious or guilty. His whole demeanour was of someone shocked and upset. Like me. Oh God, Mary Frances, either he's innocent or my world has just turned upside down and I can't trust my judgement anymore."

"Ellen, come and sleep here."

I took a deep breath. "No. Thanks. I'll be okay. I think I just needed to talk to someone."

"I should think so. Are you sure? Well, if you change your mind in the middle of the night, motor over and hammer on the door."

"Or maybe you could send Jack over with a baseball bat."

"He's a proper scary sight in those striped pyjamas."

The image of Mary Frances's portly husband being shaken out of his snoring slumbers to be my bat-wielding knight in striped pyjamas made us both laugh. Which helped. A little.

I broke the rules with Beau and Belle. It wasn't easy to get them up onto the bed. Marc and I had trained them well. In the end, I physically heaved them onto it, one at a time. And lay between them, shivering in their warmth. Wishing the warmth were Marc's. Wishing for the home of his arms. Wishing for him to yell at me for having Tim over.

In the dark, the evening replayed itself like a video in my head. On second viewing, each odd thing Tim had said and done was suddenly illuminated. He wasn't supposed to go by street signs. It was an odd quirk to begin with, but then he'd pronounced King Edward like it was a foreign word. If you weren't sure about a street name, you didn't say it like that. It sounded like he'd been trying too hard to pretend he wasn't familiar with it. And he'd known all the street signs, except, apparently, the one where I'd given him a landmark. Had that just been to make it *look* like he needed to check for directions?

He'd rhymed off Lucy's shoes. He'd deduced the shoes she'd had on her feet by a process of elimination. Why hadn't he just seen what was on her feet? The police officer had said her slippers were on the passenger side floor. Lucy was extremely fastidious. She would never have tossed her slippers in the car without putting them in a bag. Of that, I was almost certain.

And then there was his saying maybe you had to have the key in the ignition to turn on an interior light. If they dusted for fingerprints on the steering wheel, they would find Tim's. Had he been accounting for why they would show up? Had he been the one to drive the car?

He'd lifted up her bag too. Was that also to account for his fingerprints? Maybe he'd carried it to the car because Lucy hadn't planned on going anywhere. Maybe he'd been able to rhyme off what was in her bag because he had packed it.

And the lunch. We hadn't looked in the white plastic bag. It sounded like he had remembered too late he wasn't supposed to know what kind of nuts were in it when he'd corrected himself from the specific to the general. Had he packed the lunch too?

And then there was my wanting him out of my house. My impatience with his tears. That was the oddest thing of all. It wasn't like me to be impatient with someone who was so upset. Maybe he hadn't been upset. Maybe they had been crocodile tears.

Who was this man Lucy had let into her life? The man I had met tonight had not been the confident, smiling man in the photo or the man with a first-year university education who had apparently expressed himself well in court. He had not been the capable man who knew how to live off the land and who shared the details of his life in articulate, if badly spelt, letters. The man I had met tonight had been a lost little boy. The little boy from the Brudenell backwoods. What had happened to the Tim Lucy had met and fallen in love with in prison?

I shut off these thoughts. A loved one going missing would be enough to rattle anyone out of their composure. But I could not shut off the video of the evening. It kept replaying in my head. Each time, Tim appeared to be acting. Overacting. Badly acting. Getting a reaction wrong. Getting a line wrong. Correcting himself mid-sentence.

Each little thing on its own didn't amount to much. Each thing on its own was like a distant pop of a firecracker in my brain—a tiny jolt of something not quite right.

Together, they lit up the sky.

In the dark I tossed and turned. Beau and Belle shifted and moaned with me.

No. I was the one overreacting. He was a man distraught that his girl-friend was missing. That would make you say and do bizarre things.

It seemed obvious what had happened. Lucy had driven up to the Gatineaus. She had parked her car close to the railway tracks to go for a walk. Something bad had happened on that walk. The police would find her in the morning. They would probably find her in the river—not alive. It was shocking and horrifying. But it was the only logical conclusion. There was nothing more I could do. I had played my part. I had found the car. I had called the police.

I drifted, finally, off to sleep.

Lucy is sitting on my bed. She is having trouble speaking. As if she is not quite awake, or has been drugged. Her mouth is working, as if she's having a hard time formulating words. But anxious to get them out. I don't want to hear what's going to come. I want to tell her not to speak. But I can't open my mouth. I can't get out of bed. I can't even put my hands over my ears; they are weighed down by bedcovers of lead.

I try not to listen, but her words brand themselves onto my brain.

I opened my eyes. My heart was pounding. I expected to see Lucy still sitting on the side of the bed. I could still hear her voice. It took a minute to realize it had been a dream. I sat up and reached for the light. Slowed my breathing and my heart.

At some point in the past few hours, the dogs had jumped back down to the floor. They were stretched out in their usual places on either side of the bed. Beau raised his head when the light came on.

In the bathroom I splashed cold water on my face. Dreams are just the garbage dump of the mind, I told my mirror image. I was upset because she'd gone missing. My mind was playing tricks on me. But Lucy's voice was there in my head—her real voice, from last summer, regaling me with stories of people who received messages from the other side, who had psychic visions. *No.* I spoke the word out loud to the mirror. I was not one of those people.

I flicked the bathroom light off and limped back to bed. Shut my eyes. Tried to keep the dream at bay. But her words would not go away.

Three sentences that made only half sense. They repeated themselves in my head, in Lucy's voice, until I was forced to get up again and go across the hall to my office for a pen and paper. Beau followed me. To the office and then back to my bedroom. From the floor, he watched me writing. Then he lowered his head back to his paws and shut his eyes with a heavy sigh.

I looked at the three sentences I had written on the page.

> *Look in the poplar grove.*
> *Write it in a book.*
> *Tell Anna I'm safe.*

Who was Anna? What poplar grove? Why was I writing this down? I was not going to start searching for Lucy. I certainly wasn't going to let a dream image of Lucy tell me where to search. I wasn't going to be involved in this in any way.

Something told me it would be far too dangerous.

4.

I T WAS AN ORDINARY DAY on the River Road construction site. The
sun was shining. The river was sparkling in a crisp, light breeze. The
workers were on a coffee break in their truck cabs. There was no
abandoned Suzuki. There were no boats. No dogs. No helicopters. No
police. No one was searching. No one, apparently, was missing.

The construction workers shook their heads when I asked about the
police in my poor French. They had been there since seven. They had
seen no one.

I hit the bridge over to the Ontario side at eight-thirty with every other
commuter from Chelsea. The traffic annoyed me. I usually waited until
after rush hour to go in to work. I was here because I'd woken up too
early and been compelled to go for a drive.

It wasn't my business. The police knew what they were doing. Or not
doing. They had to make sure it was legitimate. Maybe Lucy had left
on her own. Maybe she didn't want to be found. I was supposed to tell
someone named Anna—if she even existed—that Lucy was safe. Maybe
she was safe because she'd taken off. Maybe she was safe because she was
dead. No. I didn't believe that. I couldn't believe that.

Then why was I supposed to look in a poplar grove?

God, a psychologist would have a field day with a missing person
showing up in my dreams, urging me to search for her.

I inched my brain back to reason as the traffic inched over the bridge.
I was going to go to work and leave the searching to the police.

Roots Research was located in an aging red-brick building above a
second-hand bookstore in Ottawa's Byward Market. Angel, the company

founder, joked that the bookstore was the company library. It did have its uses. In fact, there were quite a few "company libraries" along this stretch of Dalhousie. A few streets over, the market proper offered up fresh fruits and vegetables from local vendors during the growing season and, all year, excellent cheese, meat, fruit, and fish. There were good restaurants and bars, and live music that Marc sometimes came down to hear with me. The best part was that it was close to the interprovincial bridge. If I had to work in the city, there was no better place.

There were three of us working for Angel. He was a remnant from the hippie era, with a balding head he now shaved every day and a love of all things rock 'n' roll. I'd been with him for five years, since he'd rescued me from a government job. My ideal was to be working for myself, like Lucy. But this was the next best thing. Angel was an easy boss. The hours were flexible, the atmosphere relaxed, and I could do things like Internet searches and report write-ups from home.

"Good God, Ellen," was Angel's startled greeting.

I gave him a warning look. "I'm researching the effects of traffic jams on the moods of Ottawa commuters. I wouldn't advise talking to me yet."

My computer wouldn't boot.

"Your computer isn't used to working this early either," said Angel. "Go get a coffee or something. Don't come back for awhile." He waved me away and sat down at my desk.

I took myself across the street to Mellos. Coffee was the last thing I needed. Look how it wired Lucy. Where *was* she? Why weren't the police searching? I downed a coffee I didn't want and dodged traffic on Dalhousie, feeling a twinge down my leg as I did.

My home page was staring at me benignly when I returned to my desk. I picked up the phone. Put it down. Picked it up. Dialled. Put it down. Repeated this process until I finally got to the ringing stage.

Tim picked up on the second ring. His frustration matched mine. They'd sent only one cop up, he said. He'd filed a missing person's report in Ottawa on his way home from my house. He'd told them about his record, he said. They'd asked him to come back this morning. He'd been grilled, he said. Now they wanted to talk to me.

He gave me the number for Detective Sergeant Howard Roach of the Ottawa-Carleton Regional Police.

"Our hands are tied," said Sergeant Roach when I was put through. His voice was gruff and pleasant and cynical.

There was a click on the line. "My partner is going to listen in."

I told my story to the sergeant and his anonymous partner. My co-workers looked up from their desks and I let them listen too.

"We don't have any official capacity once we cross the border into Quebec," explained Sergeant Roach in my ear. "We've offered our 'copters and dogs, but they refused our help. We're going up to the site this afternoon. We're treating it as suspicious. Where do you work? We'll come and take your statement on our way back."

"Do you have any idea what time it will be?"

"Later this afternoon is the best I can do."

"I'm not sure if I'll be here or at home."

"Give me all your coordinates—we'll find you."

"I'd rather you found Lucy." My tone was dry.

"We're working on it, Ms. McGinn." He sounded cheerful.

I gave him directions to the office and my house.

I was too restless to work. I put my coat on to leave. I assured a now much more concerned Angel that I was fine.

I drove back to the site. I was hoping to see a full-scale search in progress. I was hoping to meet a couple of Ottawa cops.

I found a couple of Quebec cops instead, and Tim with a woman I'd never seen before. The *Sûreté* officers were just getting into cars. One of them gave me his card: Luc Godbout, *Agent*.

"Has anyone taken your statement?" asked Agent Godbout. "*Non?* I will return in half an hour. Can you *attend?*"

I could *attend*.

Tim was visibly shaking. "I didn't sleep all night," he said. "This is Marnie Baxter. She's a good friend of Lucy and me."

Marnie was a strong-looking stocky woman. Maybe the same age as Lucy. Her hair was a deep auburn with grey streaks in it. Her face was so freckled it looked permanently tanned.

This was the woman Tim had called from my house. I had never heard

Lucy mention her. But that didn't mean anything. Lucy and I had never talked about her other friends.

Marnie didn't smile. There was no expression that I could read in her pale blue eyes. Possibly there was no expression in mine either. We were, after all, in shock. All of us.

"You live on Cameron," she said. Her voice was raspy, a smoker's voice. "I know the area. I have friends on McDonald. Where are you on Cameron?"

I tried to be vague. I didn't like her knowing the name of my road. If she knew the name of my road that meant Tim had told her. But I had never mentioned the name. Which meant Tim had read the sign at the top of the road. There was no reason he couldn't have; it wasn't as if he couldn't read. Except that odd comment of Lucy's stuck in my head—that he found his way around by landmarks.

"We're going to walk down the tracks," said Tim.

I watched them go. They walked slowly, chatting, disappearing around the bend. It was all wrong, their manner of walking. They looked like they were going for a pleasant stroll. No one was supposed to be going for a stroll when Lucy was missing.

It seemed forever before they came back in view.

They got in Tim's truck. It pulled up beside me and Tim rolled down the window. "We're going to the station in Hull," he said. "I'm supposed to meet Godbout at three-thirty."

I didn't tell him Detective Godbout was coming back. The two vehicles met a little way down the road. Words were exchanged from rolled-down windows. Then the green pick-up drove off, and the dark blue unmarked *Sûreté* vehicle pulled up beside me.

The driver leaned over and opened the passenger-side door.

Detective Godbout had sad, kind blue eyes. He looked more like a family physician than a police detective. It was the eyes, the clipboard in his hand. He might have been taking my medical history. The training was the same: ask questions that will illicit the truth, no matter how bad it is.

There was a difference. A doctor will assume a headache and work towards a tumour. Detective Godbout was assuming the worst. And he was assuming Tim was involved. He wanted to know if I knew of any problems between Lucy and Tim. He wanted to know if I thought Lucy had been abused or beaten. He wanted to know if I knew of Tim's criminal record. And what I knew about the "*disparition*" of Lucy Stockman. And what Tim's reaction had been when I had talked to him on the phone and in person.

Detective Godbout wrote out his first question on a piece of foolscap and handed me the clipboard and pen. I wrote out the answer I had given verbally and handed him back the clipboard. He wrote out the next question. Back and forth we went with the clipboard and pen.

When I was done answering his questions, I had one of my own: "When are you going to start searching?"

"If we don't do it tonight, we will certainly do it tomorrow."

Tonight? Tomorrow? A woman was missing. They needed to do something *now.*

It was as if he could read my mind. Detective Godbout smiled his reassuring family physician smile. "We will do everything we can. You leave it to our hands."

I was uneasy, but I had done everything I could do. The police were on the case. I drove home.

The dogs were hyper for a walk. I started down the road, but with each uncomfortable step my nerves got more on edge. Now that I wasn't sitting in the safe unmarked car with the kindly physician cop, his questions seemed more ominous. What if Tim *had* abused her? Or worse? And what if he came after me? How would I defend myself? And the house. With the doors unlocked, it was vulnerable too.

I tried to keep walking but every nerve ending tingled. Thick bush lined the road on either side, obscuring the railway tracks that were only metres away. The nearest neighbours were below the tracks, right on the waterfront. I had never felt the isolation of where we lived before. Never felt fear. This wasn't a fear of dream ghosts. This was a fear I couldn't ignore.

I headed back to the house as quickly as my leg would allow. In the kitchen, I rummaged through drawers until I found what I was looking for: Marc's spare ring of keys and an old fishing knife. I stuck the fishing knife in my waistband and pulled my jacket back down to cover it. I worked the house key off the ring, locked the door behind me, and stuck it in my pocket.

It was still a short walk. My nerves were shot, including the actual nerve down my leg. I left the dogs outside and did some stretching exercises on the living room floor. Detective Godbout's words echoed in my mind: *If we don't do it tonight, we will certainly do it tomorrow.*

My anger took me aback. If the police weren't going to take immediate action, someone had to. The word needed to be spread, the media needed to be called. I gave up on the exercises. I pulled out food to make a sandwich, mulling as I spread butter on bread. I jumped when the phone rang. The call display was only on the phone in the office upstairs. I hesitated, then picked it up. Tim wouldn't be home yet.

I was wrong about that. At the sound of his voice, my heart raced. I forced myself to sound normal. I didn't wait to hear what he wanted. In my nervousness, I launched into my idea of getting the media involved. Horrified to hear myself suggesting that he help me.

Tim's little-boy voice calmed me down. He sounded eager, *innocent*, but out of his element. He had, he said, no idea how to start a publicity campaign. I flipped through the phone book, looking for city newspaper phone numbers to pass on to him, and offered to call CBC radio myself. Unable to avoid agreeing to check back with him. When I got off the phone, I looked at the sandwich and felt sick.

The phone rang again two minutes later. Again I hesitated and then picked up the receiver.

I wasn't prepared for the voice at the other end. Its familiarity was like a massaging hand on a muscle you suddenly realize is tight.

"Oh, Marc."

I wanted to cry. I never cried.

I told him about Tim calling. And about finding Lucy's car. I told him about being questioned by the police. I told him I was happy to leave it in their hands and not get involved. I told him I'd spent the day in complete frustration because the police weren't doing anything.

"They said they'd bring out the dogs, put a boat in the water. I went up to the site in the morning, and talked to the construction workers and nothing, *nothing* has been done. And then I talked to Tim—"

"Ellen—"

"And he was frustrated too—"

"Ellen—"

"And we decided we'd start calling the media—"

"Ellen!"

"What?"

"You just said you did not want to get involved."

"I don't. God knows I don't. But the police are dragging their asses. And Tim seems so helpless. He has no idea who to call. Someone has to do something, to—"

"It does not have to be you."

"But I just want to light a fire under their butts and then I—"

"Ellen, I do not want it to be you."

There was a silence between us.

"How was your trip there?" I asked at last.

"*Bon.* I got here Sunday. There was snow in Marathon."

Another long pause.

"Marc," I said finally. "Why did you phone?" My heart was beating fast.

Another silence. I felt him reviewing all the possible answers, rejecting most of them, and settling on the mundane: "I wanted to see how you were doing."

"I'm fine," I lied.

"You are not."

"No. I'm freaked out. Marc, I was stupid. He knows where I live."

A sharp intake of breath over the line. "You … had him to our *house*?"

I shut my eyes. Hoping that would prevent the tears that were threatening to form. "Don't," I said, "yell at me." My voice was barely audible.

Another intake of breath. This time slower. "I don't want you to stay there. I *warned* you about him."

Closing my eyes wasn't making any difference. I swiped at the tears. "Marc. That does not help. And where am I supposed to go?"

"Here."

"*There?* Thunder Bay?"

"I'll pay for your ticket."

I felt an almost physical wrenching in my arm sockets: I wanted to go. I didn't want to go. I tried to think of practical reasons why I couldn't. "The dogs."

"Mary Frances will take them."

No. It wasn't fair. He was always wanting me to go to him. "Will you come home?" The question came out sounding like a child pleading.

"Ellen. I can't. I just hired a crew. We're just getting organized. I can't leave. You know I would…."

I didn't know that at all.

Marc was silent, too.

Finally I trusted my voice. "I'll be fine. I've got the dogs."

"Oh yes, our big brave dogs."

The sarcasm was so unlike him it caught me off guard. "I've got the police."

"You think they are going to give you twenty-four-hour protection?"

"No, but maybe they could talk me out of my fears."

Marc snorted.

This also uncharacteristic response fired me up. "Right," I said. "You could give me much better protection than the police."

"*Oui.*"

The quietness of his tone threatened to spill the tears in earnest.

"How is your leg?" Marc asked.

"My leg?" The pain, I realized, had dissipated. Just since Tim's call. "The chiropractor's helping," I said, to say something.

"Did she say anything about running?"

"Yeah, she said probably in a few weeks. I'm skeptical but I'll see how I feel."

"Why don't you go to stay with Mary Frances?"

"I'm *fine*," I said. "He has no reason to—"

"But if you are scared—"

"I'm *not* scared." I was defensive. And also lying.

"Marc," I said. "I'll be fine." I was talking very fast. "I'm going to phone the *Sûreté* and find out what's going on. Tim says Lucy's family is coming up from Toronto tonight. They want to go to the site. We're meeting at the station in Hull tomorrow to demand action. I'll call you tomorrow night." The urge to hang up was so strong I made sure we actually said good-bye before I gave in to it.

On Wednesday morning I made the brief walk from the market to the Château Laurier. Ottawa's fairy-castle hotel, with its copper-topped roof and turrets, was home to the local CBC radio station. I let a liveried doorman hold a heavy glass door for me and made my way across the marble-floored lobby. An elegant elevator carried me up to the seventh floor, where I told my story, the bare bones version, to a reporter and her tape recorder.

Afterwards, I bought some food in the market and headed back to the office. I sat at my computer and pretended to work. Every fifteen minutes I checked my answering machine at home for a message from Tim.

At noon I drove back across the interprovincial bridge to the police station in Hull. There was no sign of Detective Godbout or Tim or Lucy's family. I continued on up the highway to Chelsea. No traffic to contend with now.

River Road finally looked like the scene of an investigation. Several dark blue sedans and a police van were parked on the shoulder. A German shepherd was being put into the back of the van. There was a police boat out on the river. The activity both relieved me and worried me.

Two big men in tweed sports jackets were standing with Detective Godbout. They extended their hands to me in turn: Sergeant Howard Roach and his partner, Sergeant Alan Lundy.

"Ellen McGinn," said Sergeant Roach. "Or should I pronounce that 'Mc-Gin'?" He pronounced it with a soft 'g'. "Then you could call me McScotch." He winked. He was a tall man with a shock of white hair and a ruddy complexion. A pronounced widow's peak disguised an otherwise receding hairline.

"That would be my preference, too," I said. I was used to the jokes on my name. "Did they—did they find anything?" I didn't think they would have been standing around like this if they had, but I needed to ask.

Lundy shook his head. He was the bulkier of the two. He looked like he had been squeezed into his clothes. Under his tie, the top button of his shirt was undone, and only one of his jacket buttons was done up. He didn't smile, but there was a kind of grim sympathy in his expression.

"The dogs have just finished a search," said Roach. He nodded over at the van. "They're going to bring them back this afternoon." His eyes never stopped moving. They looked everywhere except at me. But I had the feeling he was memorizing everything about me, including my vital statistics and my car make and plate number.

"Have you seen Tim Brennan today?" I asked. "I was supposed to meet him and Lucy's family in Hull but they weren't there. He said the family was coming up from Toronto last night. They wanted to see where we found Lucy's car. I thought I must have missed them."

They had not seen Tim. "We'll drop by later this afternoon to take your statement," said Roach. "I've got the directions you gave us yesterday. Will you be at work or home?"

"Home," I said. I wondered where Lucy's family was. And Tim.

When I got home, I automatically pushed against the front door, expecting it to give. It didn't. The car keys were still in my hand. I found the little-used house key and jammed it into the lock.

I was changing into jeans and a sweatshirt when the phone rang. It was CBC Television, wanting an interview. I arranged for them to come at four.

I had not been off the phone two minutes when it rang again. "I've been trying to get you," said Tim. "We're here at the Tulip Valley restaurant—me an' Anna and Doug."

"*Anna?*" The hair on the back of my neck prickled.

"Yeah, Lucy's sister and her husband Doug. That Quebec cop Godbout is supposed to come an' talk to us. D'you wanna meet us here?"

Lucy's sister. Lucy must have mentioned her sister's name to me and it had lodged somewhere in my memory. I could *not* have pulled it out of thin air.

I glanced at the clock on the stove. One o'clock. Roach and Lundy wouldn't show up for awhile. I had time to go. Maybe they would show up there, too.

The Tulip Valley restaurant sat at the intersection of Highway 105 and River Road, a ten-minute drive north of my place. It was here that Tim had gone in to ask directions the other night. I checked the road sign at the corner and smiled wryly. It said *Chemin de la Rivière*. I doubted he was bilingual. He'd probably had good reason to stop after all.

The restaurant did double duty as a coffee shop and sports bar.

Tim was sitting at a table on the restaurant side with a man and a woman. Anna thanked me for coming. Her voice had the same low timbre as Lucy's, but her colouring and features were fairer. And she emanated a milder temperament. Her eyes were big and brown, filled with gentleness and worry. "Dad wanted to come too. But he's not well. And this—" Her voice broke.

Beside her Doug put a hand over hers. He was a tall lanky man with a full beard that hid most of his face. He wanted to order me a coffee and hear every detail of my finding the car.

I described the events of Monday evening.

In the back of my head, Lucy's voice was whispering, insistent.

I tried to ignore it. I was going to sound like some kind of flaky visionary if I passed on her "message." And why give false hope? But Lucy's voice compelled me. Lucy's voice and her sister's eyes across the table.

I made my voice apologetic. I didn't tell her who had given me the dream message—just "a friend." I felt Tim listening. I wished I had waited until we were alone to speak.

Anna's eyes gleamed with tears. And gratitude. Suddenly Doug was handing over a sheaf of paper. I glanced down and was startled to see Lucy smiling at me from a photocopied photograph. I hadn't thought of posters. I promised to put them up.

Detective Godbout arrived with his kindly, now tired, physician's eyes and no reassuring news. The dogs had picked up no scent. That, said Detective Godbout in his careful English, meant it was now in the hands of the Ottawa police; that was the last place Lucy had been seen.

He asked if anyone had questions. They did. His answers were not guaranteed to satisfy. He knew this. He spread his hands in apology and left us.

We pushed back our chairs and rose to go.

Anna touched my arm. She let the others go on ahead. "Can I call you, to…?"

"Of course." I gave her my phone number. I didn't think I had anything helpful to offer, but I couldn't refuse.

"Curtis is sure he did it. But I don't know. He's so upset. I don't think he's thinking straight. Maybe—"

"Curtis?" I interrupted. That name had been in one of Tim's letters.

"Curtis," repeated Anna. She must have seen my blank look. "It was Curtis she was living with when she met Tim. Tim was so jealous."

Lucy hadn't just been seeing someone; she'd been *living* with him.

"We all wrote letters of support to the National Parole Board—me, my father, Doug, all her friends. We pledged our support. You said she was safe. Do you think she's just … got away?"

I had no answer for her. None I believed. I hugged her close. I told her I would call her if I heard anything.

She was turning to go but this time I stopped her. "Anna, I didn't want to say anything in front of the others, but the person speaking in my dream wasn't just any friend." I paused and met her eyes. "It was your sister."

A startled look came over her face. And then something like confusion. "I'm sorry," I added. "I know it sounds crazy. And I hope it doesn't upset you. But I thought you should know."

Her eyes filled with tears again. She nodded, wiping her cheek. "Thank you. I appreciate it." Through the open door we could hear Doug calling her. "I should go, but I—I just need to ask you." She hesitated, looked away. Looked back at me. "Are you sure she said, 'Anna'"?

I nodded. "I had no idea who 'Anna' was but the name was clear. I only realized it was you when Tim mentioned your name when he called this afternoon." I looked at her questioningly.

She gave me a teary smile. "Okay. Thanks. Really, thanks, Ellen." She pressed·my hand and rushed out of the restaurant.

The television crew arrived at my door just after I did. They rolled the camera while I taped one of Doug's posters to the side of the cluster of green mailboxes at the top of the road.

In the photo on the poster, Lucy is standing on her front porch. She is dressed up to go out somewhere, wearing a knee-length patterned dress and heels. She is smiling right beside the block-lettered words "MISSING PERSON" and her physical description.

> LUCY STOCKMAN
> 46 YEARS OLD
> 5'1" TALL
> 100 POUNDS
> DARK BROWN SHOULDER LENGTH HAIR
> TANNED COMPLEXION, BROWN EYES
> LAST SEEN APRIL 22 (SAT) WEARING A DARK BLUE COAT WITH SMALL RED STRIPE, BLACK OR NAVY COLOURED TIGHT PANTS, NIKE RUNNERS.
> HER YELLOW AND WHITE SUZUKI SIDEKICK WAS FOUND PARKED ON RIVER ROAD JUST SOUTH OF THE LARGE ROCK QUARRY AT THE BOTTOM OF THE HILL WHERE THE ROAD CONSTRUCTION SITE IS.

The police contact information was provided at the bottom.

There was one message waiting on my machine when I got home. It was from Curtis. He spoke in a quiet voice that seemed to mask some great emotion. He had got my number from Tim. He hoped I would call him back.

From Tim? Was he in league with Tim? That made no sense. He was, I assumed, the jilted lover. How would I feel if something happened to Marc? Devastated.

I made myself eat dinner to work up my nerve to call him back. His exchange was in the Wakefield area.

Our conversation was awkward. He wanted to hear the story of how I'd found the car. I gave him the same bare bones version I'd given the CBC. I remembered he'd gotten my phone number from Tim. "Did you call Tim?" I asked.

"I called *Lucy*," said Curtis. "On Sunday. Tim said she wasn't home and I hung up, but he called me back. He must have star-sixty-nined me." He was referring to the phone company last-number-called service. He didn't sound pleased. "He gave me some song and dance about Lucy coming to stay with me on the weekend."

"Lucy told me she was going to be in the Gatineaus on the weekend," I said.

"We never made any definite plans." He sounded adamant. And defensive, as if others had already brought this up. Then, in a disquieting tone, he added, "She wouldn't listen to me."

No, I thought. There wouldn't be many people Lucy would listen to. I thought about what she'd said about being abandoned by all her lovers. Until Tim. If she'd still been with Curtis when she started seeing Tim, he must have been absent in *some* way. I could well imagine the conflicts that would have created. Still, it must have been a slap in the face when she'd started corresponding with Tim. Had Curtis been jealous? But Anna had said it was *Tim* who'd been jealous.

"Have you talked to the police?" I asked.

"They've been here."

There was a silence. He obviously didn't want to say more. As I didn't. I tried to think of something neutral. "We're trying to get a media campaign going. I got Tim to call the papers. I talked to CBC. Anna and Doug made some posters."

"I'm knocking on doors in the area," said Curtis. Then there was a pause, and his voice became more conciliatory. "I don't have any connections to Lucy's friends anymore. If you hear anything, I'd appreciate it if you'd let me know."

I reviewed our conversation in my mind after we hung up. He had sounded as wary as I had felt. We had danced around each other, neither giving the other too much information. His reactions were the same as mine. He must be innocent. I caught myself. *What do you know? Trust no one.*

I had agreed to call him. But I didn't intend to.

I drifted in and out of sleep. Voices were filling my head with unintelligible words. There were no faces attached to the voices. They kept waking me up. And then the voices faded, and Lucy was again sitting on my bed.

Her mouth begins moving. She speaks as if with great effort. But I hear every word. "He's trying to frighten me. So I'll stay." An image comes, a silent-screen image. A small figure with long, dark hair lying on a couch, eyes closed, then opening, expression angry, her mouth moving as if yelling. Someone hovers over her. A faceless male figure. He forces something down her throat. Pills. A second, shorter figure watches. Again, no face. Then Lucy's voice, in eerie voice-over: "You've looked in her eyes."

I am in a vehicle, moving to the end of a street with houses on either side. I see stores on a busy street. Then an odometer, larger than life. The numbers click over. Five, six, seven. The odometer fades and I'm back in the car, watching it stop beside a dark shadow of a building.

Lucy's voice again. "Abandoned buildings—outbuildings. I'm wrapped in something—a man-made material. She's afraid. Follow her."

Then Lucy reappears on my bed. Looking at me. Pointing at her watch. Frantically.

I sat up in bed, and reached for the light. My heart was pounding, my T-shirt soaked. Oh God, it was happening again.

I got up to get a drink of water. Lucy's voice was still in my head. *He's trying to frighten me. So I'll stay.* "He" could only be Tim.

The images returned, vivid in my memory. Pills being forced down Lucy's throat, her anger. Tim had mentioned Lucy had a supply of Valium. My subconscious had clearly taken that idea and run with it. Because I didn't want to entertain more violent thoughts. Because I didn't want to think about why she might have needed Valium.

But there were lots of things in the dream that couldn't have come from my subconscious. The involvement of a second person. Someone whose eyes I had looked into. Who had I met that Lucy and Tim knew? Only Marnie. Was *Marnie* involved? She was the second person Tim had called from my house. She had been right there with him the next day. *Follow her.* Why? Was Marnie checking on her? Could Marnie lead the police right to her? I had been in a car, driving down a main street, stopping at a building. Abandoned outbuildings.

He's trying to frighten me. So I'll stay. Of everything in the dream, those words made the most sense. She'd been trying to get away. Maybe she *had* got away. Maybe she'd abandoned her car to make it look like Tim had done something to her. The car had been found up somewhere near where Curtis lived. Maybe Curtis was in on this. Maybe he had helped her get away. Maybe he had called Lucy on Sunday to look innocent.

Or maybe the figure in the dream was Curtis....

I splashed water on my face. It was a *dream*. Nothing more. I would get a grip.

But it was fear that had the grip. Had I locked the door? Could he get in?

At the front door, Belle and Beau waited, mouths drawn back in expectant smiles, tails wagging.

"We're *not* going out." I punctuated my words with a pull on the door knob to make sure it was locked. It was almost funny: their eagerness to go out, mine to stay in.

I started at my reflection in each window. I had never seen the need for curtains. Before.

"No one's out there," I said aloud. I looked at the dogs. "What reason would anyone have to be out there? What threat am I? No one knows I know anything. I *don't* know anything."

But I did know some things. Things that weren't the suspect messages from a bizarre dream. They were there, on the videotape of my memory, waiting to be replayed once again: the odd things from my encounter with Tim on Monday evening.

I looked at the dogs again. I wanted them to tell me I was being irrational. Instead, I heard Lucy and her second message from the previous night: *Write it in a book.*

Oh Lucy, what are you doing to me?

But I couldn't refuse her. Whether she was a figment of my imagination or not. I went in search of paper and pen.

It took an hour. I finished the description of my dealings and conversations with Tim, all the odd things he had said. But I didn't stop writing. The things Lucy had said in my dream, the scenes she'd shown me, were still vivid in my memory. The dream, hallucination, whatever it had been, it fit with all the odd things. I couldn't dismiss it. There was no way around it. I was going to have to go to the police.

I paced up and down the living room, avoiding the windows. Belle and Beau paced with me and whimpered. Every few minutes I deviated from my path to check the clock on the stove.

At two a.m. Lundy and Roach were not likely to be on duty. Was it worth getting them out of bed to hear my far-fetched tale? They would never believe me. I didn't believe myself.

But even if everything else was bunk, the odd things were probably worth something. The odd things might get their attention. And then what? Entertain them with visions visited on me by the victim? The dreams were so convoluted, so vague. The first seemed more believable, more straightforward in its messages. Maybe I should simplify the second. The kilometres must have been indicating how far from her house they had gone. I needed a map of Ottawa. Please let there be one in the house. I wasn't ready to go outside.

I found an old torn city map buried under the shoes in the coat closet. I pieced it back together on the kitchen counter and pulled up a bar stool. I found Lucy's street on the map. The nearest street with stores on it would be Bank. North would take them downtown. That made no sense. South headed out of town. I checked the map scale and measured, with my fingers, the equivalent of seven kilometres south on Bank from the intersection with Lucy's street. I noted the name of the closest main artery: Hunt Club Road.

Then I reached for a pen and paraphrased additional one-line instructions from Lucy.

I wouldn't bring her into it at all. I would just say I had heard a voice in my head. Oh God, they were going to think I was certifiable, no matter what I said.

I sat at the kitchen counter with my head in one hand and the other on the phone receiver. In my mind, I could see Lucy, pointing frantically at her watch.

Ellen. It was a voice in my head. Not an imaginary voice. My own. And it was loud and clear: *You might find her. She might still be alive.*

The words shot through my brain like a bolt of lightning. They snapped me to attention. They triggered an adrenalin rush that didn't let up for ten weeks.

———⚬⚬⚬———

THE PHONE CALLS HAD TO come collect from Tim. "The operator comes on right away," he explained. "I hate to make you pay. I got no choice. I got no choice about time either. We only have six phones in our cell block, and there's a few dozen of us who gotta share it. We have a system worked out, a schedule of who gets to talk when. I'm working during the day—doing maintenance, taking mechanics and carpentry courses. I put myself down for six-thirty p.m. on Tuesdays. We got twenty minutes. Is that okay? I don't mean to be presumptive about us talking every week—it's just easier to book it ahead. It's totally up to you."

She assured him once a week was fine. And she didn't mind paying. She didn't mind the time of day either. She found it interesting that he couldn't call during the day when Curtis was at work. It was going to have to be out in the open, this time, whether she liked it or not. She liked it. A pattern was being broken. The days of covertly running from one man to another were over. Maybe by breaking that pattern, she'd break another. Maybe this was about not expecting everything from one man. Maybe in getting the intimacy of sharing with Tim she would stop expecting it from Curtis. Maybe she could let him be. And then maybe he'd stay.

When the second phone call came, Curtis announced that he was leaving.

"I am not," he said, "accepting calls in my house from a murderer."

"It is not your house! And he's not a murderer! If you call him a murderer one more time, I'll—"

"Great." Curtis gave a grim smile. "He's teaching you well. No, you already knew the fine art of threatening. You two are obviously made for each other."

"Yes," she threw back. "We are. Which is a lot more than I can say for you and me."

There was a deep, unexpected, sigh from Curtis. And a long look.

Then that quiet voice: "You're wrong, you know. And if you weren't so pigheaded, you'd see it."

He suddenly smiled—a teasing, affectionate smile she hadn't seen in awhile.

She steeled herself against that smile. She would not let it suck her in, not anymore. She crossed her arms. "If you weren't so pigheaded, you'd show it."

Curtis shrugged. "You mean I'd show it in the way you want me to show it. You may as well be having this relationship with yourself."

"I am," she snapped.

5.

THE DETECTIVE ON THE OTHER end of the phone invited me to come down to the station to tell him my story. He even offered to send a car.

I told him I had a car. I didn't tell him it was going to take all my nerve to run to it from the front door. I didn't tell him Tim Brennan was outside my door, lurking behind every bush.

My rational mind, usually in control, could only stand by and watch. It watched me scramble behind the wheel and lean over to lock all the doors. It watched me accelerate down the dirt road, make the sharp uphill turn onto Cameron without stopping, and then speed down the highway towards Ottawa. It heard me muttering under my breath, over and over, "Hang on, Lucy. Just hang on. I'm coming."

Reason just barely stopped me from thanking God for all the green lights on the city streets and for the absence of cops stopping me for speeding. Reason watched me walk into the cavernous police station on Elgin Street with the certainty that I was going to be thrown in jail for my tall tales.

By the time Detective Sergeant Stephen Quinn of the Ottawa-Carleton Regional Police shook my hand, reason was back in control. His grip was firm and warm and attached to a man with his feet on the ground.

Sergeant Quinn was not bursting out of his suit like Lundy. He did not drink too much Scotch like Roach. He was not haggard from too many eighteen-hour shifts, or hardened from making the acquaintance of too many nasty criminal minds. He did not have an unhappy wife at home who nagged him for neglecting her and the kids.

Sergeant Quinn had a solid build and a smooth roundish face with a five o'clock shadow I suspected even a fresh shave would not completely remove. His hair was shaved close to his head. Thick chest hair showed above the neckline of the T-shirt he wore under his dress shirt. He had steel blue eyes. He looked to be barely forty.

He also looked like he had nothing better to do than to sit in an air-less interrogation room with a tensed-up woman in the middle of the night. He gestured to a chair at the table in the tiny room and pulled up another for himself. "You tell me your story, and then I'll decide if we should wake up Sergeants Lundy and Roach. They were here 'til midnight and I'm kind of reluctant to disturb their slumbers." Then he smiled. The smile put me at ease, a little.

I started with the facts. My acquaintance with Lucy. Finding her car. Dealing with Tim. I outlined all his odd comments and actions. I spoke in a monotone that kept me calm.

Sergeant Quinn didn't take his eyes from me.

I finished reciting the facts and looked at him hard. "Now we get to the part where my tale becomes what you might call fairly unbelievable, and you get to send me home."

My ability to joke startled me. Sergeant Quinn's laugh startled me even more. "Try me," he said. "Maybe I'll surprise you." He folded his hands behind his head and leaned back.

I looked at him for a moment. "Okay, but here's the deal. I want to state for the record that I don't normally pay attention to my dreams. I don't believe in dreams. Or psychics. Or telepathy. Or any of that stuff. I don't think of myself as psychic. I'm not psychic. But, unfortunately, I recently had a couple of dreams that I haven't been able to ignore."

I took my notes out from my pocket, unfolded the paper, and placed it in front of me on the table. I let in and out a deep breath. "I was hearing a voice. It dictated lines to me. It happened twice. Both times I got up and wrote down the messages. They were about Lucy." My voice had returned to that monotone that kept it from shaking. I looked at Sergeant Quinn to see how he was taking this.

Quinn's expression stayed neutral. He nodded at my notes. "Tell me what you heard."

I looked at the piece of paper in my hand. I read off the first two phrases from my first dream and then stumbled over the third. "Tell Anna I'm.... Tell Anna *she's* safe." There was no way I was going to tell him it was Lucy who had given me these messages; he would send me home for sure.

I told Sergeant Quinn what I thought they meant.

"So," he summed up, "you think this woman is in a poplar grove somewhere. And you're supposed to tell her sister she's safe." He couldn't keep the amusement out of his voice.

I gave him a wry look. "I told you...."

"Go on," Quinn prompted. His voice was very gentle.

I fought a sudden tightness in my throat. I couldn't look at him. "I got another set of messages tonight." I read the phrases I had partially made up: "Abandoned buildings. Bank and Hunt Club. Wrapped in a man-made material. Follow Marnie."

Quinn sat up straight and leaned forward. "Say all that again."

I repeated the three phrases from the first dream and the four phrases I'd made up from the second dream.

"Okay," he said. "She's wrapped in some kind of synthetic material and being held in some abandoned buildings near Bank and Hunt Club, and possibly the building is surrounded by or near a poplar grove." He kept his voice neutral. It impressed me, and disconcerted me. I couldn't read him. It didn't matter. He was listening.

"Are there poplar groves near Bank and Hunt Club? Are there abandoned buildings down there?"

Quinn looked stern. Cop stern. "Have you ever been down in that area?"

I shook my head. "No, not that I can think of."

"Never?" He had shifted to interrogation mode.

I shook my head again. Suddenly I wanted to laugh. This whole night was beginning to seem absurd.

Quinn leaned back again and sighed. "That entire area is woods, beyond the main road and the shopping malls. And in these economic times, it's full of abandoned buildings. These women's names," he went on. "Anna, you say, is her sister. Who's Marnie?"

"She's the woman Tim called from my place the night I found the car. And then she was with him the next day at the site. He said she was a friend of theirs."

"And we're supposed to follow her because—what? She's checking on Lucy?"

"That's the sense I got."

It was bad enough telling my story, not knowing if I was implicating an innocent woman. It was worse hearing it come out of Sergeant Quinn's mouth. I should never have come.

Quinn looked at me for some time without saying anything. He leaned forward again. He had his elbow on the table and his hand over his mouth. He tapped his fingers against his mouth, and breathed audibly through his nose. He never took his eyes from mine. They were narrowed, as if trying to read my mind. I didn't want him to read my mind. He'd hear the irrational voice that kept screaming: *she might be alive.*

I didn't realize I had spoken aloud until I saw the look Sergeant Quinn gave me. Then he released a breath. "I think we'd better go for a drive."

He smiled at the look on my face. "I told you I might surprise you."

The unmarked cruiser was big and blue and luxuriously comfortable. There was the faint smell of leather, coming from Sergeant Quinn's jacket.

"You say you're not psychic. Your experiences sound psychic." The voice came out of the soft darkness of the plush interior.

"You mean 'crazy.'"

"You don't have to be afraid to admit it. My grandmother was psychic. She called it having the 'sight.' She was Scottish. In your case, it sounds more like clairaudience. Hearing things—messages—"

"Oh, I'm hearing things alright." My attempt at humour came out in a shaky voice. Quinn made no response.

Ottawa's busiest street was empty. I kept my eyes on the side roads. There it was, Glen Avenue: Lucy's street. I tried to read the odometer without leaning over in a noticeable way. It wasn't easy to see it, but I wanted to make sure Hunt Club really was six or seven kilometres from Lucy's street as I'd determined from the map.

It was a silent drive. An unreal drive in a big smooth car down a deserted main artery. It was another dream. I was unsure what we were going to find. I didn't think it would come to anything. I was terrified it would.

We neared the Hunt Club area. I *had* been down here before. I saw that now. It was the shopping mall strip. The street names on the map had meant nothing to me. I didn't come this way very often.

I kept my eyes peeled for abandoned buildings on side streets. I saw how hopeless this was and understood the reasons for Sergeant Quinn's heavy sighs.

"I think it was just the general Bank and Hunt Club area." I wanted him to slow the car.

"I know that," said Sergeant Quinn. He slowed down, and held the wheel loosely, at the top, with one hand. "I also know there are dozens of abandoned buildings down here. In these economic times, everyone's abandoned something."

"I see that."

We were approaching another main artery. Hunt Club. Sergeant Quinn turned right.

It felt right to turn right. It was bizarre, that feeling. But at least the number of kilometres we'd travelled from Lucy's street to Hunt Club seemed to be correct.

I glanced to my right. There was a building at the end of a short intersecting street—a building several storeys high, with boards over the windows.

"Isn't that an abandoned building?"

Sergeant Quinn slowed the car right down and peered past me. "That's an apartment building under construction." He drove on.

"Are you sure? Those looked like boarded-up windows."

Sergeant Quinn swung the wheel around with one hand and pulled a U-turn in the middle of Hunt Club. He turned up the street. It was a court, with the building on the west side.

Quinn stopped the car so that it was facing the building. A window directly in front of us wasn't boarded up. The glass was broken at one corner. Eerie lights shone out. It took me a heart-stopping minute to realize what they were: our headlights reflecting back at us.

"There's a grove of trees over there," said Sergeant Quinn. His voice was odd.

I looked beyond the building. There was, as he said, a dark wooded area. I couldn't tell what the trees were. The skin on my arms began to feel prickly.

"Have you ever seen this building before?" Quinn's voice was cop-stern again. But pitched to a slightly higher key.

"I have never seen this building before." My voice was that monotone again. Also pitched slightly higher.

I began to shiver.

Sergeant Quinn got out of the car. I did the same. We approached the building.

The corner of the window that had appeared to be broken was merely a corner of torn plastic over the still-glassed-in window.

We cupped our hands on the plastic-covered glass and peered inside. In the dim light I made out bales of pink fibreglass strewn about the floor.

"That's a man-made material!"

"I know that's a man-made material," said Sergeant Quinn. Then he added in a calmer voice, "I'm not laughing at you."

I knew he wasn't. I knew he was as shaken as I was.

We walked around the building. All the other windows were boarded up tight. The only door was a solid metal one at the back. It had a keyhole but no handle. It couldn't be the right building if there was no way someone could get in.

I followed Sergeant Quinn back to the car.

Back in the driver's seat, he radioed the dispatcher. "I have a strange request," he said. "I'd like a police cruiser with two officers. And make sure they have flashlights."

"Can I go in with you?" My voice was peculiar. Flat.

"Yes," he said. "But do me a favour. Don't tell these officers what brought us here."

"You don't have to worry about me."

We waited in the darkness. In the silence. A few minutes later, a set of headlights arced onto the road and snapped off a short distance away.

Quinn went to speak to the officers. A moment later he was back with a flashlight.

I got out of the car. The officers made no move to get out of theirs.

I stumbled and tripped behind Quinn and his flashlight beam.

"Careful," he admonished.

We circled the entire building. There were no breaks in the windows. There were no other doors. My disappointment was acute.

We arrived back at the front of the building

"Stay here," said Sergeant Quinn. His tone softened the order into a suggestion. There was no question I would stay. He disappeared into the wooded grove behind the building.

One of the officers spoke from a rolled-down window. "What are we doing here, anyway?"

I approached the cruiser. "A friend of mine is missing and I thought she might be in this building." That didn't sound too crazy.

The two officers got out to stretch their legs.

I hung back, waiting for Sergeant Quinn to reappear from the woods. That's when Tim and Marnie strolled up the street. I could see Marnie's face under the street light from thirty metres away. Her face was clear—so clear I called out her name.

I expected them to run. But they didn't seem to hear me. I expected them to run for sure when they saw the police officers. But they had obviously thought fast. They went right up to the officers, and Tim spoke. "Officer, my girlfriend is missing."

I ran over to the police officers. I grabbed the nearest one by the arm. "Arrest these two."

The officer sent a lazy look down at me from a great height. "And why would I do that?"

I opened my mouth to explain. At the same time, I turned my head in slow motion to look at Tim and Marnie. And saw two strangers. Two completely different faces. Younger faces. Smirking faces.

I was stunned. Disoriented.

"I'm so sorry," I said.

"Hey, no problem," said the male. He was grinning, as if it were all a joke. It was a joke: a cosmic joke, on me.

I walked away. Spooked. Confused. The face had been clear. Not a hazy image that might have been Marnie's. It had been her face. And then it hadn't. I was going crazy. Truly crazy.

As if it were a film soundtrack running without the visuals, I could hear the young man telling their story to the officer. He lived just down the street. His girlfriend and this woman were best friends. They had come over for the evening. His girlfriend, a black girl, had just walked out of the house a few minutes ago. They didn't know why. They couldn't find her.

I didn't hear the police officer's response. It was an odd story. It wasn't the whole story. Why had she left? Had they had a fight? Maybe she had wanted to leave. Maybe she didn't want to be found.

Maybe the police officer thought so too. A minute later the two young people were walking back the way they had come.

I called out before I could stop myself: "Sorry!"

A cheerful "No problem!" wafted back to me from under the street light. The two disappeared in one direction, and a beam of light appeared from another. The beam of light became Sergeant Quinn and his flashlight.

There was no conversation between us. I knew he had found nothing. Maybe some poplars. Maybe not. I was afraid to ask.

We peered one more time into the windows of the building. Our beam shone back at us.

"Someone's got in there," said Sergeant Quinn suddenly.

"They have?" I jerked around so fast, I tripped. He reached out to steady me.

"Careful!" he admonished again.

The beam was not ours reflected in the window. The light emanated, hazily, from within, through the layer of plastic and glass.

I followed Sergeant Quinn at a run. He shone the flashlight behind for me. I sensed his hands ready to pick me up. My clumsiness embarrassed me.

The steel door at the back was now ajar. We stepped inside.

"We're Vanier," said one of the cops, naming a rough Ottawa suburb. "We have a key."

Quinn's laugh filled the vast black space. He shone his flashlight around.

The interior was a skeleton of wooden beams and joists and temporary walkways separating the "floors" over our heads. Everywhere were bales of fibreglass and garbage bags filled with debris. Or maybe, one of them, something else.

"Stay right behind me," ordered Quinn. It was another order I was happy to obey.

We walked all around the ground floor. We were thorough. Quinn's flashlight exposed every corner. I kicked and prodded every bale and bag. I called out Lucy's name. Self-conscious but not caring if I was embarrassing myself. I was in a state of tension I had never experienced before.

Sergeant Quinn shone his flashlight above us. A wooden ladder was nailed to a beam. I was going up into that flimsy skeletal framework. What if I fell? But I didn't hesitate. Sergeant Quinn was already halfway up the ladder. I wasn't going to be left behind. I climbed without allowing myself to think. The dark somehow made it easier.

The Vanier officers stayed below. Then Quinn and I were alone in the building. Quinn didn't reach down from the top of the ladder to give me a hand up. Professional protocol would not allow that. But I was aware that he was aware of my every move. He would have grabbed me if I'd fallen. It helped to know that.

The second "floor" was a narrow walkway with great gaps and open places where a woman, clumsy in her terror, could fall through. There were fewer bags and bales to prod. We searched for the ladder to the next floor.

I kept my eyes fixed on Quinn's leather-jacketed back, not on the gaping blackness beneath us. I walked close enough to grab hold if I needed to. Close enough to step on his heels.

"At least I know you're there," he joked in a grim voice after my third apology.

It was a slow, methodical, eerie search. I kept calling Lucy's name. My voice echoed around the black hollow shell. Every moment I expected the flashlight to expose her crumpled body in a corner, to hear a moan, or to feel the thunk of my foot on soft flesh inside a bag or bale.

And all the time I couldn't stop the irrational thought that this wasn't the right building. There was no right building.

In all, we climbed four ladders. We made our way around four narrow walkways.

We came, finally, to a metal door exiting to the flat roof.

Quinn walked to the edge and looked over the side. I stayed rooted in the centre, absorbing the solid ground into the soles of my feet. I took in long breaths of cool night air. I made them slow. Deep. It wasn't over yet. I had to go back in. Back down.

There was no way anyone else had got in here to hide a body. No one said it. No one had to. Quinn held the door open for me, and I braced myself to go back into the black cavern.

At each floor, we had to creep along the narrow walkways in search of the next ladder. Again I walked barely two steps behind Quinn. And kept my hand outstretched, ready to grab him if I tripped.

At each ladder Quinn turned to me. "Come down right after me." It was a needless request. My feet landed where his hands had just been—and sometimes on them.

At the bottom of each ladder, Quinn shone the light on the steps for the rest of my descent. His arms were outstretched. His hands all but touched me. He didn't drop them until he made sure I had safely reached the bottom.

There was no way to shut the steel door; there was no handle. There was only a keyhole, and Vanier had the "key." And Vanier was gone. We left the door slightly open.

We got in the car. We didn't speak. We drove back down to the main street. We turned right, and drove under the Airport Parkway overpass. And past another set of uninhabitable buildings.

"Aren't those abandoned buildings?" I was sounding like a broken record.

Again Sergeant Quinn pulled a U-turn in the middle of the road. A patient pulling of the steering wheel into the short incline of a driveway: to stare at the ruined barns in front of us.

They were charred black from a fire. The roofs were caved in. It didn't look recent.

"Those are burnt-out buildings," said Quinn. "And we're not going in there at night." His voice was firm, his decision final.

He backed the car out of the driveway. We headed east and turned onto the on-ramp for the Airport Parkway, back downtown.

"In these economic times," said Sergeant Quinn, for what seemed like the dozenth time.

"I know. There are a lot of abandoned buildings. I know it's a long shot. But I had to—"

"Yes, I know."

We stopped talking. The Parkway merged with Bronson Avenue and we continued north. Then we were turning onto Colonel By Drive. Beside us, the Rideau Canal was a long, dark presence. A long exposed tunnel, with a foot of water in the bottom. The water level was always lowered before winter, to transform the canal into the world's longest skating rink. The real sign of spring in Ottawa was the sky-reflecting water lapping at the top of the canal walls and rowing shells gliding effortlessly up and down its length.

I finally worked up the nerve to ask. "Could you at least follow Marnie?"

"Tomorrow morning you call Sergeant Roach and tell him what we did tonight and let him decide."

"Will you still be on duty when he comes in?"

"I hope to be home in bed. I've been on shift since one. I'm supposed to be on half time. I was supposed to leave at seven o'clock tonight. I'm still here." His voice was sharp in its weariness.

I sat in a terrible silence. It lasted the length of the long fast ride beside the canal. Through the red lights we ran at the deserted intersections. Down the ramp into the underground parking off a side street from Elgin. Into the empty parking space we'd backed out of almost two hours before.

Sergeant Quinn killed the engine. He didn't move.

"I didn't mean that to sound as harsh as it did," he said, as if the five- or six-kilometre silence since his last words had been seconds.

He turned to look at me. Thoughtful. Appraising. There were dark shadows under his eyes I hadn't noticed before. Fatigue emanated from him. I had the sudden feeling it wasn't just from the long day, but from whatever had put him onto half time. Something I hadn't noticed on first meeting him. Cop burn-out? I dismissed the thought. I had just dragged him out in the middle of the night on a wild goose chase after his shift was supposed to be over. "It's okay."

"It's not okay," he said, "when women go missing." There was anger in his voice.

He paused. "Sometimes," he said slowly, "sometimes they want to go missing. Sometimes they don't want to be found."

I nodded. "That occurred to me. I know. Like the girl in the parking lot."

He stared at me. "What girl in what parking lot?"

"I don't mean parking lot. I mean that first street we were on, outside that apartment building. And she wasn't there."

"Ellen. You need to go home and get some sleep. You're not making any sense."

"Sorry." I leaned my head back on the headrest. I was suddenly over-whelmingly weary. I turned my head without raising it from the headrest. "I forgot to tell you. It was when you were in the grove. This guy came up the street with a woman, and I—oh, it's stupid, but I could have sworn the woman was Marnie. Her face was so clear." I sat up straight. "I know it's nuts, but I saw it—her face. Clearly. The street light was shining on it. And then—to freak me out even more—the guy told the cop his girlfriend was missing. So I was sure it was them. I ran over to the cop and told him to arrest them." I let out a shaky laugh. "And then I looked at them again, and it wasn't them. They were completely different people." My voice was breaking.

Sergeant Quinn was staring at me. There was a strange look on his face. "And what's that got to do with her not wanting to be found?" he asked, finally.

"Oh, they said she'd just walked out of the house, and they couldn't find her. I thought it was an odd story, that there was lots they weren't saying. That maybe she'd left on purpose."

"Indeed," said Quinn quietly.

I turned to face him. "I know what you're thinking. But I don't think Lucy walked away of her own volition."

"But one of your dream messages was that she was safe."

I nodded. "I know. I thought maybe that was what it meant too, at first. But then I had the second dream…."

"We follow long shots all the time." Even crazy ones, I thought he wanted to add.

Before I could respond, Quinn flipped the locks on the doors from his side and got out.

We took the elevator back upstairs, back to the door on the second floor where he had met me.

He shook my hand, and then he put a card in it. "I'm back on duty tomorrow at one," he said. "I'm on 'til seven. I hope. I'm not carrying a pager these days. I'm on desk duty. But I'm usually at the end of that phone." He pointed to the card in my hand.

He paused again. Then he reached out a hand for his card, and took a pen out of his pocket and scribbled on the back of it.

He held out the card again. He didn't let go when I took it.

"Sergeants Roach and Lundy are good men," he said. "And good cops. Very good cops. If anyone can solve this case, they can. They will. But they don't give much credence to psychics. We get a lot of them, offering to help. Most of them are…."

"Kooks," I supplied.

"I don't think you're a kook," he said. "All I'm saying is: if you don't get anywhere, don't be surprised. Or frustrated. And if you need someone who'll listen, or help, call me. Anytime. And if you have another experience, I insist you call me—at work or home. Even if it's the middle of the night. I live alone. You won't be disturbing anyone but me."

The warm smile he gave me made me suddenly want to tell him everything. Instead I thanked him and pocketed the card.

In the car I took the card out of my pocket and stared at it for a long

time. On the back was another number: his home number. I committed it to memory.

I couldn't get warm, even with all the blankets on. It was five in the
morning. The alarm was set for eight. I was too exhausted and too cold
to sleep.

Would Sergeants Lundy and Roach listen to me, like Quinn had? I
wished he were one of the investigators. Whether he really thought me
crazy or not, he seemed to be giving me the benefit of the doubt. What
a relief it would be to confide in someone. But how could I confide in
him when I didn't even trust myself?

Trust. Supposedly you had to know someone to trust them. But
I trusted people every day—even people I didn't know. To a degree.
Otherwise I would never leave my house. I assumed people were who
they appeared to be. I assumed they said what they meant and meant
what they said. I looked in their eyes for verification.

I had every reason not to trust Tim. Manslaughter was an accident
but it was still taking another person's life. And now—I had to consider
the possibility—he might have taken Lucy's life, too. But when I looked
in his eyes, had I seen guilt? Cruelty? A crazed killer?

No. I had seen a lost little boy. A man who had spent the last ten
years in prison and had been back on the outside for only a year—a
year more or less in Lucy's "care." He was not going to know how to get
along without her. He'd said he didn't even know how to pay the bills.
The odd way he was acting could be as simple as his being upset that
he'd lost the person who took care of him.

But when I thought about the things he'd said, they didn't add up.
And some of his words were disturbing. I heard them over and over
again in the dull light of dawn.

*She had a recurring dream. She dreams she's being choked. She screamed
so loud she woke up the tenant two floors above us.*

*I know how easily she can be hurt—when we play-wrestle on the living
room floor.*

I tried to block out the images that shoved their way into my mind.
Whether my crazy dreams, and Detective Godbout's assumptions, were

correct or not, I knew one thing for sure: I had to end all contact with Tim.

Another thing was equally clear: I needed to search for Lucy. It was a long shot, as Sergeant Quinn had said. Such a long shot. But I needed to try. I didn't want any more dreams, or visitations, or whatever they were. I didn't want to be "taken over" that way. I would approach this logically. Maybe now that I had made the decision to search for her, maybe the dreams would go away. But at least they had given me something to go on, and I seemed to have Sergeant Quinn on side. Now if only Roach and Lundy would listen to me.

I tried to will myself to sleep. I wasn't going to be any good in the morning if I didn't get at least a few hours of rest.

I'm paddling in a red canoe on the river. Unafraid. The water is calm. I'm just below the covered bridge in Wakefield. In front of me, floating on the river, is a small barge. On it lies a figure. She is face down. Wearing gauzy lavender-coloured pants and top.

I paddle towards her, but I can't get any closer.

I come to the shore. I leave the canoe, and I'm walking in a meadow. The grass is brown.

In the distance, in the meadow, the same lavender-dressed figure is lying on some kind of a raised bed. Face up.

It is Lucy.

Her hair is spread over the end of the bed, as if someone has brushed it into that cascade. But it's not dark; it's long and blonde—strawberry blonde.

I approach slowly. She looks pale, haggard. She has no expression on her face.

When I reach her, I bend over her body and sob.

6.

THE ICE CUBES ON MY eyes helped. They reduced the puffiness and made me at least look like I'd had more than two hours sleep. The shower helped too. And the rush of adrenalin. It was becoming my daily fix.

The police station had lost its intimidating feel overnight. It wasn't just the daylight. It was my new connection to the place.

Maybe, I thought, as I took the elevator up to the second floor to Major Crimes, maybe the connections worked the same way with prisons. Maybe that explained how Lucy had been able to walk through much more daunting doors. There had been someone she knew inside. Someone she trusted. She'd had more reason to trust Tim than I had to trust Quinn, whether he was an officer of the law or not. She'd known Tim longer, had got to know him first through correspondence and phone calls. But then, it had probably made no difference. The connection, she'd said, had been immediate.

It was suddenly clear. What Lucy had been talking about. There was a big difference of course. My connection to Quinn was far from romantic. But a connection was a connection, no matter how it manifested itself. That was why the police station felt entirely different at nine o'clock on a Thursday morning than it had at two a.m. the previous night. Even though I knew Sergeant Quinn wasn't even inside.

Sergeant Roach met me on the second floor, at the same door that Quinn had. He took me into a windowless room that might, or might not, have been the same one I had been in with Quinn. He left me and returned a moment later with Sergeant Lundy.

They listened to me describe the previous night. They listened to me repeat my half-truths. They assured me they followed all leads, no matter what the source. They tried to hide their skepticism behind their kind, closed faces.

I didn't blame them for their doubt. It reflected my own. But I was angry too. At them. At myself for having dreams that were making me act like a fool. And, if I was honest, at Lucy, too, for putting me in this situation.

I kept my anger in check. I didn't get thrown out.

I didn't get anything else either. Except promises and reassurances. "And thank you for your concern. What helps us most is the concern and support of Lucy's friends."

Bullshit. What they needed most was to find her.

I stood in the middle of a chaotic room full of desks and phones and officers dealing with paperwork drudgery, and I refused to leave until they assured me they were going to put a tail on Marnie. I laughed as I said it. They laughed too.

"Shall we throw her out of here?" they joked.

But Lundy spoke to a man with long hair and blue jeans, and my impression was that he was going to be the one to follow Marnie. I tried to tell him where to look.

"Go home and get some sleep, lady," said the undercover officer in blue jeans. "Leave it to us."

I clamped my mouth shut so I wouldn't say something rude.

I headed for the phone as soon as I got in the door, to tell Angel I wasn't coming in to work. But there was no dial tone. Instead there was a woman's voice. "Hello? Is that Ellen?"

"Yes."

"This is Trish Cousins. I'm a friend of Lucy's. I give her massage and reike treatments. Counselling too." She spoke slowly but there was anything but calm in her measured tones. "I'm not sure why I'm calling. I wanted to talk to another friend of Lucy's. This whole thing is so strange. Tim called us on Sunday, and talked to Marnie—my partner. I think you met her recently."

So Marnie *was* a friend of Lucy's.

More poured out of her. Her relationship with Lucy these past ten years, both professional and personal. How she had helped Lucy work through her fears. Fears of making the trips to prison, of getting involved with Tim. And then through the relationship stresses that had followed. How she and Marnie had tried to be supportive of the relationship and to be friends with Tim after he'd got out. How she had been away at a healing workshop all weekend and had only arrived back late Sunday afternoon when Tim had called and talked to Marnie. "I found it strange they were talking so long on the phone when we knew Lucy was missing."

We knew Lucy was missing. Sunday afternoon.

Here was something Sergeants Lundy and Roach might pay attention to. I let Trish keep talking. I made sympathetic responses about how strange it was. I promised to keep in touch. We hung up and I immediately called the Ottawa police. I didn't need to look up the number anymore.

Neither Lundy nor Roach was available. I left both my home and work numbers for them.

I couldn't sleep. I took the dogs for a short walk, and then I changed and drove to work.

By one o'clock I still hadn't heard back from the police. I tried again. They were still unavailable. My heart sped up when I made the decision to ask for Sergeant Quinn.

"She said Tim called *Sunday* afternoon," I said when I had filled him in. "She said they knew Lucy was missing. But Tim told me he didn't start worrying about her until Monday. That was the reason he gave me for waiting so long before phoning me. My name was right there on the calendar for Sunday afternoon. I should have been the first person he called if he thought she was missing."

"I'll be sure to pass this on to Roach and Lundy. Do they know how to get hold of you?"

I gave him both my numbers.

He tried to reassure me. "They *are* on the case, Ellen. I know that doesn't help. You sound exhausted. Go home and get some sleep."

The familiarity somehow seemed natural. The tone wasn't condescending like the undercover cop's. The tone was concerned. And the concern was welcome.

Angel, too, wanted me to go home. But I didn't want to be at home.

"Come and stay with us," he said.

"I can't. The dogs."

Angel shrugged.

At four o'clock I drove my weary body home.

TRISH'S CONCENTRATION WAS GRATIFYING. SHE knew every knot, every sensitive spot like a lover. No, more than a lover. A lover touched you at least as much for his own pleasure as for yours. Trish's hands, her giving, her concentration, were there for her alone. This was an hour for herself. Even Trish's being gay didn't put any edge to it. There was no sexuality in this room; there was just her body—wired and knotted and electric—and Trish's strong fingers working their magic—the magic of turning electric wiring into mellow Jell-O. They call me mellow Jell-O, she sang in her head.

Not today came a more prosaic, contrary voice. Today, her muscles seemed irrevocably seized. And for good reason. During last week's phone call, she had offered to be put on Tim's visiting list.

He had sounded particularly low. His mood swings didn't bother her. They were entirely understandable; she had nothing but sympathy for them. He had much more reason than she did to be depressed. She just wished she could be there for him. Sitting at the end of a phone wire was anything but being there.

So she asked. Part of her couldn't believe she was asking. It would mean at least a four-hour drive to get to Warkworth. There wasn't even a direct route between the prison and Ottawa. She'd have to zigzag her way west on the minor highways.

She wasn't expecting Tim's laugh in response to her question. "You mean join all the others on my list? You might have to fight over time slots."

His tone was humorous but not bitter. She liked that he could laugh at himself even when he was low. Then the laughter went out of his voice. "Lu, are you sure?"

She loved the way he shortened her name. No one else ever had. There was such affection in it. "Oh, Tim," she said, "I would be honoured."

There was a long silence on the other end. She sensed he was fighting tears. She hoped he didn't sense her fight against the sudden onset of panic.

A new car would help. Her ancient Horizon would never make it to Warkworth. It was time for a reliable vehicle.

Tim went online from the prison library and together they decided on a Suzuki Sidekick. She took one for a test drive and found it a fun, spunky car. And the four-wheel drive made her feel safe. Maybe she would begin to enjoy driving. But more than the car, she needed the nerve.

Before she knew it, Trish was lifting the sheet for her to turn over. She had got nowhere near a relaxed state during the first half hour. She shifted onto her back and watched Trish work her fingers up her left arm.

"Do you think you could knead some courage into those muscles?" she asked.

Trish smiled her serene smile. "And what do you want courage for today?"

She answered, keeping her eyes on Trish's face. "The courage to visit a medium-security penitentiary two hundred miles from here."

Her words had the expected effect. She felt Trish's hands stop, watched her trying to keep the worry and wariness off her face. She smiled inside at the struggle she'd created.

"Are you doing research for Correctional Services?" The question was asked in a casual tone.

She kept watching Trish's face. She was torn between wanting to create shock and needing to receive support. "Personal research," she said.

Trish shifted her hand to her wrist. It was light, gentle. She closed her eyes to take in that gentle, caring touch. Trish was a professional; no matter what she might be thinking inside, her hands, the tools of her trade, would always emanate support.

"You're becoming more involved with this guy."

She kept her eyes closed so she wouldn't have to see what might be in Trish's eyes. A fear reflecting her own?

"You know I don't normally stop a massage halfway through," said Trish after a pause, "but it might be good if we talked for a bit before I continue. Do you want to do that?"

She did. She gathered the sheet around her and pulled herself up into a cross-legged position. She might have felt she was sitting on the doctor's examining table, except that Trish half-leaned, half-sat on the table herself, in that informal way she had. Then Trish smiled and prompted her with her usual invitation. "So tell me."

"I'm being put on his visitor's list."

"And how do you feel about that? Setting aside your fears, for the moment, do you want to go? Could you drive that distance?"

"Yes." She was answering the second question. She had no idea about the third.

"What about Curtis?"

She sighed. "The writing is on the wall and it was there long before I met Tim. You know it as well as I do." She sighed again. "I really thought things were going to work out with Curtis. I thought we were going to make it, but he bailed. Funny how he always says I'm in denial, but one thing is clear as day. He's not there. It's a slow-moving train with Tim, but I think that's better. We can't rush into anything."

Trish was nodding, but there was concern in her eyes. "But you can't ignore his history. It might have been an accident, but he was violent."

"I know. God, I know. And I'm terrified. But what else is new? It's time to face my fears, like you're always wanting me to."

"Lucy. This is one instance, anyway, where you have every reason to be afraid. I don't want to tell you what to do, but this might be one time where it would be good to listen to your fears."

"But it's not Tim I'm afraid of. It's Warkworth, it's the prison itself. It's the drive there—when have you ever known me to drive so far from home? I know it sounds crazy, but what about Lucy Stockman doesn't sound crazy? This really is an opportunity to get over my phobias. I mean once and for all. I'm tired of living my life in fear."

"So you think the answer is to stick your head in the lion's mouth?"

She grinned. "No, but couldn't I at least go look at him through the bars?"

"If you want me to help you get over your dread of *zoos* I'll gladly help," said Trish.

They laughed.

"Anyway, Tim's not a lion," she said. "I know it looks bad; he's in prison for being violent. But I believe him when he says it was an accident, and if it was an accident, then he's no more culpable, has no more capability for violence, than half a dozen other men I know. Including the one I'm living with. There's a reason I met him, Trish. I read his letters, listen to his voice on the phone, and I know, it's a certainty inside, that everything that surrounds him—the violence of his past, the violence of the institution he's in—it's all illusion. That violence is not who he is, any more than my phobias are who I am. I feel he's come into my life so that the fear I am debilitated by can meet the violence that has debilitated him, and we can each be each other's rehabilitation. I have never seen anything with more clarity."

Trish put her head in her hands and groaned. "Oh God, you're out-therapizing your therapist."

Her eyes glinted mischievously. "On the other hand, I just want to go visit a guy in prison."

Trish laughed and threw up her hands. "Okay, you win. Let's see if we can't work a little courage for the road into that frenetic bloodstream of yours."

———⁓⁓⁓———

"ELLEN." IT WAS MARY FRANCES'S voice in my ear, waking me out of a deep sleep. "What on earth is going on? I've been reading about you in the papers, and last night you were on the six o'clock news. Are you alright?"

I moved the receiver to the other ear and sat up, disoriented. "What time is it?"

"It's quarter past five. I tried you at work but they said you were here. Were you *sleeping*? Are you ill?"

"No, but I—I didn't sleep very well last night. I was having a nap."

"Tell me you aren't having anything to do with this man."

Her obvious distress, overriding apologies she would normally have made at disturbing me, woke me completely. "Well, no, not anymore. We were just trying to get the media involved. The cops are sitting on their goddamn arses."

"Ellen, forget the policemen's bloody bottoms. Think about your own. This man is more dangerous than you think."

"What d'you mean?"

"Haven't you seen today's paper? His entire criminal history is there."

"I haven't seen it yet. Why is he more dangerous than I already think? He got manslaughter. He pinched a nerve in some guy's neck."

"Girl," said Mary Frances. "He strangled his girlfriend."

"He what?" It felt like someone was choking *me*.

"He strangled his girlfriend. With her own stocking. He was originally convicted of murder but he got manslaughter on appeal."

"Oh God."

"I gather this is not what Lucy told you." Her tone managed to sound dry, cynical, and worried all at the same time.

"Um, no."

"Ellen."

"Yes?"

"Promise me you won't have anything more to do with him."

"I promise." I was only paying half attention. I told her I had to go.

I forced myself to eat something to get rid of the spaced-out feeling and the shock of Mary Frances's words. Tim had lied to Lucy. No. She must have known. There would be ways of finding out. Lucy had lied to me. Why? To lessen the shock? To bring me on side? But she had believed it was an accident. She would never have got involved with him if she hadn't.

I had walked down the pitch-black railway tracks with a man who had choked the life out of a woman. Maybe two women. I might have become the third. I might still become the third. How could I ever walk out of my house now?

I did though. I drove down the 105 to the *depanneur*. The general store, in a converted house on a big empty lot, carried all the papers. The story was on the bottom of the second page of the *Ottawa Citizen*, next to a bad photograph of Tim. He still looked like a little boy. But this boy wasn't lost. This boy was pouting. This boy had done something bad.

I drove home and took the paper up to my office couch. Beau and Belle thumped down on the carpet in front of me.

I read the story. It was all there. The murder conviction, the lesser conviction of manslaughter after he'd won his appeal. He'd served a ten-year sentence for that. And there was a litany of other crimes. When Lucy had met him he'd been in the middle of serving a five-and-a-half year combined sentence for robbery with violence, fraud, and escaped lawful custody. He had been in prison far longer than the ten years Lucy had told me. But then, she'd neglected to mention anything but the manslaughter conviction. How would I have responded if she'd told me the whole truth?

I kept reading. Tim was quoted as saying he knew he would be considered a suspect. It had been while appealing his sentence during his first year as an inmate that he had come into contact with Archie Crowe. He was worried, quoted the article, that Lucy might have been a victim of Crowe trying to get back at him. "I testified against this man at the Colin Fajber hearing. My name was used, when they promised me it wouldn't be. I heard he's out of prison now. I'm scared."

The Colin Fajber hearing. Lucy had been there. She'd been there to see justice served. Justice quite possibly had backfired on her.

I dropped the paper on my desk. The light on the phone was blinking. I stared at it. How long had it been blinking? I pressed the codes for my messages. Tim's voice sounded in my ear. "It's Thursday afternoon. I'd appreciate it if you could give me a call."

I checked the time on the call display. He had phoned while I was at the *depanneur*. He knew my phone number. He knew where I lived. He knew I knew about him....

I erased the message. I punched other numbers to get out of the answering service. I tried to dial another number. My fingers were shaking. I kept hitting the wrong keys.

⎯⎯⎯∞⎯⎯⎯

SHE HADN'T KNOWN HOW TO bring it up without sounding like she was interrogating him. But the question came out naturally. "Tell me what happened, Tim."

There was a long, slow sigh from the other end of the phone. "It was an accident. She was my business partner. She was a hooker too, but that didn't have anything to do with me. I wasn't her pimp. I wasn't her boyfriend. We were in the con business. We got in a fight one night. Arguing about something. I don't even remember. It was stupid. I was trying to get her to see some sense. Trying to scare her. I grabbed one of her stockings, pretended to choke her. Except...."

She let out an involuntary sound.

"Lu?"

"Yes, sorry. It's just—well, it is a bit shocking."

"I know. I'm not proud of it. I'm really sorry. I thought she was faking it—you know, making a face like she was choking. But she wasn't faking. I was an idiot even to think she was. I tried to revive her. I couldn't." He sounded like he was crying.

She didn't know what to say.

"I got what I deserved," Tim continued. "I didn't begrudge doing my time. Every day of my sentence I was sorry."

"But you were convicted of—murder first." She was trying to take it all in.

"Yeah, but it wasn't murder. I didn't mean to do it. I was just trying to scare her. I appealed that conviction. Anyways, they had no proof. The first trial was a total scam. I would never kill anybody. 'Specially someone I cared about. And I did care about her. Lisa was her name. She was like family to me."

A niggle of doubt: what on earth was she doing?

He was crying again, this time openly. "I served my time on that, Lu," he said through tears. "I served the whole sentence. And I deserved to. But these other sentences. I done my time and they're just screwing me around. But I can't do nothing from in here."

"No, but I can do something." The doubts had melted.

"Are you sure? I mean, are you sure you want to help me? I mean, I'd understand if you didn't want to have anything to do with me. I wouldn't blame you. I been wanting to tell you about this for a long time now." He heaved a sigh. "I just didn't know how to bring it up. And I was scared too. You been so nice to me, and I keep thinking, I don't deserve it. Not if you don't know the full story. And even now you do, I don't deserve you helping me."

She took a breath. "You do deserve it, Tim. You deserve a second chance."

7.

THE FIRST SCOTCH PROVIDED THE anaesthetic my nerves needed. I was safe in this metal box at ten thousand metres.

But Lucy isn't.

The thought was a rock dropping into the pit of my stomach. It was my first thought of Lucy since Tim's message. I had been so relieved to get a flight. I had thrown things into a bag and called Mary Frances. She had been willing to take the dogs, and drive me to the airport. The price was a half-hearted lecture on running to Marc.

I barely heard it. The blood was hammering in my ears. I couldn't miss this flight. I couldn't spend another night alone in that house. I couldn't endanger my friends' lives. Marc had been receptive. More than receptive. Relieved. He would be there to meet my plane. I willed the car to go faster.

Mary Frances dropped me at Departures just in time for me to make the connector flight to Toronto.

Now, en route to Thunder Bay, I looked around the plane as if someone had plunked me into the middle of a bad dream. I leaned back and shut my eyes. With every second I was getting farther away from Lucy. Who might be getting closer to death. Or already dead. But with every second I was also getting closer to Marc and I imagined his arms already around me, grounding me.

But I knew I couldn't stay. Marc might reground me for the moment, but that wouldn't solve anything. Not for Marc and me. And certainly not for Lucy. I resolved to get the first flight out in the morning. Then I signalled the flight attendant and ordered another Scotch.

At the Thunder Bay airport, I tried to tell Marc I needed to go to the booking desk, but exhaustion and alcohol slurred my words. And I needed some help with my bag, and with walking. Marc led me to his truck, not the ticket desk.

I had no recollection of arriving at his house or going to bed. I was only aware of Lucy visiting once again, with more of her macabre messages.

The return of consciousness brought the return of panic. It wasn't about Tim. Or Lucy. The walls of my bedroom were closing in on me.

I shut my eyes to get rid of the illusion. I opened them again. The walls were one foot from the bed on three sides. But they weren't moving. That was one relief. And it wasn't my bed, or my bedroom. That was another relief. Followed by momentous claustrophobia.

I bolted from the room. There wasn't far to bolt. Marc's bedroom opened onto the only other room in the tiny house—a combined kitchen and living room. The clock on the microwave said four o'clock. Outside it was bright daylight. I was shocked. I had slept for fourteen hours.

I took in the room around me. The unmistakable imprint of Marc was everywhere: canoe paddles propped up against the walls, posters and prints of northern rivers, scattered photographs, topographic maps pinned to the walls. All the things that had, until six days ago, cluttered up our house. The sight of all the familiar things dissolved the panic. Among the clutter I found a box of granola and a note: "Be back @ 5."

What I wanted was a phone book to call the airline. Or just a cab to get me to the airport. Lucy needed me. Marc didn't.

Marc had hidden the phone book.

When that paranoid thought occurred, I knew I was in trouble. Marc didn't have a sly bone in his body.

I wondered if he had slept beside me. The crumpled sheets on the couch answered that question. The sight depressed me. I looked out the front window. I seemed to be on a suburban street of small bungalows. White smoke billowing out from several smokestacks in the distance marred a view of striking cliffs. The sight of the smokestacks depressed me too.

Getting some food into me brought me out of my thoughts about

Marc and back to those I'd been trying to escape. I couldn't escape Lucy even if I tried. She was in my brain, right there wherever I went, waiting for me to go to sleep so she could come to me. Was this a huge guilt complex surfacing because I hadn't been there for her? I thought of how negative she had sounded all through the fall. How physically weak she had sounded just the previous week. *Some*thing had been going on this past year. Something bad.

The dream images had been briefer this time, but no less disturbing. The hazy figure of a woman peering over Lucy in a darkened building. Seeming to be worried about animals getting in through cracks in the walls, getting to Lucy, lying there, on some kind of bench. She was alive, but just barely, and only until Saturday night. On Saturday night, Lucy's weakened whispering voice had said, she was going to be dumped in the Gatineau River.

I scrounged around the house for a pen and paper. It was a fantastic story. My imagination, it seemed, had no limits. But as long as there was even a remote chance Lucy might be alive, that she might be found in time, I had no choice but to listen. And act.

I put down my pen and picked up the spoon again, still hungry. So much seemed to point to Marnie being the woman. Her arrival at the site with Tim the very next day. Their stroll together down the tracks. Tim calling her that night from my house (the only friend he called). Trish's bizarrely volunteered information: *I don't know why I'm calling.* As if something had compelled her. *I found it odd they were talking so long on the phone when we knew Lucy was missing.*

The contradiction hit me on the last spoonful.

That night at my house, Tim had told me he had left a message for Marnie, and that he had to call her because she would be worried about *why* he'd been trying to get hold of her. He'd said he was waiting for her to call back. But Trish had said that Tim had phoned late Sunday afternoon. She had said *they knew* Lucy was missing.

That would explain why Tim's first words to Marnie when he'd called from my house had been not an explanation of why he was calling but simply, "We found the car." Because Marnie already knew why he was calling. Because, while Trish had been away, and for whatever bizarre reason, Marnie had helped him do whatever he had done to Lucy.

And my vision of Marnie on that dark street? I could put it down to hallucination, but maybe—just maybe—it wasn't. Maybe it was a sign. For me. Clarification. That she *was* involved. Maybe she *was* checking on Lucy. I couldn't believe I was thinking this way. But whatever was going on with my sanity, the fact remained that Lucy's instructions had borne out; they had led me to abandoned outbuildings in a part of Ottawa I had barely ever been to.

Outbuildings. The word I had got in that second dream had been *out*buildings. Abandoned outbuildings. But I had only told Quinn abandoned "buildings." Buildings could be any kind of building. Like the one we had searched through. Outbuildings meant storage or farm buildings. And farm buildings meant barns. And barns could be burnt-out barns....

I thought back to the dark shadowy shapes of the barns and their charred, caved-in roofs and walls. There wouldn't just be "cracks" in those walls; animals could presumably roam those ruins freely. She couldn't be in those barns. But there could well be other outbuildings close by. Buildings we hadn't seen in the dark.

Had a tail been put on Marnie? They had to follow her before Saturday night. Maybe if I offered them the information about Marnie—the contradictory things people were saying, not the suspect offerings of my dreams—maybe they would finally listen.

I pushed the bowl away and reached for the phone. There was no question: I was going to have to keep making a fool of myself for Lucy.

At the other end of the line, Lundy was pleasant but preoccupied. "Are you sure he didn't call before Lucy went missing?"

"Trish said he called Sunday afternoon. She said they knew then that Lucy was missing."

He was silent. I sensed he was taking notes. Finally.

I overcame my embarrassment. "Did a tail get put on Marnie?"

"We wouldn't have had a reason to put a tail on Marnie." He said it without a trace of self-consciousness. As if our encounter the previous morning had never taken place. "But," he added, "we'll check this out. Thanks Ellen."

I hung up so angry I forgot to tell him about the outbuildings.

I punched in the numbers to access my messages. There were two new ones. I pressed 1. I dreaded the sound of Tim's voice.

But it was a woman's voice. Anna's. "I hope you don't mind my calling. I haven't been able to sleep. The police are telling us nothing. I wondered if you might have heard anything. If you get a chance, could you please call me back?"

I wrote down the number she recited, and played the next message.

"Hello. This is Kevin Hopkins calling. I'm an old friend of Lucy Stockman's. I heard you being interviewed on the radio and understand you are involved in searching for Lucy. I was wondering if you would mind giving me a call? I can be reached at…."

I wrote down the second phone number, an Ottawa exchange, under the first. His voice was so sad, it impelled me to call. And I thought he might be the easier of the two to talk to.

He was. I didn't have to talk at all. He was an outpouring of stories about Lucy. "I didn't know who else to call," he said. It was the voice on my answering machine, full of sadness and grief. "I don't know any of Lucy's other friends. I hope you don't mind. I needed to talk to someone who knew her."

"I don't mind," I said. And realized I meant it.

"I've known Lucy for over twenty years. I introduced her to yoga. She became my teacher. And she was a good friend. But in the last year or two I let that go."

"She had become so negative," I offered, in empathy.

There was a deep sigh on the line. "Yes. But she wasn't always like that. She was a bombshell in her twenties. She mesmerized us all. She was so sharp and witty and fun."

His words amazed me. And then, suddenly, I could see it. From my first meeting with her at the Gallery: the bombshell Kevin was describing. I had forgotten that Lucy.

"She could have had anyone she wanted," he said. And then he laughed. "She *did* have anyone she wanted. But she always dumped them eventually. I was never sorry. Until Curtis."

"You knew Curtis?"

"Oh yes. I had high hopes for Lucy and Curtis. He really did fit all her criteria. They had so much in common. Music. Food. Dancing. He loved to dance as much as she did. They moved in together. Worked on their issues together. He was good for her. He called her bluff, and he wouldn't let her run away. He made her stay and fight her demons."

I was relieved to hear Kevin talking about Curtis this way. Maybe I would call him. Some day when this was all over.

"But she did run away, in the end," I said. "She ran to Tim."

"Lucy was always running away," said Kevin, flatly.

"So she wouldn't be abandoned," I said. The word was suddenly there in my head, from one of our early conversations.

"She told you about that?"

"She called it her abandonment issue, didn't she? She seemed kind of, I don't know, almost excited by it."

"I know what you mean. I think it was enthusiasm to work it out. It went way back."

Back to her early childhood. I was starting to remember what Lucy had told me. She'd been quarantined in hospital with chicken pox as a toddler. She'd said her mother had never come to see her. "I confess I never really believed the part where her mother never visited her in hospital," I told Kevin now. "How could you not visit your baby in hospital?"

"I guess you never met Mrs. Stockman." His tone was wry. "She really was off in her own world. Did Lucy tell you she was a poet? She could have been a model as well. She was very poised. And very absent. That seemed to suit Lucy's father. He just wanted his wife to look beautiful and to have his dinner on the table by six-thirty every evening. I don't know how she accomplished even that. I think that was all the domesticity she *could* manage—certainly not raising two girls. I don't think Lucy was so far off the mark when she claimed the house had raised her."

"So she felt abandoned by both parents?"

"Pretty much," said Kevin. "And you know what those formative experiences can do. You end up repeating them in your adult relationships. That's what happened with Lucy. She was always choosing men who weren't there. But she was very aware of the pattern. She was determined to break it."

"But, from what you said, it sounds like Curtis *was* there. What happened?"

"Lucy Stockman's famous unrealistic expectations." The words were harsh; the tone was fond. "She wanted Curtis to be something he wasn't. She wanted him to be there all the time. On her terms. Oh, that's not entirely fair. It takes two, as they say. Curtis was no saint either. And he didn't have a very good job. Lucy was the breadwinner. She was pretty proud of being financially independent. Of being secure. Obsessed, you might say."

"So she started a relationship with Tim," I said, to get him onto Tim.

There was another heavy sigh at the other end of the phone. "Something was driving her. Even Curtis could see that. He was no match for Tim. She drove halfway across the province to visit him in prison. It might even have been in a snowstorm. Something really had to be driving her to do something like that. She rarely ever drove farther than the Gatineaus."

I remembered Lucy saying once that she had been making progress in fighting her fears. I hadn't given much thought to how much nerve it would take to actually *visit* a prison. God, she knew how to pick her cures. "But that was good, wasn't it?" My voice was doubtful. "Progress of a sort."

"I guess you could say that. By the end she was sneaking things in."

"*Sneaking things in?* To prison, you mean? Past the *guards?*"

Kevin laughed. "Don't let Lucy mislead you with all her fears. She had balls that one. She even smuggled in a bottle of wine once. Candles too, I think. I can't remember what else. She said she wanted to smuggle in some romance to that most *un*romantic of places."

"Holy cow." I couldn't imagine it.

"And after Curtis moved out, she learned how to do things for herself, how to be alone. I think it was the first time she'd ever lived on her own for that long. Two years. I think meeting Tim took her out of her self-absorption. Even Curtis hadn't been able to do that."

"You mean so she could rescue someone else?"

"No." His voice grew thoughtful. "I don't think Lucy was into rescuing anyone but herself." Then: "Do you think he did it?"

I answered before I could censor myself. "Yes."

Another sigh. "It seems obvious doesn't it? Maybe too obvious."

I steeled myself for the same question from Anna. But the call went to a machine. I left a message saying I would be back in Chelsea after the weekend.

THE LETTER CONFIRMING SHE WAS eligible to visit arrived the same day the Sidekick did. She took it as a sign. Encouragement from the Universe: Go to Warkworth. She read the list of rules. She examined the directions.

The physical directions were straightforward. There was even a list of local motels in nearby Campbellford. But where was the section called "How to get your nerve up"? She had to find the courage somewhere deeper inside herself than Trish's hands could go.

Fuck the courage. That was just a word, like "fear." Just do it.

She would have preferred the unsettled weather to be over. But it was the middle of April when anything could happen—rain, sleet, thunder, snow, a blizzard. The best she could do was pray for the day to be clear.

Her prayers were answered. There were no clouds in the sky the day of her drive. There was no storm to contend with. Not outside the car. The storm was inside the car. The storm was behind the wheel, letting nothing stand in her way—not the fear, not the panic, not the overwhelming impulse to turn the car around fifty kilometres out of town.

I WAS STARTLED OUT OF my thoughts by Marc bursting in through the door. He saw me and slumped against the door jamb. "I have been trying to call you all day. I thought you had flown the coop."

"I'm about to," I said, "if I could just find your blasted phone book."

"Why didn't you answer the phone?"

"I never heard it. I just woke up an hour ago."

Marc smiled. "And I bet you have a splitting headache."

I gave him a wry look. "Actually I don't. I guess I slept through the hangover too. Marc, thank you for … for … I appreciate your letting me come here. But I have to go back. Do you *have* a phone book?"

"It's in the truck," said Marc, as if that were the natural place to keep a phone book.

"Marc."

"You could have phoned Information." He was crossing the room toward me. He came in slow motion. It gave me too much time to think, to brace myself. If he put those arms around me, I'd be finished.

But he stopped two feet away.

"Marc, I can't stay here. I was an idiot to run away. I need to talk to the police. I need to look for Lucy."

"Ellen, there's nothing you can do." His voice was infinitely gentle. "Lucy is dead."

"You don't know that! I think she's alive. I can't explain."

"You could explain if you wanted to."

His body was too close. There was a magnetic field around it, pulling me, irresistibly, in. I took a physical step back. I shook my head. "I can't."

Marc was looking at me. "You could, though. You could stop being so stubborn for once in your life, and we could—" He stopped. "I'm sorry I left like that. I want to try again."

I shook my head again. I couldn't bear the longing on his face. I also couldn't do anything about it. Not now. "I can't deal with this right now. I need to get back—" The words got caught in my throat watching him turn on his heel and head back out the door. I heard the truck door open. And shut.

This had happened already, a week ago. It couldn't be happening again, here. I didn't want to be left here.

I ran to the door. I slammed right into Marc. Right into the phone book between us.

He pushed me away, gently, with the phone book, and held it out to me. Looking away.

I took the book. I hugged it. I walked to the phone, and sat down, and opened the book. I tried to see through the blur.

"Ellen."

I wiped my nose on my sleeve.

Arms came around me from behind. I sagged against them.

Marc's familiar voice spoke in my ear. "Stay. You're scared and you're exhausted. I won't bother you. You can stay as long as you need to."

He lifted me to my feet, turned me around, held me close.

"Oh Marc. Stop being so bloody understanding. I can't stand it." And I burst into tears for the first time ever in the arms of my now ex-lover.

I waited until Marc had gone to pick up the Chinese food. Then I made another call to the Ottawa police. If they weren't going to follow Marnie, I would just have to give them the more complete directions back to the barns.

Neither Roach nor Lundy was available. It was after six. Quinn would be gone. I told the switchboard operator it was important. I asked to speak to anyone who was available. I waited to be put through to another officer.

"Sergeant Quinn here."

I inhaled a breath. Relief and nervousness vied for the dominant place in my lungs.

"Sergeant Quinn." I made my voice formal. "It's Ellen McGinn. I have more information. The messages are getting clearer. I have more specific directions now about where Lucy is. But she's going to be moved soon. You have to act soon."

"Okay, Ellen. Slow down. I'm listening."

I told him to go six or seven kilometres south on Bank Street starting from Lucy's street. I told him there was a street off Bank; that it might be Hunt Club but I wasn't sure. "And this time," I said, continuing my half-lies, "I got *out*buildings. Not just buildings. It could be those barns, or some other outbuildings close by."

It wasn't as hard as I'd expected lying to Sergeant Quinn, though I wasn't sure anymore why I felt I had to.

"I'll have this checked out, Ellen. I promise."

"It has to be soon. The other piece of information is that Tim is sup-

posed to dump Lucy's body in the Gatineau River Saturday evening."
I felt stupid saying it, but he didn't question it.

"That's tomorrow. He'd have to go back there then to where she is."

"Yes, but it might be too late by then."

"What d'you mean? You said Saturday night."

"She's still hovering between life and death, but my sense is she's
barely coming to consciousness now. The sooner you get there—" My
voice broke.

"Are you okay? Do you want to come in?"

"Well, it might take a little while to get there." I gave a half laugh.
"I'm in Thunder Bay."

"You're *where*?"

For some reason I enjoyed taking Sergeant Quinn off his guard.

"I'm visiting … a friend."

"Isn't this a bit sudden?"

I hesitated. "I needed to get away."

"I see." Something in his voice changed. I couldn't put my finger on
it. "And when you do you plan on being back?"

"As soon as I can get a flight. Tomorrow probably."

"Pretty quick visit," he commented. "Give me the number there."

It was my turn to be taken off guard. I didn't want to give him Marc's
phone number, but there was no way to refuse. His request had not been
phrased as a question. I gave him the number.

"Lundy and Roach are going to be working through the weekend,"
he said. "Whatever it is you're doing, try to enjoy yours and leave it to
us."

"Yes," I said. Maybe, *finally*, I could.

THE SIGN FOR THE TOWN of Warkworth pointed to the right. A
much smaller, more discreet green sign with an arrow pointed left for
Warkworth Institution. How did the residents of Warkworth feel about
having their town name associated with a prison? You wouldn't want to
be going around saying, "I'm a resident of Warkworth." People might
get the wrong idea.

She considered turning right. It seemed the friendlier option. Except it didn't. Tim wasn't there. And the residents of Warkworth were likely an embittered and hardened community who didn't welcome tourists. They likely lived in prisons of their own. Prisoners of a prison town.

She shut off these pointless thoughts. At least she tried to shut them off. The brain went where it wanted. She had no control. She only had control over whether she followed where it went. Her brain could take the road to the right if it wanted and go and gawk at the Warkworthians. But she was going to turn left.

The road to the prison followed the gently rolling hills of idyllic farmland. The view from prison (were there windows in prison?) was at least peaceful. But what about the view from the farm? Maybe the farmer had made so much money from the sale he didn't care about the view. More likely, the government had expropriated the land and the farmer had to live with it. Except didn't you get money from expropriation? She thought so. Expropriation for a prison would probably have made the farmer very rich. He was probably happy to live with it.

"It" loomed in the distance—a compound of institution-grey, single-storey buildings planted in the middle of open fields and surrounded by a high chain-link fence, with coils of barbed wire at the top. As she got closer, she could feel something snake-like coil around her heart. She sounded the mantra that had got her this far from home: *Tim is in there, Tim is ahead of me, Tim is waiting for me.*

The snake uncoiled. The sudden release seemed to open something in her heart beyond what had been there before. The new openness felt remarkably like joy.

SLEEP WOULDN'T COME. I DISENTANGLED my arms and legs from Marc's. I shut the bedroom door quietly so I could turn on the light in the kitchen without waking him. He was breathing in that contented audible way of his that was not quite snoring. In fact, it usually lulled me off to sleep too. My body was relaxed. Marc had drugged it, another talent he had. But he couldn't drug my mind. Not that night. It was spinning.

Sergeant Quinn was among those in the vortex. I should have explained why I'd left Ottawa. He had known I wasn't telling it all. I should have just admitted I'd been suddenly terrified of Tim. His tone had changed after I'd said I was in Thunder Bay. Suspicious was what it had become. But suspicion of what? Oh God. Suspicion of everything. That I, someone who knew Lucy, had been the one to find her car. Why I was giving him all those directions. How I knew where to direct them. I knew because I must be involved. I'd come to him in a panic in the dead of the night. Claiming I thought she was alive. Claiming a voice in my head was telling me where she was. Then I had taken off. And when I didn't show up back in town tomorrow, as I'd said I was going to? What would he make of that?

I put the kettle on and opened cupboards, hoping Marc had tea in the house. He didn't.

On the couch, I let the mug of hot water fill my insides and made myself think rationally. Suspicious behaviour wasn't everything. What were the things you needed? Motive and opportunity. Well, I had opportunity. My live-in boyfriend had conveniently taken off the day before. Lucy had been invited to my party. Maybe she had shown up after all the guests had left. And motive? Maybe I had decided to eliminate her from Ottawa's cutthroat communications industry.

Even this ludicrous thought didn't calm me down. Everywhere my brain went, an unpleasant train of thought was waiting. I reached for the paddling magazine on the coffee table. Like the Gideon Bible in a motel room, it was the only thing around to read.

But the magazine made me think of Marc. And Marc made me think of Curtis. And Curtis made me think of Lucy. Kevin had said meeting Tim had brought her out of her self-absorption. Visiting a man in prison would do that for you.

———— ∞ ————

SHE STOOD AT HER FRONT door. She waited as she had waited in front of the gate at Warkworth the day before. She stood as if expecting the door to swing open the way the prison gate had slid open. She wasn't seeing the metal curls on the screen door; she was seeing the metal links in the prison gate and the sign posted on it: STAND CLEAR UNTIL GATE IS OPEN.

The wording had bothered her. One could stand tall, stand out, stand up, stand for … and stand clear of. How did one simply "stand clear"?

She had forced herself to ponder this question as she waited. She was standing, shaking knees notwithstanding. Was she clear?

Yes. Clarity of mind was, in fact, the only thing she did have at the moment. She didn't have "clarity" anywhere else. Her body was giving her its usual not-calm responses: dry throat, sweating palms, shaking knees. Her head ached from the long drive. But she was here, by God. And, all stress aside, she was clear. She knew why she was here and that she was supposed to be. It was another miracle. Like Tim's letter arriving in the mail.

She concentrated her attention on the block-lettered sign. Was this clarity going to abandon her after the gate was open?

According to the instructions she'd been sent, once the gate opened, she was going to have to surrender her purse to a guard. She was going to have to walk through a metal detector. She was going to have to wait for someone to phone someone else, who was going to check the photo she'd had to send in and confirm that she was who she was claiming to be. She wasn't going to be searched. It was illegal for them to do a body search unless they had reasonable cause. Knowing all these facts gave her a semblance of control. It was a semblance at best.

In front of her, the gate finally slid open on rattling wheels. She walked through the front doors and found herself at the end of a line-up of people who looked all too familiar with this procedure. No one else seemed to be nervous. They seemed bored.

It didn't help. Nor did knowing what was to come. She steeled herself, terrified that when asked to surrender her purse she was going to refuse. Which wasn't going to get her anywhere, least of all in to see Tim.

She wasn't prepared for the smile the guard offered along with his orders and outstretched hand. She handed over her purse as she might her child to a kindly caregiver. He would look after it; she would get it back.

The metal detector was simply a doorframe she had to walk through. Like at the airport. It did not reach out to hurt her. She didn't set off any alarms. She didn't have to endure the wand in the guard's hand being brushed over her body. She could swallow again.

The guard—the same or another, she could barely tell—led her through door after door. They came to a large room, where the guard pointed to an empty table. She could see his lips moving, but there was such a loud noise in her ears—a noise quite apart from the noise in the room—that she couldn't hear the words. She sat down. She was short of breath; her heart was beating too fast, too lightly. She was exhausted. But she was here.

She stared around her at the green-walled room. She might have been sitting in a public cafeteria. Snack and pop machines lining one wall. Couples and families sitting at the tables, eating cellophane-packaged sandwiches and chips and drinking canned pop. Children running around; parents yelling after them. They might have been ordinary families or couples, except for the institution green worn by the male at each table. As if a crew of janitors had sat down for a break. Except janitors didn't have numbers sewn on their shirts. Here were the inmates. Inmates. Take off the prefix and they became what they were in this room: mates.

It was also true that in ordinary cafeterias people didn't usually sit on each others' laps, or neck in the corner. The guards, watching from their observation room, seemed to be ignoring this behaviour. How far could a couple go before they were stopped? Was discreet fucking tolerated? Who was to say what was happening in that corner. Would she and Tim be necking there one day? The idea filled her with a perverse excitement.

No one had warned her about the smoke. Her shortness of breath became a physical reaction to the air. Her headache intensified.

Every time the door opened and a guard-escorted inmate walked in, she started. Was it Tim? Did she even remember what he looked like? Would he recognize her?

It was out of her hands. The gate had opened. She was inside the beast now. Clarity was no longer required. Clarity, in fact, was no longer possible. Terror held her in her chair. The terror of the first day (and many days) of school, the terror of hospitals, the terror of churches. Spaces that swallowed her. Spaces that deprived her of her ability to see.

Each inmate who entered was a blur.

Stand clear. Sit blurred.

She sat blurred until a man stood before her and brought her to her feet.

As she stood, dazed and exhausted, the screen door swung open. She had to step out of the way.

There was a man in the doorway. He looked puzzled. "Why are you just standing out there?"

She didn't respond.

"Hello?" said Curtis. "Earth to Lucy. Come in. Come *in*," he repeated, stepping aside and opening the door wider. "Did they lobotomize you while you were in jail?"

She stepped in through the door. She handed over her purse. If body searches had been legal, he would have found it was her heart, not her frontal lobe, that was gone. She was amazed at how detached she felt from him. And not amazed at all.

They sat down at the kitchen table. Curtis poured her a glass of wine. She was too tired to appreciate the gesture. She was too tired to drink it.

She was overcome by the wearying sensation of having driven not just hundreds, but seemingly thousands, of kilometres. What was she doing here? Who was this man? He sat before her, shoulders slightly slumped, avoiding her eyes. Where were the presence and confidence he had exuded in the courtroom? Where was the familiarity she had felt in meeting him there and in their letters and phone conversations? She was sitting before a prison inmate who, when he had lived in her world, had committed countless acts of fraud—and one act of manslaughter. What was she doing?

She was starting to feel dizzy. The smoke seemed to have filled not just her lungs but her entire insides. It was choking her. She was going to faint. She just needed to signal to one of the guards. She could get up and walk out without saying a word. They could pretend she had never come. She could go back to her safe, familiar world and he could stay here, in his.

In her mind, she was already summoning the guard, mentally raising her arm as if he were a waiter.

Tim cleared his throat. "Your drive here," he began.

Her horror magnified. In her mind she was tugging furiously on the guard's sleeve, to get her out of there before Tim spoke. She was terrified he was going to say something mundane about the drive, the weather. That he wouldn't be who she thought he was. That she'd made a massive mistake. Her head began to spin. Nausea overwhelmed her. She was going to throw up.

"Your drive here," repeated Tim, "means a lot to me."

The words entered her head like a peacekeeping troop and made it stop spinning. The nausea vanished. Her vision cleared. It was Tim. Thank God he was still not looking at her, had not seen her face; it was shyness, not social backwardness. It was respect. It was nothing she'd ever experienced before.

"I'm kind of overwhelmed by you sitting here in front of me." Tim gave a small, embarrassed laugh and then he met her eyes.

The guard she had summoned in her mind stood waiting. She handed him all her doubts, all her skepticism, all her fears—shitloads of fear. And then she sent him away.

"If I seem a bit stupid, and like I got nothing to say, it's … well…."

There was a long pause.

"Do you mind," he said at last, "if I just sit here and look at you for awhile?"

He was looking at her. She was supposed to be talking, spilling out the experience. She didn't want to share this. She didn't want it exposed to his cynical paintbrush, his layering of ridicule and mockery. Thinly disguised jealousy.

She met Curtis's eyes. And for the first time she saw the pain in them.

Pain. It was so clearly there. It felt like someone was squeezing her heart. Without thinking, she reached out her hand across the table. "I feel that all you want to do is cry and cry." She was speaking words she had never uttered to a man before—had never even thought. "I wish I could take you in my arms and just let you cry."

The eyes that met hers were startled, and did fill, then, with tears. "No one's ever said that to me before." He added, in a voice of wonder, "How do you see that?"

She had no answer. She didn't know. Except that maybe the clarity demanded of her at the gate had also been a warning: be sure you're ready for what you're going to see behind this gate.

She had, somehow, become ready. She had never seen anyone else's pain like this. She had—she could be honest about it now—always been so focused on her own. Had always wanted someone to look in her eyes.

But now she was looking across the table at this boyish, vulnerable man and she was suddenly *standing clear*. She had arrived here at Warkworth to meet herself.

"Pleased to meet you. I'm Curtis Frye." He stuck out his hand.

She started.

Curtis sighed. "I see you left your tongue behind too. What did they do? Cut it out so you couldn't report on the pampered conditions you found?"

She ignored his bait. She couldn't look at him. She fixed her eyes out the window on her vegetable garden at the back of the yard. It was looking neglected. It needed weeding, watering. Now that she had seen the pain in Tim's eyes, pain was everywhere, like the weeds. What was that line about the scales falling from your eyes? How was she going to bear this—this seeing what was? How was she going to contribute to the pain she saw in Curtis now, too, and watch it grow and take over?

She wasn't, not yet; it would be unbearable. Besides, she told herself, Curtis would never believe her anyway. It was too soon to speak. Too soon even to know these kinds of things. You couldn't fall in love with someone after one meeting. She wasn't even sure she had. She wasn't sure what it was she felt, but it wasn't the usual infatuation of falling in love.

So she shrugged, and the shrug let loose a lie. "The visit was okay.

He's a lonely man in prison. He needs a friend, and I can be that friend. That's all there is to say."

She made herself look at Curtis then, and she made herself believe what she had just said, so he would believe her too. It was half true anyway. She steeled herself for a sneering remark. Cynical she could deal with.

"And just how often do the pity visits take place?" Curtis was delivering, on cue.

This time she rose to the bait. "As often as I feel like it," she shot back, and felt better.

8.

MY BAG WAS WAITING FOR me when I arrived at the Ottawa airport late Sunday evening. It had been taken into custody by Sergeant Quinn, who was standing beside it.

My heart beat faster.

But Sergeant Quinn didn't look like he was here to arrest anyone. He wore the same black leather jacket he had worn the night I'd met him. But the jeans below it made me think he must be off-duty. He looked as though he were here to meet a friend or relative.

That got my heart beating even faster. I was afraid he was going to hug me or kiss my cheek.

He did neither. He came forward and stopped at the correct distance for police sergeants and civilians. "I knew you couldn't be too many flights behind your luggage."

Then he smiled and held out his hand. Its warmth shocked me as much as a kiss might have. "Hello Ellen," he said. "Welcome back."

"Hello Sergeant Quinn—"

"Steve. Or just call me Quinn, like my friends do."

"How did you know I was coming in tonight?"

"I'm disappointed you have to ask that question of Ottawa's finest. Although I did think you'd be on the previous flight"—he picked up my bag—"with your luggage."

"I missed the connector in Toronto. Sorry you had to wait." Why on earth was I apologizing? Why did I feel I had to account for anything to this man? Unless…. I hesitated. "Did they send you to meet me?"

"I assume you mean Al and Roach, as opposed to"—he sent me an amused glance—"the folks at the Royal Ottawa."

I gave him a grim smile at the mention of Ottawa's psychiatric hospital and made no reply.

"No, Ellen," he added. "No one sent me."

"So you're not here to arrest me." My attempt at a wry tone failed.

"*Arrest* you. What the devil are you talking about?"

"For, you know, leaving the city so suddenly. For dropping all sorts of bizarre clues as if I knew where Lucy was. For not coming back yesterday when I said I was going to."

I had, in fact, allowed Marc to keep me in bed all day. I had let him think he was being persuasive, but I'd already decided during the night to call a truce. Like soldiers at Christmas. Marc himself had left the bed only to bring food and beer and, once, to call the airline to book my flight. I had woken up in the morning realizing in horror that Saturday night had passed and I had never thought about Lucy once.

And now here I was, meeting my captor. Who had dropped my bag and positioned himself directly in front of me. He placed his hands on my shoulders. He stopped just short of shaking me. "You are not a suspect. Do you hear? You are the furthest thing from a suspect. I came to see you safely home. I thought you might not like to arrive at your dark house on your own."

"Since when did *you* become a mind reader?" My voice was shaky.

"Let's just say I have a cop's instincts—not to mention resource-fulness. And for better or worse, they go into overtime where you're concerned."

He reached down for my bag, did an abrupt about-face and strode ahead of me through the revolving door. I was glad he didn't see the blush that spread across my face. I had a feeling there might be one on his own.

I followed him out to the parking lot. The late April night air had a hint of warmth to it and more than a hint of unreality. And, contrary to his stated intention, Sergeant Quinn was not helping.

His car was sleek and dark. An Integra. Five-speed. It would be a fast car. But he didn't start it up right away. He leaned a forearm on the top of the steering wheel and turned to me. "Why didn't you call me when

you got scared? I meant it you know. That you could call me any time."
His smile was wry. "I don't give my home number out to just anyone.
It's unlisted for a reason."

I found myself apologizing again. He made me feel as though I'd
betrayed his trust. It made no sense at all. I wanted to ask him whether
anything had happened on the weekend. But the question was paralyzed
in my throat.

He started the engine. It purred in a way quite unlike my old Escort.
Yes, it was going to be a fast car. But we cruised out of the lot in first
gear. And then he suddenly braked and put the car in neutral. He leaned
over. My stomach somersaulted.

He reached across me and drew the seatbelt out of its holder. Snapped
it into place. "I might have had to fine you," he smiled and put the car
in gear again.

We turned onto Elgin after all.

"You *are* taking me to the station."

Quinn raised a hand off the steering wheel and gave an exasperated
laugh. "My God, woman. When are you going to learn to trust me? I'm
taking you out for a drink." He glanced sideways at me. "Something
tells me you could use one."

It was disconcerting, the potent mix I felt inside. Apprehensive. Unnerved. Excited. Like a school girl.

The bar was small and minimalist. And, except for the bartender,
empty. We sat on tall chairs with our knees all but touching under a
tiny high round table.

The drinks arrived. A single-malt Scotch for Quinn, a white wine
for me. Assumed, wrongly, by Quinn that that was what I would want.
Why hadn't he asked? Why hadn't I spoken up?

Quinn raised his glass. "Cheers." He took a long swallow, set the
glass down, looked at me and grinned. There was nothing remarkable
about his features, but the grin lit up his face. "Any plans for summer
holidays this year?"

I gave him a look. He was obviously trying for light conversation. He
didn't realize the minefield he was stepping into. "Shall I write an essay?
Ellen's mythical hiking holiday with Marc Desjardins."

"Marc. That would be who I talked to at noon."

I stared at him. "You called." Understanding clicked in. "So that's how you knew when to meet my plane."

Had he come to the airport yesterday too? Or had he called my house? Got no answer. Put two and two together. I was surprised he hadn't called us last night. And then I remembered the phone ringing. And how Marc had ignored it.

"He mentioned you'd decided to stay another day," Quinn was saying. "Had all your flight information. Sounded like a nice guy. Careful. Obviously cares for you. Your boyfriend?" His voice was casual.

"Ex. Recent. I assumed you knew. You seem to know everything else about me." What did he mean by careful? He'd said it in an approving way.

Quinn was shaking his head. There was a look of amused curiosity on his face. And something else. Something I couldn't identify.

"Marc's working in Thunder Bay this summer. The job coincided with our break-up."

"It was obviously amicable."

I took a sip of wine. Chose my words carefully. "Let's just say the situation overrode our circumstances."

Quinn cocked an eyebrow. "And was there a happy reconciliation?" His tone was mocking.

I could think of no sharp reply. Could I only dish it out?

A potent silence lay between us.

Quinn tipped back his glass for a last swallow. He looked around to catch the bartender's eyes and held up two fingers. Turned back to me. "Sorry," he said. "That was out of line. Do you do a lot of hiking?" The mocking tone was gone. This sounded like genuine interest.

I shrugged. "Well, since I met Marc. So for the past few years. It was a compromise activity. He would have much preferred me to go down rivers with him." Why was I telling him this?

"Kayaking?"

"Canoeing. White-water. But I'm af … I prefer dry land. Give me a bike or a pair of running shoes and I'm happy."

"You're a very active woman." His tone managed to be both admiring and condescending. I was both flattered and irritated.

"I used to be active when I was younger, before I became a cop and stopped having a life. Hiking, biking, backpacking. I did it all. Gotta get back to it."

The way he was looking at me made me squirm. As if he was making a suggestion. That was ridiculous. There was nothing between Sergeant Quinn and me except Lucy.

But, I couldn't deny it, the air between us was charged, and had been since he'd met my plane. Maybe since our search through the apartment building. Maybe it was natural, given the circumstances. *Everything* was supercharged. It touched me that he'd been concerned enough to come to the airport (now that it was clear it hadn't been to arrest me). And it took on greater significance since he wasn't even on duty. Maybe I could understand Lucy's attraction for Tim while she was still with Curtis. An absent partner was worse than no partner. And Marc, for all his tenderness this weekend, was absent. I'd had to go to *him*, I vehemently reminded myself. Lucy had had to go to Tim, too, but that hadn't been his choice. In fact, she'd said he was overdue for release. Why had it taken so long?

It was a relief to find a neutral question to ask Quinn.

"Well, the thing was he was serving two sentences. The system had him serving them consecutively, but there was an argument to be made that he should have been serving them at the same time. Eventually Lucy hired a lawyer to argue that case in court, and that's how he was finally released. But for those two years they were trying to go through the usual channels."

"Through the Parole Board."

"Yes, his mandatory release was this year—this month, in fact—but he'd been eligible for parole for some time. To get parole you have to have a hearing and you have to fulfill certain conditions. I'm not an expert on the process, but I think you have to have so many ETAs—escorted temporary absences—and then UTAs—*un*escorted temporary absences—before you're eligible for day parole. So you have a hearing and you get granted an ETA, then you fulfill that and you're granted at UTA, and so on. But there were all kinds of screw-ups with Brennan. They'd grant him a UTA and then there wouldn't be any record of it, and they'd have to wait to have another hearing. Stuff like that. Personally I think it was all deliberate."

"Deliberate? Why?"

"He should *never* have been let out."

I started at the vehemence in his voice. "Because he was dangerous? So why did they? If they knew how dangerous he was?"

Quinn shrugged. "Lucy."

"*Lucy?*"

"My theory is: they were trying to throw away the key, but she got on their case. She started writing to the National Parole Board. Got her family, all her friends writing too. Letters of support. From their tone, you'd think they'd put an innocent man behind bars. Another Fajber. From what I can tell, they tried to put her off, but she just kept at them. For two years. The irony is their relationship was volatile even while he was in prison."

"Volatile?" I felt suddenly sick.

"His records are full of concerns expressed about arguing during phone calls, visits. Yelling, fighting. I just don't get why she didn't see it coming."

Yelling, fighting. I thought about the Lucy I had known. She had a pretty quick temper. But she never seemed to hold a grudge. The thought came to me: maybe for Lucy, yelling and arguing were just normal. But why? Did it really all go back to her childhood?

"Lucy let me read some of the letters Tim sent when they started corresponding. Sounded like he grew up in a pretty remote part of Ontario. And she told me he was abused when he was a kid. Do you know anything about that?"

Quinn shook his head. "Probably all lies. Probably fed her some story to lure her in."

The bartender arrived with the second round of drinks. I wasn't halfway through my first. I took another swallow of the now lukewarm wine and got the question out I really wanted to ask. "I guess nothing was resolved over the weekend."

Quinn appeared unsurprised at the switch in topic. He shook his head. "They're still working on it, Ellen."

"And I don't suppose—I don't suppose they're searching the Gatineau River." I felt like an idiot saying it.

"I don't think they're concentrating directly on the river, no, but they *are* searching the general Gatineau area."

"And did you—were you able to go down to the Hunt Club area again?"

"I passed your message on to Lundy and Roach," said Quinn. "I don't know if they had a chance yet." He avoided my eyes.

"You must think I'm nuts with all my dreams and visions."

"I told you I didn't." I thought I detected a note of annoyance.

"Well, *I* do," I laughed. Before he could respond, I asked, "Are you officially on this case now? Are you working with Sergeants Lundy and Roach?"

"Not officially. But I'm not very busy with other things right now. So I'm helping out when I can. Behind the scenes stuff. I've been investigating Brennan's prison history. And," he added, "I'm getting a life back. It might even include hiking and biking. But not canoeing." He was looking at me significantly.

I narrowed my eyes at him.

Quinn saw my look. "I'm not laughing at you. There's nothing wrong with being scared."

"Who said I'm scared?"

"Hey, hey, don't get defensive on me. And don't worry, it's not obvious to the whole world. But you are, aren't you?"

I made no response.

"There's nothing wrong with having fears. It's not as if you're debilitated by them."

Like Lucy was.

I felt some weight lift. Something I hadn't even known was there. Marc had never "allowed" me to be afraid. I was being given permission to acknowledge it. To speak it out loud. I did. "I'm terrified of drowning. Especially in white water."

"See? Was that so bad to say?" He seemed pleased. As if I were a good therapy patient.

"How could you tell, anyway?"

Quinn shrugged. "I'm trained to read between the lines."

I wasn't sure how I felt about Sergeant Quinn being able to read between the lines. It was disconcerting. But I wanted him to read more.

"It's not that I can't swim," I said. "But I can't relax. Can't get my breath. I feel out of my element. And it's not because I'm not in shape." I cursed myself for sounding defensive again.

"No," said Quinn, in a way that made it clear he'd noticed that. He raised his glass. "I promise you this."

"What?" I was wary.

"Our first date will not be in a canoe."

Date? The word brought colour to my face.

"Although…." He was smiling.

"What?" I said again. Even warier.

"I think we might just be having it."

I reached for the second glass then.

I directed Quinn to the Old Chelsea exit so I could pick up my car at Mary Frances's. I would come back for the dogs in the morning. I hoped the engine sounds in the driveway wouldn't wake anyone up. Mary Frances knew I was coming home tonight; she wouldn't worry about the car being gone. She'd had a previous engagement or she would have come to pick me up herself. Interesting coincidence that she hadn't been able to come.

I opened the trunk for Quinn to throw my bag in. "Thanks, Sergeant Quinn. I'll be fine from here. And thank you for—"

"I'm seeing you home." It was not up for debate.

The Integra's headlights swung out onto the highway behind me. I was reminded of the last time I had let someone follow me home. These lights in my rear-view were giving me the same jitters.

I took a long deep breath when I turned down my road. At the airport he'd referred to my dark house, my not wanting to arrive there alone. The house *was* dark. In my panic to get to the airport I had forgotten to leave a light on. But he wouldn't know that. Unless he'd come up here already.

I was talking hard to myself as he followed me up the dark steps. So what if he had parked in my driveway before, walked up these steps, peered in the windows? It was not a *bad* thing to have a cop checking on your empty house in your absence. But why not tell me?

By the time we reached the door I was calm again. Given the circumstances, it would have been unnerving to arrive here by myself. I wondered if I could ask him to check around inside without sounding like a paranoid female.

"You don't mind living here by yourself?" His voice came out of the darkness behind me.

"That," I said, "is a relatively new phenomenon, and coinciding with these extraordinary circumstances, I have to admit it's not ideal." I shoved the key into the lock and looked around at the black shadow that was Quinn. "But under non-extraordinary circumstances, I think I wouldn't mind at all. I have the dogs for company. Usually. I'll pick them up tomorrow." I opened the door, flicked on the kitchen and outdoor lights. "I'll be alright."

Quinn stepped in the door behind me. "I know you will. But since we do have extraordinary circumstances, including, at the moment, a police sergeant in your front hall, you might like me to walk around the house with you. Make sure everything's in order."

There wasn't a hint of teasing or condescension in his tone or face. This was what he was trained for. "I wish you'd stop reading my mind," I said.

"I wish you'd *speak* your mind."

I raised my hands in surrender. "Okay, since you're here, Sergeant Quinn, I would appreciate it. But I want to state that I'm not normally a ner—"

"I know," he interrupted, and walked past me into the kitchen. There was anger in his tone. I didn't think it was directed at me.

He was thorough. And admiring of the house. But his presence, his eyes on everything, put me on edge. Every time he came near me I thought he was going to embrace me. It scared the hell out of me. That he might. That I might want him to.

At the front door, Quinn paused. He reached out, encircled my wrist with thumb and forefinger. A light but electric hold. "I'm not supposed to discuss the case with anyone, but I'll tell you this. Because I think you'll sleep better knowing. We have a tail on Brennan twenty-four hours a day. And he's a creature of habit. In by eleven, up by six. Prison habits die hard."

Then he leaned in close. I froze, waiting for the kiss. Instead his voice was soft in my ear. "Ellen," he said. "Drop the Sergeant stuff. Just Quinn."

He straightened up and let go of my wrist. Resumed his "cop" voice. "Now lock the door behind me and go to bed and get some sleep."

For once I did what I was told. Without minding.

I open my eyes. It's still dark. I feel her presence before I see her. There is a familiarity now. I want to speak but still I can't. I can only watch as more images play out in front of my eyes. The outbuilding is empty now. But there is garbage everywhere. The building is knee-deep in it. Then Lucy's voice, even fainter than before. Barely audible. "A candy-bar wrapper … fingerprints…."

She doesn't speak again. Her image is fading. I want to ask questions. This building, where is it? And where are you now? But she's gone.

I opened my eyes to the sun streaming in the window. For a moment I wondered why the dogs hadn't woken me already, weren't nosing at my hands. Then I remembered where they were. But I hadn't been alone in the night.

This time I was ready to admit Lucy's visit was not *just* a dream. She was becoming a presence in my life. She was telling me there might be a candy-bar wrapper, or something, with Tim's prints on it. Evidence he'd been in that outbuilding. Maybe there would be evidence that she had been there, too. If the police weren't going to look where I asked them to, I would just have to go look myself.

I mulled over the prospect on my walk up to the highway for the mail, enjoying the fact that my sciatic nerve barely twinged anymore. It was daylight. Tim wasn't likely to show up at the outbuilding if Lucy was no longer there. He certainly wasn't going to show up if none of this was true. What did I have to lose that wasn't already lost?

I clicked the lock shut on the mailbox. Tucked the bills and my hands deep into my pockets and trudged back down the hill to my road. I missed the dogs, but another day at Mary Frances's wouldn't hurt. I would pick them up on my way home. At the front door, I had my key ready to let myself in. I was learning.

From my upstairs office, I called Mary Frances, then Angel. I waited to be put through. From habit, I stood in the space between the desk and the window, leaning back against the desk to look out. The view was never the same twice. Today, the hills across the river looked like someone had covered them in a pale green wash. A hint of spring. In the bay, the wind was pushing the white-capped waves towards shore—*inexorably* was the word that came to mind. The river was completely open now. Marc would have already been out paddling, plowing through white-caps, dodging stray logs. They were ghosts of the drive that had been conducted on the Gatineau up until only a few years before. I'd spent hours, when I first moved in with Marc, watching the big circular booms, with their log prisoners, floating lazily downstream. Environmental concerns had put an end to that era. The river was being cleaned up now, but there were still lots of deadheads next to shore and stray logs floating downstream, especially in spring. They didn't bother Marc. I could see him in my mind's eye, stroking efficiently on the water in his sleek We-no-nah Sundowner. Five strokes on one side with a bent-shaft paddle, five strokes on the other. In a racing canoe, Marc was a machine.

Angel came on the line, and I gave myself a mental shake. More visions I did not need.

"Take as much time as you need," said Angel. "We finished up that research package on Cree myths for you. Things are pretty slow now. I'm glad you're okay."

"Nothing like a holiday with a recent ex in the lovely suburbs of a northern town to put you back on your feet."

"That's the first sarcastic remark I've heard you make in a week, you *must* be okay."

Was I? No. Sarcasm was a refuge. It always had been.

At exactly six and a half kilometres south of Lucy's street, running east

off Bank was a neighbourhood street called Delta Drive. The end of
the street backed onto the Greenbelt, the huge band of open lands and
forests surrounding Ottawa's urban areas that was intended to prevent
urban sprawl and provide a natural respite for the city's residents. This
particular section of the Greenbelt, I saw from my car, was greened (or
would soon be greened) with poplars.

I didn't get out of the car. Instead, I leaned over and locked the doors.
I looked down the path that ran between two houses into the woods.
Would Tim and Marnie have dared walk past these houses? It seemed too
public. And then there was the irrational feeling I'd had since that night
out with Quinn: that what I wanted was a road heading *west* off Bank.
It was just more voices in my head. There were way too many now.

In the rear-view mirror I watched a burgundy van with tinted windows
pull over a short distance behind me. No one got out. I started the car
and headed back to the main thoroughfare. I watched the van in my
rear-view. It stayed put, and still no one got out.

There were no streets running west off Bank this far south. I headed
back north. Another road to the east dead-ended at a run-down industrial
park. I sat looking at the warehouses in front of me. Several trucks were
backed up to them. Not isolated enough. No poplars. No point.

Back on Bank, I turned south again. That was when I noticed the
cemetery on the west side of the street. There were three gates, all open,
with narrow roadways leading in. A cemetery would be a good place to
hide a dead body. That was another voice in my head. At least this one
had a sense of humour. Of sorts.

I drove in through the first of the gates. The three roads converged
at the back of the cemetery at another roadway parallel to Bank. The
road ended at a grey prefabricated building. An outbuilding. Beyond
the building were trees. Maples.

There was no one in sight. I got out of the car and headed toward the
building. I walked all around it. There were no windows. The structure
was surrounded with junk and debris. The image I had got was of garbage
inside. I couldn't see inside. Could this be it? Could Lucy have meant
maples, not poplars? The door was secured with a padlock. It didn't look
like it had been tampered with.

My heart was thudding. I walked to the edge of the woods. They spread down a short ravine to a small creek, which was barely visible through the thicket.

Also barely visible was someone making his way up through the trees towards me.

I didn't stick around to find out who it was.

I drove home angry. Angry that I was a woman, too scared to walk through woods or buildings by myself. Angry with Marc for not being there to help me. Angry with the police for not searching where I asked them to.

I needed someone to go with me. Someone male. I couldn't imagine Angel even going for a walk, let alone a search. The one person who would do this for me wasn't someone I was sure I could ask. Or should.

I stopped in at Mary Frances's on my way home.

"I don't want to talk about anything right now," I said at the door, before she could bombard me with questions.

Her expression was sympathetic. "You've really had it from all sides, haven't you? Are you sure you wouldn't like to just move in for awhile? The dogs have already become members of the family. They just about sit on chairs at the table. Jack's been spoiling them with treats all weekend."

"Great. You've created a couple of monsters. You might just get them as permanent residents. I appreciate your offer, but I think I need to be at home. My big, brave, now fat, spoiled dogs will keep watch. I'll call you when—"

"Just tell me you're not in contact with Brennan. That's all I need to know."

I assured her I wasn't. It was not contact with Brennan I was struggling about.

There was no question I was freaked out. I was supposed to be freaked out. Under the circumstances, how could I be anything else? But it was not *Steve Quinn* I needed to be freaked out about. That fear, anyway, was completely unfounded. Quinn was someone who could help.

The light was flashing on the phone when I got in. One new message. Then Marc's voice. "It's probably just as well I have your answering machine. I probably shouldn't be calling." An audible sigh. "But I can't help it, I'm worried about you, Ellen. I got a call from a Sergeant Quinn after you left. I assume—I hope—you know the name. He was looking for you. I made him give me his number to call him back before I spoke to him or gave him your flight information. You will call me paranoid—no doubt. (No, "careful," I thought, remembering what Quinn had said. Caring.) But this whole situation is scaring the shit out of me. I know I haven't sounded very supportive; it's only because I'm scared for you." There was a pause, and another sigh, and then: "I'm glad you came last weekend. I wish you had stayed, but I *have* realized you need to search or whatever it is you're doing. I don't understand it. I just see something is driving you. Please, please, please be careful. And you know I'm here if you need anything. Okay, *ma chère. Je t'aime.*"

Tears were streaming down my face by the end of the message. And then I wiped them away. Marc was in Thunder Bay. Where he was choosing to be. He wouldn't come home. He couldn't help me. I picked up the phone, pressed a now familiar sequence of numbers, and asked for my call to be put through.

"What can I do for you, Ellen?" asked Quinn.

He sounded so business-like I almost lost my nerve. Tears were still dangerously close to the surface. "Um, I wanted to ask for your help, but—"

"Anything," said Quinn. He somehow managed to sound jokingly flippant and dead serious at the same time.

I pulled myself together. "I have more details now. About where Lucy may have been hidden. If we could find it, I think there might be some evidence." I didn't tell him what it might be. "I went down to the area this morning, and there are a couple of places that might have been it, but I lost my nerve. If I were a *man*—"

"You don't want to be a man; you just need a man," said Quinn.

He was so matter-of-fact, I ignored his proprietary tone. He was a cop. He had competencies I lacked. And, for this task, anyway, I needed someone with competencies. It was why I had called, wasn't it?

"But," Quinn was saying, "it will be on my time off. We'll go Saturday. And you will not say anything to Sergeants Lundy or Roach about my going with you."

"But what if we find something?"

Quinn hesitated. I thought he was going to say, 'we aren't going to find anything.' But he said, "It will be you that finds it and reports it."

⸎

"WHERE HAVE YOU BEEN? I'VE been trying all day. Where were you last night? You said you'd be home by six."

The assault in her ear was the last thing she needed after the drive she had just made, but his anger was understandable; she should have been home twenty-four hours ago. She pulled the bath towel around her more securely and kept her voice calm. "Tim, I'm sorry. I got delayed in Toronto. It was pouring rain yesterday; I couldn't drive in that. I just got back half an hour ago. Listen I just got out of the bath, can you—"

"Well, why didn't you let me know? You could have left a message."

"I thought it had to be an emergency—"

"I've been worried sick. I thought Curtis had come back, had done something." His voice faltered.

She was bewildered. "Tim? Are you alright? What in the world has Curtis got to do with anything? He's not going to hurt me."

"But you said yourself, he abused you. I worry about you, Lu." He sounded like he was fighting tears.

She was starting to shiver. She descended the stairs to her bedroom to find her robe. "Listen, you really don't have anything to worry about Curtis. He's gone. And why would he hurt me? I never meant he was physically abusive. He just fucked with my brain. Anyway, he's the one who wanted out." She regretted those last seven words as soon as they were out of her mouth.

There was a moment's pause, then, in a different voice Tim said, "What do you mean, he wanted out? You said you kicked him out. You said you wanted the relationship to end. What are you saying? Do you want him back?"

"Oh my God, Tim, slow down, you're jumping to massive conclusions. Hang on a sec. I just need to put on my robe." She put down the phone, knotted her robe around her waist and wrapped her hair in the towel. It wasn't her hair towel, but under the circumstances, warmth won out over hygiene. She could hear Tim speaking before she got the phone back to her ear.

"Don't tell me I'm jumping to conclusions. You just said—"

"First of all, this has nothing to do with Curtis. I was delayed by rain. Second of all, I had—I thought I had no way of letting you know." They were going around in circles; this was anything but a constructive conversation.

"Well, that's all very well to say now," Tim said. "I've been worried sick."

"Stop saying you've been worried sick—"

"I *have* been worried sick. Do you know how frustrating it is to be on this end of the fucking phone? Not to be able to take calls or leave messages? Not to be there with you to know what's going on?"

His voice was getting louder. Lucy had to raise hers to be heard. "I do know—"

"To hell you know. You have no idea. But I'll give you—" He was past it now. Lucy held the phone away from her ear. There would be no reasoning with him. There was so much anger inside him. The so-called "therapy" he got in prison was useless. He couldn't just learn to "manage" his anger; there was so much inside him already; it had to come out. It often did, now that their phone calls had become daily.

Half the time he had to yell just to be heard above the din in the room. The whole prison seemed like it was a time bomb of anger. The narrow phone wires to loved ones seemed to be the only real outlet. That was the unfair part. Why should she be on the receiving end of it? She hadn't done anything. She was trying to help him, for God's sake. She had, in fact, just made this long stressful trip to Toronto for him. And this was what she got for her trouble—this earful of abuse. Goddamn it, she didn't have to take this.

She shouted back. It felt good to yell. A release of tension from the drive, from the weekend, from tiptoeing around her father and trying to bring him onside. She shouted until she was hoarse. She shouted until she heard a click in her ear, followed by the buzz of the disconnected line.

She stared in disbelief at the portable in her hand. He had never hung up on her before. Their shouting matches were supposed to give them each a chance to vent. No one was supposed to take it personally. Hanging up was not part of the contract. But at least she could now get dressed. He would call back.

She pulled on a sweatsuit, hung up the towel in the laundry room, and carried the portable back up to the kitchen. A glass of water from the Brita pitcher in the fridge soothed her throat.

The phone rang. She grabbed it.

"Oh God, I'm sorry, baby." He sounded like he'd been crying. "I know I lose it. I can't help it. I don't mean to take it out on you. God, you're the last person I should be yelling at. I was just upset and worried—*not* worried sick.*"

The sudden laughter from both of them broke the tension. "I know," said Lucy. "It's okay. I like you being worried about me—as long as you don't make yourself sick about it." Or yell at me about it, she thought, biting her tongue.

They laughed again. "But," she went on, "you have to trust me. I'm not going to screw you around. I was completely open with you about Curtis. You know that. I didn't hide anything from you, even the uncomfortable stuff. And it's over. One hundred and fifty percent over. I have no reason to lie to you. Give me one good reason why I would lie to you."

In her ear there was a sigh so deep it seemed to fill her own being.

"Everything sounds so fucking rational when you tell me," said Tim. "When you're there, talking to me. It's when I'm here alone and you're not there, and the phone just rings and you don't pick up. That's when my brain starts going crazy. Everyone else has always lied to me, why wouldn't you?"

"But don't you see? That's exactly what I've been talking about. It's an opportunity for you. Just like I'm starting to break my patterns, this is an opportunity for you to break yours. For you to stop your brain from going crazy with those thoughts. For you to learn how to trust again."

"Well, it sounds easy when you say it. You try being here inside my cell, inside my brain."

She couldn't help laughing and was relieved when Tim laughed too. She was excited, almost giddy with relief. "I didn't say it was easy. My

God, I just drove to Toronto. Negotiated the 401. I've never been able to do that before. I'm breaking my fears. We can do this, Tim. We can help each other. I feel it. I don't mind it when you lose it. I know you need to vent. I like that. We both get to vent. But ... just don't hang up on me, okay? I can't take that."

"Yeah, I know. I shouldn't have done that. It wasn't fair. I'm sorry, Lu. I was just so scared for you, I had to let it out. How was it at your dad's anyway?"

"Well it's about time you asked," she said, with humour in her voice. The words almost tumbled over each other she was so relieved. Everything was fine. This was what it was about—communication, peace after a fight, *personal progress*. She told him about the weekend, about getting Anna and Doug to agree to write letters on his behalf. "And I know Dad's going to come around," she added. "It's just a matter of time."

"Time," said Tim, "I got plenty of."

She was afraid he was going to spiral down, but he added: "Lu?"

"Mmm?"

"I love you. You know?"

Warmth spread through her chest. She did know. That was the most amazing thing of all.

9.

STEVE QUINN'S PLACE WAS A second-storey walk-up apartment in an Edwardian house not many blocks from the police station. I was nervous knocking on the door. Pleased by the smile in his eyes when he opened it. And relieved when he said he was ready and didn't invite me in. Also slightly disappointed.

I wasn't surprised when he suggested we take my car and held out his hand for my keys. I handed them over without even thinking about it. "It's not your Integra," I warned him. I felt self-conscious about my battered old Escort.

"Hey, it's got a stick, that's all that matters." He sent an approving look my way and started the engine. "Most women don't drive stick shift."

"That's bullshit."

Quinn laughed. "Okay, most women *I* know don't drive stick shift. Where to, Boss?"

I directed him to the end of Delta Drive. He stopped the car close to the place I had parked a few days before, where a path between two houses disappeared into the woods. He made no move to get out. He turned to me. The car felt very close. "Where are you getting your information from, Ellen?"

"I told you, I've been having these dreams."

"But there's something you're *not* telling me."

"That cop instinct at work again?"

"Or maybe you're just not very good at lying."

"Are you saying I'm lying?"

He gave me an appraising look. "No," he said, "not outright lying.

But I think you've been editing the truth."

"And you want the *whole* truth."

"And nothing but the truth, preferably."

I smiled, I couldn't help it. "Well, that I can't guarantee. I don't have a clue what's true and what's not true anymore."

"Okay, then, just tell me what you've been experiencing. Without censoring yourself. Call it a dry run for the court."

"The *court*?"

"One day you're going to be a witness, sweetheart, no doubt about that. So let's start with those dreams you keep telling me about. What's really going on?"

My brain was racing. Doing a quick edit to see what I could still leave out without arousing suspicion. "Well, the dreams are true," I said. "At least, I'm not sure their *contents* are true, but I have been having them. And, as you say, I've been editing the contents. They've been much more elaborate than I've made them out to be. It's not just messages I've been getting but images. I've had to interpret the images. I was trying to simplify it, make it easier, more coherent, but…."

"You said it was some anonymous voice giving you the messages. That's not true, is it?"

I looked out the window, prepared to watch until the buds opened on the trees. Quinn seemed prepared to wait with me. Why did he have to be so perceptive? Finally I turned back to him. "It's Lucy who's speaking to me."

Quinn's expression didn't change, but he breathed in, and out, a long breath. "I can see why you might have been reluctant to volunteer that information."

"Because it seems like the product of an overwrought mind?"

It was Quinn's turn to watch the buds on the trees open. "Let's just say," he said at last, "that I can see how you might think I might think that."

I laughed a bitter laugh. "It's *me* who thinks that."

"Yet, you came to the police station at two in the morning."

"That was the hell of it. Not putting any credence in the dreams but feeling compelled. The crux was realizing Lucy might still be alive." I was embarrassed to hear my voice choke up.

Quinn put a hand over mine. It was a clichéd gesture, and that embarrassed me too. "I would have done the same," he said. He took his hand away and leaned back against the door. "Why don't you give me the unedited version of the dreams—word for word and image for image. If you can remember."

"Well," he said, when I had finished giving him the description of each dream. "This is as good a place to start as any. Shall we go look for an outbuilding in a poplar grove and a candy bar with an incriminating fingerprint on it?"

We did. It was a surprisingly pleasant walk, in the warm sunshine of a Saturday afternoon in early May. The green wash over the trees and shrubs was a shade darker here than it was up in Chelsea. We might have been friends out for a stroll. Or, yes, on a first date. We asked each other the kinds of questions you ask someone of the opposite sex you want to get to know better. He was easy to talk to. Receptive. I had misunderstood his attitude about Marc and me. He was nothing but sympathetic. And he was willing to reveal things about himself. His recent divorce after a lengthy and painful separation. His desire to get out of the city and buy a house in the Gatineaus once the finances had been sorted out. He wanted a house like mine. A partner with similar interests.

"My wife—ex-wife—lives entirely in an emotional, and urban, world. She was never interested in doing anything outdoors. Just art galleries and theatre. Which is okay in small doses, but…. She doesn't approach anything logically. She comes at things sideways. It was exhausting to deal with. I used to think that was the way all of you were. But I've begun to realize not all Ellens are created equal."

He was glancing down at me with a significant look.

I started. "What d'you mean, 'all Ellens'?"

Quinn hesitated. Then shrugged. "I just mean all women aren't the same. Some of you are rational."

I rolled my eyes. "Yeah, right. I've been very rational lately."

"You've had very rational reasons to be irrational. But I can read you. Underneath." He smiled. "Call my psychic."

I laughed. "Or psycho—like me." But I was enjoying the idea of

Quinn being able to read me. He certainly had an uncanny ability in that department.

We turned around. There were no outbuildings in the woods, nothing out of the ordinary. Back at the car, Quinn looked at me over the roof before he unlocked the door. "Where to next, Boss?"

I directed him to the cemetery. He turned in at the first entrance and parked on the roadway at the back. There was no one else in sight. "Shall I refrain from making jokes about the graveyard?"

"Go ahead, get them out of your system. I already did."

The cemetery had a whole different feel to it with Quinn with me. Like the Greenbelt, it was an enjoyable stroll. Nothing sinister at all.

We couldn't get inside the storage building. It was locked up tight.

"It doesn't look like anyone else has got in here either," was Quinn's comment.

"And there are no poplar trees," I added. "But can we go down there anyway?" I nodded to the woods.

We found a trail and wandered along the creek in the ravine. The only thing out of the ordinary was my feeling that Quinn secretly thought this whole exercise was pointless.

We headed back to the car. Quinn paused beside me on the passenger side after he unlocked my door. "You're pretty quiet. Disappointed?"

I narrowed my eyes at him. "Are you just humouring me?"

He reached out and shook me by the shoulders. "I'm going to throttle you, woman."

He must have seen my stricken face. He let me go. "I'm *kidding*."

I laughed to hide the adrenalin rush and got in the car. "I know. Anyway, if you do, you'll have a handy place to hide my body."

"That's not," said Quinn, "what I'd like to—" He cut himself off and shut the door after me.

The drive back up Bank Street was a déjà vu. I could still feel Quinn's hands shaking me. He'd been joking. I was being paranoid. I sat and stewed in silence.

"I don't think anyone will recognize us here." I jumped at the sound of his voice. He had pulled into a small strip mall just north of Hunt Club.

"What are we doing?"

"We're having dinner. Me taking you." He looked at me out of the corner of his eye. "Mind?"

I shook my head. Dinner in a public place. It was probably just what I needed.

The tavern—a separate building in the corner of the parking lot—was dimly lit and starting to fill up. Quinn directed me to a table at the back.

The waiter greeted us with a big friendly grin. Quinn ordered a Jack Daniel's and a steak. I ordered just the steak.

When his drink arrived, Quinn leaned back in his chair. "So tell me something, Ellen McGinn."

"Uh oh," I said.

"I think this is a harmless question. As opposed to some others I could think of asking you."

I looked at him in wary amusement. I had been right. There was a normalcy here I needed: the people around us talking and laughing, the waiter setting down the drink on a napkin, a relaxed-looking man across the table from me, sipping from his glass and, it was becoming obvious, deriving a personal enjoyment from my company.

"Shoot," I said.

"Why are you so skeptical about psychic phenomena?"

I shrugged. "I can't verify it. I can't prove it or disprove it. It seems better to leave it alone." *Because it's scary. Because something else has control. Something I don't understand.*

"But it's not leaving you alone."

"Apparently not. But I can ignore it."

"But you're not."

"I *told* you why not."

Quinn put a hand up. "I'm not here to argue with you."

"Why *are* you here with me?" I couldn't believe I'd let that question out of my mouth.

Quinn looked at me, his eyes wide. "Because I believe in you."

I cringed at the cliché. "Even when I don't believe in myself?"

"Especially because you don't believe in yourself."

I shook my head. I had no idea what he meant by that.

Our steaks arrived. We ate, making mostly small talk. He was attentive, making sure my steak was to my liking, my water glass was filled, was I sure I didn't want a glass of wine.

I finished my last bite. "My turn to ask a question."

Quinn smiled. "Shoot."

"You mentioned the courtroom. Are you guys really going to get Tim?"

Quinn was shaking his head, a glint in his eyes. "Nope, not going to answer."

I looked at him, indignant. "I answered your question."

"And I will answer yours. Just not here. Too public. Wait 'til we get back to the car. Do you want dessert? Coffee?"

"No thanks, I'm fine."

Quinn turned in his chair, scouting for the waiter and the bill.

Outside there was a chill in the darkness. Quinn pulled out onto Hunt Club and headed west to the on-ramp for the Airport Parkway, retracing the route we had taken a week and a half before, up the canal and back to Elgin.

We didn't speak until we reached his house. Quinn expertly manoeuvred the car into a tight spot at the curb. He turned off the ignition and settled back in his seat, his body turned towards me. A street light across the road gave his face odd angles of shadow and light. I tried to find the face I knew in the odd angles. I couldn't. I had to look away. It was too disconcerting.

"No question Lundy and Roach are going to get him. It's just a matter of time."

"But do they have any evidence?"

"I keep forgetting you don't know what they've been doing. I'm going to tell you because I think it will alleviate some of your fears. But we are not having this conversation." The stern expression on his shadowed face made him even more unrecognizable.

I spoke to the windshield. "Okay. No."

Quinn seemed oblivious to my unease. He was working up to his story. "They figure Brennan strangled Lucy Saturday morning in her house. Maybe while she was having a shower. Then he dumped her body somewhere up in the Gatineaus and abandoned her car on River Road. Where you found it two days later. In his witness statement, Brennan said he put the bike rack on the car, and her bike, but that she changed her mind, and he took the bike off. They figure he actually put the bike rack on the car for his own bike, and cycled the rest of the way to town after he ditched the car."

"I don't remember a bike rack on the car."

"No, there wasn't one there. But Stupid mentioned it in his witness statement. Maybe he took the rack with him on the bike. Maybe he ditched it. Maybe he just fucked up."

I couldn't imagine Tim carrying a bike rack on a bike. "It would take him quite awhile to bike to town. It takes me an hour, and I'm on a road bike. I think Lucy bought Tim a mountain bike. That would be a lot slower."

"You bike to town?"

"Well, I haven't this year because I've had this sciatica bugging me, but, yeah, normally lots of times to work in the summer." I hoped he wasn't going to make any more condescendingly appreciative remarks about my activeness.

"Did you ever bike to Lucy's?"

I looked at him but I was seeing Lucy in her garden as I wheeled my bike around to the back of her house. "Yes, actually. At least once. Why?"

"Was Brennan there?" He seemed excited.

"He came in later." I spoke slowly, remembering how the three of us had eaten together and how Lucy had told Tim I'd biked all the way from Chelsea. "You think I gave him the *idea?*"

Quinn shrugged. "Could be."

I tried to imagine Tim parking the car and taking a bike off the back. It seemed unlikely. "Maybe he had someone else drive with him in another car."

"Still stuck on the accomplice theory, huh?"

"I'm not stuck on any—"

"Hey," His voice was soft. "Ease up, girl. It's all theory at this point. But we've pretty well tracked his movements through that whole Saturday.

His movements don't match his witness statement."

"How did you track his movements? You mean talking to his friends?" I thought about Marnie. If she were involved, wouldn't she protect him? She'd have to, in order to protect herself.

"That and a lot more. You'd be surprised." He ticked items off on the fingers of one hand. "Surveillance cameras at corner stores, bank machine statements that record the time of transaction, pay-per-view movie records. His alibi doesn't hold up."

"Is it enough to prove him guilty?"

"Not on its own. We need the body. Fortunately Brennan needs the body too."

"What d'you mean, he needs the body? Why?"

"In order to get control of Lucy's estate. You knew he was the sole beneficiary of her estate?"

"Oh God, no, I didn't." The sole beneficiary. "*There's* a compelling motive for…."

Quinn was nodding. "Damn right it is. Everything is his. The house alone is worth a quarter million. But in order to get it all, he has to produce a body. To prove Lucy's dead. Otherwise he has to wait something like seven years. And I can guarantee you, Stupid isn't going to wait that long. He's already gone through over twenty thousand dollars of Lucy's money. And since she went missing he's been pawning off her office equipment." He grinned. "He brings her fax machine and computer in the front door of a pawn shop and we're at the back door ready to take it."

"*Twenty thousand dollars?* I don't understand. How did he—"

"Twenty-two thousand, actually. He was defrauding her this whole last year. No doubt he was planning it from the moment she made contact in prison."

I closed my eyes. For an instant I could feel Lucy's panic. What had her friend Kevin said? She prided herself on being financially secure. No wonder she'd been so negative last fall. God, it must have been a nightmare.

"How come she didn't go to the police?"

He shrugged. "He said he was going to pay it back. He'd met a guy in prison, Bill Torrence, who got out before him. Or after. I can't remember. They were going to go into business together. Cattle transport or something. That never happened. But then, suddenly, Torrence is going to give him a big fat loan. Going to wire the money. It was a big fat lie."

I'm on the phone with my bank manager and it's taken me ages to get through.

"She was waiting for the money," I said. *Right to the end.*

Quinn nodded.

"But I don't understand. How's Tim going to produce her body?"

"Ellen, Ellen, you disappoint me. You know how diligently he's been searching."

I shook my head, but he didn't seem to notice. "One of these days, he's just going to 'happen' across it." He made quotation marks in the air. "And then…." He mimed the motion of hanging himself with a rope.

Hanging, strangling…. An involuntary shiver crackled the back of my neck. Lucy was so small. *I know how easily she can be hurt when we play-wrestle on the living room floor.*

I turned to Quinn. "When I talked to Lucy the week before she went missing, she sounded terrible. She didn't explain why, but obviously—from what you say—she was upset about the money. But it sounded like something beyond—mental stress. Do you know, or have you guys any theories about what was going on that week? Do you know if Tim was…."

Quinn was looking at me.

I tried again. "Detective Godbout asked me if I knew if Lucy was being abused. I just said no automatically. I mean, I had never seen any evidence myself. But I hadn't seen her."

Quinn's face was inscrutable in the shadows. But he was nodding. "Lundy and Roach have been talking to some of Lucy's friends. It appears she was being abused, that she was trying to get out."

I closed my eyes. It would explain a lot. Lucy's becoming more and more negative after Tim moved in. The way she had sounded that day. *You may not need me, but I need you.* I wanted to cry.

"We are not," said Quinn again, "having this conversation."

I swallowed and made my voice casual. "What conversation?"

"Okay," he said. "Now." His tone had changed completely. "If I promise not to ask impertinent questions about your psychic abilities, will you come up for a coffee before you go home?"

The idea made my heart pound. "No. Thanks. I really should get home. The dogs—"

"Those damn' dogs." The words were spoken in a low voice. It was a teasing voice. A tantalizing voice. A menacing voice. I had a sudden image of his hands on Belle and Beau. Violent hands. Getting the dogs out of the way. So he could get to me. Where was this *coming* from?

I squeezed my eyes shut to block the images. Opened them again and gripped the door handle. "I have to go." My voice was near panic.

Quinn put a restraining hand on my arm. "Ellen, Ellen. What's the matter?"

"Nothing." I was breathing hard. "I can't explain."

He let me get out of the car, got out his own side and came around to me. I was afraid he was going to embrace me. There was a rigid band of steel around me. He couldn't fail to notice. But if he did, he made no sign. He faced me, his expression full of concern. His concern confused me. It made me want to take down the barrier. I wanted to trust him. I needed to go home.

"I'm sorry," I said.

He put two fingers against my lips. Pressed them gently.

I couldn't move. His fingers held me as still as if he'd taken my head in a vice grip.

He took them away. "No, I'm the one who's sorry. It's my fault. I shouldn't have told you all that about Tim while you were alone with me here. Nor about Lucy. I know it's disturbing. And you don't know me." He gave a rueful smile. "As much as I'd like you to. I should have been more sensitive. Call me when you get home. So I know you got there safe. Are you okay to drive?"

I nodded. I avoided his eyes. He put the car keys in my hand. I walked around to the driver's side, got in, started the engine. Pulled away from the curb. I think I remembered to wave.

Heading up the highway into the hills, I shook off the night-time traffic. But I couldn't shake off my thoughts. My brain turned around and around the theory Quinn had given me, trying to fit it with my own. It was an awkward fit at best. The cops' theory was so much more logical than the fragments I was piecing together from Lucy's suspect messages. So much less complicated. Also more disturbing. More violent. More calculated. Had Tim planned this all along? Had he been conning Lucy since the very beginning? The story in my visions made it an accident. Was that just because I wanted it to be an accident? Lucy's story—my story—was a much gentler, more forgiving version. Who was I kidding?

There's violence out there. Evil. Face it. That's what Quinn was doing. Trying to get me to face it. Those visions of him with my dogs were just my paranoia. It was the situation that was violent; his work was *surrounded* by violence. But *he* wasn't violent. If I could just keep that straight.

I arrived in my own driveway with the heat still blasting out of the vents. I was still shivering. I took the steps to the lighted deck two at a time. Just short of the top, I felt a sharp twinge in my leg. Damn. I stopped to pick the house key out of the ring. I approached the door, rubbing my leg.

That's when I heard it. The faint droning of an outboard motor on the river.

I limped around to the front of the deck and looked out in the direction of the water. The night was so black there was no distinguishing trees from open water. The air was cold but still. The sound carried clearly. It grew louder until it seemed to be out in the middle of the river, straight out from the bay. But there was no light.

And, suddenly, no sound either. As if the motor had been killed.

I stood on the deck, straining my eyes and ears. Hugging myself to stop the shivering. Had I imagined the sound?

I forced myself to stand there in the chill of the night. Listening. But the silence continued. And in the dark, the images began to crowd my brain: Tim and his hands on Lucy, Quinn and his hands on me, a boat drifting on the water at night, doing God knew what. I ran for the safety of my lighted kitchen and my golden-furred dogs.

The ringing of the phone woke me up. I picked up the receiver with a groggy hello and some trepidation. There was no call display on the bedroom phone.

"I'm on my way over with the weekend papers and steaming cappuccinos," said a familiar British voice. "Don't even think about going anywhere today."

"Coffee and the crossword sound just about like heaven today."

I dressed and walked the dogs up the hill to meet the car. In the bright sunshine, the motorboat incident, Steve Quinn's confusing energy, and my dreams seemed distant and unreal. What remained was a strong desire to see Quinn again. Which I was going to block out in about five minutes. I didn't want Mary Frances picking up any vibes. Vibes I shouldn't even have been having. Nor did I want us to go anywhere near the conversations Quinn and I weren't supposed to have been having in my car last night. I would tell her I didn't want to talk about Lucy. She wouldn't pry. The sight of the silver Cressida turning down the hill brought relief. A day off from fear and imaginings.

On Monday I went back to work and found I could concentrate. Life could go on.

⚬⚬⚬

THE GRABBA JAVA WAS HUMMING with the chatter of patrons and clatter of dishes. Most mornings she loved it. She could tune it out while she wrote in her journal. But today her veins were humming with the caffeine of her second extra-large latte—the one she should never have consumed. She had come here, as she did every morning, to feed two habits—coffee and journal-writing. Today she had also come to escape the house. Not the emptiness, but the noise. The new tenant upstairs was, it turned out, very heavy-footed.

Be careful what you ask for, she wrote. With Curtis, and then the tenant, moving out, the silence had screamed at her. She had wanted signs of a heartbeat in the house again. She hadn't bargained on a foot-beat. And a world-weary foot-beat at that. How had she missed it during the interview—the darkness surrounding Denise? But now it was obvious. The unattractiveness of her face wasn't just the disfavour of Nature; it was her own dark spirit. It emanated now through the floorboards. How was she going to survive a year of that overhead? The *Landlord-Tenant's Act* didn't list "dark spirit" as grounds for eviction.

The Grabba Java was as wired as she was. She wasn't going to last much longer.

She was impatient with herself. Why could she never be satisfied with where she was? Was this a metaphor for her life? It always seemed to be just up ahead of her—just beyond reach—the life she envisioned. Why did she always find herself waiting? Waiting for Curtis to come back. Waiting for Curtis to go. Waiting for Tim to call. Waiting for Tim to get out of prison. Waiting for someone to come and participate in her life.

Why couldn't she just accept what was, this minute, right now? Sitting in this café, enjoying the coffee, hating the noise. She couldn't bring Curtis back. She couldn't get Tim out of prison. But she could leave the café.

So much for acceptance. She stuffed her journal in her purse and headed for home.

10.

THE NEXT DAY, THE NINTH of May, the chiropractor's office called to remind me of my four o'clock appointment. I had forgotten. That was a good sign. It meant I was walking without pain. I could probably start running and biking again.

"There's no reason you can't," said the chiropractor after she'd treated me. "Just don't go out and try to do a ten-k run tomorrow."

There was no risk of that.

I took River Road home. It had been two weeks since I'd been down this way. My stomach muscles knotted on my approach to the construction zone. The embankment was almost finished. There was no yellow Sidekick parked by the side of the road.

I pulled off the road and parked my car where the Sidekick had been. I got out and locked the doors. I took my wallet and keys with me. Lucy had apparently taken her keys but not her wallet. Was that likely? I'd asked Tim if he had a second set of keys. What if the ones he had brought had been the only set? What if Lucy had been in no position to take anything with her. What if Lucy herself had never been here?

I looked all around the area where her car had been. And then I went for a walk down the railway tracks. I retraced the route Tim and I had taken in the dark. I felt a heightened sense of awareness. Not fear. I looked carefully in the pond water where he had shone his flashlight. The water was opaque with mud. The stumps and weeds sat benignly in the sun.

I found the rotting dock. I stood on the relatively solid bottom step. In the water the frayed rope end washed back and forth. Even in daylight it still looked uncannily like human hair. But I watched it with surprising detachment.

I strolled back up the tracks. I paused to look down at the river. I kept hearing Tim's voice in my head. "It's so shallow here. See how shallow it is?" Why had he kept saying that?

Back at the car I stood looking down the road past the construction zone. A forest-green half-ton pick-up appeared around the bend and cruised down the hill towards me. I stood calmly. Resolute. Waiting for Tim to stop and tell me why he was here.

But the driver didn't stop. And it wasn't Tim. It was a man I'd never seen before. And it wasn't a forest-green pick-up; it was a teal-green van.

I looked after the van after it passed me. I could see not only where it was going, but where it had come from as well. And who was lying in the back.

"Slow down, Ellen. Take it easy. I'm listening. Where are you? What happened?"

I leaned my forehead against the glass of the phone booth, trying to catch my breath. "I'm at the Tulip Valley restaurant. At a pay phone. I was up on River Road just now and I stopped to look around. I thought I saw Tim's truck coming towards me. But then suddenly it wasn't Tim's truck; it was a van. A different shade of green. But it wasn't real. Oh God, it wasn't a dream either. I was standing in the middle of the road in broad daylight. I—I think I had some kind of vision or something. I saw—I saw what happened to Lucy on Saturday night. God, this sounds loony—"

"Cut the commentary. Just tell me what you saw."

The sharpness of Quinn's tone snapped me out of my embarrassment. I recounted what I had seen. "It wasn't Tim driving; it was someone else. A man. I didn't recognize him. But I could see inside the van as it went by. I could see Lucy. She was lying in the back, in a sleeping bag. I think that was the man-made material I got before. And, I can't explain this, but I knew where they had come from. It *was* down in Hunt Club. I got an image of them driving away from those burnt-out barns. I've been thinking about them. I meant to have us look—" I stopped myself;

who knew who was listening in? "I mean, I meant to ask you to look there earlier, but I didn't see how they could have four walls and a roof. But now I'm wondering if there's another shed or something somewhere close by. I was wondering if you—if someone could check. Check for that candy-bar wrapper. God knows," I added in a self-mocking tone, "you might even find one with an actual fingerprint on it."

Quinn ignored that. "What else?"

"I saw where they were going. I saw the van drive to a bridge and stop and the man went around to the back and lifted Lucy out. He—" I stopped. It was sounding like the plot of a cheap thriller.

"He what?"

"He dropped her off the bridge—into the water. Oh God, I think I must be losing my mind."

"You are not losing your mind, Ellen. You are in a highly emotional state. This whole experience has been traumatic."

"You think I'm hallucinating."

There was a slight pause. "I think you're in an extra-sensitive state. Anything can happen."

I slumped back against the glass of the phone booth, holding my head in my hand. What Quinn really meant was that I was overwrought, imagining things. But on Saturday he had made it sound like he might even believe in this kind of phenomena. Words came out of his mouth and I didn't know what to make of them. I didn't know what to make of myself, either. Maybe I *had* been hallucinating. Maybe I was losing my mind altogether.

"Ellen. Are you still there?"

"I'm here."

"Ellen, stop questioning yourself. There's something to what you're experiencing. No question. You're the sanest woman I know. And you said yourself, if there's a chance Lucy is still alive…."

My words repeated back to myself pulled me out of my confusion. So did Quinn's words: *you're the sanest woman I know*. Not that it mattered what he thought. It didn't matter what *I* thought. Whatever had just happened, I had to follow up on it.

"There's more," I said in a wry tone.

"I'm listening."

"It looked like he might have dropped something of hers on the bridge. I saw something fall but couldn't make out what it was. Maybe a shoe. Something like that."

"Could you identify the bridge?"

"No, just that it was a bridge for cars—not the railway bridge. There's three up here that I can think of. Philemon Wright, Wakefield, and Farrellton."

"I don't suppose…."

"What?"

"I don't suppose you got the licence plate number of that van."

I couldn't tell if he was laughing at me—or at himself. But I found my sense of humour. "Sergeant Quinn, you know that would be too much to ask of a visionary. It wasn't like seeing a truck go by in the usual way. I was seeing right into the van. *Past* it."

My voice must have sounded odd. "Are you alright?" His voice was sharp again. This time with concern.

"I'm alright. I'm going to go search those bridges."

"No."

"But I have to—"

"No. Not by yourself."

His words were like melted butter seeping into my jittery veins. I drank in his concern, his insistence that I wasn't to go by myself. His caring. And if he was expressing that kind of concern, he must think there was something to this story. I thought about the possibility of meeting someone on the bridge. Some friend of Tim's. The melted butter congealed.

"I'm not trying to scare you," he added. "I just think it's too risky. I'll send someone up. I'll come up myself. I'm off in half an hour."

His words melted butter again. But automatically I protested. "Really, you don't have to. I don't think I'm going to meet anyone. *If* this really happened, I'm pretty sure it already happened. There was darkness all around the edges of the images. I don't think it had to do with the way I was seeing the images. I think it was supposed to be night. Saturday night, maybe."

"You're not to go up there on your own."

I drank in his orders. Without shame. Someone taking charge was exactly what I needed right now. "What about the barns?"

I heard Quinn let out a breath through his nose. I imagined him tapping his fingers against his mouth as he had done in the interrogation room the night we'd met. "Okay, here's the deal," he said finally. "I'll go check out those barns when I leave here. And you go home and wait for me. It doesn't get dark 'til eight-thirty or nine these days. We have lots of time. I'll come and get you and we'll search those bridges this evening. And then…."

I was almost afraid to ask. "And then?"

"And then you'll feed me dinner."

There it was again—that word, this time implied: *date*. I had to admit it. I wanted to have another meal with him. One less fraught. But I had no food in the house. And…. "I don't think I can—"

"You *can*," said Quinn. "You will." There was humour in his tone.

He was right. It was the least I could do. I lightened up. "Yes sir."

His voice changed back to concern. "Are you okay now?"

"Yes. Thank you. I am." It was only a half-lie. The jangling in my veins was settling down. I was starting to get an entirely different case of nerves. The anticipating kind.

"Good girl," said Quinn. "I'll see you about seven or seven-thirty." Neither of us mentioned our last contact. His comment on my "highly emotional state" when "anything can happen" had clearly been an allusion to it. He had understood. There was nothing more to say.

At home I dug my runners out of the back of my closet and pulled my windbreaker off the hook. There would be time for an inaugural run before he arrived.

I shut the front door behind me and stood for a moment with my hand on the handle. With Quinn coming up it felt alright to leave the door unlocked. Though he'd probably give me grief if he discovered it before I came back.

I was back well before seven. I wanted time for a shower. And a snack. There was a pizza in the freezer we could heat up later.

It was seven-forty when the black Integra pulled into the yard. I had forgotten to ask if he remembered the way. There had clearly been no need.

"There was a million years of debris in those buildings," he said when we headed north on the 105. "Let's hope we have better luck on those bridges. Couldn't you have a vision of where she is now?"

I laughed, a bitter laugh. "It's not my fault there's a time lag. But I appreciate your humouring me."

"For the last time, I am *not* humouring you."

He looked anything but in good humour. I kept silent, except for directing him to the Farrellton Bridge, a few kilometres north of Wakefield. Quinn parked the car at the end of the bridge and we walked up one side and down the other. We didn't speak. I had my eyes on the ground, scanning for any item that might belong to Lucy. We found nothing.

In the middle of the Wakefield bridge I leaned over the railing. I looked into the water below. The current was fast but the water was deep. It made sense for her to be thrown off a bridge.

Here she would sink to the bottom. She wouldn't just wash ashore.

It came to me with a certainty that had nothing to do with any vision: the night I had walked with Tim along the tracks he *hadn't* put her in the river. But he had been thinking about it. He had, in fact, been thinking out loud. That was why he had kept saying, "It's so shallow here." He was realizing she would simply wash ashore. But she wouldn't from the middle of a bridge.

I caught up to Quinn. Told him my theory. He made no comment. He seemed preoccupied with his own thoughts. We drove in silence to the last bridge, Philemon Wright, the one closest to the Ontario border. This was the one with the most traffic. The least likely candidate. By the time we got back to the car I was frustrated. Angry.

"I'm sorry," I said as Quinn pulled away from the shoulder.

He looked at me in surprise. "What are you sorry about now?"

I waved my hand in the air. "For wasting your time."

Quinn smiled. "How could an evening stroll on three bridges in the lovely Gatineau Hills with you be a waste of time?"

My face coloured as if he had said I was the lovely one.

At the turn back onto the 105 highway, he turned south rather than north. "Where are you going? There aren't anymore bridges south of here—not over the Gatineau."

"There's a little place I know in town," said Quinn, not taking his eyes off the road.

"A restaurant?" But I knew the answer before he gave it.

"My place."

My heart rate sped up.

"We took a bit of a risk down there at Hunt Club. I don't want to push it. You're going to be a witness when Lundy and Roach finally crack this case. I wouldn't want to give the defence any unnecessary ammunition."

"*Are* they going to crack this case?"

"You bet those electrifying eyes of yours," said Quinn. "But let's not talk about that right now."

The case? Or my eyes? "But then you'll have to drive me home."

"I'd rather do that than…."

"Than what?"

Quinn sent a quick glance my way. "Than eat in your boyfriend's house."

"It's my house too." I was indignant. Though it wasn't, technically, true. I would get my own. Soon.

"I'd rather have you at my place." He shrugged. "Call it male territoriality. I don't mind driving you home."

Under my too-light jacket, I was starting to shiver.

"What do your tastes run to?"

I looked around Quinn's living room. It was sparsely furnished, and needed a carpet, though the hardwood floors were beautiful. "Well, I think I'd prefer red wine, if you have any." Wine, more than Scotch, would take the chill out of my bones. And hopefully slow my pulse too. What was I *doing* here?

Quinn laughed. "In music, my girl. I meant in music." He gestured to his CD cabinet. "Pick anything you like. And you can even have red wine. I'll be back in a sec."

I listened to his footsteps retreating on the hardwood of the long narrow hallway. The stairs inside the walk-up had led us to an apartment on the second floor, with rooms off the long narrow hall. The kitchen was at the back, south-facing. The living room was in the front, with a small glassed-in balcony jutting out from it above the front porch. In between were two rooms. Quinn had opened the door to each in turn, his bedroom and the guest room. I had given the first room only a quick self-conscious glance. At the second, Quinn had said, "If I have too much to drink you can stay here."

"If *you* have too much to drink?" Then I realized what he meant. I was here without my car. My *getaway* car.

Something must have shown on my face. Quinn gave me a light punch on the arm. "I'm kidding, El. I promise I'll get you home tonight. Something to drink?"

He led the way down the hall.

"Are you giving me a choice this time?"

"You always have a choice," he said over his shoulder. "As long as it's Scotch. And here's the living room."

I had Blue Rodeo's *Five Days in July* playing when he returned with two bulbous glasses of wine. Between the two of them, they looked like they held the contents of the entire bottle. Quinn handed me one and gestured to the couch. Blue Rodeo's familiar distinctive sound was calming me down. The wine would do the rest. Quinn was a cop, for God's sake; who would I be safer with?

Facing me from a decorous distance, my cop held his glass out. "To nailing Brennan."

The toast undid my newly achieved calm. "To finding Lucy," I said.

Quinn clinked his glass to mine and took a sip. "Hmm, not bad for something I found in the bottom of my liquor cabinet."

"You could have had Scotch. *I* could have had Scotch."

He held up a hand. "I like wine. Just don't have it very often. Wine you need someone to drink with." He gave me a significant look.

I took a large swallow then and offered to put some food together to go with the wine.

"Relax. To be honest I'm not very hungry. Unless you are."

I shrugged. "I ate something before you came."

"Then there's no rush. This is nice. Good music choice. I haven't had a guest here since…."

"How long *have* you been here?" I couldn't remember when he had said he'd split up with his wife.

"Bordering on a year now. It's not really my kind of place, but it'll do for now."

"Oh, don't you like it? I love these older buildings."

Quinn looked around the living room and his face brightened. "It's not bad, is it? I haven't had much chance to do much in the way of decorating yet. I'm barely here."

"But you're—" On half-time, I was going to say, but it didn't feel like a topic I should initiate.

"I'm just not the kind of guy who spends much time at home when it's just me. Was different when I was married."

"Do you have kids?" I wasn't sure if this was safer ground or not.

Quinn shook his head. "No, thank God for that. I mean, if it wasn't going to work out."

His comment brought to memory something Lucy had said early on about a pregnancy scare while Tim had still been in prison. I took another swallow of wine. The bottle had been in the bottom of Quinn's liquor cabinet just a bit too long, I guessed, but I welcomed the relaxing buzz it was giving me. "How does that work in prison, anyway—exercising your conjugal rights?" I was willing myself not to blush.

"Ah yes, the notorious private family visits. PFVs they call them. They take place in the fuck trailers. Pardon my language."

"Fuck trailers?" God, why had I asked?

"They used to be actual trailers, but at Warkworth—that's where Tim was transferred after Lucy met him—they had started building small semi-detached houses by the time she was visiting."

"So how would it work? I mean getting a PFV?"

I couldn't bring myself to look at him, but his voice sounded amused. "Tell me you haven't got your eye on someone serving time in the slammer, Ellen McGinn."

"*No.* Forget I—"

"Sorry. I'm being a brat. You want to know. You have a right. The way it works, as far as I understand, is: in Lucy's case, meeting Tim after he was already behind bars, they'd have to know each other for a year before they could declare themselves common law. Then they could apply to have PFVs. You're eligible every six weeks. You go for a weekend—three days actually, I think, Friday to Monday. Or Tuesday to Thursday. Lucy would have ordered—and paid for—all the food. Tim would have brought it from the kitchen. They would be locked into one of the fuck—sorry, I mean one of the houses—for the duration. Private time. He'd be allowed to wear civilian clothes."

Locked into a small house on prison grounds for three days with an inmate. I couldn't imagine it. Though of course it would be entirely different if the inmate was your partner or husband. But for a person like Lucy, with all her fears. She must have felt supremely comfortable with Tim to risk doing that. I looked at Quinn then. I thought about visiting him in a prison. Being locked up for three days. Something in my abdomen, and lower, responded. I took a sip of wine, hoping the big glass would hide my face.

⬧⬧⬧

SHE FOLLOWED THE SENIOR VISITS and Correspondence Officer outside into the bright May sunshine and along a narrow flagstone path that bisected the lawn. High in the corners of the prison yard the cameras watched her every move.

They watched her follow the officer toward the row of semi-detached houses. He stopped at one of two gates right next to each other. The gates led to two walkways across two tiny front lawns up to two front doors. A high chain-link fence surrounded both yards and ran between them. A green nylon sheet covered the portion of the fence between the two small patches of lawn.

Except for the unusual highness of the fence and the heavy mesh covering the windows, the building looked like a normal house—a white clapboard bungalow, with a small cement stoop; it might have been out of the fifties. Lucy could pretend she was a war bride—as her mother had been, more or less. Except that her mother's incarceration, starting out in a small post-war bungalow in North Toronto, had been permanent. Not a three-day visit.

Lucy banished the thoughts of her mother; she had not invited her on this weekend. She watched the officer beside her. He shook out his ring of keys, selected one, and unlocked the gate. He swung it open and smiled for Lucy to go through. Inside the yard, she turned to watch him shut the gate between them. She watched, in horrified fascination, as the lock snapped shut.

She looked up to the top of the fence and was suddenly dizzy. Before her eyes the fence seemed to be stretching upward higher and higher. The panic was rising inside her along with the fence. She reached out to grasp the metal and looked down at the grass. She was aware of the officer watching her. She concentrated on the blades of grass at her feet. If they could thrive in here, continue to grow and live, so could she. She wouldn't need to scream. The guard would not have to re-open the gate and take her away.

And, she reminded herself, there was a phone inside. All she needed to do was pick it up and a guard would be at the other end. Twice a day, a guard would be coming around to do a count, to see that everything was alright. She wasn't being abandoned; there was an out if she needed it.

She was so intent on bracing herself for her voluntary incarceration, she didn't hear the front door open. It was the officer looking beyond her that made her turn.

Tim stood on the cement stoop, in a white T-shirt and blue-jeans.

Lucy stared up at the man on the stoop. This was not a numbered prisoner. This was Tim Brennan of Brudenell. And on his face were reflected all her own fear and excitement, anticipation and terror.

She turned back to the V. and C. Officer. He was looking at her with a question in his eyes. A kind concern. And encouragement.

She nodded and made her way up the walkway to Tim and the open door behind him.

"WHAT IS IT ABOUT YOU women, anyway?" Quinn was shaking his head. "There are so many documented cases of women befriending—and marrying—losers in prison. Trying to rescue them. And then ending up dead."

Lucy wasn't trying to rescue anyone but herself.

Lucy's old friend Kevin's words. I had a feeling they might be true. But Quinn's view was probably going to be the prevailing view. That she had walked into a trap, possibly had deserved what she got. "She wasn't trying to rescue him," I said, knowing I couldn't defend myself.

"Well, I just don't get it. Especially since his records show there was evidence of yelling and fighting even when he was in prison. He probably physically abused her there. Why would a smart, sane woman continue in a relationship like that?"

I let out an audible sigh through my nose. I didn't have any answer to that. I had no experience of violence. My impression of abused women had always been one of helpless women who got battered around by much stronger men. But Lucy was not helpless. Despite her fears. Despite her size. I knew how feisty she was. Even in my second dream she had not been lying there passively. Each time she'd come to, she'd been furious. Yelling at Tim. Provoking him so that he'd drugged her again and again. I had been assuming that whatever Tim had done to her—drugged her, strangled her, whatever it had been—had been an isolated act of violence. Now, here was Quinn telling me there had been violence even while he was still in prison. They would have been alone during their PFVs. Had it started there?

"Anyway, enough about those two," Quinn added. "I don't want to talk about any of that disturbing stuff tonight."

You don't want me running away. There was, I mused, no chance of that tonight. The wine was having its intended effect. I felt my body and my mind relaxing. I pulled a leg up onto the couch, tucked it under my other leg. I concentrated on the man beside me. He wasn't a handsome man. His face was too round, his features too blunt. But he had physical presence. A confidence exuded from him. And there was no denying the chemical energy between us.

He smiled at me now. "Tell me more about yourself, Ellen McGinn. You want kids?"

I shrugged. "Maybe some day, before I'm forty."

"You've got years then."

"Flatterer."

"You can't be more than twenty-eight."

I laughed and made a "keep it coming" gesture with my free hand. "I thought cops were supposed to be able to see through all that."

"We see through *everything*, Ellen. Make no mistake about it."

"So, how old am I?" I gave him a challenging look.

He pretended to scrutinize me. I enjoyed the scrutiny.

"You're thirty-three," he said.

"You read my driver's licence."

Quinn adopted an innocent look. "Now when would I have seen your driver's licence?"

"I don't know, it must be on a computer system somewhere."

"Yes, all your vitals are there, for the entire force to read: single—newly single—beautiful strawberry blonde, five foot, hmmm, eight. Very fit. Likes biking, skiing, running, but *not* canoeing or swimming or anything related to water." He was checking off the items on his fingers. Strong-looking square fingers.

I couldn't quite hide my smile. I didn't even mind him mentioning the water. It was an understanding kind of teasing. Not a mocking. "Quite the system you've got there," I commented.

"You have no idea. Want to know what else is in there?"

I shook my head, but I did.

Quinn looked straight at me with that wide-eyed look of his. "It says you've been underappreciated. That you're looking for someone who appreciates you for who you are, who shares your interests. Who believes in you."

"Okay, stop," I said. The clichés, as true as they were, were making me squirm. I reached for my glass and took another long swallow.

I put the glass down on the coffee table and stood up. "Mind if I go see if you've got any cheese and crackers or anything to munch on?" I wasn't hungry in the least but I needed a break from the intensity.

Quinn made to get to his feet, but I put a hand out to stop him. "Let me. You did say I was going to feed you."

He shrugged and sat back. "That was just an excuse, but go ahead." He called out after me: "You'll probably have better luck in the cupboards than the fridge."

I came back with a bag of chips and what little remained of the wine. "Strange bedfellows," I said before I thought. I put the chips down on the coffee table and willed him not to make an innuendo.

"It'll hit the spot," said Quinn. He stood up, I thought, to take the bottle from me. But it was me he reached for. "But this will hit the spot even more," he murmured. "Mind?"

Mind? I wasn't capable of minding. I wasn't capable of thought at all. I was enveloped in a shock of sensation. The sensation of being engulfed, no enfolded, in much bigger arms and body than Marc's. I wrapped my arms around his back. There was solidity, overlaid with the softness that came from not working out. But under the softness there was strength, no question. For the first time, possibly in my life, I felt small, vulnerable. Vulnerable in a good way. This was a man who could take care of me. Who could sweep me up into his arms and carry me to safety. Something I didn't even know I wanted. I leaned into him. I think I even moaned a little. Quinn didn't try to kiss me. There was a tension in his body, though, as if he were fighting every impulse to do just that, or to run his hands everywhere over me. But when he pulled back it was to push the hair back from my face, and to let out a long slow breath. "Oh God, Ellen McGinn, what have you done to me?"

"Me?" My voice came out sounding like a little girl's. I couldn't shake the sensation that I had shrunk to half my size. It was strange. Exhilarating in the way of strange new things. I was a dainty feminine creature. How did he *do* that?

"I think the question is what you've done to *me*." I spoke against his chest. And felt the vibration of laughter inside. His arms tightened around me again.

I don't know how long we stood like that. In the tight, tense embrace. I could barely breathe. I wanted him to kiss me. And more. How far would protocol allow him to go? Was this whole night off the record? I found myself hoping it was. "We are not," I could imagine Quinn saying in his stern cop voice, "having this intercourse." I had to smother the impulse to laugh.

In that uncanny way he had of reading my mind, Quinn loosened his hold again. "Come and sit down, we need to talk."

He pulled me down onto the couch beside him and turned towards me. He was brushing my hair with his fingers again. There was another sigh. "What am I going to do with you?"

A voice I gave no permission to speak said, "What would you like to do with me?"

His expression managed to be both lustful and wry. "Nothing so very original, I'm afraid," he said. "Though I have no doubt it would be extraordinary. But…."

"But." I had pulled back, was looking directly at him. I knew he wanted me. It made me euphoric. Bold.

Quinn groaned. "God, woman, don't look at me like that. I can't. *We* can't."

"Because?" Of the case? Or something else?

"You know why. This damned case. I can't get involved with you. Not yet."

"And yet."

"And yet, what?"

I shrugged. The wine had loosened my inhibitions, and my tongue. "And yet, I'm here."

"So you are," said Quinn, and he looked so wary I did laugh then.

"What's so funny?"

"Your face," I said. "Scared."

For a moment he looked angry. Then it passed. I had imagined it. "Me?" he said. "Scared of a minx like you? C'mere. I'll show you who's scared."

In a second he had pulled me onto his lap, was kissing me, not gently, gripping the hair close to my head, pushing my hips down to his, pressing me into his hard groin. I kissed him back with the same ferocity. A need had met a need. Quinn's felt like it was the need for raw sexual release. I wasn't sure what mine was. It wasn't as if I hadn't been having satisfying sex. God, only a few days before! This was different. It would be. Of course. I was the object of passion. I might even have called it a violent passion. But scared didn't enter my mind. For one heavenly moment in this whole nightmare, there was no fear. It felt good to be wanted like this. Possessed.

I put my hands down to the belt of Quinn's jeans. A hand suddenly clenched around mine. The other pushed my head back. For a moment fear was back. But then I heard the whispered "Holy fuck." I wasn't the scared one.

The next instant I found myself back beside him on the couch. Quinn was leaning forward, elbows on his knees, breathing hard. He turned his head to me. "You pack a pretty lethal charge, don't you?"

I pulled my legs up to a bent-kneed position on the couch, grasped my ankles with my hands. My breathing wasn't that regular either. "I'd say it was mutual."

I watched him run his hands through his close-shaven hair. "Ellen, I'm sorry. I'd love to be able to say screw my job, the case, the whole effing force. God, there's nothing I'd like to do more than throw you down on that coffee table. But I can't. I can't get involved with you—that way. Not yet. But. When this is over…."

He was looking at me with a hopeful expression. "When this case is over, and I've wrapped up some loose ends, and I've found a place in the Gatineaus, we can do this properly."

He spoke in a determined voice. So determined it unnerved me. I tried to keep the conversation light. "What's properly? Candlelight and wine?"

"Anything you want."

THE HOUSE, NO BIGGER THAN a small apartment, consisted of an open-plan living room and kitchen in the front, two small bedrooms in the back, and an ugly beige bathroom. It was too small, too impersonal, too sterile to be a home. She stared at the empty hangers in the bedroom closet, the empty drawers she had pulled open in the dresser. Whose clothes had been there before? Was it worse to keep her clothes in the institutional suitcase she'd had to transfer her clothes into in the personal search room, or to put them in drawers that had held someone else's? Why was she so neurotic about these things?

She was aware of Tim standing behind her in the doorway. She felt trapped in the room, too close to the bed. She wanted to pull back the covers, make sure the sheets were clean (the rules had indicated that each family was responsible for washing all the linens after each visit; there was a washer and dryer in the kitchen, of course they were clean). But she didn't want to give Tim the wrong idea.

She could stand the confined space no longer. She brushed past Tim, leaving the suitcase open, unpacked, on the bed. In the kitchen she opened cupboards, inspecting their contents. Tim had followed; she was aware of him standing awkwardly by the Formica table.

"I got all the food you asked me to."

Such as it was, she thought, remembering the list of items available. Anyway, it wasn't the food she was checking but the cooking supplies, the dishes. She wasn't sure what she had been expecting (the Hyatt Regency, no less, her brain mocked her).

"There's no colander. How can I make pasta when there's no colander?" She was slamming the cupboards shut; she couldn't stop herself. Tim's awkwardness unnerved her even more. She wanted to say, "Just let me do this. Let me complain about the lack of utensils and the size of the pots. Just let me settle in."

As if he read her mind, Tim left off watching her. She heard the electronic click of the TV, the tinned voices. The sound increased her irritation. She hadn't come here to watch TV—or to watch him watch TV.

She stood at the kitchen sink, running the water for a drink. What were they going to do for three days? It was only ten in the morning on Friday. What were they going to find to talk about until nine o'clock Monday morning? Stop, she told herself. This wasn't a stranger, it was Tim. They'd known each other for a year. It was just the circumstances that were strange, that made them strange to each other. It was so forced, this so-called private family visit. They had never been a family before, had never had even a semblance of privacy. They didn't know how to sit companionably together in a living room.

She made herself go to the couch. She sat down next to Tim, not too close, but not too far away either. She reached over for the remote and took it out of his hand. Found the mute button.

"Hey, what are you—"

He stopped when he saw her face.

"Tim." She didn't know how to continue; she didn't know what to say.

There was a long silence. She opened her mouth again, and the words came. "Do you mind," she asked in a soft voice, "if I just sit here and look at you for awhile?"

She woke up to bright sunlight. She rolled over into Tim's arms and breathed in the musky smell of his chest. "Oh God," she groaned happily, "you snore. I barely slept."

"At least you slept. I ain't shared a bed with a woman in fifteen years."

"You must have slept—you were snoring."

"How could I snore when I didn't sleep?"

She smiled sleepily. "Okay, you were snoring while you lay there awake. Go to sleep now."

"I don't think so. I think I'm going to have to skin-search you."

She laughed and pressed herself in closer. "How far are you going to have to go?"

"I'm going to have to search every crevice you have," he whispered.

And he did. With surprising tenderness. As he had the night before. She had underestimated him on several counts—his size, his sensitivity, his fit. He filled her being. Somehow the physical transmuted into the emotional. She let herself become lost in feeling—physical, emotional, it was all one. She and Tim were one. She had never known this kind of merging before. She forgot where she was. She almost forgot who she was.

He didn't stop after he'd come. He caressed her until he was aroused again. And again. They almost didn't get out onto the porch in time for the morning count.

———

IT WAS ALMOST ONE A.M. when Quinn drove me home. He had graduated to the Scotch after the wine was gone. I had graduated to water.

And an instant headache. I didn't ask if he was okay to drive. He didn't seem affected by the alcohol at all. He'd probably just have to wave his badge if we were stopped anyway.

"For a second date, that was a pretty supercharged one." Quinn's voice came out of the darkness beside me. "Or was that the third?"

I blew out a breath. "That," I said, "felt like we jumped right to the fourth or fifth."

"Is that when it happens for you? The fourth?" There was amusement in his voice. "I'll remember that. That and the romantic paraphernalia. Candles and wine. Anything you want."

Romantic paraphernalia. Lucy had smuggled romantic paraphernalia into prison. Kevin's description was suddenly in my head. Of course she would have been smuggling it into their PFVs. It was beginning to make more sense.

"There aren't any rules," I said to Quinn.

"Clearly not." He laughed. I made myself laugh with him. But I was back to my edgy state. In the car, Steve Quinn had gone back to being Sergeant Quinn. I wanted to be home. I also wished Steve Quinn would stay with me.

In my mind, he did.

———— ∞∞∞ ————

SHE WAS STANDING IN THE line-up for her third PFV. She felt weighed down today. She *was* weighted down. Literally. With "romantic paraphernalia," all stashed in the deep pockets in her baggy pants. Everyone did it. She'd discovered that last time, chatting in the parking lot with the wife of another inmate. They couldn't body search you unless they had "reasonable cause," which usually meant someone had tipped them off that you were trying to bring in drugs.

She was shaking in her boots but she was going to walk by this guard anyway. And she was going to get away with it. Big deal. Where was it getting her? Into a depressing sham of a house surrounded by a high chain-link fence, which was surrounded by an even higher chain-link fence, and barbed wire and surveillance cameras and security guards. There was always—still, ever—something standing between her and what she wanted. The barriers, in fact, were getting more literal and solid. Maybe that was progress—that they had arrived in the material world. Maybe getting through concrete barriers was the final test.

She was intent on analyzing this new idea and didn't notice how close she was getting to the front of the line. Before she had time to think about it, she was walking undetected through the metal detector and following the guard to the personal search room.

And it was something after all. A small step toward her future. Which in this one minor instance meant a romantic weekend with Tim. Baby steps, she told herself, watching her belongings being transferred into the vile institutional suitcase. Baby steps so you don't spill the wine.

Fifteen minutes later, she sagged against the front door. Her smile at Tim felt like the smile of a Cheshire cat recovering from a bad LSD trip. But Tim seemed barely to notice her paranoid triumph. Instead he pulled her to him and immediately guided her hands under his sweatshirt. It was a sweatshirt she'd just sent him, but he'd cut the sleeves out of it. She was opening her mouth to berate him for ruining a perfectly good piece of clothing, but what was under her hands and before her eyes, and in Tim's gleaming eyes, all registered at once. "My God, you weren't kidding when you said you've been working out." She ran her hands over the smooth ridges of his abdomen and hard biceps.

"You think that's hard? Feel this." He pushed her hand down jeans that were sexily loose. He must have lost a couple of inches off his waist.

She almost forgot what was down her own pants. His cock was as smooth and hard as the rest of him. "Did the guard find this when he strip searched you?" she said against his mouth.

Tim looked shocked. Angry even. Then he let out a laugh. "No, baby, I saved this for you." He started to unzip his jeans.

She pulled away. She hadn't gone to all that effort and stress for nothing. "Not yet. Let's wait."

"Wait? Are you crazy? I been waiting six weeks. What's to wait for?"

There was no better cue. "This," she said, and pulled out the weighty contents of her pockets and lined them up on the kitchen table: two pairs of beeswax candles, a cassette tape of Keith Jarrett's Köln Concert, a flat packet of bubblebath crystals, and—from a pocket she'd specially sewn into the inside lining halfway down her leg—her *coup de grâce*: a half-bottle of Valpolicella.

Tim picked up the wine and held it away from himself as if it were a ticking bomb. "How the fuck did you get this in? Fuck, you're going to get us in fucking shit."

"Stop swearing at me." She reigned in her temper and reached under his shirt again. "I'm not going to get us in shit," she said, with a seductive smile. "I'm going to cook us a dinner you're not going to forget."

They had to drink the wine out of tumblers. She fashioned tin foil into candle holders and lit the candles. She stood back and looked at the table with satisfaction. Keith Jarrett was playing on the blaster. She served up the pasta.

Across the table from Tim she raised her glass. "To us."

Tim took a swallow of wine, made a face. "How do you drink this stuff?"

She watched him swallow another large mouthful. "Don't drink it if you don't like it." She spoke sharply. Had she been a fool? He hadn't had a drink in fifteen years. Between them one of the candles flickered out.

She was doing the dishes when Tim came up behind her. In a shot he had her twisted around with her arm pinned behind her.

She yelled with the sudden pain but couldn't help the simultaneous electric response in her groin. "What are you doing?"

"Showing you how strong I've gotten. Quick too."

In another instant she was on her back, her wrists gripped in Tim's hands, her sides pinned by his thighs.

"You're hurting me."

Tim loosened his grip immediately. He eased his weight off her. She started to her feet. And was instantly knocked off them again.

"Never let up your guard," said Tim in her ear. "First rule of wrestling."

She struggled against his weight. There was a sharp pain in her arm, pinned underneath her. She could feel Tim's erection through his jeans. "Let me go!"

"You want romance. I'll give you romance."

"No! Tim! Let me go! You're hurting me!"

She sat in the warm bath, hugging her knees to her chin. Watching the shadows from the candles play on walls. Her tears fell into the bubbles soothing her sore limbs. Tim's remorseful apologies reverberated in her ears.

He sat on the closed lid of the toilet, his face turned to look at her. In the candlelight, his eyes glistened. In them she could see reflected the tears and love that were in her own.

11.

I WOKE UP THE NEXT morning to Steve Quinn's voice in my head. Not the things he'd said late into the night, but something he'd said when he first arrived at my house: "There's a million years of debris in those buildings."

A million years of debris. The phrase repeated in my head all day at work, like one of the mantras Lucy used to tell me about, chanting behind my thoughts of Quinn.

I tried not to think about him, but that was a hopeless endeavour. In the sober light of day, I was relieved we hadn't slept together. God, he'd had to stop *me*. Thank God he had some self-control. Did they train cops in that too? They were put in some pretty intense situations. Was I just another intense situation? No. I refused to believe that. He'd talked about the future. And not a pie in the sky future either. Not a "some day I'll leave my wife" future. He was already on his way there. Lucy had waited two years for hers to begin. Would I have to wait that long?

I stopped that train of thought. None of this was relevant right now. Only Lucy was relevant. Finding her. Convicting Tim.

Every time the office phone rang, I looked up to see if it was for me. Every hour I checked my messages at home. It was completely irrational. If he was going to phone at all, he would most likely wait 'til evening. *If* he was going to phone. The fifth time I checked my home answering machine, I was startled to hear the voice intoning that I had "one new message." Impatiently, I pressed the buttons. But it wasn't a male voice. It was Anna. Anna! I had forgotten all about her. I had told her I would call her a week ago. I wrote down the number she'd left. I would phone her tonight.

I forced myself to work. Accompanied by the incessant mantra: *a million years of debris*.

I left the office at four. I headed south in a light rain and heavy traffic on Bank Street. Hunt Club was not quite as busy. I drove past the blackened barns and turned right at the first street. It curved through a suburban neighbourhood northwest of the barns. The houses backed onto a field, which backed onto the Airport Parkway. I couldn't get behind the houses from here. And I couldn't see any other buildings. I drove back to Hunt Club.

I felt self-conscious pulling into the driveway in front of the barns. It was so close to the street. Would Tim, or Marnie, have had the nerve to pull up here? Maybe, in the dead of night.

I worked up my own nerve and got out of the car. The rain had stopped. We weren't getting nearly enough for this time of year. Despite the lack of rain, the huge overgrown lilac bushes in front of the car were already in leaf, the buds about to open. Temperatures had soared in the last few days, painting Ottawa in full spring green.

I walked past the barns, eyeing their charred caved-in walls. I came to the field I had seen from the neighbourhood. To the west were the backyards and the backs of the houses. Their upstairs windows were rows of huge eyes watching me.

I turned back. And stopped in sudden surprise. In front of me was a small rectangular building. I had walked between it and the barns without even seeing it. How had I missed it? I went back to look from the vantage point of my car. The building was right in front of the driveway, but the overgrown lilac bushes obscured its view.

The building was, in fact, the garage at the end of the driveway. It had not been destroyed by fire. It was a building a person could walk into: there were three walls and, in front, a mangled metal garage door that didn't quite shut. And at the side, near the back, a door.

I wasn't ready to look inside. I walked all around the building instead.

More surprises. Beyond the trees on the other side of the garage was a house, with its own driveway—one of the few residences on Hunt

Club. If you drove up that driveway, you could nose a car through a narrow opening in the trees and park it behind the garage where it couldn't be seen.

I stood behind the garage and glanced down at the overgrown grass rising up around my knees. What I saw caused the hair to rise on the back of my neck. The long grass was pressed down in two defined tracks—spaced the width of car tires.

And then I looked up. Several trees hugged the back of the garage. They were skinny, spindly trees, with newly unfolding fresh green leaves. Where two or three are gathered, did that constitute a grove? I looked up into the poplars, and I smiled a small sad smile.

At the side door, I hesitated, then pushed at it. The debris met me at the door—a million years of it, rising a foot deep, covering the entire floor. Exactly as I had seen in my dream.

My heart began to thud.

Light filtered into the garage from the cracks in the big metal door at the front. Cracks an animal could squeeze through.

I didn't dare go in. I didn't want to disturb anything.

But something had been disturbed. Just inside the door, spanning the width of the back wall, was a raised platform, maybe two feet off the ground and two feet wide. It too was piled high with debris. Except at the end closest to the door, a place had been cleared. The dust was swirled as if something had been pressed against it. Something that could have been the size and shape of a small person wrapped in a sleeping bag.

I felt no fear looking into the garage. What I felt was sick to my stomach. Sick at the thought of Tim casually eating a candy bar while Lucy lay unconscious in a sleeping bag nearby.

Even stronger was the remorse. At the thought of Quinn and me sitting in a blue unmarked cruiser in the driveway, pointing our head-lights, unseeing, at this building, while Lucy lay within fifteen feet of us, grasping at the hope of light through the cracks.

You may not need me, but I need you.

I was exhausted by the time I got home. Too exhausted to walk the dogs. I let them out and took a pizza out of the freezer and turned on the oven. The pizza I was going to feed Quinn the previous night. Would things have turned out differently if he had come here? Probably not. I remembered the way he'd checked around the house the night I'd arrived back from Thunder Bay. The electricity in the air. It was better the tension had been broken. The jumpiness that had returned in the car on the way home had been—what? The dregs of former fears. There was nothing to fear in Quinn. He made it okay to feel vulnerable. I smiled, remembering his orders to lock up after he'd seen me to my door. His looking out for my safety was a welcome relief. If he was a little authoritarian about it, I could live with that. He was someone I could turn to, lean on during this time that was becoming more and more traumatic. I should forget about the future. He was what I needed *now*. But the future wouldn't go away. Not when he was presenting possibilities himself. It was crazy. I wasn't even done with Marc yet.

Maybe you are. Marc isn't here. Steve Quinn is.

I was letting the dogs back in the door when the phone rang. I ran upstairs to the office. The call display read Unknown Name/Unknown Number. It could well be Quinn, calling from home. But it was a female voice, with an Irish accent, that asked for me.

"Speaking."

"Ellen. Hello. My name is Bryn O'Connor. I'm calling with regard to the Lucy Stockman case. I've just got my private investigator's licence and I'd like to help. It's not the money," she added, "it's a woman's thing."

Her lilting accent made me want to believe her. But she sounded too much like she was trying to take me into her confidence. I let her talk.

"I read about the case in the papers a couple weeks back. I contacted Mr. Brennan, but he said he had no money to pay for a private investigator. But he gave me your number—yours and some other friends of Lucy's. I hope you don't mind my calling. I understand you were the one who found her car after she went missing."

I was silent. Warning bells were going off in my head.

"I know it's hard on the phone. Maybe if we could meet?"

I made up my mind. "I'm sorry. I can't talk to you right now. I'll have to think about it."

She didn't press me. But she gave me her phone number, an exchange farther north in the Gatineaus. I would ask Quinn if he knew anything about her.

The call reminded me about Anna. I rescued the pizza from the oven and went searching in my knapsack for her number.

She answered on the first ring. "Oh, Ellen, thank you for calling back. I'm sorry to keep bothering you."

I assured her it was no bother. I apologized for not having called back sooner. But I didn't have anything reassuring to tell her. I didn't have anything I could tell her at all. Just that I knew the police were keeping up the search.

"I feel helpless being so far away. I keep having these dreams about her."

"You *do*?"

"Yes, in one I asked her, 'What happened?'"

"What did she say?" I held my breath.

"She just kept shaking her head, saying 'I don't know, I don't know.'"

Like Anna didn't know. Surely this, more than anything, was proof that "my" Lucy was a figment of my imagination. And yet … the garbage I had seen in the garage was exactly as I had dreamt it. The directions I had dreamed had led me there. There was *something* to all this.

"Would such a dream be a—a *usual* thing for you?" I rushed on. "I ask because before Lucy came to me that night and gave me that message to give you, I had never had that kind of dream where someone was speaking to me like that." I had to stop myself from adding, "Especially someone dead—or nearly dead."

"Not usual at all," said Anna. "But nothing that's going on is normal."

"No," I agreed.

There was a pause, then she said, "I don't mean this to sound vain, but did you find it odd that you didn't know who I was? I mean that Lucy never mentioned me—assuming she didn't."

"It was a bit of a surprise to find out she had a sister," I admitted. "If someone had asked me I would have said she was an only child. I didn't mean that to—"

"It's okay," said Anna. "We weren't very close. Lucy was...." She paused again.

"Self-absorbed?" The word was out before I could stop myself.

There was a sigh. "That pretty much describes her. That's why I asked you before if you were sure she said my name in your dream. To be honest, I would have thought I was the last person she would want to reassure." Her voice started to break.

I was helpless to say anything. I felt forty or more years of hurt and bewilderment seeping toward me through the phone line.

"I'm sorry," she said. "I know this isn't about me. Mostly I just wanted to tell you that you probably have no idea how much comfort I have been getting from that message. That she—oh it sounds silly to say it—but that she would think of me in whatever state she's in, wherever she is. And this probably sounds silly too, but the fact that you didn't know who I was makes it seem more real."

"That I didn't make it all up," I laughed.

"I didn't mean it that way." Her voice was apologetic.

"It's okay. You don't know how much I've been wondering if I *have* been making everything up."

"*Everything?*"

I hadn't meant to say that. "I've had a few other dreams too," I admitted. "But nothing that really makes sense. It helps to know you've been dreaming about her too."

"Do you think she really is trying to get messages to us? I've never really believed in this kind of thing."

"Me neither. But that doesn't seem to matter." We laughed.

"Thank you, Ellen. Will you keep in touch with me? Let me know if you hear anything?"

I promised I would.

The phone call, and the pizza afterward, reenergized me. I called Belle and Beau. Grabbed their leads. The sun had set; I would take them just to the end of the road.

But outside, it was darker than I'd anticipated. No moon. I nixed the walk. I stayed up on the deck while Belle and Beau ran down to the yard. I could hear them crashing about in the bushes below, their tags jingling.

I crossed my arms over my chest and walked around to the river side of the deck. And heard it again: the unmistakable hum of a motor.

An electric current of dread zapped through my bloodstream. It was not my imagination. The dogs' tags jingled somewhere below me on the hill, grounding me in reality.

Out on the water, the hum continued. It seemed to be out in the middle, straight out from the bay. If there was a light, I should be able to see it. The river stayed obsidian black.

This time the boat didn't stop; the puttering continued, getting fainter and fainter, towards the dam to the south. Then silence.

What would someone be *doing* out there? This wasn't the weather for evening outings. And, anyway, not without lights. Was someone out there searching for Lucy in the dark? Why put her in the water and then search for her? And how long did it take a drowned person to rise to the surface anyway?

The last question, anyway, was a rational one. It would have an answer. It was time to do a little research. Research was something I knew how to do. And *reading* about drowning shouldn't scare me.

I whistled for the dogs.

Up in my office, I booted up the computer and dialled the modem. My home page came up. I typed the word "drowning" into the search engine.

The website for the Drowning Accident Rescue Team—DART—seemed as good a place to start as any. I clicked on the link and waited for it to come up on the screen.

The DART home page appeared on my screen. I clicked on an option called "Rescue vs. Recovery." I started to read. "The Rescue Call Mode is used when there is a chance to save a human life." We were definitely past rescue mode. I skimmed to the next paragraph.

"The Recovery Call Mode is used without the goal of saving a human life."

The page went on to give the two scenarios. They both began with a swimmer who begins to tire. I scrolled down the paragraph, reading in horrified fascination.

"Her breathing comes in short and irregular gasps. She takes a small amount of water into her mouth and she coughs…."

My muscles tensed. My throat constricted; I had to catch my breath.

"She flounders for only a few seconds before more water enters her mouth and throat. She begins to cough violently, fighting to keep her head above water. As she coughs, she expels more and more air from her lungs and her breathing becomes shallow, rapid, and less efficient…."

My chest felt like something was squeezing it. I couldn't get enough air.

"She slips below the surface of the water. Sinking slowly, she loses her ability to hold her breath and carbon dioxide build-up forces her diaphragm to contract uncontrollably. A deep inspiration of water occurs."

Something was pushing against my lap. The sensation, and the whining, brought me to. I was soaked in a cold sweat, gasping, choking. But I was *breathing*. Air.

I sat stroking Beau's head with shaking, grateful hands. I slowed my breathing, took in the room around me, staved off the panic. I focused on the mundane surroundings of my office: desk, bookcase, patterned carpet on the floor. The experience faded, my body's responses returned to normal.

I went downstairs to the kitchen and made a mug of tea. Back at the computer, I cupped my hands around the hot mug, staring at the screen. Then I scrolled back to the top of the page, working up my nerve to read it again, to read to the end this time.

I made myself reread the description of the girl's drowning. At the first mention of her breathing coming in short irregular gasps, mine began to choke up as well. I stopped reading and forced myself to breathe normally. I made myself go back to the words on the screen. I read the entire description over and over until I could do it without having a physical reaction. I breathed in deep even breaths. I got to the end of the passage again. I read: "As her desire to breathe comes back under control, dreaming loses its horror."

Dreaming?

I squeezed my eyes shut and then stared back at the words on the screen. "As her desire to breathe comes back under control," I read this time, "drowning loses its horror."

I sipped the tea. The warm liquid filled my insides with calm. I continued with the rest of the description.

"She sinks faster, not realizing she is quickly losing all voluntary muscle control. In her dazed state she may not feel the effects of the water pressure on her body. She reaches the bottom and as she becomes unconscious, she instinctively grasps at it."

On the screen I see the drowning swimmer sink to the bottom of the lake. She's reaching out, naturally, calmly, for the bottom, as if she has found her resting place.

She hasn't, not yet. The current nudges her along, her long dark hair undulating around her head. The current carries her past the weeds that live at the bottom of rivers, past logs that have been down there for twenty-five, fifty, a hundred years. I'm on the water, above, looking down; the water is clear right to the bottom. Crystal clear. I follow her progress. I see the surface landmarks she passes—the village of Wakefield, the cottages lining the river downstream from the village, my own bay. She is carried on her journey just above the river bottom, eyes wide open, but not seeing. She drifts past my bay, on her way downstream. She skirts around a small island and then something reaches out, snags her. An errant branch of a fifty-year-old log. She settles in to wait for new currents to break her loose—currents stirred up by heavy rains. By the time the new currents come for her, she'll be buoyant, ready to rise to the surface. She'll join the deadheads somewhere along the shoreline of the big island in the bay above the dam. Then she'll wait for me to find her.

I ate my morning toast thinking about the bay above the Chelsea Dam and the big Hydro-Québec-owned island that sat in the middle of it. And divers. I had a specific location now.

But for divers I would need assistance. To get assistance, I would need to come clean.

I called the police station and was put through to Sergeant Roach.

"Can you be here in half an hour?" he asked.

I could.

I glanced at myself in the hall mirror before running out the door. I definitely looked more rested than the last time Roach and Lundy had seen me. Did I look different? Did I look like a kook?

If Roach and Lundy saw a different me, they gave no sign. Nor did they react to my embarrassed admission that I hadn't been completely truthful about how my information had come to me or in what detail. Sergeant Lundy said "Oh," and looked a little sad. That was all.

But they took notes. It was the first time I had seen them take notes. It gave me courage to tell them more. I gave them the new information from my experiences of seeing into the van and from sitting at the computer. I cringed when I used the word "vision" but I had no choice.

They would, they said, definitely check out the garage. And they talked about putting divers in above the dam. But they didn't promise.

What they did promise was that they were going to get Brennan. It was just a matter of time, they said.

In a break at work later in the morning, I continued my Internet research. There were, I read, no rules about when a body came to the surface. It was putrefactive gas formation that caused the body to rise. The rate at which that happened depended on water temperatures. In warm water it could happen in a couple of days. In winter it might be slowed for weeks or until the spring. It also happened at a slower rate in running water than in stagnant water. And depended on whether the body was weighted down, whether it got caught on anything on the bottom. If the body were prevented from rising, the gases that had formed would eventually escape and the body would lose its buoyancy. It might stay down forever.

The Gatineau was still almost winter cold, I figured. And there was definitely a current. Slow but steady. She apparently hadn't been weighted down, but a branch had snagged her. It might be awhile before she came up. If she came up at all. If someone hadn't already taken her out of the river—and that seemed like such a remote possibility—I needed heavy rains to stir up the water and dislodge her.

At lunch I went downstairs to the "company library." The musty smell of second-hand books hit me as soon as I opened the door.

Zak, the pony-tailed owner, looked up from the mountain of books and papers piled on the old wooden teacher's desk he used as a counter. He nodded when he saw it was me and bent back over his book.

I went to the fiction wall and found the Cs spread over several floor-to-ceiling shelves. I got the step-ladder to see the top rows. Zak didn't bother to alphabetize under each letter. If you couldn't find a book he knew he had, he would simply come over and pull out what you were looking for. But I didn't want to ask. I wanted to find it myself. Or not.

I found *The Long Goodbye* and a few minutes later *The Big Sleep*. I was almost to the Ds when it jumped out at me: a faded paperback copy of *The Lady in the Lake*.

Zak waved me away when I tried to pay. "Bring it back when you're done."

Standard Roots practice.

I put the book in my knapsack. Preparatory reading for a boat excursion I was going to have to make.

12.

THE WEEKEND ARRIVED WITH STILL no call from Quinn. There was no reason he *should* call. He'd made no promises. Had not, now that I thought about it, even said the non-committal "I'll call you." He'd said, "Lock your doors." I'd said, "Yessir." Maybe he was taking it literally that we should wait. Would he really curtail all contact until this case was over? I hoped not. I needed him *now*. But I couldn't bring myself to be the one to call. Although if the other night had never happened, I wouldn't hesitate. Damn. Why had I let that happen? I needed him to go out on the river with me.

I also needed a boat.

I wished Marc had been able to put in our dock before he'd left. Even more, I wished our neighbours would put their dock in. And their motorboat. It lay upside down beside the dock on shore. I wanted to borrow that boat.

There was, really, no reason to wait for the boat, or for Quinn. I had a fleet of boats to choose from, in my own front yard.

I spent the weekend contemplating the idea. But I couldn't bring myself to take a canoe down to the water. Not yet.

On Saturday night I was restless. Despite my longest run yet. I came back at eight to discover a Private Caller had phoned not five minutes before. But not left a message. Damn! I was sure it was Quinn. He'd said his number was unlisted. That would probably show up as "Private."

I was not going to call him back. I didn't even know for sure it was him. I needed a distraction. On the night table in the bedroom I found a book I had started, and abandoned, weeks ago: Timothy Findley's memoir, *Inside Memory*. I took the book and a cup of tea to the living room couch. I opened it to the page where I had marked my place and forced myself to read. A line jumped out at me. Findley quoting the American actress Ruth Gordon: "*Be yourself—but know who you are. Being yourself is not a licence. It's a responsibility.*"

I couldn't settle into the book. My thoughts kept spinning around. Quinn, Tim, Lucy…. If Quinn was right, Lucy had already experienced Tim's violence even when I'd first met her. But she'd looked happy. Maybe physical fighting was "normal" for her. No big deal. But there must have been happy, harmonious times too. Obviously. He'd proposed. I'd seen the glow on her face. It couldn't have been all bad.

I forced myself back to the book and eventually dozed off.

I woke up, much later, to Belle nosing in my lap. The light was still on, the book still in my lap. The blue-lit digital clock on the video player glowed the time: 2:22. I had been out for hours. In a deep—mercifully dreamless—sleep.

One I was ready to return to. I didn't have the energy to go up to bed. I set the book on the floor, pulled the afghan over me and reached up to turn off the lamp beside the couch.

As if one switch had activated another, an eerie light swept through the living room. Then the room was dark again, as if the light had been shut off.

I shot off the couch and ran to the window. Beside me in the dark, the dogs whined softly. On the road just beyond the front yard shone two small yellow lights. Parking lights. My heart was pumping in my throat. Was it Brennan? His accomplice? Should I call the police?

Or *was* it the police?

On duty? Or off?

With that thought, my pulse slowed. A little.

The yellow lights began to move, the vehicle obviously backing up. It was a shadowy black form moving in the black night. But not a truck. Not a van. A car, possibly compact.

The car backed down the road, hesitated for a moment, then the headlights came back on and swung in erratic curves—the car turning around. The lights moved down the road and disappeared around the bend.

When I was sure it was gone, I went upstairs to check the phone in my office. The light was flashing. And the call display again registered a Private Caller. At 10:19 and 10:47 and 11:55. Now I was sure my Private Caller was Quinn. I couldn't believe I hadn't heard the phone. Clearly, I had been in a deep sleep.

I retrieved my messages. There was only one. "Ellen. I'm worried about you. Call me, no matter how late it is."

I was pleased to hear his voice. But it made me more certain the car had been his. And that made me uneasy—that and the usual bossiness. Tonight it bothered me. I didn't have to report to him. But these were, I reminded myself, "extraordinary circumstances." A cop checking on me was not a bad thing.

I waited twenty-five minutes. Long enough for him to get home, if it had been him. And then I called.

He sounded out of breath when he answered. As if he'd run up the stairs to catch the phone. I felt a small feeling of triumph. The car *had* been his. I was sure now. But he didn't have to know I knew.

"I was asleep," I explained. And then suddenly felt bold. "Were you calling for a reason?"

"Just keeping tabs on you, McGinn. Making sure you're keeping out of trouble."

"And if I weren't?" I matched his light tone. "Would you come and visit me in a medium-security prison?" I might as well have been suggesting we meet in the fuck trailers. At almost three in the morning, it seemed I had no control over my tongue.

"I can't imagine you'd do anything that would get you to medium security. You're no more than a minimum-security gal."

"Oh yeah? Says who?"

I could hear the smile in his voice. "Says me. You're a pussy cat. I'd put you in Pittsburgh. Anyway, it would be more convenient to visit than Warkworth."

"How can Pittsburgh be more convenient than Warkworth?"

"Not the city. It's a minimum-security institution near Kingston.

That's where Brennan was for the last six or seven months of his term. He got transferred sometime in the fall." He didn't sound like he wanted to talk about Tim. "I'd be very happy to drive to Pittsburgh to see you. The only problem would be there wouldn't be anywhere *private* for us to visit."

The suggestiveness in his voice unnerved me, but I couldn't help asking what he meant.

"Just what I said. There aren't any PFV facilities there. You have to go next door to Joyceville. Joyceville's medium security, like Warkworth, but that's one scary place. You'd have to submit to a body search."

A body search. I couldn't imagine Lucy submitting to a body search.

"She didn't," said Quinn, reading my thoughts. "At least that's what I understand."

"They didn't have PFVs after he got there? But then how…." I was mentally matching timelines with something Lucy had told me.

"How what?"

"Well, Lucy told me she had a pregnancy scare that spring. We talked in May and I'm sure she said it had been a couple of months before that. He must have been in Pittsburgh by then. So how—"

"Could she have had her pregnancy scare?" I could hear the amusement in Quinn's voice. "Use your imagination. Minimum-security institutions are about minimum supervision. Sounds like she had more balls than I've given her credit for."

More balls than *you* have, I wanted to say. It was time to end this conversation before I really got myself into trouble. I thanked him for checking on me and we said good night. I wasn't sure whether I should have thanked him. Whether I wanted to encourage him. I should be getting used to these internal contradictions. I should also be reconciling them.

Know who you are.

The canoe sat half in, half out of the water on the grassy shore. The early morning sunlight bathed the faded red paint of the canoe in a surreal glow. My heart was beating as if I were five kilometres into a run. I had not picked the lightest canoe to carry down the path from Marc's rack. I had picked the heaviest. Intentionally. An old reliable fibreglass tub. I squatted beside it, one hand on the gunwale, the other rubbing my shoulders.

I glanced over at the neighbours' motorboat. There was so much more to it, more surface in the water, more stability. I wished it was ready for use. But wishing wasn't going to change anything.

I looked back at the canoe and then out at the river beyond the bay. A fine mist rose off a mirror of blue and green. This was safe, flat, *still* water. I wasn't going to tip. I wasn't going to fall in. I wasn't going to drown. I was going to be fine.

I stood up and zipped up my life-jacket. I took in, and released, a breath. I pushed the canoe farther into the water. Then I laid the paddle across the gunwales and stepped in, bracing myself with the paddle stem the way Marc had taught me. As I did so I pushed off with my foot, to launch the boat completely. So far so good.

The air over the water was a degree or two cooler than on land. But it was still spring air: gentle, promising.

My paddle cut through the water. I heard Marc's voice giving me calm instruction: Dig, pull, pry, sweep. Breathe. Dig, pull, pry. Dig. *Breathe*.

The strokes came back to me. Not very expertly, but sufficiently enough that the canoe responded. Marc had taught me well. In spite of myself.

I headed the canoe south, towards the Chelsea Dam. I stayed as close to shore as I could, keeping my eye out for stray logs, and especially for deadheads. They collected in the shallower waters near shore. I needed to check shorelines. I also needed them for safety.

Right at the place where the river widened into a big bay above the dam sat a tiny island, out in the middle. I paused in my paddling, brought the boat to a standstill. Took my time working up my nerve. The water was mirror calm. I would be fine.

I turned the boat and headed, slowly, out toward the island. I paddled a slow circle around it. I peered carefully over the side of the boat, as if I might actually be able to see into the murky depths.

Then I headed south for the big Hydro-Québec-owned island in the bay. It was the perfect size for a private cottage retreat. It was ringed with good sunning rocks, but also signs that prevented sunbathers: *Privée. Défense de passer.* I had never set foot on it. But I was about to become familiar with its shoreline.

On the northeast side was an inlet that over the years had collected a substantial population of deadheads. Another deadhead might be inclined to join them, should it have resurfaced somewhere upstream, not too far away.

I was prepared for how it would look: "a bloated hand that was the hand of a freak." A face that was "a swollen pulpy gray white mass without features, without eyes, without mouth. A blotch of gray dough, a nightmare with human hair on it." Blonde in Raymond Chandler's case, dark in mine.

I knew from my Internet research that Chandler's description wasn't entirely accurate. The head of a floating body would most likely be hanging down. But I had deliberately sought out Chandler's description for its emotional impact. I wanted to carry this image, make myself *see* it, so that when I came across the real thing I would not freak out. That, at least, was the theory.

I returned home an hour and a quarter later, bringing back with me only the images I had started out with and a mixture of disappointment and relief.

I hefted the canoe back up on shore and left it there, upside down next to our dock, the paddle and life-jacket stowed underneath. There was a satisfying ache in my biceps. That would be gone soon. My new morning exercise would take care of that. I could do this. I could paddle. I could search. I would not go out unless the water was completely calm. I would not scare myself more than necessary.

The river in the early mornings of late May was murky. Murky and still. The weather held. We were having a record dry spring. It was a two-edged sword. The good weather meant I could be out paddling every day, not worrying yet about blackflies. But for Lucy to surface, a heavy rain was needed to stir up the currents.

I was getting used to the canoe. My strokes were getting less awkward, more efficient. My arms were getting strong. I cut minutes off my time, down around the Hydro-Québec island and back.

I kept watch for stray logs. The tugs had cleared most of them by now, but one occasionally floated downstream, dislodged from some winter holding place. When I saw a floating shape on the water, I approached with pounding heart. I approached expecting to see the grotesquery that was now Lucy and to be haunted for the rest of my life.

It was near the Hydro-Québec island one morning that I found the hand. It was a hand cut off at the wrist, floating like something out of a David Lynch movie. It was a pale white hand, lying languidly on the surface of the water.

Heart-twisting horror. A cautious approach. And then recognition. It was not a human hand. It was a rubber glove—a dirty, flesh-coloured rubber glove, given substance by the water.

Relief. Even a chuckle at the cosmic joke.

And then a thought. A practical one. Maybe the man in the teal-green van had used gloves to handle Lucy's body and, stupidly, thrown them in the river after her.

I tried to land the glove on the blade of my paddle. Every time I got the paddle underneath and tried to lift it, the glove slid off, disappeared momentarily, resurfaced. It was an elusive hand.

This could go on forever. I drew the boat in close and reached over the side to pluck the glove between my thumb and forefinger. It became a lifeless mound of rubber in the bottom of the canoe.

A sudden gusting wind came up just before I reached my bay. It whipped up the waves. I paddled harder. To get around the point into the bay I was going to have to turn the boat so the waves came broadside. Oh God, please don't let me tip! But there was Marc's calm voice, telling me what to do. I knelt down, off the seat, and, staying low, slid forward to the middle thwart. I crouched down low, the water right there beside me now. I watched in alarm as the waves came rolling against the side of the canoe, but the boat was imperturbable. I soaked my arm digging the paddle in deep. A few minutes later I was in calm waters.

I sat on the shore for a good ten minutes, absorbing the solid ground into my being. Only one molded piece of fibreglass had separated me from the river. Yet putting my weight low in the boat, at surface level, even just below, had made me safer. So that I wasn't an object *on* the water, but somehow part of it, rolling with it, not resisting. My pulse returned to normal.

I left the glove in the boat and went up to the house for a plastic bag. And then what to do? Offer it to the police on the slim chance it had incriminating fingerprints on it? Or accept it as a macabre message from Lucy: *I am down below.*

I wished I could leave it at that. Why did I have to keep embarrassing myself? Why couldn't I stop myself from making that phone call?

I laughed when I told Sergeant Lundy what I had found.

"Is it a surgical glove?" He sounded interested.

"No, it's a rubber glove. The kind you use to wash dishes."

"There wouldn't be any prints left on it," he said. "But I'll come up and get it anyway." He didn't miss a beat. "I can use it for doing the dishes. My wife will have a fit. I've never done the dishes in twenty-two years."

I laughed. "Come on up. I'd like to help you give your wife a fit." I liked the fact that he had a sense of humour. A wife. A life beyond "Major Crime."

"Did anything—were you able to send anyone to look in that garage?" I was embarrassed to ask.

"I'm not sure," he said. "I haven't seen Sergeant Roach since yesterday."

So much for police assistance. Not that I blamed them. Not really. I was on my own. The search was mine, my undertaking. And, it came as a kind of surprise, that was okay.

Being yourself is not a licence. It's a responsibility.

———— ✺ ————

ALL THE GROGGINESS FROM THE bad motel sleep vanished when she came up the drive, past the Pittsburgh Institution sign. She couldn't believe her eyes: Tim was there waiting. In civilian clothes. Outside. There was no gate, no line-up, no security check. There was only a low chain-link fence around a large picnic area. They were free to walk around outside, to eat the lunch she'd brought in a cooler, to snuggle together against the November wind at the picnic table, to pretend they were in a park on the "outside." A little taste of freedom.

Tim was looking well and happy. He'd been transferred from the slaughterhouse; he was getting to drive the tractor. He was starting to work out again. He was happy she'd come to see him. He pulled her onto his lap. She could feel his hardness while they talked and ate the cheese and fruit she'd brought. She loved that neither of them acknowledged it. That it was just there—an unspoken message of desire answered by her own secret response. Why had she put off coming? This was what she needed—to be reconnected to his physical being. No wonder they'd both been so screwy the last few months. They needed physical contact. It was a shot in the arm. Ballast. She was drugged on the heat of him amid the frigid air.

"I met a guy the other day. Bill Torrence. Rich."

"What's he in for?"

"Fraud," said Tim. He popped one half of a muscat grape in his mouth, removed the seeds of the other half, and popped it into her mouth. "He defrauded some guy out of a few million. He'll probably be out on parole in six months."

Tim himself had just been denied day parole. Again. "I don't want to talk about parole," she grumbled. She didn't want to talk period. She just wanted to be held. To immerse herself in Tim's physical presence.

"But he can probably help me. After I get out. He says he can set me up in his cattle transporting business."

"*Cattle* transporting? You'd need a truck."

"Yeah, he says he can give me info on how to lease one through his brother-in-law—he's a money man."

"Legitimate money?"

Tim looked hurt. "Yeah, legitimate. You know I'm going legit after I get out."

"I didn't mean you. I meant Mr. Money Man." She was running her hands under Tim's shirt. Revelling in the warmth of his skin. She wished she could have all of her skin next to his.

"Well, anyways, it's just an idea we're rolling around."

"We?"

"Bill and me."

"How old a guy is he?"

Tim shrugged. "Late fifties? Real classy guy. Just wants to get back to his golf and country club. Who else is going to hire me?"

Lucy sighed. "I know. Those bloody application forms. 'Previous place of employment: Pittsburgh Institution.' Maybe we could just put 'Pittsburgh' and they'd think you were a paint mixer."

"Huh?"

"Forget it. I still think our best bet is to set you up in your own handyman business." She was sliding her hand down below his belly. Down into his underwear. His jeans were so lovely and loose. She didn't even have to undo the zipper.

"I'd need equipment, tools."

"Oh, you've got the tool." She grasped his warm cock in her hand, smiled when she felt it respond.

Tim kissed her hard. "I'll show you my tool."

Lucy sighed. "I wish you could."

"I can," he said. His voice was lost somewhere in her hair. His hands found their way under her jacket. Her nipples hardened under his fingertip squeeze. "Meet me in the bathroom."

"The bathroom!" She pulled back, stared at him.

"Everyone does it. We won't get in trouble. People even do it in the corner of the visiting room. Staff are pretty human here; they turn a blind eye. But the bathroom's more private."

She was horrified. "I can't do it in a bathroom, it's sordid. It's—"

"Sh-shh," he whispered, his hands in her hair. "It's me and you. Nowhere is sordid when it's me and you. I love you." His voice held a softness she hadn't heard in months.

Her eyes filled up with tears. The horror abated. She buried her face in his jacket. Her cheeks were hot—from shame, from desire. Mostly desire.

In the echoey, tiled bathroom, Tim turned her around at the sink so they could see themselves in the mirror. She reached down and guided him inside her from behind. He was already hard. Ready. She was ready too. She couldn't take him in deep enough. He gripped her pelvis and pulled her off the floor, pulling her hard against him. She felt light and loved in his strong arms. They *fit*.

They were meant to be together. There was no greater proof than this—this intimacy achieved in this most cold and sterile of locations.

Oh joy to her body and soul, being with Tim.

13.

I STOPPED CARRYING MARC'S FISHING knife with me everywhere I went. There was no humming of motorboats out on the black river. No more cars (that I saw) arrived in the middle of the night. Some nights I even forgot to lock the door.

My neighbours put their dock in, and, kindly, ours too. But the motorboat remained up on shore. I still couldn't bring myself to ask.

The weather stayed dry. June arrived in a rare heat wave. Forests burned.

I stopped dreaming. I stopped having visions. But I didn't stop paddling.

The rain came one night a week into June. It beat down on the metal roof and woke me up. I welcomed the disruption to my sleep. The rain was putting out fires and stirring up currents. In the morning the world would be soaked and the water calm. But only on the surface. Under the surface, colder and warmer waters were already exchanging places. New currents were flowing. The currents were stirring things up, dislodging things. Sending things to the surface. The resurrection of the deadheads.

The drumming of the rain lulled me back to sleep.

I woke to the sound of birds singing and water dripping from the roof overhang onto the deck.

I was dressed in an instant.

The sun paused for a moment to sit on top of the hills across the river. Belle and Beau barked after me from the dock.

I had gotten the trip to the Hydro-Québec island down to half an hour. I made my usual circle counter-clockwise around the island, ending at the enclave of deadheads on the northeast side. I found an opening among the logs and manoeuvred the boat in. I entered with trepidation. If I saw Lucy, I could not bolt.

The water here was shallow. She could very well have washed up here. She would be protected in this pen of logs, kept safe for those who were looking for her. Maybe only her foot or hand would come up, the way only one end of the logs surfaced. She had spent so much time with them down below, maybe she had become one of them. Maybe she was here and I just didn't recognize her.

I arrived down at the river one morning at the end of the second week of June to find the neighbours' motorboat tied to their dock. I looked at the boat with a grim satisfaction.

That evening I worked up my nerve. I had received permission to borrow the boat. Now I just had to make the call. I got ready to leave a message. It was a Friday evening; he probably wouldn't even be home. I would tell him I had some further information on Lucy's whereabouts, that I wanted to ask if he would do one more search with me. I would be friendly, but formal. I would *not* say, "Why haven't you called me in the last three weeks?"

He didn't say hello when he picked up the phone. He said, "When are you going to get your own life?"

I was so taken aback all my rehearsed lines vanished. "What d'you mean?"

"My call display says Marc Desjardins is calling me. You're living in his house. You're calling on his phone. You're looking after his dogs—"

"They're *our* dogs."

"Oh?" His tone was knowing.

I was silent. Pissed off. Why had I phoned?

"Sorry Ellen. Call it sour grapes. Male territoriality."

That term again. But I couldn't stop myself from repeating, "What d'you mean?" I was starting to sound like a broken record.

That made him laugh. "An attractive woman calls me up, and I have to see her ex-boyfriend's name on my call display. As if you're still *his*."

"I'm not his." I was indignant. "I'm not anybody's." This conversation was going nowhere I had predicted.

"Well, that must be lonely," said Quinn. "What are you doing tomorrow evening?"

I took a breath. "That's actually why I called. I wanted to ask you a favour."

"Shoot."

"I wondered if you'd come for a motorboat ride with me tomorrow evening."

"A motorboat ride with Ms. I'm Afraid of the Water? What gives?"

I ignored his put-down; I was keen to launch into the tale of my experience at the computer, my search on the river.

"You've actually been out on the water?" said Quinn when I was done. "This is a big step for you."

"Yes, Marc would be proud of me—if he knew."

"You haven't been talking to him?" There seemed to be relief in his voice.

"No, not lately."

"Why don't you come and have dinner at my place and we'll talk about it." He said it without a trace of self-consciousness. As if the last several weeks of silence had never happened. How did men *do* that? And how had he managed to sidestep my request?

"Okay. But couldn't you come here? Then we'd be—" closer to the boat, I was going to say, but Quinn interrupted me. And misinterpreted my reluctance.

"I promise I won't molest you again."

It seemed safest not to respond to that comment. "What time?" I asked, resigned. And, in spite of myself, excited.

I woke up Saturday morning with the familiar current coursing through my veins. The one that had just let up. *You know you want to go.*

Relax, I told myself. Go with the flow. Let the future take care of itself. God, I was starting to sound like Lucy. What was it she had always been at me about? Learning to live in the present moment. Accepting what *is*. I suddenly remembered a book she had given me for my birthday the previous summer. What was it called? The *Tao Te Ching*. One day I would pull it out and read it. I had a feeling it was all in there. And that maybe Lucy had read it like a Bible. That it had gotten her through the two years of frustration waiting for Tim to get out.

I was in the bathroom applying rare make-up when the phone rang. I raced to the office. I stopped my hand on the receiver when I saw the area code. It had been much longer than a few weeks since *we'd* spoken. On the fourth ring, I picked up the receiver.

"Were you outside?"

"I just got out of the shower," I lied. "Just finished a run."

Silence. Then: "Your sciatica must be better."

"Yes."

Another pause. "I'm sorry I haven't called before now."

"It was my turn. I got your message. I—I appreciated it."

"It's okay. We probably both needed a break. How is everything?"

"Fine. Oh, they haven't found Lucy yet, but—"

"The reason I'm calling is my contract is finishing up here in a few weeks."

"*Weeks*? I thought it was supposed to go 'til the end of the summer?"

"The client changed his mind about a few things. That's a polite way of saying he ran out of money. So it looks like I will be home in the middle of July."

Home. July. *When are you going to get your own life, Ellen?* Sooner than I thought. "I guess I'd better start looking for a place to live then."

"Yes," said Marc. "But there's no rush. I mean I know it's short notice. If you don't find anything for July first, you don't have to worry. I won't boot you out."

"Thanks." The laugh got choked in my throat. I was *not* going to cry. "I've been thinking it's time to find my own place anyway. And now I know when you're coming back."

The words hung between us. They hung in the air long after we'd hung up the phone.

The thought of moving so soon overwhelmed me. July was only two weeks away. I wasn't sure I could find a place that quickly. But the thought of staying with Marc even for a couple of weeks was worse. He would be back to trying to tell me what to do—and not do. No, it *was* time to get my own life.

My new thoughts about moving calmed me down about Quinn.

I had my car keys in hand, hollering for the dogs, when the phone rang again. This time it was a Private Caller. I picked up the receiver.

"Ellen, glad I caught you. I hate to do this to you, but something's come up. I'm going to have to cancel our dinner plans. And I'm sorry I can't talk right now either. I'll call you Monday."

I barely had time to make polite reassurances before he hung up.

I took myself out to the deck to sit and absorb my disappointment. And to wonder: had they found Lucy?

SHE WAITED UNTIL SHE HUNG up the phone to vent her frustration. Why did all her plans have to get screwed up on her? Now what was she going to do tomorrow for New Year's Eve? There was no way she was going to go skating on the canal by herself. Damn Kevin, anyway. It wasn't as if she had called him. It had been his idea. It had been so long since she'd heard from him—from any of her friends—she hadn't even minded the short notice of the invitation. She'd been elated that he'd reached out to her. That she was going to have some company on the last night of the year. She'd taken her skates over to Bank Street to get them sharpened. Even walked over to Queen Elizabeth Drive afterwards to check out the ice conditions in the daylight. She didn't want to be tripping over cracks and holes in the dark. But the ice was freshly flooded, smooth. It would be fine.

It *would* have been fine.

She continued to grip the receiver. At least she hadn't lit into Kevin. It wasn't his fault his father had taken ill. She was proud of herself; she'd found a calm voice to extend her sympathy, and her concern for the long drive he was going to have to make to get to his father. Kevin had sounded grateful. Relieved. And no wonder. He knew all too well what she was like when plans had to be cancelled at the last minute.

She let go of the receiver and let out a yell of frustration into the empty room. Why couldn't *anything* go the way she wanted? Why was Tim's parole constantly denied? Why was she spending yet another winter alone? Was there some karmic lesson she was supposed to learn from this? Yes, of course there was. She was supposed to learn to go with the flow. To let go. Not hold on so tight. Her anger turned to slow tears of self-pity. And then she chided herself. Love was a choice. She had chosen Tim. She couldn't—clearly!—change the circumstances. But she could change her mind. The Buddhists and Taoists had it right. Even if she didn't like it, she could accept what existed: winter, her fatigue, her aloneness. If she accepted it, things would start to change. She felt the truth of it, like a small spark of excitement inside her.

And she could make her own plans.

When Tim called early the next evening to wish her a happy new year, she returned a whole-hearted wish for his release in the new year.

Half an hour short of midnight, she bundled up and carried her skates out to her car, and drove to a street near the canal. She laced up her skates in one of the change huts. The temperature was holding at a miraculous minus eight and there was only a light breeze. She took a hesitant step out into the darkness, felt the sharpened blade of her skate take to the smooth unseen surface.

She glided out to the middle of the canal, avoiding the other bulky faceless skaters. The waning moon came out from behind a cloud. Its light turned the black ice a dull glistening dark grey. After a few minutes of hard going, she turned her back to the wind. At the moment of her pivoting, the moon disappeared behind a cloud. But she didn't need the light. She spread her arms and let the gusting wind propel her into the unknown new year.

THERE WAS NOTHING IN THE morning news, or in the Sunday *Citizen*. So that wasn't why Quinn had cancelled.

I picked up the previous week's edition of the *Low Down* at the *depanneur* along with the *Citizen*. I turned to the classifieds in the back.

The last time I had done this had been for Lucy, two months before. The similarities were not lost on me. We were both trying to leave relationships. We were both looking for a place on the river. I felt a sudden pang.

A wish that we could be talking, sharing our pain and disappointment. Although mine was nothing compared to what hers likely had been. She had risked everything to be with Tim. Had he really been conning her from the start? He'd proposed before he'd got out. It could have been a ploy to entrap her, but there had been no quick prison chapel wedding. *He's giving me two years to decide.* Like Lucy had given him two years. That sounded like someone who was appreciative of what she had done, not someone simply after her money. It sounded genuine. On the other hand, she'd made him her beneficiary anyway. So maybe it didn't matter. But then why propose at all? Unless it was for real.

There wasn't much in the local paper in the way of permanent rentals. They were mostly cottages. There were lots for Lucy. Lucy no longer needed a cottage on the river. The whole river was hers.

SHE DIDN'T MENTION TO TIM that it was their anniversary. Two years since they'd met at the Supreme Court. She was going to save that for the appropriate moment—the post-climax denouement. She had it all planned in her mind. For two days, in fact, and for the duration of the two-hour drive, she thought of nothing else. God, two years ago who would have thought she'd be ecstatically fantasizing about having sex with a convict in the corner of a prison visiting room.

She was going to arrive in her longest, fullest skirt, and nothing underneath. She was going to sit on Tim's lap and watch his eyes light up when he realized there was nothing between his hardness and her wetness. She was going to take him deep, deep, deep, and ride him slow (there had to be some discretion!), and he would go crazy. And his cock would slide over her clitoris in just the right way, in a slow hard way, and she would go crazy too. And then they would come, together, with a yell rising in each that they would have to mask by kissing each other hard.

She was wet for two days thinking about it. It was all she could do to keep from satisfying herself. On the trip down she got herself so wound up, she decided to check in to the motel first; she didn't want to arrive at Pittsburgh looking like a sex-crazed female.

As soon as she got into the motel room she knew it had been a mistake to come here first. In the stale dank room, reality raised its ugly fear-filled head. She felt herself go dry. She tried to fantasize herself back to wetness but fear had done its work.

She was even more dismayed half an hour later when she walked into the visiting room. It was crowded, noisy. She hadn't imagined actual faces and personalities in the room. Obviously no one wanted to be outside on a damp cold afternoon in early March. But weekdays weren't usually so busy. Was everyone having an anniversary? The only silver lining was that, when Tim arrived a few minutes later, it was easy to creep into a corner unnoticed.

She could barely meet Tim's eye. He seemed equally ill at ease. He sat down against the wall and pulled her onto his lap. She was grateful to be facing away from the room. She felt Tim fumbling under her skirt, unzipping himself, trying to press himself into her. She was still dry; he was soft. She wrapped her arms around him, lifted herself slightly so he could find his way inside, ignored the pain of being so dry. Achieving semi-hardness, he pumped hard. He seemed caught between the need and the shame, where she now felt only the shame.

She had forgotten the mess of sex. She hadn't thought to bring any tissues. A condom would have taken care of it, but to avoid awkward fumbling around she had opted to go without. Now the possibility of pregnancy sent panic through her veins. She could barely wait for Tim to zip himself back up so she could get to the bathroom and get his cum out. This was not the right time to get pregnant.

Cleaning herself up, she was filled with self-loathing. Here was an abject lesson in the futility of desire; things never turned out the way you envisioned them. She hadn't even come close to coming. And of course she'd entirely forgotten to whisper "happy anniversary" in Tim's ear. What had possessed her to believe for a minute she could enjoy such a private act in such a public place?

She cut the visit short. She'd forgotten to bring underwear to put on afterwards, and she felt naked and exposed, even with the long full skirt on. She had to promise Tim she'd be back at six. He seemed unusually anxious about her return, which further irritated her. Did he think she was going to turn around and go home at this time of day?

Outside, the frigid dampness hit with full force and she pulled her coat tight around her and walked quickly down the drive to the parking lot. To her right loomed Joyceville, its high electric fence and small-windowed cell blocks looking even more ominous in the encroaching dusk. Although it was a medium-security institution like Warkworth, it made Warkworth look like a country resort. The thought of voluntarily incarcerating herself behind that fence for a weekend gave her the creeps. Her groin, already sore and now chilled, felt suddenly colder. Violated. The whole property—Pittsburgh so open, Joyceville so closed—suddenly had the feel of a dark, malevolent force. What the hell was she doing here?

It took all her willpower and a double layer of underwear to get herself back to Pittsburgh. She parked as close as she could to the door, and arrived at the Visitor Control Point out of breath from running. She signed the registry and pulled open the double doors to the visiting room. Tonight, it was silent and almost empty. If only they had waited until the evening. But she knew the room would have seemed too empty, their actions too noticeable.

She picked out a couch on the other side of the room from the only other couple and waited for Tim to arrive. When he did, minutes later, it was obvious he was hiding something behind his back. He was also looking, for some reason, even more nervous than in the afternoon.

She stood up, and then took a sudden step back when a long-stem red rose was thrust under her nose. She was shocked. "Where did you get this?"

Tim smiled a secret smile. "Happy anniversary, sweetheart," he said and bent and kissed her.

She pulled back in astonishment. "You remembered!"

"How could I forget?" The words were spoken with such devastating simplicity she sat back down on the couch. She buried her nose in the rose to hide her emotion. She felt Tim sit down beside her. Felt his arm come around her. He spoke in her ear. "You didn't think I'd forget? Two years ago today, you changed my life."

The softness in his voice seemed to match the delicateness of the rose.

She heard him clear his throat. "Lucy?"

She looked up, wiped tears off her cheeks.

Tim was looking around, as if to make sure no one was listening. He turned back to her, took both of her hands in his. His hands, usually dry and warm, were cold and clammy. Was he sick? She looked at him anxiously.

He took in a deep breath. "Lucy, will you marry me?"

She stared at him. Something rose up, caught in her throat. Not words. A feeling. Could one gag on joy? Gag for joy?

Her eyes filled with tears again. She wrapped her arms around his neck, trying to stifle the choking sounds in his shoulder.

Tim's arms came around her. She could feel tension and fear through the tenderness and love.

Someone loved her. Someone had asked her to marry him. Someone was terrified she was going to say no. She was overwhelmed.

"Don't answer me now," Tim said, finally.

She sat back and met his eyes.

"I mean it," he said. "You don't have to give me an answer now. Take the time you need. Take two years. Any time between now and then you want to tell me is okay, but I figure you've given me two years of your life—I can wait two years."

Before she could speak, he brought an envelope out of his pocket. "I wrote you a letter. That's how much I love you; I'm willing to risk the grammar police hammering on my door, arresting me for double negatives and criminal spelling."

She was relieved to laugh. "Should I read it now?"

"If you want." His voice was suddenly shy.

She opened the envelope, unfolded the lined foolscap paper. By the time she got to the end, the words were a blur.

Back in the motel room, she reread the letter by the inadequate forty-watt bulb in the bedside lamp. This time it made her cringe. Not just the grammar mistakes and clichés, but the impracticality of Tim's dreams and promises in the face of their (her) current financial reality. He was promising to build her a house in the country on a private lake and said she could stop working for the government and do her own writing. Did he really think they could afford all this on what little money he would be able to bring in?

She was angry with herself; he'd even said he was willing to risk her criticism. That was how much he loved her. She made herself look past the surface to the sentiment, the deep feeling, underneath. He was giving her two years. That meant more than the proposal itself. No one had ever said they would wait. Decisions were supposed to be quick and irrevocable. And, always, on the other's terms.

She would not tell him she thought he was idealizing her—she had not "saved" him. She would not tell him his dreams for their future were unrealistic. She would not tell him she was no longer sure they even had a future. They had a "now." And from the "now," she had a marriage proposal. A letter of commitment. A red rose. A full heart. And two years. What more could she desire from the "now?"

She slid between the crisp clean sheets she'd brought for the bed and shut off the light.

14.

ON MONDAY MORNING I DROVE to the office. I tried not to think about Quinn calling. This time he'd said he'd call. But it didn't look like he was going to come out on the river with me. I would make other plans.

I phoned some friends to put out the word that I was looking for a place to live. I made calls for business. I stayed on the phone so I would not be waiting for it to ring. I told myself, again, that if he called it would be in the evening. At home. And I wasn't planning to be at home in the evening. At six o'clock I drove up the highway, took the turn-off for the village, and knocked on Mary Frances's door.

"What are you doing tonight? I want you to come with me out on the river. I've arranged to borrow the neighbours' motorboat."

"Ellen McGinn, in a *boat*."

"These are strange times." I smiled.

"Why do I sense there is a macabre reason behind this excursion."

"Because there is." I smiled again.

Mary Frances regarded me with pursed lips. "I'll go with you. But we are not going to find anything." She spoke accusingly.

"Maybe not," I said. "But I can't promise."

"Well, God help us if we do."

"Yes," I said.

But I felt a gap between us. I had crossed a line. There was no turning back now. In fact, every day I was more and more certain I was going to find Lucy. With the motorboat we could cover more ground in less time. And with someone with me, the sight of Lucy wouldn't be such a shock. I hoped. And if Steve Quinn wasn't going to cooperate….

Mary Frances arrived an hour later.

We putted our way down to the dam in the ten-horsepower boat. It was a beautiful evening. Mild. The trees glowed in the evening sunlight. We hugged the shore.

In the bow, Mary Frances smoked cigarette after cigarette. It was a lazy-looking gesture that betrayed the tension I knew she was holding inside. She was skeptical but she wasn't immune to the possibilities.

We entered every bay. We strained our eyes. We followed the length of the huge boom that stretched across the river just above the dam. We traced the perimeter of the Hydro-Québec island. And then we returned home on the opposite shore in the still-warm twilight.

"Well, my dear, that was a most pleasant evening," said Mary Frances, kissing the air near my cheeks when we got back to her car. "I feel I know every inch of the Gatineau now."

"Every resident should," I said. "By the way, keep your eyes peeled."

"For a body? Me? I think not."

"For a house. For me."

Mary Frances looked sympathetic. But under it I knew what she was thinking: it's about time; we knew from the start it would come to this.

"And thank you for not saying anything," I added.

"You know I have only your best interests at heart."

"If I could only be as sure as you what they are."

"One thing I'm certain of," she said, getting into the Cressida.

"What's that?"

"The house, you'll find." She pulled the door shut and gave me a wave.

I made a face after the retreating car.

There was no message from Quinn when I got home, or indication that a Private Caller had called.

—∞∞∞—

TIM HAD BEEN DENIED BOTH day parole and a UTA. The denial was a brick wall. Four brick walls and no door. There was no recourse. He wouldn't be eligible for another hearing for months, and even then there was no guarantee that the same answer wouldn't be given. The system was hell-bent on screwing him around. Only Tim's Classification Officer held out a ray of hope. There was, he said, little chance for Tim through the usual channels. But there was another way: through the legal system. She could hire a lawyer to get time off his sentence, to argue that his sentences should have been served concurrently, not consecutively.

Her father gave her the name of a lawyer.

The lawyer said he'd look into the case and get back to her in a week.

A week. What could she do in that week that would not be waiting? There was the Emily Carr guide to finish up over the next couple of days to meet her deadline. That was doable. And then what? Something for herself. Something social. Something new. Someone new.

Ellen McGinn.

She had been enjoying their steady if infrequent contact these past few months. With the last of the material coming a couple of weeks ago, that contact had stopped. But it didn't have to. She felt from Ellen some need, or curiosity at the very least, to learn about the more spiritual, contemplative side of life. A wary curiosity, yes, but there was something Ellen was looking for, though she denied it. She would simply invite her over. And if Ellen accepted, and if it felt right, she would tell Ellen about Tim. She felt wonderful detachment about the "ifs"—open to them, not defeated by them. Ellen was free to make an excuse if she needed to, but she was also free to say yes.

When Ellen's "yes" came, she was euphoric.

She was still into the flow of the moment—almost high on it, though she knew that was as dangerous as trying to control it—when Ellen came over a few days later to sip wine at the kitchen table. She let the conversation come around naturally to the topic of men, boyfriends—and Tim. She had already decided on what version—and quantity—of the truth she thought Ellen could handle: most of it, but not all. Now she watched Ellen closely as she told her story, gratified to see she was not going to freak out and run away. She scrutinized Ellen's face, her body language, looking for judgement, doubt. Ellen was the kind of person who kept a mask over her feelings. But at least her initial skepticism was no longer there. What she felt now from Ellen was an air of receptivity and acceptance. It made her even more euphoric. It was, she knew, a sign of her own acceptance of herself. At last.

On Monday, the call from the lawyer came: Tim definitely had a year coming to him. And there was a court precedent on his side. He could be out within weeks. But the lawyer couldn't—or wouldn't—take it on. He gave her the name of the lawyer who had won the precedent-setting case.

She hung up the phone. She made herself breathe. Hold on to the centre, she told herself.

I MADE THE ROUNDS OF the available rentals. There was nothing worth considering. I took a phone number from a notice pinned to the board at the Kirk's Ferry *depanneur.* Beside it Lucy's face mocked me from a torn poster. *Do you really think you're going to find a house? Or me?* I pulled the poster off the board. I folded Lucy up and put her in my pocket.

At home, I phoned the number I'd taken off the notice. The house had been rented. I took Lucy's photo out of my pocket and looked at it again. She wasn't mocking me at all. She was smiling in encouragement. *Keep looking.*

The first of July came and went. Marc would be home in a week and a half. I didn't even bother to buy the new edition of the *Low Down.* The same houses were listed every week—the ones I'd already looked at and dismissed. I resigned myself to being at the house when he came home.

SUDDENLY TIM WAS GOING TO be out. In eight days. The new lawyer was definite on that. He wasn't giving her any caveats. No maybes. No "cautious optimism." A court hearing had been set for Friday, May twenty-seventh.

"F-day" she called it. Free or fucked again.

The lawyer might be sure, but she wasn't making any assumptions. They had been screwed over too many times. She wasn't going to tell anyone. Just her father and Anna. She held back from formulating any plans in her head, from buying the Champagne. She kept herself busy. She had a deadline to meet. Things to buy for Tim. The upstairs apartment to get ready for the new tenant. Denise had managed to trash it before she disappeared. The new tenant, Lakshmi, was moving in at the end of the month. Lakshmi: the Goddess of Prosperity. It was a good omen.

Saturday afternoon found her kneeling over the apartment bathtub, scrubbing, trying not to gag. She didn't want to think about the source of the filthy ring, the dirt and grime that had come off Denise's pallid skin.

She rinsed the tub, stood slowly to stretch the kinks out of her ankles. She surveyed the bathroom with satisfaction. Not a speck of Denise left. The mirror her boyfriend had smashed had been replaced. She made a face in the new mirror. Just what she had needed, more expenses. She had enough expenses already.

She didn't, she reminded herself, begrudge the expenses. What was three thousand dollars in lawyer's fees when it virtually guaranteed Tim would be here in a week?

A week. She felt like someone had just shot her up with caffeine. Tim. Here. An actuality in her life. What if he didn't fit in? What if he embarrassed her with his manners, his grammar, his lack of intellectual conversation?

She switched off the bathroom light, paused in the doorway of the bedroom. The floor still needed doing but the windows were clean. What a difference clean windows made. She would do the ones downstairs too. You never realized how much dirt was building up on windows; you just got used to looking out through filtered layers. You got used to clouded vision.

She filled a bucket with hot soapy water and started on the bedroom floor. Tim wanted her to go down on Friday to wait with him for the results of the hearing. The lawyer had said the legal papers would be delivered by noon. And then he would be free to go.

She scrubbed at the black scuff marks on the floor. Free to go. God!

She could hardly believe it. Hardly dared to believe it. She had tried to suggest driving down after he heard the results, but that had led to a massive misunderstanding. He'd tried to tell her to stay home, not come at all; he would get the bus. But she could hear the fear in his voice. And the guilt. Guilt that, as he said, she had already done so much for him, but at the same time fear that she would abandon him at the last minute. That was what had made him assert his control, try to push her away. She knew that tactic well. If I insist you not be there, you won't disappoint me.

And didn't she have the same guilt and fear? Guilt for suggesting that she only get in the car when he got the decision. Fear that they were just too different, that it was never going to work.

A sweat broke out on her forehead. She had to sit back on her heels, wait for the dizzy spell to pass. The fear had raised its head from time to time, but she had always been able to work her way through it. She'd always had the ironic luxury of time. Now it came and smacked her in the face. Knocked her off her feet. Choked off her breathing. She beat it back with her rag, her broom, her bucket of soapy water.

At the end of the day she was exhausted but triumphant. She stood in the middle of the apartment, surveying all her hard work. Savouring the clean, light energy. She was optimistic about the new tenant; she'd looked quiet and kind.

The timing of it all was no coincidence. No coincidence that Denise and her dark energy were gone. She could admit it now: Denise had been a mirror for her former negative self. But the apartment was now clean. Every fear and dark thought had been cleared out of every corner. A new mirror was even hanging in the bathroom. A mirror of her new self. She was thrilled by the metaphor. So thrilled she went into the bathroom and this time smiled at her reflection.

Fear and negativity be gone. She had slain all the dragons. She was ready to be with Tim.

ON THURSDAY, JULY SIXTH, I stopped at the *depanneur* on my way home from work to pick up a few items. A pile of the week's edition of the *Low Down* was sitting on the counter. I shrugged and tossed one in with my groceries.

Sitting on the deck with a beer, I skimmed my eye down the For Rent column on the back page. I almost missed the new listing: *Small house on Gatineau River. Former church. Hardwood floors, four appliances, $650 per month. Avail. immed.*

I knew it was mine. The blind certainty was uncharacteristic of me. But the certainty, at any rate, was refreshing. And so was the joy when I saw it an hour later, the delight I felt in everything about it. From its high ceilings to its polished wood floors. From its view of the Canadian Shield cliffs on the opposite shore to the yard that sloped down to the railway tracks and the point of land that jutted out onto the water on the other side of the tracks.

The price was right. The size was right. The location was right. The location, in fact, was uncanny. It was on River Road, less than a kilometre from where I had found Lucy's car.

The timing was perfect. A tenant had fallen through at the last minute.

I tried to restrain my jubilance when I left a message for Marc that night. I could hear the disappointment in his voice when he returned my call the next morning. It was a short conversation. There was nothing left to say. I would be gone when he came home.

The red light began flashing on the phone when I hung up. The automated voice announcing there were four messages shocked me. I hadn't been on the line more than five minutes. It wasn't even 8:30. Who would be trying to get me so early?

I punched in the codes to listen to the messages. The first was from a CBC reporter. The next was a reporter from the *Sun*. The one after that was from the *Citizen*. And the last was from Steve Quinn. None of them gave a reason for phoning. None of them needed to.

I couldn't get hold of Quinn. Or Lundy or Roach. I turned on the radio.

It was the second story on the local newscast. "A skull and some bones were found yesterday in an isolated woodlot in the Gatineau Hills. The remains have been sent to Montreal for identification. A forty-one-year-old white male has been arrested. Charges are pending."

A woodlot. Earth. Bones. I was stunned. The images had all been wrong. Dead wrong. But Lucy had been found. At last.

Before the news was over, the phone began to ring. The first caller was Mary Frances. "Oh, Ellen, I'm so sorry."

"Sorry?" I repeated her word, stupidly.

"My dear, sorry that it was the worst possible news."

That shook me. I was supposed to have been hoping she was still alive, not assuming my dreams had been correct. I was supposed to be grieving her death, not feeling this overriding relief that her body had finally been found.

The phone kept ringing. I stayed in my office so I could monitor the call display. I let the media calls ring through to the machine. I took the calls from friends. Angel told me to stay home for as long as I needed. I didn't know how long I needed. I didn't know what I needed.

The noon newscast had more details. "An Ottawa man has been arrested for the murder of Lucy Stockman. Ms. Stockman had been missing since April twenty-second. Remains believed to belong to the victim were found in a secluded area of woods in the Masham area by her common-law husband. He was accompanied by a woman believed to be an undercover police officer. Following the discovery, Tim Brennan, forty-one, walked into the police station and was immediately arrested. An hour ago, Mr. Brennan was formally charged with first-degree murder."

Accompanied by a woman. Why hadn't I done a useful thing like that?

All those dreams, so-called visions. It had all been bullshit. The cops had been right. Of course. They were trained to come up with plausible theories and solve crimes. Quinn had said they knew Tim needed to produce the body. They had assumed he knew where the body was. They had worked on that assumption. They had arranged for someone to go undercover. To befriend Tim. To keep up the "search" with him. It had paid off. It all made perfect sense.

What a fool I'd been. Searching south of the city. Searching in abandoned buildings. Searching in the water. She hadn't been in the water at all. She'd been nowhere near water. She'd been in dense woods, buried in a shallow grave.

As dry as her bones were now.

PART II: FINDING

Being one with the Tao
when you seek, you find.
                    —Tao Te Ching

15.

THERE WAS ONE NAME AND number on my call display I was not expecting to see ever again. Lucy's remains had been positively identified in Montreal two days before. The day before that, Tim Brennan had been charged with her murder and put behind bars without bail. There was no one who should be calling me from Lucy's house.

I made myself pick up the receiver.

Lucy's voice asked for me.

"Speaking," I whispered.

"Ellen. Hello. It's Anna Stockman."

I sat down hard on my office chair and let out an audible breath. "Anna—I'm sorry. I never phoned. To say—"

"That's okay. I'm calling to let you know there's going to be a memorial service for Lucy on the thirteenth." There was a briskness in her tone. Briskness would carry her through. "I'm calling you from Lucy's. Doug and I drove up from Toronto last night. We brought my father. We've been trying to plan a service. We want to find someone who will speak. But I don't know any of Lucy's friends. You're the only one I've met. I was wondering if we could ask for your help."

"Of course." My response was automatic. Then I added, "I didn't know Lucy very well. I don't think I could—"

"I know. But we were wondering if you would mind calling some of her other friends for us. Maybe find two or three people who would be able to speak."

"Of course," I said again.

The first surprise was the sheer volume of names and numbers Anna dictated to me. The second—when I started my phone calls—was the discovery that none of Lucy's other friends knew each other either. I was not the only one outside the circle. There was no circle. If we were a circle, we were each spokes. Spokes without a wheel joining them together. Spokes whose centre was Lucy. That was my third surprise—that Lucy had been such a hub. She had reached far and wide: artists, massage therapists, lawyers, government clients who'd become personal friends, teenage children of friends, the range was endless. And they all had stories.

But none was willing to speak. They were nervous. Or shy. Or, like Kevin, afraid they'd cry.

Lucy's friends could not tell their stories in public, but they needed to share them with someone. Someone who would listen. Someone who would glean. Someone who would pull it all together and deliver it back to them. I could listen and glean. That was "research." The second part—the pulling it all together, the delivering it back—that part I wasn't as qualified for. But I couldn't bear the disappointment in Anna's voice when I called her back the next day.

"I'll speak, if you like." I had already decided to offer. "I was thinking I could gather stories from her friends and present them as a collective memory. If you think it's a good idea."

Anna thought it was a wonderful idea. I wasn't so sure. But somewhere behind it, I felt Lucy scheming.

I spent two evenings on the phone. I explained what I was doing. I felt gratitude—and need—emanating from the other end of the line. The stories spilled out. They matched Kevin's stories of the dynamo she had been. They described her passion for fairness, her enthusiasm for learning, for throwing herself into everything she did, for teaching others. The stories were imbued with warmth, gratitude, admiration. They were coloured, now, with confusion, pain, guilt.

Only one person refused to speak to me.

"I do appreciate what you're doing," said Curtis. "But it's not something I can participate in." The wariness I had been expecting from our previous conversation. The warmth took me by surprise. "The grieving masses," he added, "do not want to hear what I have to say about Lucy." No, they probably didn't. Here was the bitter ex-lover. Who else had I been expecting?

"I'm sorry I bothered you," I said. "I understand."

"No. You don't. You just think you do." His directness also took me aback. It seemed bold, in a conversation between strangers. "You and everyone else already have a construct of what Lucy did, and why, and where I fit in, and how I feel," he continued. "Lucy, by the way, was the queen of constructs. That's why I don't want to talk to you. Because no one wants to hear the truth, especially my version of it. I've already been labelled the jilted lover."

"No," I said. Then I corrected myself. "Yes."

There was a pause. Then: "Thank you."

"For what?" This conversation was getting more and more bizarre.

"For not denying what you're thinking."

His next words were the most unbelievable of the entire conversation. "What time," he asked, "does the memorial service start?"

There was no ventilation in the church. The hundreds of bodies in the pews added their own heat to the already close air. Our entrance had been documented by a row of television cameras out on the sidewalk. Journalists had been requested to stay outside. Those who had come in were requested not to take notes. The only movement in the church was the fanning of leaflets, like so many small white flags.

I sat close to the front. The two pages of my speech were getting damp between my fingers. Somewhere behind me, Marc sat sweltering in a winter-weight suit, his only one. He had arrived home just the night before—only a day after I had moved out. Had called me in the morning to offer to go with me. "Marc, you don't have to. I'm sure you need to recover from all that driving."

"I'm coming," he said. "I'll pick you up at noon." His words, and his decisiveness, brought me surprising relief. And, after we hung up, tears. I sat among all my unpacked boxes and cried out my frustration. What was I doing here? Was I doing the right thing?

By the time Marc arrived at the door, I had pulled myself together. I *was* doing the right thing. I needed time to sort everything out. Not just Marc and me, and Steve Quinn and me, but, most of all, Lucy's death and the last ten traumatic weeks. I needed my own place to do that from.

Just as the service was starting, a man with red eyes and a fist of tissues slipped into the pew beside me. We exchanged a sympathetic glance.

The minister was a woman. She had never met Lucy, even though geography would have put Lucy in her parish. Lucy had not been a churchgoer. Even the United Church would have been appalled at most of Lucy's beliefs. The minister was appalled at her death. The minister seemed to be appalled at the death of all women, no matter how they met their end.

"Five thousand women this year will die of breast cancer," she shouted to the congregation. There was a pause for emphasis. "*Five* thousand." Another pause. Then she volleyed another statistic into the church: "One in two women will be a victim of violence."

She paused to reload her ammunition. "Look around you. Which woman would you choose?"

Her words angered me. It was not the anger she intended. Lucy had not died of breast cancer. And this was not a political rally. The men in the congregation had not come to be accused. They had come with the rest of us to mourn the death of Lucy Stockman.

The man beside me was openly weeping. I reached over and took his hand. He didn't withdraw it. I let go only when it was my turn to make my way to the front to deliver my distilled memory of Lucy.

I unfolded the pages, took a breath and spoke in as clear a voice as I could manage. "The story goes that when Lucy was a little girl she danced so much she wore out the living room carpet. Lucy lived her whole life with that exuberance—and with that *thoroughness*—that made her wear down the carpet…."

Halfway through my rehearsed speech I relaxed enough to look down into the congregation. In the first row, Anna and Doug, and an older man who was obviously Lucy's father, sat linked by their hands and the identical expressions of grief on their faces. Beside them were Sergeants Lundy and Roach. Their hands were in their laps, their faces composed. That they were here touched me. I had not expected them.

My eyes swept over them and beyond, into the throng of anonymous faces that packed the church.

"She got right into the fight to get Tim Brennan out of prison," I recited. "And we have to give her credit for her incredible energy and courage and faith, no matter what we might think of her wisdom."

At my mention of Tim Brennan's name, I could almost feel the reporters in the congregation memorizing my words. There was no question I would be quoted in tomorrow's papers.

It wasn't until I was heading back down the steps to my pew that I spotted Quinn. He was sitting directly behind Lundy and Roach. My heart, which had just stopped pounding from nerves, began pounding again. I hadn't expected to see him here either. Our eyes met briefly—he gave me a half-smile of encouragement—and then I turned to re-enter my pew across the aisle. Would he stay for the reception? Would he and Marc meet? I barely heard the next speaker.

And then Lucy herself breezed up to the front of the church.

I didn't hear the name she gave. She had been, she said, a university friend. She might have been Lucy's twin. A slightly bigger build, and heavy-rimmed glasses, but the same dark hair and complexion, the same energy. She wasn't, that I knew of, on the official list of speakers. She had, she said, just got into town. That would explain it. She hadn't seen Lucy in years, but in university they had been inseparable.

She wore a flowing dress of Indian cotton and as she paced up and down at the front of the church it swirled around her, as if imbued with an energy of its own. She regaled us with stories—mischief they'd created, trips they'd taken. She made us laugh, the only laughter the church heard during that service. And then just as quickly she breezed out. I didn't see her again. I wasn't even sure she'd been real. It seemed just as plausible that the ghost of the mischievous Lucy we'd just heard described had briefly appeared among us to remind us that life prevailed. But it also seemed a mockery. One so alive, the other so dead.

By a miracle Marc found me in the mass making its way, as one body, to the back of the church and down the stairs to the reception room. Then we got separated.

Someone touched my shoulder. I turned to face the man with the red-rimmed eyes. He took my hand. "Thank you for speaking so honestly about Lucy. You were the only one who had the courage to mention Brennan."

"You're Curtis." His words and responses were still throwing me.

"Are you doing anything after this?" My hand was still in his. His eyes were holding mine. He was my height, with a lean build and shaggy hair. He kept pushing his bangs back from his eyes. His mouth turned up naturally at the corners. "Would you go for a beer with me? I have a feeling we have a lot to talk about." His smile went deep into his sad eyes.

"But I thought you didn't want…."

"I didn't want to talk to a stranger over the phone and have my words twisted in a speech. But," he smiled again, "you didn't do any twisting."

"I'm glad you think so." I glanced around and located Marc … talking to Quinn. Shit! Of all the hundreds of people in the room they'd had to find each other.

Curtis's eyes had followed mine. He had probably seen my alarm too. He smiled his understanding. "Some other time then." The smile came from his eyes. Beyond the redness and the obvious pain, there was kindness. This wasn't the distant, aloof man I had envisioned.

I wanted to cry then, and it wasn't just about Lucy. "Yes," I said. "I'd like that."

"I have your number," he said. "I'll call you."

I disengaged my hand but there was someone else with her hand outstretched to take it, a woman who emanated serenity through her grief. A woman with short brown hair and delicate features. "I'm Trish."

Trish Cousins. Lucy's massage therapist and counsellor—and Marnie's partner.

"I couldn't help hearing what Curtis said. I want to thank you for speaking so honestly too. What you said about Lucy taking risks for Tim. It's true. She did think life wasn't worth living if you didn't take risks.

And in Tim's case she considered them calculated risks—as you said."

"And what did *you* think?" I hadn't been able to get hold of her when I was making my calls.

Trish's smile was as gentle as her voice. "I'm paid to listen, not to judge."

"But still—you heard maybe more than anyone else about her relationship, about what was really going on."

Trish was nodding. Over her shoulder, I saw Marc and Quinn shake hands and Marc move away.

"I know this isn't the time to talk about it," I added. "But I've heard so many theories and opinions in the last few days as I've been talking to everyone. Would it be okay to call you?"

"Yes. I think I probably need to talk about it too. You have my number still?"

"Yes."

We smiled at each other. It wasn't until she had disappeared in the crowd that I thought to wonder if Marnie were here. I turned to scope the room again. Quinn was standing where Marc had left him. But before I could reach him, I came to Lundy and Roach holding small plastic cups of juice.

I held out my hand to Sergeant Lundy. "I'm sure it means a lot to the family that you came."

"We couldn't not come," said Lundy. "We feel we know Lucy now too."

Yes, I could understand that. I had done them an injustice. Their job was more than theories and investigations and arrests. Their job was involvement with people in unspeakable pain, people they had never met before, and people they would never meet.

"We're going to be calling on some people again in light of what we now know," added Roach.

"I guess there's going to be a trial."

Roach nodded. "Like I said. We'll be calling you."

Marc arrived at my side at that moment and I introduced him to the two detectives. And then stood beside him not hearing the conversation. Looking again for Quinn.

"I'm going to go get a juice," I murmured to Marc. I turned and bumped against someone coming up right behind me. "Oh, sorry," I said and then I looked up. "Oh!"

Close up, Quinn looked tired and slightly on edge. I wished I could get him to open up to me. Something was going on in his life. I wasn't making *that* up.

But his smile was so obviously filled with pleasure at seeing me I hoped Marc didn't suddenly turn around to see it. "I was hoping I'd bump into you here," he joked. "You did a good job up there."

I felt myself blush in the awareness of Marc behind me, his arm brushing against mine. "I was speaking for a whole bunch of her friends."

"But you were the one who pulled it all together."

I made a gesture of assent.

"So we can add speaking to your many talents."

I acknowledged the compliment. *We're not back together*, I wanted to say. But the unconscious pressure of Marc's arm against mine paralyzed me.

But then I looked Quinn in the eye and willed my face to remain its normal colour. It didn't matter if Marc heard my next words; they were "legitimate." "I didn't get a chance to tell Sergeants Lundy and Roach. I've just moved. They said they'd be calling me. Maybe I could give you my phone number to pass on to them."

Quinn's eyes glinted in amusement. He gave a brief nod. "Give me a call at the station on Monday. I'll make sure they get it." His voice was brisk.

"Are you ready to go?" It was Marc, beside me.

"Oh. Not quite. I haven't spoken to Lucy's family yet."

I nodded good-bye to Quinn. His whole demeanour had stiffened up at Marc speaking to me. But they seemed to have been talking amicably enough earlier. I looked at Marc to see if he had noticed, but he was looking as relaxed as ever, holding out his hand again to Quinn. Quinn shook it, unwillingly it seemed to me. Perversely I was enjoying this display of—what had he called it before?—male territoriality.

"I'll speak to you Monday, Ellen," he said in his stern cop's voice and turned away. I hid my smile from Marc. In any case, the sight of Anna and her father erased my momentary amusement. Anna's face was tear-streaked but calm. She was playing the consummate hostess, maintaining her poise, speaking a few words to each person. She emanated control, calm, decorum. She would probably remember nothing tomorrow.

There was nothing controlled about Mr. Stockman. It was impossible to tell what sort of a man he was in normal circumstances. Grief had taken up residence and torn down all the retaining walls. But I remembered Lucy describing him as a stern, austere man. She resembled him in features, though his complexion was fairer. What had she said? Her mother had been the Hungarian; her father was English. A typically self-controlled people. Not today. Maybe not ever again. His tears fell without restraint. He seemed to hear nothing that was said to him. His response was the same for everyone. "Thank you for coming." It was a recorded message for someone who couldn't be there in person.

I half expected Anna not to recognize me, but she stretched out her hands when I approached, thanked me for my words.

I hugged her close and spoke in her ear. "She's safe now," I heard myself say. We drew apart. Her eyes gleamed with tears.

Out on the sidewalk, a reporter called my name.

"Ignore them," said Marc. His arm around my shoulders was a shield.

I leaned into it. I was exhausted.

In the truck, we wound down the windows to let in the hot breeze.

"What were you talking about with Sergeant Quinn?" I asked. No beating around the bush.

"You."

"What about me?"

Marc kept his eyes on the road. "I was telling him how freaked out you were—that that's why you came to Thunder Bay. He said you didn't seem the type to freak out. I told him I had never seen you like that before."

"I'm fine now," I said to his profile. "I'm not acting from fear anymore."

He glanced at me. "I never said you were."

"Marc, I'm not running away."

There was a two-kilometre pause. "Is there someone else?"

The question took me aback. My response was quick. Maybe too quick. "No."

Back at home, I peeled off my damp dress, twisted the cap off a beer, and stretched out on my new futon couch with a fan aimed at my feet.

I stared out the window at the imposing rock cliff on the other side of the river. In the bright afternoon sun, it seemed harsh, unyielding. A wall of rock, not a rock of comfort. Marc had invited me to come over before he dropped me off. I had been tempted until he'd asked if I would take the dogs for the next few weekends and a week in August when he was going paddling down the Dumoine. No, nothing was different. I asked him to take me right home.

I took large swallows of the beer, felt it cool my throat and dull my brain. Had that service helped? The Minister, certainly, had not helped. Lucy's "ghost" had helped—maybe for a minute. And we had all got to tell our story. Even if some people had done it vicariously through me.

I thought back to the opinions I'd heard expressed on the phone. As I'd told Trish, everyone had a different theory.

"She was incredibly dynamic. A bombshell. She attracted men to her like a magnet. But she was also incredibly stubborn. She refused to admit when she was in trouble. I had no idea what was going on. If I'd known I would have called the police months ago. Now I look back and it's obvious she was in trouble. If only she had confided in me."

"She was a rescuer. She emanated this aura that she knew what she was doing, but she was being naive. She believed all those lies he told her. She didn't see what he really was. He was unredeemable. I have to admit I'm not surprised it came to this."

"She was taken in. We were all taken in. It's pretty scary, when you come right down to it. How come none of us saw it?"

"I don't know what happened to her, but Tim didn't do it. Someone has tried to frame him. She and Tim had an incredible love for each other. She'd found her soulmate. It wasn't easy, they had so many dif- ferences. But they were working it through. They had a bond most of us yearn for. They've got the wrong guy. I'd stake my money on it. Not my life, but my money."

Everyone, it seemed, had a reason why they'd lost touch with her in the last year. Or seen her only sporadically. Had no one really known Lucy? Had she confided in no one? Did even Trish know the truth? Lucy, it seemed, had isolated herself from everyone. Or had everyone abandoned her, the way I had?

Abandoned. It had been what she called her "core wound." And her ultimate fear. Had she ended life the way she had begun it—abandoned by everyone she loved?

⊶⊷

SHE WAS FLOATING AROUND THE living room. Her arms had become wings. She was a note of music suspended in the room. The tips of her toes touched the ground only long enough to lift her off again. She rose and fell, as notes do, within the confines of their song. Her own confines—self-imposed—were the parameters of the kilim carpet that covered the living room's hardwood floor.

When her father was home, no music was tolerated. It was understood that this was because it disturbed her mother. This made no sense: the records were her mother's own Hungarian dances. And when her father wasn't home, she could turn up the volume as loud as she liked; she never got a negative reaction. She never got any reaction at all. As if her mother weren't home either.

But there was someone who occupied the dining room most late afternoons when she arrived home from school. The dining room was separated from the living room by a set of French doors left permanently open. In spite of the open doors, it was hard to see in the room. The north-facing lead-paned windows did not let much light in, and the gumwood wainscotting and heavy oak furniture gave the room an even darker, gloomier air.

This did not seem to bother the occupant. She sat, straight-backed, on the edge of a dining room chair at the table, close to the windows. Her dark hair was captured in a chignon at the nape of her neck. She wore a linen sheath dress. It fit close about her knees, which were pressed together. Her long legs were pulled in under her and at an angle to the side. In one hand she held a fountain pen. In the other she held the stem of a small glass, cut in such a way that it appeared to be filled with glinting diamonds. Amber-coloured diamonds. Liquid diamonds.

Except for the arm that raised the glass to her lips, the woman didn't appear to move. Today, the paper on the table before her remained blank. She stared straight ahead but seemed to see nothing. Nothing in the room anyway.

To the casual listener, the room would have seemed silent. It wasn't. Emanating from the chair was a soft humming. Tuneless but tireless.

This sipping, humming, unmoving person was Lucy's mother.

No matter how many hours her mother sat at the table, at five-thirty every evening she put down her pen and rose from the chair. She straightened her dress and put a hand up to her hair to make sure no strands had fallen. She also put a manicured finger delicately to the corners of her mouth, as if to wipe away excess lipstick. Or perhaps the amber liquid.

She did this all on cue. The cue was the opening and closing of the front door.

Before the click of the latch on the inner door of the vestibule, Lucy's mother would be in the kitchen.

Before the click of the latch on a third door—the coat closet—her mother would have rinsed the crystal glass and put it in a kitchen cupboard her father would never open.

The only cupboard her father ever opened was the liquor cabinet in the dining room. He never noticed the difference in the level of the bottles. There was a good reason for this. Lucy's mother had her own bottle, in one of the kitchen cupboards her father would never look in.

Her father took a long-stemmed glass from the sideboard. He didn't notice that one of the glasses was missing. There were so many of them, after all. "Company" glasses. He poured into his glass the same amber-coloured liquid, took one sip, then left the glass on the sideboard to go into the kitchen to kiss Lucy's mother's cheek. It was not the same quick peck he occasionally sent Lucy's way when she was saying good night. This lingering kiss on her mother's cheek made Lucy look away.

Her father never said anything about the lack of evidence of dinner preparations. Dinner would be on the table by six-thirty. It always was. Lucy never questioned how her mother did this. Mothers did this. That was what they were for. Lucy wasn't sure they were for sitting at the dining room table in a dark room in the late afternoon sipping from a glass, writing or not writing. At least she had never seen other mothers do this. But her father didn't object. It had occurred to Lucy he maybe didn't know.

It occurred to her that as long as he got his dinner by six-thirty, he maybe didn't mind.

Lucy wasn't anywhere to be seen when her father came home. At the sound of the front door opening, she took the needle off the record, shut off the hi-fi, and ran soundlessly upstairs. Up two flights to her favourite room in the house, the attic. The stairs to the attic were behind a narrow door next to the twin narrow door of the linen closet on the second floor. Tonight, as many evenings, the slope-ceilinged room with the musty smell and the one gabled window was a hospital room. Lucy was the nurse. Over her mouth she tied a white tea towel stolen from the kitchen. The tea towel mask over her face was so she wouldn't get the chicken pox and high fever of her baby doll patient. Sometimes the doll cried; sometimes she was quiet. Sometimes she was hot, then cold; sometimes shivering, then drenched in sweat (water that Lucy poured over her).

The doll's mother never came. Lucy, the nurse, was the only person who came into the hospital room, and she didn't care about the doll. She let the doll cry out her misery. She didn't love her. She was angry with the doll's mother, who never came to visit.

16.

"MS. MCGINN, YOU MAINTAIN THAT Lucy Stockman visited you in a number of so-called 'visions,' and gave you information about her whereabouts. Would you agree, Ms. McGinn, that feeling as guilty as you did about abandoning her in her hour of need, your hallucinations were your psyche's way of trying to save the day?"

"No."

"Explain, then, if you will...."

I could never explain.

The cross-examinations started playing out in my head almost immediately after the memorial service. They were relentless. The defence lawyer took me to pieces every time.

I had taken three weeks off to unpack, settle in, and try to resume "normal" life. I was enjoying my new home and a different view of the river. The sciatica was gone. I was back to my regular running routine. The quiet, flat River Road was perfect, and I could also run on the tracks—even this particular stretch—without fear of Tim Brennan. But where Brennan had stopped pursuing me, the defence had started. Every time I set out for a run, the grilling and accusations began.

The guilt of letting Lucy down pursued me too. I was supposed to have found her. It had become the driving force of those ten weeks—after my initial reluctance. And I had failed her.

But I also felt betrayed. By Lucy. By myself. Everything had turned out so differently from where my dreams had been leading me. *What is the good of a search when there is no result?*

I had no answer. I had only a disturbing image of Lucy's remains found in a woodlot near Masham. I wanted to go to the site, but I had no idea where it was. I would ask Quinn when he called. Maybe he would take me. Maybe something would become clearer there.

There was another set of questions in my head that wouldn't go away. The questions about what Lucy had been doing with Tim. What had happened during the year he had been out. Why she had ended up where she had. I didn't have those answers either. But I had a means of at least attempting to find out.

First I gave myself two weeks to relax. To try, anyway. I deserved that much. The questions would wait. Nothing was going to change in two weeks. And no one called me. Except Steve Quinn.

In fact, he woke me up. It was the Monday after the memorial service. I glanced at the clock, fumbling for the phone. Eight-fifteen. I pushed the on button and was greeted by a brusque "Are you alone?"

At the sound of the familiar voice, I was instantly awake. "What do you think? I just moved into my own place."

"But what's 'is name was at the memorial service with you."

So I hadn't imagined his reaction at the service.

"His name is Marc," I said, pushing my tangled hair off my face. "And he was with me because he insisted on coming. And I was grateful for his support." *He was there for me.* The thought was startling.

I sat up. "We aren't seeing each other, if that's what you're thinking. How did you get my number anyway? I was going to call you today." *Just not so early.*

"It didn't take a lot of detective work. Where am I calling, anyway? You've got a Wakefield exchange."

He was incredulous when I told him. "Don't tell me you bought the Rivests' house."

"No, but I'm not that far away."

"Right on River Road? Where exactly? Give me the 911 number."

I gave him the house number, and the landmarks: I was on the straight stretch, just after the long hill that wound down to the river; if he got to the place where I'd found Lucy's car, he'd gone too far. He wanted to know so he could visit, of course, but I had to shake off a vision of him arriving in the dark, secretly watching the house. That paranoia was *over*.

"I'll just have to make a trip up one day to see your new digs."

"I'm around. I'm on holiday for a few weeks."

He hesitated. "Things are pretty busy right now. I don't know when I'll be able to get up there. They've got me officially on the case now. We're working with the Crown, gathering more information. But I will come."

"Have you learned anything new about the case? Have you got enough to convict Tim?"

"Trust me," he said ambiguously. Then he lowered his voice. "Wait 'til we see each other. I promise that will be soon." There was a pause and then he added, "Now do me a favour and keep away from your ex."

If it had been anyone else I would have come up with a sarcastic reply. For some reason I couldn't do that with Quinn. "I'm not seeing him!"

"Good. Keep it that way." There was humour in his voice, but under it was something I didn't like.

I made myself respond with a flippant "Yessir!" and we hung up.

I didn't keep my promise about Marc, though it wasn't to spite Quinn. The dogs naturally brought us together. Marc got another renovation contract locally, and began dropping them off for the day. He always invited me to come in when I brought them back, and after the first few awkward times I stopped refusing him. I did miss him. I knew he missed me. And I *liked* him—now that I didn't have to compete with his canoeing obsession. I hoped we could be friends. But we didn't talk about that. We didn't define what we were doing. We didn't talk about "us" at all. We stayed away from all sensitive topics. We sat on the deck in the cool evenings drinking beer, or we watched videos, sitting a discreet distance apart on the couch. Then I went home.

It was a relief to be enjoying each other's company without it being fraught. Marc seemed to have come out of his self-absorption, his obsession with canoeing. We talked about things we'd barely ever talked about—events that were happening in town, or in the world, the mundane details of our day. It was possibly a mutual ploy to keep ourselves away from the sensitive topics, but if so it was a good one. We seemed to be getting to know each other all over again. Or for the first time. I wasn't sure. I certainly wasn't going to try to explain it to Steve Quinn. I didn't owe him *any* explanation, I reminded myself. I wished I had asked him when the trial was going to start. Just how long was I going to be torturing myself with cross-examinations? And—a more secret question inside myself—how long were we going to have to wait?

Marc didn't ask me about Lucy or the upcoming trial. But I was plagued with thoughts anyway. All the conversations Quinn and I weren't supposed to have had. The things her friends had told me. I spent hours in a lawn chair on my little grassy point of land beside the water, making notes in a journal.

And reading the book Lucy had given me for my birthday. *The Tao Te Ching.* I had found it squeezed into my bookcase. And felt overwhelming emotion when I opened it to find an inscription in Lucy's handwriting I had completely forgotten about.

> *To Ellen,*
> *May this be a goad and a comfort on your journey through life.*
> *Affectionately Lucy.*

I remembered mispronouncing the title when I'd unwrapped the book and Lucy correcting me. I remembered asking what the Tao was, and then laughing: "Or did I just open myself up to an hour-long dissertation." She'd given me a friendly whack on the arm. "I can tell you in one sentence. It means 'The Way.'"

"The way to … salvation?"

"Something like that. I'll let you read it—or not."

I hadn't read it. Not until now. Now I absorbed every word.

> *Immersed in the wonder of the Tao,*
> *you can deal with whatever life brings you,*
> *and when death comes you are ready.*

I wrote and I wept and I wrote some more. The writing seemed to help. It also raised more questions.

When the third week of my holidays arrived, I dug out the phone numbers I had collected. Remembering Marnie and her possible role made me nervous about calling her partner, Trish. I started with Curtis. I expected to have to leave a message for him, but he picked up.

"I only work part time. Come on up now if you like. You can bring your bathing suit and go for a swim."

"Not necessary." My tone was dry.

"Stupid of me—you live on water too. I'm used to offering a haven for city folk."

I didn't correct him on my reason for declining. A thought had struck me. Had he been a haven for Lucy?

"Funny you should ask," said Curtis. "We can talk about that when you come up."

He gave me directions.

An hour later he was eyeing me speculatively. "What do you think?"

I scanned my eyes over the view and then back to Curtis. "It's amazing up here."

"Up here" was on a platform—the second "storey" of two platforms actually—in a giant, unusually wide-branched white pine crowning a hill that overlooked a small lake north of Wakefield. I was sitting in a vintage bamboo sixties or seventies tub swing that hung from a branch near the middle of the platform. The Beaujolais in my glass had been nicely chilled to make it a refreshing summer drink. The tree's branches shaded us from the hot afternoon sun. "I always wanted a tree-house as a kid."

"So did I," said Curtis from his perch on the wide railing surrounding the platform. "That's why I built it. That was Lucy's seat you're sitting in. In fact, she's the reason it's there; she didn't like being too close to the edge."

I smiled sadly. "Kind of ironic, isn't it?"

I enjoyed the way understanding registered on his face. He nodded. "She was wilfully blind sometimes. *Most* times, maybe."

"Is that what you believe?"

Curtis's laugh was harsh. "You want to know what I believe? Have you got a few hours?"

I smiled at him over my wine glass. "That was the idea wasn't it?"

"She was sitting right where you are now a week before she died. The Easter weekend."

I almost choked on the wine. "She was with *you?*"

"Not in the way you're thinking, but, yes, she was here."

"*Were* you providing a haven?"

"You could say that," came the measured reply.

"I'm sorry. I hope this doesn't sound like an interrogation. You don't have to tell me anything you don't want to."

Curtis smiled then. The first real smile I'd seen on his face. Or perhaps just the first smile without the red eyes. It transformed his face. "Are you really worried about that after the way I put you off?"

"I guess not. But why are you telling me now?"

Curtis gave a slow shrug. Everything about him was deliberate. The way he chose his words and put his sentences together. The way he moved his body. "You seem to have a need to know," he said. "And you don't seem to have come armed with preconceived notions."

I laughed. "All my preconceived notions got knocked out of me the day Lucy went missing." I paused. "Actually, I think my preconceptions started to get knocked out of me the day I *met* Lucy."

Curtis was nodding. He had an air about him of really listening. I found myself telling him how I'd met Lucy. How we'd become friends. How we'd stopped being friends.

"You weren't the first," he said. "She—I don't know if this is the right word, but I'll use it anyway. She *systematically* attracted people to her, and then alienated them."

"I did my part," I said. "I rejected her."

"You wouldn't have rejected her if she hadn't alienated you."

"You make it sound like I had no choice."

"And did you have any choice after Tim killed her? You found the car, you have to testify at the trial. You have no choice. You're a victim, I'm a victim. We're all victims."

His vehemence took me aback. Was I a victim? I didn't feel like one. "I could have chosen not to go back up to the car. I didn't want to."

"I bet you're sorry now you did."

I gave a wry smile. "I was sorry for awhile. But not anymore."

"But what choice did I have?" he said. "What fuckin' choice did I have that my girlfriend leaves me for a fuckin' murderer and endangers all our lives?"

"Maybe you'd already made your choice. By getting involved with Lucy in the first place." It was something Lucy might have said. I wondered if she, too, had been irritated by his refusal to take any responsibility.

"I understand what you're trying to say about choice," said Curtis, in a calmer voice. "But the truth is, if I tried to overpower you right now, you wouldn't stand a chance."

His example shocked me. I tried not to show it. I responded in a calm voice. Pedantic even. "But the question isn't *if* you did, but *would* you. And, call me naive, but it seems like it would be out of character for you to suddenly come at me. But," I added, "if you do suddenly decide to act out of character, can you give me some warning so I can choose to go home?"

He laughed then, and his laugh—a warm, genuine laugh—dissipated my unease. "Touché."

I changed the subject. "So did you stay in contact with Lucy after…." I trailed off.

"After she ditched me for another guy? No, I'm not that much of a masochist. I took a few months to get some emotional distance. But I liked the woman. As it happens I like most of my exes. I always try to stay friends. So after a healthy amount of time, I contacted her."

"Before Tim got out."

"Before Tim got out," he confirmed. "We saw each other now and then. She asked me to have dinner with her a night or two before he was released."

"Didn't you find that a bit … odd?"

Curtis barked out a laugh. "Well, at first I flattered myself that she'd come to her senses. She didn't announce until we were in the middle of dinner that Tim was about to be released. I realized she wanted to…." He paused, searching for the right word. He seemed to pick his words with care. "Gloat," he said at last.

"Gloat? I can't believe that. It seems heartless."

"It depends on what she was gloating about. It wasn't so much about Tim. I sensed she wanted to show me how well she'd got on without me since I'd left. She'd been living on her own for almost a year."

"That's when I met her. When she was on her own. I admired her. She seemed so self-sufficient."

Curtis was nodding. "I can see how she would have come across that way. But that was a first for Lucy. Her pattern was always to have a man waiting in the wings. She chased me and chased me. I've always been slow to commit. And then when I finally stopped running and said, 'okay,' she dumped me for Tim."

"But Tim wasn't free to move in." But he was *there*, I added, to myself. Maybe in a way no one else ever had been. He couldn't be anywhere else. His being in prison, ironically, had ensured he was always there. It had probably been quite easy to offer her unconditional love from prison.

A FIGURE STOOD BESIDE THE highway in the distance, at the end of the drive. He didn't move, didn't pace or fidget or look at his watch. But he watched the highway with an air of unease, as if he had no idea where he was or where he was going. He looked like he was hoping someone would come along and pick him up and take him home.

She pulled the Suzuki over onto the shoulder. Their eyes met through the windshield. The fear in his eyes met the fear in hers. But then she saw relief shear through his fear. Someone had come for him after all.

The first few drops of rain began to fall as they turned onto Highway 15. She stuck to the eighty-kilometre-per-hour limit, but even so sensed everything was going by too fast for her passenger.

There was, she thought, too much space around him.

She was overwhelmed by the anxiety filling the car. Her own, driving in the rain with a line of cars building behind her, bringing a newly released convict to live in her home. And his. She felt his almost more than her own: fear of the open space, the speed of the car, the unknown destination. Anxieties she knew all too well. The difference was: Tim would grow used to it all. He would become at home in the world again. But maybe, just maybe, as he overcame his terror of being out in the world, so would she.

Two and a half hours later, she pulled into the driveway and pulled the key out of the ignition. She closed her eyes and with one long exhalation tried to release all the tension of the drive. Then she turned and smiled at her passenger. "Welcome home, baby."

But Tim wasn't looking at her. He was letting himself out of the car. He seemed mesmerized by his surroundings, the neighbourhood, the house, even though he'd seen it all before when he'd been allowed to visit on his ETA. He stepped onto the porch as if in a daze.

She reached into the back for his forgotten duffel bag. It was even lighter than she was expecting. What did it feel like to carry all your earthly goods in one small bag? For a moment—the moment between the car and the front door—it was her bag, her life. There was something incredibly freeing about the lightness of this bag. You could, she thought, go anywhere you wanted. No mortgage payments, no bills, no clients, no deadlines, no responsibilities, no "things" to worry about. For a split second she envied Tim his freedom. Until she remembered the invisible cord that still connected this bag, and its contents and its owner, to prison. He wasn't free—not yet. There was a parole officer to report to, mandatory counselling to take, a job to find, or for her to create for him, adjustments to make to living in the "real" world. And when he had adjusted, what then? Then he would be bound by other bonds—work, car payments, financial responsibilities. All the trappings of "normal" life. Who, really, was ever free?

She vowed, climbing the front steps to let Tim in the front door, that in the intervening time, in her house, in her care, she would give him a taste of real freedom.

"I COULD SEE SHE WAS stronger for having been on her own," said Curtis. "She seemed more sure of herself. I was impressed. And I told her so. I also gave her a hard time for not seeing the light about Brennan. But she seemed to have grown up a lot." He sighed. "There were so many times when I felt like a parent with a four-year-old."

"Yet you stayed with her."

He shrugged. "I was waiting for her to grow up." He paused, then added, in that deliberate way of his, as if he were delivering a line on stage: "No one has ever loved Lucy the way I loved her."

His words hung in the air between us for a few silent minutes. I wanted to ask him if he believed in unconditional love. Instead I said, "It must have been a blow when she said Tim was getting out."

"Don't misunderstand me. I didn't accept her invitation to dinner thinking she was coming back to me. I just hoped for her own sake that she wasn't continuing on with Brennan."

"And after he got out. Did you continue to see her?" I thought about what Anna had said. That Tim had been jealous. If Lucy had continued having contact with Curtis, that would have been a hotbed of conflict.

"I ran into them on Bank Street the day after he was released."

"The day *after?* My God."

"Completely by accident. I was getting my morning coffee at the 7-11 on my way to work. When I lived with her, Lucy wasn't even awake at that hour."

"Where do you work, anyway?"

"At that time I was a mechanic in a garage." He grinned. "Now I'm working part-time in a second-hand bookstore."

"Quite the renaissance man," I smiled back. "It must have been a shock to run into them." But what I was really wondering was how it had been for Lucy.

"Well, at least I now knew what Brennan looked like." He said it in a quiet but significant voice.

I gave him a sharp look. "Were you worried? I mean for your own safety?"

"The man had been in prison for murder."

Manslaughter, I corrected in my head. But I knew Curtis would tell me there was no difference. There were definitely some similarities between him and Marc. Maybe that was why I liked him.

"I wouldn't say I was worried," Curtis was saying. "Just more aware."

"But you still kept in contact with Lucy."

He shrugged. "What can I say? I liked the woman. We were friends. But it wasn't like we saw each other all the time. It was mostly phone calls, and not all that often."

"Did she … did she say anything about Tim and her? How things were going?"

Curtis wiped a hand over his eyes as if remembering was an effort. "Yes and no. I remember the first thing she complained about was his grammar."

I gave a wry smile, remembering Tim's letters. "But he wrote to her. She would have known he was no English major."

"I think she made excuses for him while he was in prison. You know, being surrounded by all those other bohunks—that was her term, by the way—he wouldn't be able to help himself. But when he was living in her house, and she was introducing him to her friends and had to listen to him every day…."

I was nodding. "It would be a whole other story."

"That and his redneck attitudes. She found herself with a country-music loving, gay-hating, sports-loving bohunk. There was no point in saying 'I told you so.'"

I was suddenly taken back to my second visit to Lucy's after Tim had got out. The time I had cycled down. Early September. I had been elated that Marc and I seemed to have come to a place of acceptance about our differences. Lucy had tried to tell me we were on a journey to acceptance of "the other." I had laughed at her. I was just trying to get along with my guy. But when Tim had joined us at dinner, she'd said, "Ellen and Marc are going through *exactly* what we are." I remembered I'd had no idea what she was referring to; she had let me do all the talking that day. Had it been about their different interests? Their contradictory attitudes? It would make sense. But in prison he'd claimed to be a jazz lover and to be interested in all the metaphysical things she was. Had he lied?

"Where are you?" asked Curtis.

I started, and laughed. "Being haunted by a ghost."

"As are we all," he said wryly. "Are you hungry? I've got the fixings for a Greek salad."

I *was* hungry. I had lost track of time. It must be going on eight. The sun was lighting up the pine tree in a golden green glow.

The salad was good. It fortified us for another several hours of talking, this time in the cottage. It had been the family cottage, Curtis explained, but he'd moved in permanently after he and Lucy had broken up. The furniture was cottage furniture. Outdated but comfortable. We sat end to end on the lime-green couch.

It was after eleven when I finally took my leave. We had been talking for almost seven hours. My head was full. I needed to go home and unload it.

"You're still tense," Curtis said when we stood at my car saying good-bye. "I thought you said you were on holiday."

I made a gesture with my hand that reminded me of Marc. A gesture that said: Are you surprised?

Before I could stop him, Curtis had turned me around and was massaging my shoulders. "This isn't a come-on. You look like you're carrying around a plank in your shoulders. Maybe you should see a massage therapist."

The only massages I'd ever had before had been a method of foreplay. But I believed him that this wasn't a pass. We had spent an enjoyable evening together, but our common point of interest was Lucy, not each other. And his hands meant business. They weren't caressing, they were digging, finding all my trigger points.

"Ouch!"

"You have to relax and go into the pain," said Curtis.

"I cannot pretend to enjoy pain."

"Okay." I could feel him grinning behind me. "Really enjoy it then. You've got so many knots. It would be my pleasure to get at them."

"To torture me you mean." I scrunched up my neck when he pressed on one particularly painful spot.

"Okay, call me your torturer if you must. It's for your own good."

"Would that make me a vic—*ouch!*" This time I pulled away, half grimacing, half laughing. Rubbing my shoulder. "Okay, okay, I need a massage. You've convinced me. But not from you. Is there a professional you recommend? Trish Cousins maybe?"

"Kendra MacKenzie," said Curtis, without hesitation. "She's right in the market—didn't you say you work in the market? I'll give you her phone number. I've had a lot of massages in my life and she's the best."

The phone was flashing when I got home. A Private Caller had phoned at four, just after I had left for Curtis's. "Hello, Ellen," said my private caller's voice. "I'm sorry you're not there. I'll call you in the morning. At ten."

Don't call me. He didn't say it, but it was implicit in his tone. So was the order: *Make sure you're there.*

I couldn't believe he had called the moment I'd left to see Curtis. He seemed to have a sixth sense when it came to men and me. But maybe he was going to come and see me at last. We could finally talk. I had a thousand questions. And only half of them were about Lucy.

I slipped out the back door in my bare feet and felt my way in the dark to one of the Muskoka chairs on the lawn. Wispy clouds obscured the full impact of the starry night sky. I filtered Curtis's stories through what I already knew—or thought I knew—about Lucy. Back in the house I continued with my notes late into the night.

❦

SHE WOKE, WOOZY AND HEADACHEY, from a fitful sleep. Tim's snoring had kept her awake, not to mention their sexual hunger for each other after all these months. She felt raw inside but satiated. It hadn't exactly been romantic, tender love-making. But the urgency, she had to admit, had been on both sides. And at least they'd been in a bed, not in the corner or the bathroom of the prison visiting room. There would be plenty of time for tender romance. A life time.

The other side of the bed was empty. It was only seven-thirty. She was tempted to try to sleep awhile longer, maybe even just to sit up and do her meditation right there in bed. But she could hear cupboards banging overhead.

She rushed upstairs. A loud announcer on the radio was telling the Joke of the Day.

"Morning, sunshine," Tim said, turning to smile at her. He looked sleepy too, unshaven, puffy-eyed. "'Bout time you got up; I been up for hours. You got any coffee in the house?"

"What on earth have you got on the radio? Where's CBC?"

"I don't want to listen to that crap. I found a decent station."

"But it's *country*. Since when do you listen to country?"

Tim shrugged. "Just my whole life."

Her mouth gaped. Who was this man, standing in her kitchen? "But I thought you liked jazz and classical."

Tim shrugged again. "That's okay too. What do I gotta do to get a coffee?"

She clamped her mouth shut and turned to push the curtains back on the kitchen window. The sun was shining. It was going to be a beautiful day. Tim was allowed to have interests she didn't share. Didn't *know* about. "Let's go over to Bank Street," she said. "We can find coffee and a croissant."

She went back downstairs to dress. She would be patient. There was clearly going to be an adjustment period. Meditation and yoga could wait 'til later.

Outside in the sunshine, Tim took her hand. Such a simple thing to bring her such pleasure—a man who liked to hold hands.

At the corner of Bank Street, Tim paused and her hand was suddenly gripped hard. She was about to protest when it dawned on her: he was terrified. Of the traffic, the noise, the busyness. She understood this kind of terror. And she hadn't spent the last fifteen years in a penal institution. She gave his hand a reassuring squeeze.

They walked along the store-lined street. She pointed out the shops—the Fresh Fruit Company, the antique store, the outdoor store where she had bought the mountain bike she'd given to him last night.

Tim was saying something in response, but she didn't hear it. There was a rushing wind in her ears. Because there he was, coming out of the 7-11 with a styrofoam cup: Curtis.

For a moment, she thought she was seeing things. She never ran into Curtis on Bank Street. The coincidence was astounding. And, by the startled look on his face, very real.

For a second they met each other's eyes, sharing the knowledge of knowing each other and knowing that Tim didn't know they did. There was a moment of what seemed to Lucy a silent debate of whether they would let him in on that knowledge. For a second she was happy for Curtis just to see them walking together, holding hands, as he rarely had. She would have been satisfied with that silent gloat if she hadn't seen the wariness in his eyes when she and Tim drew closer. He didn't want to be introduced.

That clinched it.

Neither man offered his hand to the other. Tim looked startled, then equally wary.

She wished she hadn't said anything. What had been fun as knowledge between Curtis and herself was awkward and embarrassing among the three of them.

Curtis raised his coffee, as if in a mocking toast, and got into his truck, parked at the curb right beside them.

Tim stared down the street after the truck. Then he turned back to Lucy, dropped her hand. "I thought you said he didn't live around here." His voice was angry.

"He doesn't. I never see him around here. He must have stopped on his way to work." It was ludicrous. She was being defensive—apologizing for Curtis.

She took Tim into the Second Cup. She left him at a table and went to the counter to order two lattes.

Tim made a face when he took a sip. "What is this yuppie crap? Alls I want is a coffee and doughnut."

"All," she said automatically.

The bewildered look on Tim's face irritated her. He should know that one; she had corrected him enough times. But she knew it wasn't just about his grammar, that bewilderment. It was about being in a yuppie coffee place on a city street. He looked like a biker in a tea room—an annoyed biker at that. Tim stood up—to go, Lucy thought, to the counter to order a plain coffee. He was at the door before she realized he was leaving.

"Where are you going?"

Half a dozen startled heads turned at her raised voice.

Tim didn't turn around. The next instant he was gone.

She grabbed her bag and ran out the door. There was no sign of him in the direction of her house. She turned to scan the other way. And spotted him several doors down, frozen on the spot. He looked, she realized, like herself, having a panic attack. Except it was even worse for him: he wanted to go home but he had no idea where that was.

She arrived at his side, out of breath. Took his arm. "Tim," she said gently, "it's the other way."

Tim came out of his daze. The look in his eyes shifted. He shrugged off her hand. "I know it's the other way. I'm looking for an effing coffee." (Lying to save his pride, she knew.) "And after I get some, I'm going to turn myself in to the police."

"What?"

"I obviously don't fit in here. And you don't care. I'm goin' back."

"You can't do that." It was Lucy's turn to panic. Everything she had worked for, for so long … admitting to everyone she had failed. She wasn't sure he even had the option of going back. She didn't want him to go back.

"Let's go home. I'll make coffee there. Then we'll go to the Welfare office."

17.

STEVE QUINN SEEMED TO FILL the house. He also seemed ill at ease. I was in my own place, on my own. And yet there was still a barrier. The barrier of the case. And Quinn didn't step over that barrier. He didn't hug me or kiss me. As usual, I was conflicted about that.

It was four o'clock on a hot August afternoon. I was back at work now, but had come home early to meet him. He had an hour, he'd said on the phone. He couldn't come any later. He had to be somewhere by five-thirty. If I hadn't known better I would have thought by his tone that he meant home for dinner.

He was in work clothes, but the sleeves of his white dress-shirt were rolled up to his elbows and the top button undone, revealing even more of that thick mat of chest hair. "Now this," he said, looking up at the tongue-in-groove ceiling, "is exactly the kind of place I'm looking for."

I was pleased to hear it, but surprised. It seemed too small, too "quaint" for him. Belle and Beau came and nosed at him. Marc had dropped them off that morning, his truck already loaded for his trip down the Dumoine. For the first time, the sight of the canoe in the back of the truck didn't fill me with dread. I told him to enjoy himself and realized I meant it. There was nothing at stake anymore. I could be generous. It felt good. On impulse I hugged him good-bye. And then wished I hadn't. The physical memories were too fresh, too tender. And his response too warm. Now, in Quinn's presence, I banished him from my head.

"So the dogs *are* yours," said Quinn, giving Belle a pat on the head. "Did you get custody?"

"Shared," I admitted.

"So you are having contact with Marc?" Was there a note of anger in his voice? I gave him a quick look but his face wore an expression of mild curiosity.

"Just over the dogs."

I took him out to the backyard and through the break in the trees at the bottom of the yard. We crossed the railway tracks and I led him through a narrow opening in thick bushes. You had to know it was there. I liked that. The path opened onto the small grassy point. Shrubs lined the southeast side. In them I had stashed a folded lawn chair. The northwest side sloped down to the water, lined by rock and small boulders.

I gestured to the point as we came through. "This, in theory, is my access point."

"If you wanted access," Quinn said, nodding his understanding. Then he gestured at the lawn chair in the bushes. "Nice secluded place to sunbathe."

I ignored his suggestive tone.

We crossed back over the tracks and ducked through the break in the trees into my yard. I spoke over my shoulder. "I'd offer you a beer, but I doubt you're allowed on duty. Would you like a—"

"Beer, yes."

He shrugged when I turned to look at him. "I've taken the rest of the day off."

We sat in the Muskoka chairs in the backyard with the dogs at our feet and clinked beer bottles. "To your new life," he said. "You've got a really nice set-up here. I'm envious." Then he added in a more serious tone, "I hope you've been able to put all this behind you. Though I realize you can't really until the trial is over. But take a break while you can. It was a stressful few months for you."

"When is the trial going to be? I've been going crazy over it. The defence is going to take me to pieces over my witness statement to the Quebec *Sûreté*. I wish you guys had taken my statement later that week when I was thinking more clearly."

"Stop worrying. You'll be fine."

"They won't ask me about the—dreams will they?"

"El, I honestly don't know."

I didn't normally like my name being shortened, but it came so naturally out of Quinn's mouth—sounded so *familiar*—I didn't mind.

"But why are you worried?" he added. "We often use psychics."

I sighed. "And you think they're kooks."

"Well, when they're sexy kooks, we don't mind." He was laughing at me. "You'll be subpoenaed," he added. "As for when?" He gave an exaggerated shrug. "The wheels of justice."

He saw my look of dismay. "Don't worry, they *are* moving. There will be a pre-trial hearing first. Probably this fall or winter. I can't say for sure when, but *soon*." He gave me a significant look and repeated, "*Soon*."

Then it was his turn to sigh. He punctuated it with a long swig of beer. "Anyway, stop stewing about it, Ellen." He sounded annoyed. "Put it out of your mind."

"You've got to be joking. I think about it all the time. I have a thousand questions."

He spread his hands. "Well, take advantage of the fact that I'm here then. Ask away."

But my mind went blank. I spread my own hands in a gesture of futility. Where to begin?

"How are you doing here on your own? You're not nervous? Not afraid?"

"No. You've got him safely in custody, haven't you?"

"Yes, the bastard. Just give me five minutes with him."

He must have seen the look of alarm on my face. "It boils my blood when I think about men like him beating up on women, and frightening other ones. I hope they throw away the key this time."

"Just how bad was it—Tim beating up on Lucy?" Curtis too had hinted at abuse. But he hadn't known any details. Did *I* want to know them?

"Pretty bad. A couple of trips to the hospital that we've been able to ascertain so far. Once for a sprained ankle. That was in the fall. The other for a sternum injury. Much more serious. That was at Easter. Just the week before she went missing. God knows how many injuries didn't make it to the hospital."

I cringed. "What were they fighting about?" The differences Curtis and I had talked about didn't seem serious enough to warrant physical violence. Did the injuries correspond with her contact with Curtis? She'd been with *him* at Easter. I tried to hide the shudder that ran through me.

"What weren't they fighting about?" said Quinn. "Money was a *major* issue. And it's clear he was jealous. Of all Lucy's male friends but especially her ex, Curtis Fry." He nodded at me. "You met him. You were talking to him at the memorial."

Did he notice everything? I nodded. I didn't trust myself to talk about Curtis. For various reasons. "You said before he defrauded her. How did he do that?"

Quinn was shaking his head. He glanced at his watch. "That's a longer story than I've got time for now. But you know she set him up in a handyman business."

I nodded.

"Well, that took a lot of money—according to Brennan. He told us he kept saying to Lucy 'you gotta spend money to make money.' He claimed to be buying tools, supplies. And he needed a truck. But funnily enough, the first truck got stolen—and all the tools with it. That was in the fall I think. So of course he needs another truck, and more tools. And then—lo and behold—that one gets stolen too."

"So I don't see how that's defrauding her."

"Sweetheart, it wasn't really stolen. The first truck was found burnt out in a field. He probably set fire to it himself. Him and his friends. The tools were gone. No doubt he got money for them. And probably for the second truck too—it was a van, a Curbmaster, all set up as a portable workshop. I can't remember how much Lucy poured into the business. Something like nine thousand dollars in the first month alone. And the thefts, and the burnt-out truck, provided a convenient excuse for another scam of his."

"Which was?"

"He was being threatened—he said—by a biker gang. They were—he said—extorting money from him." He snorted.

"How do you know it's not true?"

Quinn just shook his head at my naiveté. "It's all lies. Everything he fed her was lies."

"So he told her about the threats?"

"Probably not at first. But when the money started disappearing from her account, she no doubt confronted him. And he had his story ready."

"He had access to her account?"

"She tried to get him his own account but—funnily enough—the bank wouldn't give him one. So she gave him full access to her own. Including a bank card and a cheque book. So he was writing cheques left, right and centre. She had a thirty-thousand-dollar line of credit. But she never used it except very occasionally. And always paid it back within a week or two at the most. Suddenly, for the first time in her life, she finds herself in the red. And it just keeps getting deeper and deeper."

"How do you know all this?"

"We've got a forensics accountant looking into her financial affairs. And the asshole's being questioned, and giving us his bullshit stories. We've just started talking to her friends too. The picture's beginning to come together. It's not a pretty one. Then there are the forged cheques and the whole Bill Torrence scenario. But," he looked at his watch again. "I'm afraid I've got to get going."

His mention of the forensics accountant reminded me of the other kind of forensics. "Was there any evidence found on her body?"

Quinn had got to his feet. "Well, I'd say 'remains.'" His eyes were trained on mine as I stood up. "There wasn't much left of her. It was a hot spring. And she hadn't been buried."

I put a hand on the back of the chair. "And is there any hard evidence in the—remains?"

Quinn shook his head. "No, the hyoid bone was never found."

"The what bone?"

Quinn took a step closer. "Hyoid. It's the bone under here." His hands were suddenly around my neck. He pressed his thumbs lightly on the front of my throat. "It's a small horseshoe-shaped thing. The one that breaks when you choke someone."

"Don't press too hard then," I joked. I wondered if he could feel my pulse hammering in my throat. I could still feel his hands after he took them away. They were warm and dry. Gentle. Presuming.

It was a moment before he stepped back. An electric moment.

He spoke in a neutral tone. "The only thing we have to go on is the teeth."

"You mean her dental records?"

He shook his head. "No. Their colour. They were pink."

"*Pink?*" I felt sick.

"There are three things that make the teeth go pink." He spoke in a detached scientist's voice. "Choking, asphyxiation, and drowning." He checked them off one by one on his fingers. "The pressure causes red cells from the blood vessels that supply the teeth to seep into the enamel. It stains them pink. We're running some further tests now."

We walked back up to the house in silence. The vision of Lucy's pink teeth had made me feel sick. And angry.

"We are not—" said Quinn, beside his car.

"Having this conversation," I finished. "I know. I do appreciate your telling me the things you do."

"You deserve to know. And it really doesn't have any bearing on your own testimony, so there's no reason you shouldn't know. Except the Crown would have a fit. As he would if he knew I was here." He began to jiggle his keys. "El." He avoided my eyes. "I'm not going to be able to see you for awhile. Or call."

I should have been relieved, but my heart jolted in disappointment. "Because of the case."

He looked as though he was going to say something else, but he repeated my words: "Because of the case. One of us will be calling you when the hearing gets under way. You'll be called in for an interview to review your testimony. But until then…."

"I understand," I said. I opened my mouth to say it was probably better this way. But it got covered, briefly, by Quinn's mouth.

"Now be good, " he said, pulling back. And he was into his car almost before I had time to register the kiss.

I took myself down to the point to do just that. In the warm sun I leaned back in the lawn chair and closed my eyes. Replayed his kiss. It had been brief but warm. *Claiming*. He had no right to claim me, but there it was. I was letting myself be claimed. There had been no chance to ask him what was going on with us. Or with him. The slightly stressed air still hung about him.

His stresses probably didn't hold a candle to Lucy's. Her stresses wouldn't have started with money—or even, likely, Curtis. They would have been about the simple everyday things. A man gets out of prison after fifteen years and comes to live with you. He has little experience of the outside world. You have to show him how to do everything. Even how to get around. He has a lousy sense of direction and keeps getting lost. It would be like having a child suddenly on your hands. Worse, because you'd be expecting him to act like an adult.

Compound all that with your own fears and idiosyncrasies—and temper—and there would have been frequent fireworks.

⚬⚬⚬

JULY FIRST ARRIVED. SHE HAD never made much of Canada Day. She certainly wasn't keen on fireworks. But Tim was excited about the celebrations, and his excitement was contagious. They planned to go to Parliament Hill that evening, to watch the display. During the day, the festive atmosphere permeating the city infected them both. They had a peaceful day of kind words and affectionate hugs; she even let Tim take her off to bed for an hour in the afternoon. She dozed contentedly in his arms afterward. It was worth being reminded that they did fit, sexually. More than with any other lover, even if he didn't kiss as well as Curtis.

When dusk came, she packed up a blanket and extra jackets for both of them. "I guess I should drive, shouldn't I?"

Tim nodded.

But she found herself wishing he could handle driving at night. On the way to the city centre, he did nothing but criticize: she wasn't watching carefully enough, she was following too closely, she wasn't quick enough off the mark when the light turned green. She reigned in her retorts, needing all her concentration to navigate through the traffic around the Hill. "Just find me a parking spot."

There were no available street spots. The expensive lot they finally found was miles away, and the cars were squeezed in so tight she was afraid she was going to scratch her car. It didn't help to have Tim yelling at her to watch out every time she turned the wheel.

The crowds on the Hill were suffocating. The exhaust fumes from all the cars that had driven into the downtown core seemed to hang in the air. They found a place to sit, but barely had space to spread out the blanket.

"Why didn't we come earlier?" asked Tim. "You shoulda known it was gonna be this crowded."

"I didn't know," she retorted. "I never come here."

The music from the performers was hundreds of decibels too loud. The fireworks sounded like rifle shots. She couldn't relax. Every time another firecracker went whistling up into the air, she grabbed Tim's arm, waiting for the explosion. She wished she'd brought her earplugs; she could have enjoyed the displays without the sound. Without the noise they were spectacular. She could feel her tension affecting Tim, making him tense too. Why hadn't they just stayed home and watched it on TV?

Finally the show was over. She pushed the panic away as people pushed at her, everyone wanting to get off the Hill at once.

She wanted a frozen yogurt, something to soothe her insides, but they couldn't find one on Bank Street. She was voluble in her complaints. It seemed unjust that after all she had just suffered she couldn't get a simple soothing snack.

And then Tim disappeared. She was walking down the street with him one minute, and the next he was gone. She stopped in her tracks, letting the crowd stream by her, her eyes searching frantically. But he was gone. As if he'd just walked away from her. Maybe he had. There was nothing to do but keep walking to the parking lot and go home. He'd call from a pay phone eventually.

There were no messages on the answering machine. She opened up the bag of popcorn she'd bought at the 7-11 on her way home and sat down on the couch to wait. She had devoured half the bag before the phone rang.

Tim's voice yelled in her ear. She held the receiver a foot away and could still hear him. This time, he said, he was really going to the police station. He was fed up. All she did was complain—about the crowds, and the firecracker noise, and the traffic fumes, and not getting her precious frozen yogurt. And not being able to take constructive criticism about her driving.

She did her own share of yelling. His "constructive criticism" had been back-seat driving. She didn't need his criticism.

"Some of your own medicine," he shot back.

When he was finally done, forty-five minutes later, she got back in the car to bring him home.

18.

THE IMAGE OF LUCY'S PINK teeth haunted me. It had been a hot spring, Quinn had said, and she hadn't been buried. But as disturbing as they were, the pink teeth were also oddly reassuring. Drowning had not been ruled out as a possibility. Maybe there *was* some truth to my visions. Even though they felt unreal now. I decided I would concentrate on finding out what had happened to Lucy *before* she'd gone missing. There were concrete answers out there somewhere.

Marc called as soon as he got back from the Dumoine. I could hear the excitement, the *rush*, of the river in his voice. These trips always energized him. I had been selfish to begrudge him. Except it had been all he *ever* wanted to do and talk about. I wasn't entirely to blame. Now he wanted to get together for dinner. But I was ready for him. Or rather, I *wasn't* ready for him. Curtis's words about taking the time to gain some emotional distance had hit a nerve. And Quinn, in his inimitable way, had been recommending distance too. The hug I'd given Marc before he'd left had shown me I needed it.

I felt his rush deflate when I told him. "We can still share the dogs, but I just don't think it's a good idea to spend time together right now. I need some time. *We* need some time. To adjust."

I prepared myself for protests, or even silence, but to my surprise I got agreement. He admitted the hug had confused him, he had thought about me all week. I felt a pang of warmth for him, for this new openness. Why did closeness always come when you were on your way out? I had a sudden feeling that Lucy had probably felt the same way with Curtis. He'd said that as soon as he'd committed, she'd dumped him for Tim. But maybe as soon as he'd committed he'd stopped trying. *Until* she'd dumped him for Tim. And by then it would have been too late.

Marc and I came up with an amicable agreement for sharing the dogs while minimizing our own contact. But when I got off the phone I felt flat rather than relieved. It was necessary, I told myself. With Steve Quinn too. It would be good for me to have time away from both of them. And there were other people to call.

Curtis was a rare male who liked to talk on the phone. He enjoyed talking, period. I could see why Lucy had been attracted to him. Much more than I could see why she'd been attracted to Tim. Tonight I asked Curtis about his attraction to *her*. I leaned back on the futon couch, enjoying the sound of his voice in my ear. It was ten o'clock. We often called each other late in the evening and talked long into the night on our one-track topic.

"We were very compatible," he was saying. "We were both vegetarians. We both loved the country. And downtown. We loved riding our bikes around. We both loved jazz. We loved to dance. To fuck. To talk and debate. No subject was taboo. You knew her—she had the quickest mind of just about any woman I've ever known. It was the negative dovetail that got in the way."

"The what dovetail?"

"The negative dovetail. We fit together in a way that reinforced all the negative stuff we each had inside."

"Oh, you mean bringing out the worst in each other."

"Yeah," said Curtis. "That too." He paused. Then, "She was fuckin' crazy."

"What were you doing with her then?"

Another pause. "I was attracted to the woman."

"Is that all?"

"She was smart. She could make you believe black was white and up was down. She was in fuckin' denial." He was scornful. And full of admiration. In spite of himself, it seemed. "What can I say? She turned my crank."

"Sooo," I drew out the word, hesitating. But I could feel Curtis waiting for me to speak. He liked me to challenge him. In this, too, he was a rare male. He didn't often change his mind, but at least he listened. I could see how this might have driven Lucy crazy. Someone listens, you think maybe they'll get your point, give one over to you. I had a feeling Curtis had rarely given one over to Lucy. He'd never given one over to me in all the weeks we'd been calling each other or getting together. But he let me talk.

"What were you going to say?" he prompted now. He was enjoying this. I could hear it in his voice.

"Well, just that you've given me compelling reasons why you got involved with Lucy. You made a choice. You can't blame her for that." Our argument about victims was ongoing.

"I agree there's no point in blaming anyone," he said. "I agree everyone is responsible for their actions. But I won't agree no one is a victim. I could drive down there and throw you across the room and you couldn't do anything about it, because I'm stronger than you."

"Yes, but you wouldn't," I said calmly. I was used to this violent example by now. It no longer shocked or worried me. I wasn't sure how I knew. But there was a certainty inside me that he was just blustering, *theorizing*, as disturbing as it was. "Anyway, you and your victims," I added. "You sound just like the minister at the memorial service."

"Why? Because you thought you were at a service for a woman who'd died of breast cancer?" I could hear the amusement in his voice.

I grimaced. "That and her assumption that Lucy had been a helpless victim. I didn't know Lucy very well, but she didn't come across to me as a victim of violence."

Curtis gave a laugh that had no humour in it. "Lucy was not a victim of violence. You're right about that. But there was violence. I think she was *born* with it. She surrounded herself in it."

I felt a kind of excitement rising in me. Had I been right that yelling and fighting had been a normal part of her interaction with people? But *why?*

"Lucy wasn't a victim of violence," he repeated. He made the most of his sentences. He would have made a good stage actor. He paused to make sure I was listening. Then he let fly the zinger: "She was the perpetrator."

—— ≈≈≈ ——

THE FIRST PERSON SHE EVER hit was her mother. She hadn't meant to. It was six o'clock. Her father was in the sunroom with his paper. Her mother was in the kitchen. Anna was in her room, her stuffed animals arranged on the bed as if on a boat.

She ran downstairs to the kitchen. She wanted to help. She wanted to make her favourite *süti*—cookies—the ones that were actually two stuck together with jam.

"I want to make *legényfogó*," she said to her mother's back.

It didn't come out right. She'd meant to ask nicely, not demand.

Her mother's back remained turned to her. "I'm making your father's dinner."

She ran up to the counter. She almost touched her mother's skirt. She looked up with a big grin on her face. Playful. "Not mine too?"

No response.

"Not mine? Not Anna's?"

There was a sigh from her mother. She wasn't supposed to sigh. She was supposed to laugh, to get the joke.

"Mine too," she insisted. "You're making my dinner, too. Right? And Anna's. Right?"

It was a joke. She wanted her mother to laugh. And it was true. She wanted her mother to say yes!

Still no response. Her frustration escalated. "You're making my dinner too! And Anna's. And yours. We're all eating!"

Her mother turned and stared down at her.

She waited. She held her breath. She had yelled, so now her mother was supposed to get mad. She was supposed to smack her. That's what happened in other people's houses.

But not in her house. Her mother just kept staring. As if she wasn't there. Or as if her mother wasn't there.

Her mother was supposed to be there. She reached out to touch her. She wanted to make sure her mother was really there. She was so anxious, her hand extended faster than she intended. And in a fist. Right in her mother's stomach. Hard.

There was a soft thud. A groan from her mother. An expulsion of air. Her mother's hand gripping her own stomach. And then the air was suddenly charged with tension, fear, excitement. The kitchen door was swinging with it; her father was in the room.

This was it. He was going to come over and wallop her for sure. And she'd be able to kick and punch and yell. And then it would be over. And everyone would feel better.

But her father just stood in the doorway. Newspaper folded in one hand.

"What is going on, Susan?"

Everything was in slow motion. The way she turned her head to look up at her mother. The way she had to wait—fear, hope, fear, hope—for her response. The way her mother removed her hand from her stomach and took in a long breath.

"It's alright, Michael. Lucy just wanted to help."

Disbelief. Disappointment. Rage. "I did not! I did not!"

She threw herself down on the floor, where she could kick and punch and yell. If only the floor would fight back. If only she would feel better after.

When she was spent, tear-stained, bruised, she found herself alone on the kitchen floor. Everything was still. Even the kitchen door had stopped swinging.

The floor was hard. She pressed herself against it. She wanted it to yield. When it didn't, she picked herself up and took her bruised bones up to her room. She threw herself face down on the bed. The bed yielded only a little.

She couldn't believe she had punched her mother. That no one had punched her back. She thought about her fist sinking into her mother's stomach. It had been softer than she'd expected. Her fist had gone in deeper than she'd expected.

It was the first physical contact she could remember ever having with her mother. She replayed it over and over in her mind. She slowed it down. She made it gentle.

She put her hand on her own bare tummy and pretended it was her mother's tummy. Her mother's stomach got even softer. It pulled her fist in gently, surrounded it with softness. It loosened her fingers and made them relax, so there was no more fist. There were just her fingers caressing her tummy.

It felt good to have her hand on her tummy. She pretended her hand was her mother's hand. Stroking. Comforting.

And then the hand slipped farther down her tummy, to the place where things started to tingle. And even farther down, to the place that created the warmth and the tingling. She crawled under the covers and pulled them up around her chin, and stroked herself to sleep.

QUINN'S FINGERS STROKED ME AWAKE. They knew their instrument. They played it delicately, eliciting a yearning song of sensation from every nerve ending. Warmth spread from my groin to my whole body. And then I was burning up.

I opened my eyes and found myself in my own bed. Alone. Soaked in sweat. There were no sensitive fingers on my groin. Not even my own. The heat was from the duvet I must have pulled over me sometime in the night. It was still night. Four a.m.

I got up, exchanging my damp T-shirt for a dry one. It wasn't the first time I wished I had the nerve just to go down to the river on a hot night and jump in. This August was a hotter one than usual, even the nights. A shower would have to do. A *cold* one.

The face in the dream had been Quinn's, but the touch ... I had to admit, the touch had been Marc's. I put the dream out of my mind and returned my thoughts to my conversation with Curtis.

I had never experienced the kind of anger and frustration he had described. Thank God. I thought back to the few times I had been the target of Lucy's wrath. It wasn't anything to take personally. It warranted sympathy—for the little girl inside Lucy who was only looking for a sign, any sign—a slap was as good as a hug—that she was loved. But over the years, all anger had brought was disaster. Unfulfilled relationships. Physical and verbal abuse heaped on her head. The stripping away of her money, her dignity. Regret, possibly, that she'd ever left Curtis. A slow road to hell. Was that all there had been to the last year of her life? All the evidence pointed to it. All the evidence, at least, that I'd gathered so far.

It was, I decided, as I cooled my frustrated flesh under the shower, time to call Trish.

SHE WAS READING OVER AN ad he'd put together to advertise his handyman business. It was full of spelling errors. She had a red pen in her hand. Circling them, she felt like her father. Exacting. Relentless. But she couldn't help herself.

Tim was looking over her shoulder. "Give me a fucking break! I can't do this right, I can't do that right. You're a fucking nit-picking bitch. Curtis should get a prize for putting up with you for so long."

She was on her feet, coming at him with her fists. How dare he call her a bitch. How dare he bring Curtis into this.

Tim knocked her fists away from him as if they were flies. She stumbled and he grabbed her hair and pulled her back to her feet. Flung her back into the kitchen chair.

She was so enraged she picked up a glass from the table and aimed it at him. It went whizzing past him and smashed against the fridge.

Tim pulled her to her feet again, his hand a vice clamped around her wrists. He held her away from him. "Now cool down." She didn't see him reach for his can of beer. The next minute, she was gasping as cold sticky liquid came pouring over her head and down her face and shirt.

She kicked at him. "Fuck off!"

"You fuck off!" He held her farther away and poured the rest of the beer over her head.

"There—now you don't need to lay into me anymore. You're all calm and cool." He shoved her away and stormed out the door.

She picked herself up off the floor and took herself into the bathroom. She turned on the shower and stepped in. Water, beer, and tears ran together down the drain. She peeled off her clothes, item by item, and let them fall in a sodden heap in the bottom of the tub. She wished she could keep peeling off the layers, the layers of self-importance, of self-righteousness. She was disgusted with herself—with her sanctimonious attempts at "improving" Tim, her lame wrist-wringing, her holier-than-thou nit-picking. Who was she fooling? It wasn't Tim's behaviour she couldn't stand. It was herself. She wasn't where she wanted to be, or who she wanted to be. This relationship was supposed to get her there, but it only seemed to be getting her further and further away. None of it made sense. She had chosen to be healed through this relationship but didn't want to accept the medicine she was being given.

She gave a sudden yank on the taps, turning the water from hot to extreme cold and made herself stand under it until she had become a numbed mass of ice.

Dressed in clean dry clothes, her insides warmed by a mug of tea, she swept up the glass and got on her hands and knees to mop up the beer. She deserved to have beer poured over her head. She deserved to be cleaning it up. She couldn't believe she was having these thoughts. The realization hit her with a shock: she was being abused.

She wrung out the rag into the bucket one last time, wincing at her sore wrists. She resolved to let Tim be. Not to react to the things that bugged her. To let him speak and act in his own way. It wasn't his fault if he couldn't speak about the more philosophical things in life; he had never had the luxury of such thought. She would focus on the good things: his affection, his optimism about the money he was going to make, his willingness to help out around the house.

Even more, she resolved to be gentle with herself. That was going to be the hardest of all.

19.

TRISH AND MARNIE SHARED A condominium in a high-rise on Queen Elizabeth Drive. The condo was spacious and luxurious, with hardwood floors and floor-to-ceiling windows that offered a panoramic view of the canal and the city beyond.

"Marnie's the reason we can be here," explained Trish when I admired it. "She works for Nortel."

We smiled knowingly at each other. The high-tech company was doing exceptionally well.

Trish took me through the living room to her massage and counselling rooms. Next to the modern scarcity of furniture in the living room, these were small, intimate, carpeted rooms. Both were decorated in warm colours, with Native art on the walls and New Age music playing softly, with a mild background hiss, on a tape deck in the massage room. The rooms were warm as Trish was warm. I could imagine Lucy coming here to relax (as much as she was able) and bare her soul in safety. There was a vaguely familiar aroma in the air.

"Shall we sit in here?" asked Trish. She gestured to the couch in the counselling room. "If you can forget it's for counselling, I find it the most comfortable room in the house."

She bade me sit down while she went off to make a pot of tea.

"What's that scent?" I asked when she came back with a tray. "It's driving me crazy. I can't identify it."

"It's patchouli," said Trish with a smile. "I used patchouli massage oil on my last client, and it's still permeating the air. I used to use patchouli on Lucy, too; it has relaxing properties in it." She set the tray down on the coffee table and poured tea into two mugs and handed me one. Her hands were elegant but looked strong.

I thanked her and cupped my hands around the mug. "That's why it smells familiar then. Lucy sometimes had that aroma around her. And it was in her bathroom too. I never knew what it was."

Trish smiled again. "It's not that common anymore. It was a sixties thing."

"Lucy was pretty hyper, wasn't she?" I took a sip of the hot tea.

Trish nodded. "She used to tell me she wished she could sit still for five fidgetless minutes. Her coffee-drinking habit didn't help, but she said it woke up her brain and got the ideas crackling. But it got her body crackling too. She had a love-hate relationship with coffee." She gave a soft laugh. "I sometimes felt like I was doing battle more with the caffeine in Lucy's veins than with Lucy."

"The stillest moments she ever had were probably right in the next room, lying on your table."

"I had to work hard to get her to those moments," said Trish. She herself sat very still, her hands in her lap. She projected the same aura of serenity as she had at the church.

"Was it…." I hesitated. Now that I was here, it didn't feel right to be asking her about Lucy. It felt like it might be breaking a counsellor's confidence. I looked at her. "I have a zillion questions, but I don't want to put you in a compromising position. I'm not sure what's appropriate to ask, or how much you feel you can tell me."

Trish nodded. "I've been thinking about that since you called. If Lucy were still alive, it would be an entirely different matter, but under the circumstances … well, I know you knew her and it doesn't feel like you've come here to smell out a sensational story." She angled her head to one side, looking at me. "And now that you're here, I sense it will help *you* in some way to hear about Lucy. So I don't mind telling you what I can."

Her words echoed Curtis's. Was my need so obvious? And what was behind it anyway? If asked, I wouldn't be able to explain why it all seemed so urgent to me. "I appreciate that. Though I don't know where to start."

"What were you just about to ask me?" She picked up her mug and took a sip. Then the mug went back to the coffee table and her hands back into her lap.

I shook my head, trying to think. Then I remembered. "Oh, I was going to ask you whether Lucy's jitteriness got worse towards the end—or even after Tim got out? I guess what I really want to know is what happened in that last year. I've been thinking about how stressful it would be to suddenly be sharing your house—your life—with someone who'd lived so many years in prison."

Trish was nodding. "It was extremely stressful—for both of them. Tim had no idea how to live in the outside world. And by that time Lucy was so used to living alone it would have been an adjustment for her to live with anyone, let alone someone just out of prison. She had to show him how to do everything, even things like using debit machines and bank machines."

"I remember Lucy telling me. I hadn't thought about how much technology would have changed by the time he got out."

"A huge adjustment," nodded Trish. "For Lucy too. I don't think she realized just how huge it would be. They were on completely different schedules. She had no time to meditate or do yoga, which were the main things she did to centre herself. Tim didn't want her out of his sight. He was so insecure and afraid in those first weeks. And they had to keep the light on in the bedroom for a long time. He hadn't slept in the dark in fifteen years. So that deprived her of sleep."

I shook my head. "It sounds extremely difficult. For both of them. Did she regret it? Did she ever say?"

Trish smiled. "There's a loaded question. She had *moments* of regretting it, like anyone would. But she also strongly believed—I do too—that they were on a very specific journey together. A journey to healing."

I'm hell-bent on healing the traumas of my past.

"She was determined to heal all her fears," I said.

"Yes, and also determined not to run away this time."

"She told me she was always the one to break up her relationships. She said it was so she wouldn't be abandoned. And I know she was still seeing Curtis when she met Tim."

Trish was nodding. "That was her safety valve. But with Tim she realized that running wasn't going to get her anywhere. As difficult as it was. She was determined to stay and work it through."

"And to get Tim to work through his stuff too?"

"Well, not in a forceful way," she smiled. "He knew he needed help. I saw him a few times too, as a client."

"You did? I didn't realize that."

She nodded. "I can't talk to you about what we talked about, except it probably can't hurt to say he suffered a lot of abuse as a child. And he suffered from bouts of serious depression. He checked himself into the Royal Ottawa once. And he was always threatening to turn himself in to the police. It was very upsetting for Lucy. She thought she was failing to provide him with a safe house while he got back on his feet."

"What about Lucy—did *she* have a safe house?" I was thinking of the violence, the possibility of abuse.

Trish shook her head. "I suggested she go to a shelter once. But she thought I was betraying her. Since I was also encouraging her to be patient with Tim." She paused. "They were both going through an intense healing crisis."

"A healing crisis? What's that? It sounds like a contradiction in terms."

"It's something that can happen when someone is being healed—or afterwards. The healing may bring up emotions and issues that have been buried deep inside, and the healing brings them to the surface in a sudden way that puts the person into emotional—or sometimes even physical—trauma." She paused. "I can't discuss the details of Tim's healing but I never meant it to come at Lucy's expense."

"But it sounds like it was—literally," I said. "I've heard she was thousands of dollars in debt when she died." I didn't word it as "fraud." I wasn't sure how much Trish knew.

She compressed her lips into a sad smile. "Money was a huge issue. Money was very important to Lucy. Her *security* was very important. She suffered from panic attacks—you probably know. She needed to create a safe environment for herself, which meant knowing she had enough money, having a rigid schedule, planning ahead. She didn't like surprises or changes in plans. The two years she spent getting Tim out were an incredible test of that, because she couldn't plan anything—since his parole kept getting denied. She learned to let go a little. It was good for her. The handyman business was an even greater test. It meant she had to put out a certain amount of capital before seeing a return. I felt it was a good test for her, to risk an investment like that. To let go of holding on so tight. As a counsellor, I was there to support her decision. It was unfortunate it never paid off."

Unfortunate, I mused, wasn't the word.

She seemed to read my mind. "I don't know whether all the money she lost was intentional theft by Tim or not. She was becoming more detached about it. But it was a long time before she got there. The more in debt she got, the more stressed out she got. Tim had no concept of how to handle money." She sighed. "The last time I saw her it seemed like she was getting closer to being ready to move on, even without the money."

"And then there was Curtis," I said.

"Curtis. Yes. He was the other big issue. Tim was very jealous that Lucy was still friends with him. I tried to get her to see that. She was very drawn to Curtis again and Tim was afraid he was going to lose her. That may be why he started hurting her."

"You mean physically."

She sighed. "Sometime late in the summer she came to me with a badly sprained ankle. She ended up in the hospital. I did a reiki treatment on her the week after."

"What *is* reiki anyway?" I asked.

Trish smiled. "It's a healing treatment that originated in Japan. It involves moving the body's energy fields around, replacing the negative energy with positive."

"But how do you move the energy fields around?"

"With my hands. I hold them just over the body, not touching. It helps with physical healing and can improve your emotional well-being. Lucy responded to the treatment really well."

"Do you know how she got the injury?"

Trish cocked her head, as if trying to remember. "I don't take notes, but I'm pretty sure they fought about Curtis. She'd been to the Gatineaus. Oh, yes." She looked at me with a smile. "She'd gone up to your house, actually."

"*My* house?" I was shaking my head. I hadn't had a visit from Lucy the previous summer.

"Yes, I remember she said you weren't there. I think they were supposed to go to the racetrack or somewhere that day. Lucy hated the noise and dust and the crowds. I think she refused to go at the last minute. They had a big fight and he stormed out of the house. And she went up to your place to find some quiet by the river. You apparently gave her an open invitation to go up and use your dock?"

I looked at her in amazement. "I guess I did. I'd forgotten that."

———— ∞∞∞ ————

NO ONE ANSWERED THE DOOR. She was glad. She didn't want to have to tell Ellen about Tim's antics. She remembered where the path was beside the canoe rack. She made her way down to the river.

Only when she had written out the morning's episode could she relax. She looked out over the river. Absorbed its stillness. There was barely a breath of wind. Even so, there was relief from the city's heat. She was glad she wasn't at the Speedway. She doubted Tim had gone on his own. No doubt there would be another fight about it when she got home. But at least she would be fortified by this hour of stillness. Maybe it would keep her calm even if he lost it. Somehow she had to convince him that her needing time alone didn't mean she was rejecting him. She wondered how much longer she could go on living like this. It was getting claustrophobic. Was this progress? To exchange the fear of open spaces and abandonment for the fear of being smothered and controlled?

She thought back to what Trish had said to her the other day—that her energy was different, better. She found it hard to believe. She was in just as fucked-up a relationship as ever. But her digestion was better too. Tangible proof. So what was different? That she wasn't running away? Wasn't distracting herself with other men to avoid the pain? Was facing it head on?

She sighed. She longed to be alone. She could handle being alone now.

The truth was this relationship was not what she had expected. And the rage she felt about that was stronger than anything Tim could direct at her—raging anger at herself that it might be just another painful, unhealthy, dead-end relationship.

She looked out at the river. Who would have thought a river could be so stagnant. But of course it wasn't. The stillness was an illusion. If she threw a stick into the middle it would get downstream, eventually. And somewhere underneath there were currents. Strong currents. Currents people couldn't see. Currents of forgiveness. They were inside her. Somewhere. For Tim. For herself.

She thought about Ellen and Marc's house up on the hill behind her. Did Ellen feel abandoned when he left her every summer? What kind of relationship was it, anyway, when he was away so much?

A motorboat carved into the bay, made a big circle, and sped out. The waves from its wake rolled in and rocked the dock. The swaying made her feel sick. She stuck her journal back in her bag and headed back up the path.

—∞∞∞—

"LET ME GUESS," I SAID. "When she came home Tim accused her of being at Curtis's. He lives up in the Gatineaus too."

"Yes," nodded Trish, "that's exactly what happened." She related the events in a calm voice. Her hands were still, never straying from her lap. She seemed somehow detached from the events she was telling me about. "Tim was convinced Lucy was having an affair with Curtis. She told me he forced her down on the bed, said he wanted her to show him how Curtis had done it. She struggled and the futon came partly off the frame. Her foot got caught in the slats. She wrenched it so badly she blacked out for a moment or two." She looked at me then and I realized I was wrong. She wasn't detached at all.

She swallowed and continued. "When she came to, he forced her. Told her he was in control now and she had to do whatever he said."

I closed my eyes. *Oh God.*

Trish's voice came as from a distance. "She managed to get him to take her to the hospital, even though she hated hospitals. On principle. Because of her experience as a toddler. Did she tell you about that?"

I nodded. "You mean being in isolation with the chicken pox. She said her mother never came to visit her."

Trish was nodding. "But she also hated hospitals because her mother died in one. And she had never made her peace with her mother. Being in the hospital with her sprained ankle brought that whole experience back. Her mother was an alcoholic."

"I didn't know that."

"But she died of cancer," Trish continued. "I think it was cirrhosis that developed into liver cancer. That would have been a dozen years ago."

"Do you mean Lucy was upset at her mother all through her life because of that one time she was left alone in the hospital?"

Trish gave a sad smile. "She felt unwanted and abandoned all her growing up years. She used to say she was brought up by a house and four walls. Her father was stern and demanding and her mother wasn't *there*. She just did what was expected of her in that generation. It was after the war. As far as I remember, her mother was escaping from Hungary. I guess it was sometime during the revolution. She met Lucy's father on the boat. He was English. They were both coming to Canada. They got married and she got pregnant with Lucy. It wasn't an easy birth. Her mother had to have a caesarian. Lucy used to say it was because she didn't want to leave the safety of the womb."

I smiled. "I bet she came out kicking and screaming."

Trish smiled too. "I imagine she did. Her mother couldn't handle someone as…." She paused. "As volatile as Lucy. She was a poet, with a poet's sensibility. It sounds like she may never have wanted to have children. But by the time she realized that, she'd had two."

⟡

SHE WAS ON HER BIKE, on her way to deliver a report to Health Canada in Tunney's Pasture—the "bureaucratic ghetto" she called it—in the city's west end. It was the beginning of August. The worst of July's heat and humidity were gone. She should have been enjoying the bike ride in the cooler air, but the farther she got from home, the stronger the panic grew. Her stomach was going into a knot, her heart was beating faster, her mind racing out of control. The world was a dangerous place. The city, the roads, the cars, the people, they were all dangerous. She wanted to be back home, back to safety.

She forced herself to concentrate on making the pedals go around, to stop at stop signs, stay close to the curb. She had to get the report delivered, had to go into the very kind of building she dreaded.

She turned into Tunney's and took in the maze of low-rise box buildings and the one high-rise that towered over the others. She made herself take deep breaths and find a parking meter to lock her bike to. One step at a time, she told herself. Lock the bike, take your bag out of the carrier, walk to the door of this ugly brown building, open the door, sign the visitor book at the security desk. Focus on what you're doing right now. Don't think about what's to come. It's safe to be walking through this door.

She made herself navigate the maze of corridors and cubbyholes to reach the one that belonged to her client. Made herself block out the glare of the fluorescent lights and the intimidating clicking of high heels on the unyielding floor. The sight of her client, smiling from behind her desk, forced her out of her fearful self. She plastered a confident smile on her face, shook the proffered hand with a firm grip, made a joke as she handed over the work.

Under the professional facade, her twelve-year-old self was trembling, and silently pleading, "Can I go home now?"

<hr/>

I TOLD TRISH HOW I had always assumed Lucy was an only child, that she had never even mentioned Anna to me.

"I think in a lot of ways she did think of herself as an only child," said Trish. "Or at least the only abandoned child. Her mother may not have been as distant with Anna, simply because she was younger. Or maybe because she wasn't as hard to handle as Lucy." She smiled. "I'm treading on dangerous ground here—it's just speculation. Lucy rarely ever talked to me about her sister. But having met Anna at the funeral, I can imagine there were a lot of reasons Lucy might have had for secretly resenting her."

"Like what?"

Trish paused, considering, I suspected, whether she should continue with her speculation. After a moment, she said, "Anna has a poise and control very much the same as Lucy described her mother having. That would have been a minefield for her."

"Seeing her mother mirrored in her sister." I was remembering Anna at the funeral. Playing the consummate hostess. I could imagine Lucy's mother being like that. But Anna had been controlled only on the outside. I knew how upset she was about Lucy. And how hurt by her sister's rejection of her all these years.

Trish echoed my thoughts. "I suspect the mirror was only physical and that Anna didn't act as distantly as her mother."

I nodded. "Little sisters tend to look up to their big sisters. But if that was the case, wouldn't that make them closer?"

Trish smiled a sad smile. "You'd think so. But family relationships are never rational."

"Nor any relationship," I laughed.

"As I say, I'm just speculating and I think I'd better stop," said Trish.

<hr/>

SHE WAS IN HER ROOM again. Face down on her bed. Sent by her father for yelling at her mother. Yelling seemed to be the only way to make her mother notice her. Except it didn't. Her mother seemed to look right through her. As if she didn't know where the sound was coming from. Which made her yell louder. Which brought her father running.

She heard a sound and turned over. A small figure stood in the doorway. Eyes big with distress and concern. Eyes expressing everything she wanted her mother to express. Her sister took a tentative step into the room.

"Go away." It came out more harshly than she intended. But she couldn't comfort her sister, and her sister certainly couldn't comfort her.

Anna turned and ran. Slamming the door behind her.

She knew Anna hadn't meant to bang it so hard, but it gave her a perverse satisfaction anyway. To get a rise out of someone. Even if it was just her sister, who didn't deserve the way she treated her.

———— ✑ ————

I TOOK A SWALLOW OF my rapidly cooling tea and looked at Trish. "You said before that you and Marnie were friends with Lucy, and with Tim after he got out." I wasn't sure how far to take this line of questioning—or how far she would let me take it. I didn't want to give away my suspicions about Marnie being the second person Tim had called from my house, or about Tim and Marnie already knowing Lucy was missing on the Sunday. If Trish mentioned that to Marnie….

Trish began fidgeting with her ear, pulling on the lobe. It was the first time I'd seen her hands move. "We had them over to dinner a couple of times. Marnie's from the Sudbury area, and she and Tim found they had a lot in common—he's from somewhere in rural Ontario. They had similar upbringings, both came from poor families and lived mostly off the land. Marnie's a bow hunter and when she found out Tim used to hunt she tried to get him interested in the club she belongs to. She invited him to go with her on several occasions, but he never took her up on it. We were trying to help him to feel part of the community, but he wouldn't respond. I think his fear ultimately blocked him."

I was tired of that word. It seemed to be an excuse for everything.

"When was the last time you saw her?"

The hand went up to the ear again, pulling on the lobe. "I gave her a treatment just a few days before she went missing."

The day I had found her the cottage in the paper, she'd mentioned she'd had a massage. "We spoke that day," I said. "She told me she felt better for it." I hesitated. "I heard Tim injured her pretty badly."

Trish nodded. "He punched her in the sternum. She was in pretty rough shape—so much so that I went to her house instead of her coming to me. She was in a lot of pain, and dazed from the painkillers. But upbeat. Things seemed to be looking up. You asked if she seemed more jittery toward the end. In fact, she was calmer than I'd ever known her to be. It was like she had a lot of surface static. Which was understandable given everything that was going on that last week. But underneath

I could feel a calm." She smiled. "I told her it was like hearing a radio station under all the static, and she said, 'As long as it's CBC, not some twangy country station.' That was one thing about Lucy—she never lost her sense of humour, no matter how bad it got."

I gave a wry smile. "Did you talk to her again after that?" I might be getting to dangerous territory, but it seemed an innocent enough question.

"Yes," said Trish. "She called me on the Friday evening. Tim was having some kind of breakdown and she wanted me to see him. But they called back later to cancel. That was the last time I heard from her." She looked at me and her eyes were brimming with tears. "She thanked me for all I'd done for them, and for her, over the years. It was almost as if she *knew*."

I touched her hand. "You did a lot for her. There wasn't anything else you could have done."

She blinked away the tears and wiped her nose. "I know." *But.* She didn't have to say it. "That was the last time I talked to her. I had a workshop that weekend. But Marnie—" She stopped abruptly. And she stood up just as abruptly.

I got to my feet too. Opened my mouth to ask her what she had been about to say. But the look on her face told me our interview was over. I looked at my watch. It was nearly five o'clock; we'd been talking for over an hour. "I've taken up way too much of your time. But thank you. This has helped a lot. You've filled in a lot of the pieces."

At the door, I remembered Lucy's choking dream. I turned to Trish. "When Tim phoned me that Monday evening, he told me Lucy had a recurring dream. That she dreamt she was being choked. Was that true? Did she have such a dream?"

Trish nodded. "It started after Tim moved in."

My intake of breath was audible. We looked at each other.

"You know the police's theory is that she was strangled." I spoke slowly.

Trish nodded again. "It does seem like it might have turned out to have been precognitive, but at the time Lucy thought it was a past-life experience coming to the fore. Me, I took it as symbolic. And even in spite of what's happened, I still do."

"Symbolic? Of what?"

"Of Tim trying to choke off her will."

Outside, I headed across the street to my car. The coolness in the air surprised me. Maybe our unusual August heat wave was over. My head was full again, as it had been with Curtis. Everything Trish had said made sense. Except it was all very well to talk about the progress Lucy was making, but in the end she'd been abandoned in a much worse way than she'd ever experienced before. So what was the point of her progress? And the talk of Tim's fears. No doubt he had fears, but there were deeper things going on with Tim, I was sure. Was he the clever con artist the police took him for? Or was there something more serious going on? Something pathological? And what had she been about to say about Marnie?

———— ✺ ————

IT WAS TIM'S REGULAR PSYCHOLOGIST who suggested they get couples counselling. They lasted two sessions with the counsellor. The woman refused to see them again after they described a recent episode of violence. Tim, the counsellor said, had to get control of his rage first. The counsellor strongly advised her to find a refuge, adamant that they couldn't make any progress together until Tim got his anger under control.

In the car she cried out her frustration. How was he supposed to get his anger under control when he couldn't get help? Now even the therapists wouldn't see them. What were they going to do?

Tim said nothing.

At home she went into the sitting room and turned on the TV. She made sure she left the door open. For once she welcomed the mindlessness of the television. Maybe they needed to do more of this. Maybe Tim had the right idea—keep conversation and activities to the inane and innocuous. Keep their focus off all the red-hot areas. Fill their minds with irrelevance and just coast along in a vacuum.

She heard Tim's footsteps heading down the stairs to the bedroom.

Ten minutes later she heard him come back upstairs. She automatically moved over to make room for him on the small couch. When she looked up he was standing in the doorway, carrying his duffel bag in one hand. In the other he held something out to her. "Here—take these."

She got to her feet. He was holding out his bank card and cheque book.

"What are you doing?"

"I'm leaving. For good this time."

Her heart began to pound. Tim had threatened to turn himself in to the police so often the past four months, she'd stopped believing him. But this seemed different. This didn't sound like an empty threat. He sounded calm. Resolute. And devoid of hope.

"Where will you go?"

"Who cares?" he flung back. She heard him striding through the kitchen. A minute later the front door slammed.

She raced to the door, yanked it open, expecting to see his truck pulling away from the curb. He was standing on the front steps, his back to her.

She opened the screen tentatively.

Tim turned his head. There were tears streaming down his face.

She took his hand and they sat down on the porch steps.

"I got nowhere to go, Lu. I only got you."

"Hush. I know, I know."

She rocked him and waited for the tears and the shaking to stop.

On the fridge the next morning, she found a note:

Lucy,

Please don't give up on me now. My life is just now beginning to take shape. Something I have not experienced in a long while. I'm not sure I deserve your patience especially based on my behaviour of late. I do know you deserve much better than you have received and I fully intend to do all I can to produce for myself and for you. I love you babe.

T.

20.

SEPTEMBER BURNISHED INTO OCTOBER, AND I thought about what had been happening in Lucy's life a year ago at this time. Each leaf falling off the trees would have been like another dollar bill—*hundred* dollar bill—dropping out of her line of credit. I sat down with the notes I'd made from all my conversations, and tried to assemble them into some kind of chronological order. But I didn't have any dates or many details. Just that the trucks had been stolen and then the biker threats had started. And Bill Torrence had promised money. I wondered if Curtis would know anything about these things.

"The trucks were stolen in the fall," said Curtis. We were sitting at my tiny kitchen table, a bottle of wine and two flickering candles between us. It was my turn to cook dinner. I didn't know anything about vegetarian cooking, so I stuck to pasta. Curtis was always gracious in his praise. Now he waved his fork in the air, as if he were pointing at notes on an imaginary chalkboard. "First it was the pick-up. They found it in a field somewhere outside of town. Lucy said Tim wouldn't let her call the police. He didn't want to have anything to do with the police. He'd get in trouble with his parole officer. But I think it was the police who ended up finding it. Lucy never said if Tim got into any kind of trouble.

"Then," he said, pointing the fork again, "it was the van."

"A Curbmaster, I heard."

Curtis raised an eyebrow at me. "Who've you been talking to?"

I smiled. "I can't reveal my sources."

"Fair enough," said Curtis in his measured way, meeting my eyes. "As long as you don't reveal this source either."

"I promise. You were never here eating pasta in my house."

"It's pretty good for pasta I never ate."

"You're such a bullshitter." We had, by now, reached a comfortable teasing sort of relationship, though our topic of conversation remained obsessively focused on Lucy. I wasn't the only one with a need to talk about her.

"When was the van stolen?"

"You're asking the wrong guy for dates, but it seems to me it wasn't that long after the truck. Maybe within a few weeks."

"Do you know where the biker gang threats fit in?"

Curtis smiled. "Your source told you about those too? We had a conversation about that. I was trying to get her to see the unlikelihood of random theft happening within weeks like that, and she told me it might not have been random. Tim told her he thought it might be deliberate. I told her it was more likely Tim's lies were deliberate. But of course she wouldn't listen." He took a long slow swallow of wine.

"What I do remember," he went on, putting the glass down, "is that she phoned me some time before Christmas. November maybe. And she said Tim was being blackmailed. I told her it was extortion, not blackmail—if it was even true."

Lucy, I mused, would not have liked to be corrected. Curtis seemed like her match in many ways. It was sad they hadn't been able to make it work.

"Some biker-types were coming up to him and demanding money," Curtis was saying. "He'd gone into her account and withdrawn some substantial sums to pay them off."

"And you think he was making it up?"

"Do you doubt it, in light of what happened?"

I shrugged. "It seems obvious from where we sit now. But maybe not then. He would have made enemies in prison, especially over the Archie Crowe thing. What came of it?"

It was Curtis's turn to shrug. "Nothing, of course. Except for more money disappearing out of her account without being replaced. And I think that's when Tim started talking about his pal—someone named Torrence, I think."

"Torrence? Who was that?" I asked it in my most innocent voice.

"Oh, some figment of Tim's psycho imagination, no doubt," said Curtis. He paused with his fork in mid-air. "Supposedly he was some rich guy Tim knew in prison. Who had some influence. Torrence was going to make sure the threats stopped. And, guess what, they did."

―――∞∞∞―――

THE NOVEMBER STATEMENTS WERE LATE. All the other bills had arrived. She checked the mail every morning, but there was no sign.

Tim shrugged and shook his head when she asked him if he'd seen them. "I don't pay attention to your mail. It's none of my business."

"It *is* your business. You're in charge of paying back the line of credit."

She rummaged furiously through the papers on her desk. They must have arrived—the other batch of bills were there.

She shifted through the wastepaper basket.

"They're not going to be in there." There was scorn in Tim's voice.

She pulled a statement out of the garbage, checked the date, and sucked in an angry breath. "They are," she said between gritted teeth, "if you put them there."

"Why do you hafta blame me for everything? You must've thrown them out by accident."

She barely heard him. The room was suddenly spinning. The negative balance in her line of credit was even bigger than she was expecting, almost seven thousand dollars. She steadied herself against the desk. Then she fished in the garbage for the other statement. The room started to spin again. She sat down hard.

"You've been taking money again, Tim. There's seven hundred here, and another five hundred two days later. I never said you could take those amounts out." Her voice was shaking.

Tim grabbed the statement from her hand. "Lemme see that. That can't be right. The bank made a mistake."

"The bank did not make a mistake." She glared at him. And was shocked to see his righteous indignation transform into terror. There was no other word for it. It was an emotion she knew all too well.

"I need money, Lu—"

She exploded. "You always need—"

"I'm being blackmailed." It came out in a shout over her voice. It was a shout ragged with fear.

She stopped her tirade in mid-sentence. *"What?"*

"It was two biker-types. I heard Archie Crowe got outta the joint recently. I think he put them on to me. I don't know how they found out where I live. They come right up the driveway with a knife. In broad daylight. I didn't want to tell you. I didn't want to scare you."

He was strangely excited as he poured out the story, obviously relieved to finally be telling her. "I never even seen 'em coming. I was working in the garage. They were big guys—lot bigger'n me."

Her heart was racing. "What did they say?"

"One of them said he was going to put a bullet between my eyes unless I gave him seven hundred dollars."

"A *bullet?* I thought you said he had a knife?"

There was momentary confusion on Tim's face. "Well, he musta had a gun too. I never seen it. That's what he said. I told him I didn't have the money, that I needed time to get it. I told them I'd have the money in an hour—that I'd meet them at Rick's Bar. Then I went to the bank machine. I had no choice, Lu. I had to take it out of your account."

She was breathing fast, feeling the first signs of panic. "What happened when you showed up? They didn't try to hurt you?"

"No, I waited outside, and they came out and I handed them the money, then I got the hell out of there. I didn't tell you cuz I didn't want to worry you."

"And the second amount?"

Tim looked down at the statement, as if that would help him remember. "They found me at Hurley's two days later—made me go to the bank machine and get five hundred more."

She watched him register the shock on her face. "I think that's all, Lu. I don't think they'll bug me anymore."

"How do you know?"

"It was just the feeling I got."

She stared at him.

"I called Bill Torrence," he added. "He's got influence. He said he'd check into it. I don't think it'll happen again."

"And is this related to the car thefts too?"

Tim looked startled. "Yeah," he said slowly. "They were trying to scare me."

She was starting to shake, her mouth was dry. She swallowed hard. "This has got to stop. They could clean us out. They could hurt you. They could hurt me."

Tim put his arms around her. "Hey, baby, relax, it's okay. Bill's going to take care of it. I promise you. They won't bother me again."

She pulled herself out of his arms, wiping tears away. She felt overwhelmed, out of her depth. They needed help. "I think we should call the police."

"No!" It was Tim's turn to panic. "No police. Please Lu, it'll just get all screwed up."

"But it's theft. They're stealing from me!" She thought she was going to start hyperventilating. Money just kept leaking out of her account. Everything was spinning out of control.

"I talked to Bill about money too," said Tim. "He says he might be able to give me a loan—a big loan. Enough to cover my debt to you and give me some capital to get a business going."

"He has that kind of money? *Clean* money?"

"We're still working out the amount. When we do, I'll pay you back everything I owe you. Even for the money they blackmailed out of me. You shouldn't have to suffer because of my past. It's not fair to you."

"Nothing's fair," she said. But a glimmer of hope came into her heart. Bill Torrence sounded almost too good to be true. But a mentor, a wealthy mentor, was exactly what Tim needed. Someone to support him, get him on his feet again. And someone who'd been in prison would be doubly understanding. Maybe everything was going to be alright after all.

———∞———

CURTIS AND I MOVED TO the futon couch with the remainder of the wine, leaning back on cushions, facing each other. Our favourite position for Lucy conversations. Sometimes Curtis reached out and performed reflexology on my feet. He usually found painful trigger points, but I didn't pull away. I would never have admitted it to him, but I usually felt better for it afterward. My left foot was in his hands now, being subjected to what I called his torture treatments.

"Have you gone to see Kendra yet?" he asked me.

"Not yet. I'm thinking about it."

Curtis shook his head. "Stop resisting, McGinn. You and Lucy are opposite poles—you resisting everything you can't explain, she way too willing to believe the unbelievable."

I pulled my foot away then, annoyed. "What's my foot doing in your torturing hands if I'm resisting everything I can't explain?"

Curtis grinned. "It's not. You just pulled it away."

"Because you're so provoking."

"I think you like being provoked."

"I think you like being provoking."

Curtis reached for my foot again. "Give it back. I promise to provoke you only physically."

I laughed then and relented. "Did you provoke Lucy this way too?"

"Lucy needed provoking. It was the only way to get her to see any sense."

"But it sounds like she was starting to see through Tim. Didn't he move out sometime around Christmas? She told me he was moving out. That he needed to gain some independence, and she needed her space. She didn't make it sound like they were breaking up. But maybe that's only what she told me. Was she trying to end it then, do you think?"

Curtis gave an exaggerated shrug. "Who knows? She gave me the same story. And there was the snowplowing thing too. Tim supposedly had a bunch of snowplowing contracts for the winter, which meant he had to get up at something like four a.m., and Lucy didn't want her sleep disturbed. So I think that was part of the rationale for getting separate places. She might have been secretly hoping they'd end up going their separate ways eventually, but she would never have admitted that to me either. And I gather money was still an issue. I think he was still stealing from her, because she told me she went over to his place and made him sign an agreement that he would stop taking money out of her account and would pay her back everything he owed her. She finally took him off her account around Christmas time."

———⊶⊷⊷———

SHE WOKE UP TO SILENCE and daylight—the little that winter could siphon into her basement windows. Winter: her worst time of year. She'd endured two winters on her own, waiting for Tim, cursing the system that was keeping them apart. How ironic that now that they were finally free to be together, she was alone in winter's hell again. The lesser of two evils.

She couldn't bring herself to get up. The silence was a drug. Tim wasn't banging around upstairs or slamming the front door at four in the morning. He wasn't even slamming the door on his way back in to see her. She had forbidden him to come before noon. Even when there were no driveways to plow. Mornings were to be hers again.

In fact, he wasn't coming over as often as she'd been expecting. It made her want to go see him. She was glad to find this desire back in her heart. It was a necessary shift: to be granted enough separation to breed the desire for reunion. Maybe they could start over from two separate houses, the way most people started. Begin dating. See if there was enough there to draw them together again. And keep them together. It wouldn't be so in-your-face. She could see other men, he could start meeting other women….

She dressed and went upstairs to do her meditation in the little sitting room. Her earplugs weren't where she thought she'd left them, but she didn't search very hard. She didn't need them. There was no one else inside, and only sound-deadening snow outside.

Dead snow. There hadn't been a snowfall for the past week. More ironies: as soon as he'd moved out he'd stopped needing to get up at four a.m. But this separation, she reminded herself, wasn't just about getting uninterrupted sleep. And meditation was not about letting her thoughts run wherever they wanted. She slowed her breathing and focused on each intake and release of air.

The sound of the front door closing brought her back with a jolt. Darn him. She'd told him not to come before noon.

She met him in the front hall, taking off his boots. "What are you doing here?"

She knew from the look on his face before he opened his mouth. He needed money. Three thousand dollars.

"For God's sake, where is it going? This is the last time I'm bailing you out."

She wrote the cheque and stewed all afternoon, Tim's cliché mocking her in her head: *You gotta spend money to make money.*

No. Not her money. Not anymore. This was going to stop.

She ran downstairs to the computer.

Then she drove over to Tim's, let herself into the dark apartment when he didn't answer the door.

Tim was a lump in front of the TV.

She screamed out the conditions on the agreement she was going to make him sign: "You will pay back the ten thousand into my line of credit. You will pay thirty percent of your income to me over the year. You will disclose all the sources of your income to me. You will pay all the interest on the line of credit. This is the last time I will pay it. It's your responsibility. You will not ask for, or take, one more cent from me."

She shoved the contract and the pen in front of him.

"I'm doing the best I can, Lu—honest! The truck broke down. I had to get it fixed right away—I can't not have my plow working. I got commitments."

"You *got* a commitment to me. Now sign that contract. I'm fed up."

She watched the tears stream down his face. She hardened her heart against those tears. She watched him sign his name. She scrawled hers next to it. She felt nothing but a cold hard emptiness. Emptiness that even her own tears on her way home couldn't fill.

———— ∞ ————

"THE CONVERSATION I REMEMBER THE most from that time," said Curtis, "was when he was just about to move back in."

"So he did come back. That explains his calling me from her house when she went missing. I never heard anything more about their relationship after she told me he'd moved out. Sometime around Christmas, right? Maybe early January?"

Curtis laughed in a self-deprecating way. "Don't ask me about dates. Whenever it was, I don't think he lasted much more than a month on his own. We had dinner just before he moved back in. It was in February. That I remember because we had an unusual deep freeze that month, and her pipes froze. I always warned her that might happen. The basement wasn't very well insulated. I was working at the bookstore by then and she called me there to ask me to come over to fix them."

<hr>

"WHERE'S MR. BROCKMAN REPAIRS?" HIS voice was mocking, but she could tell he was pleased she had called him and not Tim.

"I'll tell you about that when you get here." She stopped herself. "That is, if you wouldn't mind coming over."

"No problem," said Curtis in his lazy, seductive voice.

"I'll cook you supper."

"You're not serving up Tim Bourguignon are you?"

She laughed. "No, Tim is still very much alive. He's not likely to be here this evening, but if you're worried, we could go out."

"I'm not worried if you're not worried." She could almost see the shrug that would have accompanied these words.

She wasn't worried. Since moving out, Tim never came over on Friday evenings. He had finally made some friends and usually went with them to Hurley's or another bar. She wasn't sorry not to have to deal with his coming in at three a.m. or his morning-after hangover.

She also wasn't sorry the pipes had frozen. She'd been so busy catching up with work after Tim had moved out that she hadn't had time to socialize the way she'd intended. But she also hadn't thought there was any urgent need to take advantage of his absence. Unfortunately now there was: he was moving back.

By seven she had running water again. By seven-thirty she and Curtis were ensconced in a booth at My Cousins on Elgin Street, sipping wine and waiting for their dinners to arrive. Curtis had convinced her she didn't feel like cooking. Now he slouched back in the booth. The familiarity of his lean frame and posture gave Lucy a pang.

"So have you guys broken up, or what?"

She recited her stock line. "Tim's had his own place for a month now. We're still seeing each other. We just needed our own space." Then she leaned forward. "I understand now."

Curtis sat up, smiled his slow smile. "What do you understand now?"

"I understand why you needed your space. Understand how needy I was, how I drove you crazy." She sighed. "The shoe's on the other foot now. Big time."

She half expected a smug retort. She almost wanted Curtis to judge her. But there was sympathy in his eyes, and his voice was gentle. "It's tough having someone in your face all the time, isn't it?"

She felt her throat tighten and hoped she wouldn't cry. "I guess I had to draw someone needy to me to make me finally see it."

Curtis was nodding. "Mirrors—they're our healing. So," he added, "the official line is you've got separate places now to have your own space, but really you're easing out. Right?"

For a moment she was annoyed by his presumptuousness. But it was refreshing to have someone read her inner thoughts. He did know her. He always had.

But she shook her head. "Actually, it looks like he might be moving back next week."

Curtis raised an eyebrow. "So much for getting your own space."

"I don't really have a choice. There was a break-in where Tim lives. He's in the basement. The landlord lives upstairs. The landlord's TV and VCR and stereo were stolen. He's asking Tim to move out because—"

"Because he thinks Tim did it?" Curtis looked amused

"Because," she repeated, "he wants his son to move in."

"And why do you feel obligated to take him back? He's not your legal responsibility."

"He's got nowhere else to go."

"But you're enjoying having your place on your own."

"Yes, but…."

Curtis's eyes held hers. He spoke in a quiet voice. "Rescuing isn't always a good idea."

She bristled. "I'm not rescuing."

"Doing something for someone when you don't want to be doing it is a form of rescuing." His smile was rueful.

"It would just be temporary."

Curtis was shaking his head. "Once he comes back—"

She cut him off. "I'm still thinking about it."

"Think carefully," said Curtis.

She did think carefully. She wasn't trying to rescue Tim. She was trying to contain him. She couldn't—wouldn't—do it forever, but for a little while longer she would protect the world from Tim Brennan.

And get her money back.

———— ∞ ————

CURTIS DIDN'T SEEM TO KNOW anything more about Bill Torrence. But I needed to know how Torrence had fit in at the end. And what had Quinn said about forged cheques?

I wondered if Trish knew? I called her the next day from work.

She seemed reluctant to talk to me. I didn't press her.

That left only one person who could tell me.

I stewed about it for days. He'd said he couldn't call me, but he'd never said I couldn't call him. I would do it at work, of course, but I needed a legitimate reason. I couldn't just call up and say, "I need to hear more about the case you're not supposed to be talking to me about."

I made up my mind. I would tell him I needed to talk to him about Lucy—that I had more information. He would, I hoped, forgive me when he found out my real reason for calling. He'd always been sympathetic to my needing to know the story.

I called the station. My heart was pounding.

Sergeant Quinn wasn't available, I was told. Would I like to leave a message?

I didn't have the nerve.

21.

THE TEMPERATURE PLUMMETED. THE CURRENT slowed the freezing of this section of the river, but thin ice built up along shore. Snow piled around the house. Many days I worked from home to avoid the treacherous drive. I was antsy for the trial to get under way, but I heard nothing from Lundy or Roach. Or Quinn. Curtis took off to Mexico at the invitation of a friend who lived there. It was after he left and I was trying to flesh out the information I knew about Lucy that I realized I'd never asked him about her Easter visit. How had that slipped through the cracks? I knew the answer. There had been so much ground to cover.

I called Trish again. We hadn't talked much about the sternum injury or what had caused it. But this time Trish was more than just reluctant to speak to me. "I'm sorry, Ellen, I can't meet with you. I never thought about the trial. But I realize we're all going to be witnesses, and I shouldn't be speaking to you."

"I would keep it confidential. I would never reveal we'd talked."

"I'm sorry, I just can't take the risk."

I hung up the phone, wondering if Marnie was the real reason she wouldn't talk to me. If Marnie *had* been involved, it couldn't have been premeditated on her part. She must have got caught up in something. Through contact with Tim that weekend maybe? Had Trish started to tell me Marnie had seen him on the weekend? She'd said Marnie and Tim had lots in common. Like hunting. The word gave me the creeps. Had Marnie gone over to Tim's that weekend for something to do with bow hunting? I had no answers. And, now, no means of finding them.

All my sources had been cut off. There was, as Quinn said, no point in stewing. The truth would come out eventually. But I might have to wait for the trial for that. And the hearing hadn't even been set yet.

Without Lucy to concentrate on, my head filled again with cross-examination scenarios. Now, in addition to exposing me for a flake, the defence lawyer in my head discredited me for talking with other witnesses and, worse, for having intimate contact with Sergeant Steve Quinn. I threw myself into work and winter activities. Skiing in the park. Snowshoeing on the railway tracks with the dogs. Coffee with Mary Frances.

Slowly, gradually, I relaxed into the white dormancy of winter.

The call came, finally, in late March. It came from Quinn. He was formal, business-like, and brief. The pre-trial hearing was going to get going in April. He had been assigned to line up the witnesses. Could I come in for an interview with the Assistant Crown next week?

Three days later another call came. This time from Marc. Belle had had a stroke.

I was shocked. I hadn't even known it was possible for dogs to have a stroke. And she was still young. Marc assured me there was every chance of her recovering. I was going to make sure. Over his half-hearted objections I brought her to my place.

After a few days, Belle's appetite came back and, after a week, her bark. I stopped having to carry her up and down the stairs. She was able to walk, slowly, down to the river and back. Her head had a decided lean to the left.

On the ninth evening after I had brought her home, she had another stroke.

I sat with her on her quilt, talking to her, running my hands over her soft fur. She lay still. Too still. I pressed my head against her chest. Frantically I felt for her heartbeat.

And then I smelled something. A fragrance. Familiar. And I knew its name: patchouli.

I looked around for the source of the scent. And saw Lucy standing in the doorway.

Belle suddenly sat up and sniffed the air. She looked across the room to Lucy.

I looked down at Belle. I looked back at Lucy.

Lucy smiled at me. Then she beckoned to Belle.

Belle stirred in my arms. She struggled to her feet. She licked my nose. And then she trotted over to Lucy. She didn't hobble, her head didn't lean. She stopped in front of my dead friend and wagged her tail.

Lucy gave me another reassuring smile. Then she turned, and Belle followed her out of the room. Out of space and time.

I found myself on the floor, holding my Belle's still-warm, unmoving body in my arms.

Lucy's presence stayed in the room. I had never seen her so calm. Had never seen such a beautiful smile on her face. Her fears were gone. And mine, now, too. There was nothing to be afraid of. Her visit wasn't a hallucination or my imagination. It was a gift. The gift of knowing that Belle was in good hands. And that Lucy was okay now too.

But they were both gone.

I buried my face in Belle's fur and let the tears flow, unchecked. She was too young.

Lucy had been too young too. Why hadn't I insisted Quinn and I search those barns that first night? Why hadn't I made more of an effort? Why had I let my doubts get in the way?

Grief came rising to the surface. At last.

I rocked myself back and forth and sobbed as I had never in my life sobbed.

22.

"DO YOU SWEAR TO TELL the truth, the whole truth, and nothing but the truth?"

I had opted to swear on a book I didn't hold sacred. The court attendant holding it out was smiling. She seemed to know the procedure was unavoidable, the question ludicrous, and my answer necessarily the first lie. The court's interest was only in the bare bones of the truth: the "facts." I hoped that was as far as I would have to go. The pre-trial hearing had begun.

Above and to my right sat the judge. Facing me were the two Assistant Crown attorneys, Steve Quinn, and Mr. Blair, who would have the pleasure of cross-examining me later. The rest of the courtroom was filled with high-school students, here to learn the workings of the Ontario court system.

They were dispassionate observers, a role I had given up a year ago.

Before I sat down, I glanced beyond the Crown's bench to a glassed-in box. It was the first time I had laid eyes on Tim Brennan in almost a year. It was important to meet his eyes. I couldn't speak in this court unless I did. That was the only thing I had any certainty about—that I had to, that I could.

He looked straight back at me. No expression on his face.

I took my seat then, out of his line of vision.

The Assistant Crown, Deanne Fortier, rose from the bench. She was blonde and petite and had a sympathetic smile and the trace of a Québecois accent.

"Ms. McGinn, I understand you are a researcher here in Ottawa?"

It was the end of class for the high-school students. They filed out of the courtroom. They weren't drained or shaky, or anxious for the Assistant Crown's smile of reassurance. They were looking forward to their weekend. They weren't worried about being cross-examined on Monday.

I glanced at Tim sitting in his glassed-in box, waiting to be led away. He raised his eyebrows and adopted a sympathetic expression. I didn't return it.

I approached Deanne Fortier. I was keeping both Steve Quinn and the defence lawyer deliberate blurs in my peripheral vision. For different reasons. But it wasn't making any difference. I could feel their focus on me. Also for different reasons.

Deanne was in a rush. She gave me a kind look over the load of thick binders in her arms. "Technically I'm not supposed to speak with you now that I'm finished the examination. But don't worry, you did fine." She lowered her voice. "Don't let Blair intimidate you on Monday. Answer only what he asks you. Don't volunteer anything."

I couldn't help looking over at the defence lawyer. He was speaking in low tones to his assistant. Every few minutes they sent glances my way. They were clearly planning their strategy, confident they could expose me.

Deanne started down the aisle. "*Bonne fin de semaine*," she called back over her shoulder in a teasing sing-song voice.

I sent a quick glance in the direction of the other source of attention on me. And felt my face flush when his eyes met mine. Aside from the brief phone call, it was our first contact in over six months. He hadn't been present at my interview with the Crown.

I was too self-conscious to speak to him in the courtroom. I headed down the aisle after Deanne Fortier, all too aware of him following me.

He caught up at the door to the anteroom and held it open for me. At the second door, he took the handle but stood with the door still closed. "You look like you could use a drink. And maybe something to eat. I've got an hour before I have to be somewhere else. I'll take you across the street to the Lord Elgin."

He opened the door for the defence lawyer and his assistant to go past us. He seemed not to care if he was heard. This wasn't, I told myself,

Steve Quinn, the man who was not supposed to be interested in Ellen McGinn. This was Sergeant Quinn, the police detective concerned about a witness who had just been on the stand for two hours. His concern was legitimate. And accurate. The witness could use a drink, and an opportunity to unload the tension of the day.

At four o'clock on a Friday afternoon in April, the lobby bar at the Lord Elgin Hotel was filled with suited business people and a few casually dressed tourists. Quinn and I settled into two comfortable wingback chairs kitty corner to each other at a round table. He let me order my own drink. A few moments later the waiter set down two single malts in elegant snifters.

Quinn raised his glass to me. "You can relax those tight muscles, McGinn. You did fine. You were a wealth of information."

His reference to my muscles made me blush. I took a swallow of the warm liquid and tried not to watch his lips on the rim of his glass. He had let his hair grow in a quarter-inch or so and had the beginnings of a trim beard. He was blonder than I would have expected. He'd also shed a few pounds. Was looking more relaxed. The strain from last summer seemed to be gone. But the chemistry was still there. Possibly more intense.

The case was the only safe topic of conversation. I sent a wry look across the table. "I'm not done yet, you know. Blair was having a field day in there, scribbling away every time I said the word 'dream' and 'vision.' And don't you think he's going to take me to the cleaners on the statement I gave the *Sûreté*? It says nothing incriminating about Tim. He's going to make it sound like I changed everything in hindsight. God, I wish you guys had taken my statement that first week."

"Yeah, too bad we never did. But the last thing Lundy and Roach had time for was running around getting witness statements. They were busy concentrating on Brennan. But I told you before, don't worry about it."

"They probably avoided taking my statement on purpose. They thought it was going to be full of hocus pocus."

"Here we go again. Are you still apologizing for being psychic?"

"I'm not—" I stopped the automatic denial. "I'm just acutely aware that other people might be skeptical."

Quinn met my eyes. "That's *their* problem."

And yours. The thought zinged through my brain like a bullet. For the first time, there was no doubt.

I changed the subject before he could read my mind. "I've been wanting to know. At least can you tell me…. Can we have one of those conversations we're not supposed to be having?"

Quinn looked around and seemed satisfied that there was no one who knew us, no one listening. "What do you want to know?"

"A few things. About Bill Torrence and the forged cheques for one thing. And about the woman who went searching with Tim."

Quinn stared at me. "I didn't tell you about that last summer?"

"No, you didn't have much time. Remember?" I looked him in the eye, feeling suddenly bold.

"Or maybe you were just asking too many questions."

"And not getting any answers." The Scotch was loosening my tongue. I braced myself for the rebuke.

But he grinned. "Well, you'll get your answers soon enough in the papers. Bryn's going to be on the stand in a few days."

"Bryn?" My voice was sharp. "Did she have an Irish accent? Was she a private detective?"

Quinn was nodding, a question in his eyes.

"She phoned me. Sometime last May. I meant to ask you about her then, but you—I forgot." *Because you disappeared.* "I was too scared to talk to her."

"You were too scared to talk to anyone," said Quinn.

His mocking tone pissed me off. "So, what if I was?"

Quinn raised his arms in surrender. "Easy, girl. I was just teasing. I'm not putting you down."

You are. It was another clear thought.

I put him back on track. "So it was Bryn who was with Tim, not an undercover officer?"

"Yes, as you say, she's a private investigator. She heard about the case and called Brennan. Offered to help him search. But then Lundy and Roach got in touch with her and convinced her to work for them. She went searching with Brennan—the few times he actually went." He shook his head, smiling. "What a woman. You should get Lundy to tell it. I'm not familiar with all the details of how they set it up, but it's a pretty amazing story."

"But she was with him when they found Lucy's remains?" I felt sick and angry whenever I thought about the little of Lucy that had remained. It must have been even worse for Bryn, to actually see it.

"Yes, she was with him."

"Did the forensic testing ever reveal anything more?"

"No, we still have nothing except the teeth to go on."

"So she could have drowned."

Quinn looked at me, uncomprehending.

"You said drowning was one of the things that could account for the pink teeth." In a dry voice I added, "In one of my visions, she'd been put in the river. Remember?"

"Masham's a long way from the river," said Quinn.

I spread my hands. "You see why I get embarrassed when I talk about the so-called psychic stuff."

"But there *are* parallels. You don't have to be embarrassed. We think she was strangled in the bath or the shower—that's water. And remember you talked about her being wrapped in a synthetic material? In the first interview Lundy and Roach did with Brennan, he kept mentioning the shower curtain. Said Lucy had told him to wash it. He said it had torn to shreds in the washer and he'd had to replace it. Lundy and Roach just let him talk. They never questioned him about it, but he mentioned it about three times. Sure enough, there's a brand spanking new shower curtain in the bathtub when the house is searched. And one or two of the shower hooks were reversed. Which seems very unlike Lucy; from what I understand she was very meticulous. It's likely the curtain tore when he attacked her. He may well have wrapped her up in it to carry her to the car."

I shook my head. "Don't you remember? I got later that it was a sleeping bag she was wrapped in." And there was no way I was confusing bath water with a river.

I looked straight at him. "She could have been taken out of the river. If they realized she had resurfaced." I hesitated. "I heard a motorboat out on the river a couple of times—in the pitch dark."

Quinn was shaking his head. I didn't blame him. His theory, the cops' theory, was so logical. So reasonable. Unbelievably reasonable.

"I'm going to be laughed out of court when Blair brings up my visions. He'll have a field day."

"So what?" There was impatience in his voice. "I've told you before, we often use psychics."

But you don't believe them.

It was another zinging bullet of truth.

"Well," I said to test him, "this psychic had it as an accident."

Quinn stared at me. His expression said, don't be naive. But his words were: "What if I told you that on the evening before he called you, the man who is so worried about his missing girlfriend rents a video called *Wolf.* A video about a werewolf."

My stomach turned. "It sounds sick."

"Not sick," said Quinn. "Evil. Do you know what I see when I look in Brennan's eyes?"

I shook my head. I couldn't look in Quinn's eyes.

"Nothing. This guy is the most evil character I've ever dealt with—and I've dealt with a lot of bad characters."

"Speaking of potentially bad characters. Can you tell me about Bill Torrence?" I wanted to change the subject.

"What do you want to know?"

"Well, I remember you saying he was offering Tim a big loan to pay off his debt to Lucy. Or at least Tim said he was. Was it just a lie?"

Quinn nodded. "A big fat lie about a big fat mythical loan. We've talked to Torrence. He was in contact with Tim at Lucy's about the cattle transport idea, but Tim turned him down. He never offered any loan at all, let alone one for thirty-five thousand dollars."

He told me what he knew.

—⟨∞⟩—

SOME NIGHTS TIM DIDN'T COME home. When he did come in, waking her up at dawn, he was drunk or stoned. She stopped asking where he'd been. Stopped reminding him he was violating his parole. He could deal with his parole officer on his own. She wasn't going to try to make it better.

No one could make it better for her either. There was no one to call. No one besides Trish. Kevin had all but disappeared. There was no point in calling her father or Anna: what would she say? And Ellen was keeping their relationship brutally professional. Ellen seemed to have barely heard last week when she had asked her to keep an eye out for a cottage in the Gats. Where was Bill Torrence and his money?

She kept asking Tim. And came upstairs one morning to find him talking in animated tones on the phone. When he got off, he looked ecstatic. He swung her around so fast she got dizzy.

"What? What is it? Stop!"

Tim put her down. He was beaming. "Bill's just leaving Toronto. He's got a cheque for thirty-five thousand smackeroos. Made out to you, baby. He'll be here in five hours."

She stared at him. Her heart began to pound. In five hours her troubles would be over. She could hardly believe it.

She couldn't concentrate on work. She kept looking at the clock. Counting down the hours.

In three hours she would be celebrating. They would be celebrating. With three hours to go, with Torrence actually on the road, she could buy a bottle of Champagne. That wouldn't jinx it. It would be perfectly chilled by the time he arrived. They could *all* celebrate.

She arrived back from the liquor store with her brown-paper bag. She had splurged on the real thing: Pol Roger, thirty-five dollars. One one-thousandth of the amount they were going to receive.

Tim was sitting at the kitchen table. He looked up when she came in. His face said it all. "They got as far as Kingston. His wife took sick. Real bad. She was hemorrhaging. They had to go home. She's got cancer."

No. He was not coming. Nothing else registered. The room began to go black at the edges. She almost dropped the bottle.

"He's going to come as soon as he can. But he's gotta look after his wife first. He said maybe in another week."

Another week.

She made herself breathe.

Okay. She could wait another week. For thirty-five thousand dollars, she could wait one more week.

She put the Champagne in the fridge.

———— ∞∞∞ ————

QUINN TOOK A LONG SWALLOW of Scotch and set the snifter down. He looked at me. "After he didn't come, Brennan changed his story to say that Torrence was going to wire the money instead. It was probably Lucy who planted the idea in his thick head—asking why he couldn't simply wire the money. But the wire, of course, never came either."

"What was she planning to do after the money arrived? My sense was she was trying to leave." I didn't mention my sense was from one of my first dreams.

"Brennan, of course, maintains they were going to live happily ever after, that there were no problems, that he had no reason to harm her. But we found evidence that he was, in fact, going to be moving out. Probably at Lucy's insistence."

"Evidence? What evidence?"

Quinn grinned. "One of the neighbours had the foresight to sneak over to Lucy's house in the middle of the night and take a green garbage bag Tim had put out for collection the week after she went missing. He brought it to the police and we sifted through it. And voila, we found the torn-up copy of a lease, signed by Tim and witnessed by Lucy. It was dated the nineteenth, the Wednesday before she went missing."

"That's brilliant. Amazing Tim didn't think to burn it."

Quinn snorted. "That would take more brains than Stupid has in his head."

"And what about the forged cheques? Where do they fit in?"

"The cheques." He nodded. "First there were a couple of cheques he wrote on her account in January and February. She'd taken him off her account shortly before Christmas, so he obviously stole the cheques. They were for something like seven thousand and five thousand dollars. Enough to get her line of credit up over the twenty thousand mark."

"But what were they for?"

Quinn shrugged. "He claims his truck crapped out on him, that he needed a new one right away to keep up with his snowplowing contracts. He's also claiming Lucy knew about them. It's all bullshit—they've determined her signature was forged. Then there were the Kyle Smythe cheques. The day before Lucy went missing, the Friday, her bank called to say her account was overdrawn, that the cheque she'd received from a Kyle Smythe for a thousand dollars had non-sufficient funds. Lucy told the manager she'd never received such a cheque—didn't even know a Kyle Smythe. But the bank manager said her signature was on the back of the cheque."

"Tim had forged it again? But I don't understand. Who's Kyle Smythe?"

"A friend of Brennan's. He had Smythe write a bogus cheque, deposited it into Lucy's account at one machine, and withdrew six hundred dollars from another one. We've questioned Smythe. He says he got fifty bucks for his trouble. Lucy must have realized Tim was behind it because she told the manager she'd take care of it." He took another sip of Scotch and continued. "She probably confronted Brennan, and he probably held the carrot of the Torrence money out to her yet again. He'd been doing it for weeks. That last week, Lucy was calling the bank every day, asking if the wire transfer had been made yet."

Oh hi, Ellen, I'm on the other line with my bank manager and it's taken me ages to get through.

"She didn't know before she died that there was a second cheque from Smythe," Quinn continued. "Also with her forged signature on the back. Brennan had taken out more money against it. That one bounced the following week. So her line of credit ended up being around the twenty-two thousand mark." He shook his head and muttered, "I hope they hang him.

"Now," he said, changing the subject. "I can see you're going to stew about Blair all weekend. Believe me, he's not worth it. All you need to do is listen to his questions carefully. Be wary any time he says, 'May I suggest that....' Or he may not even start a question that way, but may try to get you to agree to something that goes along with a scenario he's trying to paint. Don't let him get under your skin." He smiled. "You'll be fine. You could have a support person in the court with you, you know."

I shrugged. "I'd prefer not to." I didn't want anyone else hearing me being taken to pieces and shown to be a flake.

"Well, I'll be there. Look at me whenever you need to."

I wasn't sure that would help, but I gave him a smile.

Quinn's expression changed somehow from one of professional interest to personal. "You and what's 'is name never got back together, I hope."

"No, what's 'is name and I did not get back together." I was annoyed.

"Sorry. I'm not trying to be insolent. I just can never remember his name." His smile was cajoling. "How *have* you been? You haven't got anyone new in your life, have you?" His eyes willed me to say no.

"No, I'm enjoying being on my own." I was not going to sound like I was waiting. I was suddenly not sure I should be. It was obvious now that he had been humouring me about my dreams and visions. I was back to my confused state: attraction, repulsion, mistrust, desire. What *was* it with this man?

"How's the new place?"

"I love it."

He was shaking his head. "I still can't believe you moved just down the road from where you found the car. I suppose you're communing with Lucy's ghost or something."

"Or something." I tried to keep my tone light.

"How's work going?"

"Fine. I work more from home now. And I'm doing some writing on my own."

"You *must* be communing with Lucy's ghost," he teased. "You're sounding more and more like her."

I started.

He seemed not to notice. "There's one way you're not the same though." The teasing note was gone.

"What's that?"

"If you got into an abusive relationship you'd leave."

I met his eyes. "I don't know if I would."

Quinn glared at me.

I shrugged. "I've learned not to make assumptions—even about myself."

"You wouldn't stay. You'd fight back. You'd get out." His vehemence took me aback.

"Well, I can say this much." I kept my voice calm, if not my thoughts. "I believe I wouldn't get into an abusive relationship in the first place."

Quinn was nodding. "That I believe. *You* are not going to end up in a pine grove near Masham."

His words shook me. But I kept my voice calm. "Exactly where were Lucy's remains found, anyway?"

"You mean you've never gone to the site?"

"How could I? I've never known where it is. I've been wanting to go, but—"

"You and I will go. After the hearing."

My adrenalin started pumping.

"Or." Quinn raised his eyebrows as if struck by a sudden thought. "What are you doing this weekend? Tomorrow say?"

My pulse sped up even more. It made sense for Quinn to take me. I wanted to go. I didn't want to go alone. He knew the spot. And he was offering.

"Sorry. Stupid of me," Quinn was saying. "What you need this weekend is to relax—not go on a morbid hike in the woods. We'll go after the hearing. Whenever you're ready."

"No," I said, "I'd like to go tomorrow. But," I looked directly at him. "Are you free to take me?"

Quinn met my eyes. "I'm free." Then he looked away.

———— ∞∞∞ ————

THE DOORBELL WAS RINGING. SHE lay in bed, spaced out from the sleeping pill, too aching to move. Let Tim get it.

Through the floorboards, she could hear voices. Male voices.

Bill. Bill Torrence had arrived.

She eased her body out of bed.

A minute later Tim was calling down from the top of the stairs. "Lu. I need you up here."

She pulled on her housecoat. She climbed the stairs as fast as she could.

A short balding man almost skinnier than she was sat in the cold living room. Papers lay on his briefcase on the coffee table. Legal-looking papers. Relief seeped into her aching bones.

But the scene wasn't right. It was Tim who was writing the cheques.

The man got to his feet and held out his hand. "Hi, I'm Vaughan Hendricks."

She looked from Mr. Hendricks to Tim. Tim didn't pause in his writing. "Mr. Hendricks is renting me the apartment. He needs you to witness the lease."

From relief to disappointment back to relief in seconds. She eased herself into a chair in the chilly room.

She watched Tim hand over the cheques to Mr. Hendricks. She didn't ask him if there was money in his new account to cover them. Vaughan Hendricks was here. He was real. The apartment was real. And Bill Torrence was real too. The money was coming. And then there would be more than enough money. And then she would be free.

Tim handed her the lease agreement and the pen. She signed him over to Mr. Hendricks. She signed him out of her life.

THERE WAS A PHONE MESSAGE waiting for me when I got home. Curtis. He'd been home for a few weeks now, he said. He'd come home to a subpoena. He assumed I had one too. He'd been trying to avoid contact, but…. "Hell, I missed you, McGinn." I could almost see his slow smile as he said the words. "Come up for dinner tonight if you get this message in time."

I called ahead. I let Curtis feed me a Spanish omelette and pour me a glass of wine. We assumed our usual places at each end of the lime-green couch.

"I don't want to talk about the hearing," I said. "I want to hear about Easter. *Last* Easter."

"Easter," Curtis repeated, with a sigh. There was a silence while he brought Easter back. Then he spoke. "She called me the Thursday before Easter. She needed a break. I invited her to come up to the cottage. She said she'd bring the wine."

THEY CLIMBED UP THE LADDER to the tree-house. From under the wide canopy of pine branches the lake, still frozen white, was just barely visible. Lucy sat in the bamboo bucket swing—her seat. She wore her navy pea coat against the chill of the April air and held her wine glass in gloved hands. Curtis sat on the wide railing.

She watched his easy posture and his sexy body in his jean jacket with appreciative eyes.

She didn't tell Curtis that Tim didn't know where she was—exactly. She'd left a note that she was driving up to the Gatineaus to go for a walk. That she would be back by six for dinner.

"So did the money come yet?"

"No. Can you *believe* it?"

"Yes," laughed Curtis.

Lucy watched his beautiful smile and ignored his skeptical reply. She didn't want to talk about her life. She asked questions instead. About how he was doing, about his work, his family. She could see he was taken aback. Impressed that she had made some progress out of her self-absorption.

Lucy was impressed too: at the way he expressed himself, at his serenity, his confidence. Why had she given this up? She knew why. She hadn't been able to appreciate him then. She had been too busy trying to meld him into her idea of who he should be. But the chemistry was still there—patently there. Who was to say that when Tim was out of her life…. They could take it slow this time. Maybe she could rent a cottage nearby….

No. She pressed down hard on those thoughts. There was no going back.

But couldn't they go on?

She didn't know. She didn't have to know.

That was new.

Curtis was giving her a queer look. "Did you hear me?" he asked.

She started as if he had shouted. Met his eyes. And started again. They were filled with kindness and concern.

He leaned forward. "I said, are you *safe?*"

The expression in his eyes was suddenly irritating. Condescending.

"Yes," she snapped. "I'm safer with Tim than I ever would be with you."

She said it to be contrary. She knew he didn't believe her. But in fact it was true. Tim had no power to hurt her. No power over her at all. Not anymore. Whereas Curtis ... if she let him back in to her heart....

In that moment she was overcome by compassion for the man sitting across from her on the wooden platform high in the tree. There was no space. No time. Just compassion and love. For Curtis. For his honesty and integrity. For how hard he'd tried—in his own way—when they'd been together. For how frustrating he must have found it dealing with her needy, demanding ways. She did love him. Not for who he could be for her. Just for who he was. She listened to him talk. She watched the way his eyes sparkled and the way his voice warmed to his topic, and she smiled, unseen, in the deepening twilight.

It was the dusk masking his face that finally brought her around, panicking about the time. It was almost seven o'clock. It would take her the better part of an hour to get home. Shit.

Down below the tree-house, in the darkness, Curtis held her close. Something old and familiar stirred between them, and he abruptly let her go. "We should not sleep together," he said.

"No." Under the surface disappointment she felt a small surge of happiness. They were on the same wavelength. At last.

Curtis walked her to her car. He closed the door firmly after she got behind the wheel.

—⚭—

"I CALLED A FEW DAYS later to see how she was doing," said Curtis. "She would have been pretty late getting home, and I had a bad feeling about Tim."

The sternum injury.

"She didn't tell me Tim had physically hurt her, but he had." His fingers, which had been pressing on a trigger point on my foot, pressed harder. Then he released my foot. And looked at me. "I didn't find out until the police told me. But I can imagine exactly how it happened. I think when she got home he confronted her about where she'd been, and knowing Lucy, she probably told him outright and he lost it."

I closed my eyes against the image of Tim sending a powerful fist into her sternum. No wonder she had sounded so bad on the phone that day I had called her. She would have been in terrible pain. And then I remembered something from our next phone conversation. I looked at Curtis. "Lucy told me she might be in the Gatineaus the next weekend. That's why I invited her to my ice-breaking-up party. Was she going back to your place?"

Curtis shook his head. "We talked about her coming, but we never firmed anything up. I wasn't expecting her. But I've heard since then that she apparently *was* on her way to my place."

"But she never arrived."

Curtis looked up, and there was unbearable pain in his eyes. "She never arrived."

The house was dark. I had forgotten to leave a light on in my rush to get to Curtis's. At least it was only a few steps from the car to my door. And there was nowhere for anyone to be watching me from; I was so close to the main road. But the thoughts wouldn't go away. Quinn spying on me. Tim hurting Lucy. Lucy lying in pain in bed. Calling the bank. Calling me. Calling how many other people, reaching out for help?

I stuck the key in the door and flicked on the hall light. I was spooked tonight, there was no question. I hadn't told Curtis I was going to the site since I couldn't tell him I was going with Quinn. That was definitely off the record. There was no one I could tell where I was going.

I gave myself a shake. There was no reason to worry. My unease was from hearing more about Tim's violence. Quinn had said Lucy had ended up in the hospital with the sternum injury. The hospital again. A place she dreaded. A place that had brought back memories of her mother.

———— ∞∞∞ ————

THE EMERGENCY WAITING ROOM WAS becoming a familiar place. In the middle of the night it was relatively quiet. And then a pregnant woman was ushered in on a stretcher. Lucy heard the words "emergency caesarian." At the words, the woman, already in distress, became visibly distraught. Lucy tried to block out the woman's cries, her sudden yell as a contraction hit. The woman had become her mother, crying out at the child who would not come out on her own. She was relieved when the stretcher was wheeled away. Relieved and also sorry for the woman.

Would hospitals forever be a place of horror for her? And … had her mother felt the same way?

She was absorbed in this new thought—it felt important—and didn't hear her name called. Tim elbowed her in the arm. "That's us." He got up to go with her.

But the nurse wouldn't let him into the examining room.

In the car on the way home, he demanded to know what the doctor had asked her. "What did you tell him?"

She let out a long jagged sigh that hurt her chest. "I didn't tell him anything." She turned her head to the window and looked out into the street-lit night. "Just take me to the drugstore so we can get the prescription filled."

Back home, Tim headed for the sitting room. She heard the TV come on. Sounds of gunfire and screeching tires.

She eased her aching body down the stairs. Crawled into bed.

The pain ebbed with the painkillers. Where were the painkillers for the emotional pain?

She began to cry. Not her usual tantrum tears. Not hiccoughing can't-catch-your-breath tears, but long, slow, despairing sobs. So deep, so drawn out, they were almost a relief. She had heard these sounds before. Had her mother's pain been similar? The cancer, in the end, would have been much more painful. What really had she known of her mother's pain? What had she tried to know?

Her father had been the one to call. Followed by Anna to stress that her father hadn't exaggerated the seriousness of their mother's condition. She was in hospital. It wasn't likely she would come out.

At the word "hospital," she balked. There should now be an opportunity for poetic justice. Her mother was the one in hospital now, wanting her. She should be able to refuse to go.

But she couldn't. Of course she couldn't.

She was so focused on getting herself to Toronto—huge, noisy, unbreathable Toronto—and into the beast, the hospital itself, that she was unprepared for what she found there. There was a ghost lying in the bed. A ghost who was not her mother.

She choked back the tears. No amount of preparation would have readied her for this sallow, gaunt figure with the laboured breathing, barely taking up any space in the bed. Her mother's features were still there in the ghost face—the high cheekbones, even more prominent now, the naturally pursed lips. This was what her life had come to, at fifty-nine. The alcohol, her own dissatisfaction and unhappiness, had slowly eaten away at her insides.

She looked across the bed to Anna, whose eyes were also brimming. And then, without warning, she was filled with anger—anger she hadn't summoned. She wasn't sure what she'd come here to do or say—what was there to do or say?—but it wasn't to rage. She couldn't rage at a ghost. It would blow her mother to kingdom come. And it was meant for her father, anyway, who wasn't there this evening. Thank God.

But her hands, which should have taken her mother's, were clenched, and she couldn't unclench them. To unclench them would have been to unleash the demon.

She could feel Anna looking at her in hurt and bewilderment, wondering why she wasn't reaching out to their mother.

At that moment, her mother's eyes opened. For an instant—an instant only—they lit up. Was it because she'd thought she'd seen Anna? Her lips parted, as if to speak.

She couldn't bear to hear whatever the ghost mouth was going to say. Words that might haunt her forever: What are you doing here?

She bolted to the lounge.

Anna came after her. She didn't open her eyes, but sensed her sister sitting down beside her. She kept her concentration on her breathing, not on the presence beside her. But she couldn't block it out. It was a warm and gentle presence, completely devoid of reproach or disappointment. She scrunched her eyes tighter. How dare Anna be so forgiving when she was being so impossible?

She couldn't will her sister away by keeping her eyes closed. There was a soft sigh, and then a hand touched hers—a feather touch. At the touch, her eyes fluttered open, and she turned to face Anna. But the seat beside her was empty.

23.

WEARING BLUE JEANS AND A white T-shirt, Quinn arrived on the stroke of nine. In the sunlight his eyes were bluer than I had seen them before. Cobalt blue.

It was a Saturday in mid-April masquerading as a warm day in June. I was, I realized, dressed too warmly.

In his car I talked too much, too fast, to make up for the blueness of his eyes and my paranoid thoughts of the night before.

We headed northwest on River Road, past the site where I'd found Lucy's car, a full year ago. In Wakefield we took the road linking the village with Highway 105. Not far up the 105, we turned again at the junction with the highway to Masham. Just before the village we turned right. We drove north for a few more kilometres and turned left onto a dirt road. Irwin. I memorized all the turns. So I could come back on my own, I told myself.

Quinn drove slowly down Irwin. A funereal pace. He was looking for a road on the left. A break in the trees. An even narrower dirt road. He turned the car down the road. We manoeuvred our way around potholes and rocks. We came to a roundabout, encircling an enormous white pine. It reminded me of Curtis's tree-house pine. I wished I had told him where I was going today. I could have trusted him. And I could trust Quinn. I put my paranoid thoughts out of my mind.

Quinn braked. "I'm trying to remember. I was only here once. We brought Bryn back up here a week after Tim led her to the body. To do a video statement. To retrace their route that day. I just saw the video

again a few weeks ago. It's pretty powerful. We filmed from the back of
a pick-up. You can see that the whole area is just bush and forest. They
go down all these roads. They drive and drive. This was only the second
time they'd gone searching, and they never get out of the car once. Bryn
has no idea where she is. Then they come here, and—that's right...."
He was talking more to himself than to me, remembering. "They went
down this road." He pointed to an even smaller track beyond the circle.
He nosed the car down the track.

We drove a short distance, until we reached a fence. Quinn stopped
the car, turned off the ignition, yanked up on the hand brake.

He turned to me. "This was the first place they got out to search that
day. After driving around for two or three hours. And wouldn't you
know, within twenty minutes they've found Lucy's remains."

"It's pretty compelling evidence, isn't it?" I asked. "His leading her
right here."

"Damn right it is. Stupid son of a bitch."

We got out of the car. Quinn pointed to a pile of wood in a small
meadow in the distance. "He led Bryn that way first. Told her Lucy was
likely under a pile of brush or wood. Now how would he know that?
She said they didn't even search under the wood pile. You can see an
incline just beyond it—leads up into some woods. They got that far,
then he suddenly wants to turn around. She follows him back. They
do a cursory search on the way back—they look under the wood pile.
Then he brings her back this way, and they go through here, into the
woods along the fence." He turned and gestured the other way. Then
he looked at me. "Shall we?"

I nodded.

He led the way through the dense bush. He held branches for me.
He pointed out barbed wire half buried in the brush under my feet.
"Careful."

I concentrated on my footing. Not on my thoughts. Not on Tim
leading Bryn in this same way, holding the branches for her, pointing
out the barbed wire.

The dense brush gave way to a grove of pines. The forest floor was soft
with pine needles. Sunlight barely filtered through the trees. I wasn't sure

how Quinn knew where to go. We seemed to be going in circles.

"Sorry," said Quinn, pausing to look around. "It all looks the same."

Then I saw it: a red ribbon tied around a thick pine trunk. A memorial. I touched Quinn's arm and pointed.

"Right—there it is." He looked around again. "Tim and Bryn were about here when she spotted something over there." He pointed toward the pine tree. "A dark mound, she said, something that looked out of place. She pointed it out, and Tim said, 'That's Lucy.'"

"He *said* that? How could he tell from this distance?"

"It's great, eh? That's what she asked him. He pointed out a running shoe—it was even farther away—said, 'That's Lucy's running shoe.'"

I stared at him. "He saw that from here? No way. He's going to hang himself for sure, isn't he?"

"We're going to get the bastard."

Again that hardness in his voice. I walked away from him, toward the tree.

The ribbon was police tape. It was wrapped several times around the thick trunk. X marks the spot.

At the base of the tree was a pile of brush and pine needles. Nearby was a darker patch of earth, where the pine needles had been cleared away. It was dark still, months after forensic experts had sifted painstakingly through the soil and branches in search of evidence.

I crouched down. I put my hand palm down on the dark earth.

"There wasn't much," came Quinn's voice above me. "A skull, a few bones, some flesh hanging off them. Some clothing. What got Bryn was the clump of hair on the wood pile."

The hairs on the back of my neck stood on end. I was on my feet in an instant. I stared at him in horror. "Her hair?" I whispered.

Quinn was nodding. "Her hair." Then he saw my face. "Oh God, I'm such an insensitive idiot. I thought you already knew all this."

"No. I didn't." I couldn't keep my voice from shaking. "It's okay. Can you—could you leave me here—for a few minutes?"

"Are you sure? You'll be alright?" His eyes looked normal again. Not cobalt blue. Just worried.

"Yes. Please." Then I looked around. "Wait—I'm not sure how to find my way out."

Quinn pointed to a gap in the trees. "Through there. You can see the beginnings of a trail. It's a well worn path. You can't go wrong. That will take you straight to the circle where that big white pine is. I brought you in the long way—the way Brennan brought Bryn in. After they spotted Lucy's remains, they decided to take pictures, and went back to the car for the camera. She said he led her out this way. It's a much more direct route. But how would he know that? Unless he'd been here before. Of course, bringing her *in* this way would have been too obvious. But Stupid fucked up, going out and returning by the more direct route. More damning evidence."

He touched my shoulder and his voice lost its edge. "I'll bring the car to the circle and wait for you there. You're sure you'll be okay?"

I nodded and thanked him. And watched him go.

Then I sat down on the pine-carpeted forest floor, trying to keep the images of Lucy's remains at bay. A life had ended here. A will—a life—had been choked off. An exuberant life. It had come down to a few bits of flesh and bone and hair. I let the horror work its way through me. Gradually, it ebbed. And was replaced by ... nothing. I wanted to feel grief, sadness for Lucy. Understanding. But there was nothing. As if this place had nothing to do with her.

I sat with a blank mind and an empty heart. I wanted a flash of understanding. A vision. Anything but this emptiness at the end of my too-long-postponed pilgrimage.

I sat until my legs went numb. Then I stood up. The numbness ebbed, both from my legs and from my brain. I turned slowly and then I could see it—the hair on the wood pile. But the hair wasn't dark. It was blonde. Strawberry blonde. Strawberry blonde hair cascading over a raised bed in a meadow. A raised bed that could have been a wood pile.... The dream from last summer slowly came back: Lucy floating on water, but my finding her on dry land.

But I hadn't found her at all. Anywhere.

Emotion finally crept in: it should have been grief. It was *apprehension*, and *fear*.

I turned again. In slow motion. To the place we had come in. To where we had stood. The colours of the woods had changed. They were the intense colours of a dream.

I am facing Tim. He is speaking. I am replying. But I can't hear the words. I can only feel the terror in both of us.

Hands reach for my throat. Only it's not my throat. I am not me.

My arms, arms that aren't mine, reach out. Not to defend. They pull him in. They hold him. My voice, a voice that isn't mine, speaks. Comforting words that hold no comfort.

The fear releases. But no relief replaces it.

I let him go. I step back. I look in his eyes. I am me, looking in his eyes. And they are cobalt blue.

The colours of the pine grove returned to their muted sunlight-deprived tones. I stood rooted to the spot. Not daring to move, but turning my head in every direction. Had Quinn come back into the grove? Was he right now hiding behind a tree? Watching? *Why?*

Reason answered: *Steve Quinn did not bring you here to kill you.*

Saying the words—almost out loud—made me see how ridiculous they were.

I made myself sit down again, my back against Lucy's tree, knowing now that it would forever be Lucy's tree. I made my breathing slow down, and as it slowed my pulse slowed too. I closed my eyes and let rise up what was under the surface tension and confusion. It wasn't anything I was expecting. But there it was: A steely resolution.

Bright sunlight hit my eyes, and I paused at the edge of the woods to let them adjust. Quinn was leaning against the trunk of the car beside the huge white pine in the circle, facing the direction we had hiked in. Looking relaxed. A lit cigarette in his hand. I had never seen him smoke before. There was a lot about him I had never seen before.

At the sound of my boots crunching on the gravel, he turned his head, pushed himself away from the car and tossed the butt. He came toward me, and the relaxed stance shifted to attention. To concern.

"There you are. I was about to come looking for you. I was worried you'd got lost."

I made myself meet the eyes from my vision. "I'm not lost."

He looked at me for a long moment and opened his mouth to say something. Then he shook his head. "Come on. I'll take you home."

In the driveway, Quinn turned off the ignition. "You're pretty quiet."

I turned to face him. I had my story ready. "I think I just saw what happened to Lucy. You—the police—were right. I had another vision, or whatever you want to call it. Tim's hands reached out to choke me—only it wasn't me. It must have been—"

"Oh God," said Quinn. "Bryn."

"*Bryn?*" I stared at him.

"I wasn't going to tell you that part while we were in the woods."

I waited for him to continue. My heart was pounding again.

Quinn exhaled. "Just after they spotted Lucy, Bryn said Brennan got this odd look on his face, like he suddenly was thinking he'd made a mistake bringing her there. She was suddenly afraid for her life. He actually started to reach for her neck and she made the spontaneous decision to pull him to her in a huge bear hug, pretending to be shocked and sorry for him. It probably saved her life. It snapped him out of it."

I took in and let out a long, slow breath. Absorbing what he had just said. Absorbing what I had just seen. I had got it. I had got it all. All of it and more.

Quinn looked at me as if he had seen a ghost. "I should never have taken you there."

"No, it's okay. I'm glad you did. I'm okay."

"Are you sure? I think I should stay with you for awhile." The dictatorial tone was gone. He seemed unsure of himself. Hesitant.

"No." This was not a man I wanted with me. This was not a man I wanted in my life. I made him go home.

The water was completely open, the current steady. It sent tiny ice flows on their way downstream, unperturbed. The breeze was from the south.

I stood on the point, holding my face to the warm wind, taking it deep into my lungs.

Finally, I saw it—the violence hovering around Quinn. He had tried, all along, to hide the truth: saying things he thought I wanted to hear, playing the protector, trying to gain my trust. Needing to be in control.

My vision had given me a glimpse—a glimpse in the strange, *safe* way of my visions—of the lengths he was capable of to ensure that control. In his eyes I had seen his own fear of those capabilities. It was that fear that, day by day, kept them in check.

Finally, I understood all the contradictory feelings and responses in me. I had capabilities too. It was time to stop denying them.

I watched the tiny ice flows bobbing past the point. Before they reached the dam down at Chelsea, they would have melted into the water.

The river was ready for Belle's ashes. There was someone who would want to be part of that ritual. I headed back up to the house to make a phone call.

24.

I SAT OUTSIDE COURTROOM 32. I had a response rehearsed for Sergeant Quinn. I would be cool, polite. I wouldn't get drawn into conversation, or flirting, or whatever approach he tried. As for Mr. Blair....

The sound of heels clicking on the granite floor brought me out of my thoughts. The Assistant Crown Attorney, Deanne Fortier, was coming toward me, her sympathetic smile at the ready.

She sat down beside me and spoke *sotto voce* in her slight accent. "I am not supposed to be talking to you, but I just wanted to tell you not to worry. You were fine on Friday. Are you alright?"

I nodded my lie.

Deanne stood up and looked down the hall. "There's Sergeant Lundy. I will leave you to him, then." She smiled again. "Don't let Mr. Blair unravel you."

I looked down the hall. Sergeant Lundy was strolling toward us. I hadn't seen him since the memorial service, months ago. I wondered if his coming here today meant....

Deanne paused long enough to speak a few words to Lundy, then she flashed one more smile my way and went back to her office.

Lundy eased himself into the seat beside me. He never quite smiled, but the natural expression on his face was kind. "Ellen," he nodded, by way of greeting.

"Hi, Sergeant Lundy."

"Al," he said and suddenly grinned. It was a full-on grin. One eye-tooth was chipped. For a moment the tough guy was gone.

I took the hand he offered. It was the size and texture of a leather work glove. "Are you taking over witness hand-holding today?"

Lundy dropped my hand. "Yeah, and general slave to the Crown. Quinn called in sick this morning."

"Oh," I said. Intense relief.

"Yeah, so they fished me out of my bed." Lundy heaved a sigh that made his belly balloon out and in. He shrugged.

"Naive of me to think they'd let me sleep. Even if there's been a bit of a lull lately. The murderers in town have killed everyone they want to. And those we haven't caught seem to have gone on vacation." He winked. "The wife wanted to go on vacation too. She was kind of reluctant to let me out of bed this morning." He spoke without a trace of self-consciousness.

I couldn't help laughing. "I don't think I'd like to be a cop's wife. When you're never home." *When you might not come home.*

He shrugged again. "She knew what she was getting in for when she signed up. We went through a rough patch last year, when we were trying to gather evidence on Brennan. Seemed like me and the Roach were on the case twenty-four hours a day—no rest for the wicked. Yeah, yeah, yeah." He sucked in the words in quick succession. "Had to have a talk with the wife."

I suppressed a smile at the thought of Al Lundy being a communicator in a relationship. But what did I know?

"Must have been tough," I said.

He shrugged. "She's young, she'll heal."

And he was young too. The realization was something of a shock. Beyond the extra weight and standard haggard cop look, he was probably not much more than forty-five. The same age as Lucy.

I watched the lawyers file past us into the courtroom. The Senior Assistant Crown Attorney nodded at me solemnly, respectfully, from behind his owl glasses.

"Technically," Lundy was saying, "I should be here every day—me or the Roach. But before all the town murderers went on holiday it was pretty busy for us, and Quinn was familiar enough with the case." He nodded at me. "You had some dealings with him one night, I recall.

That's what got him in on it in the first place." He seemed not to notice the sudden colour on my face.

"Doesn't he have his own cases?" I tried for a casual tone.

"Naw—not our Quinn. Not now anyway."

"Ms. McGinn."

I jumped.

The court attendant was standing at the door.

I drew in and let out a deep breath and stood up. "Well, at least there are no high-school students today."

"Oh, they'll be in after the break."

He held the door for me. "Roach'll probably be by later. If you're done by noon, we'll take you to lunch."

I couldn't imagine ever being done.

The judge was nodding at me as I came up the aisle. "Good morning, Ms. McGinn. I hope you had a good weekend." Her friendliness took me aback.

"Oh, yes." I couldn't help the wry tone.

"You haven't been sworn in yet, Ms. McGinn, but we still like to hear the truth."

I laughed in spite of myself and took my seat in the witness box. Appreciating her attempt to help me relax.

The judge turned to the clerk. "I think we'd better swear in Ms. McGinn as soon as possible," she joked.

The Crown's side of the court was all smiles. The defence looked disapproving. I glanced over at Tim Brennan in his glass box. He sat without expression. Gone was the sympathetic innocent. Quinn had called him evil. Was he? Today he just looked sullen and guilty.

Mr. Blair stood up. He put on his glasses and peered at his notes. Then he took off his glasses and aimed volley number one my way.

"Ms. McGinn, I understand from what you've told us that you don't consider yourself to be a close friend of Lucy."

I took a deep breath. *Answer only the question asked, Ellen.* "That's correct," I said.

"But you had gone through at least a period of time where she would confide in you."

"That's correct," I said again.

"And confided to the extent that you were familiar with her relationship with Tim Brennan."

"I was familiar with his past. I wasn't familiar…. After Tim got out of prison and moved in with her, I didn't hear very much about their relationship from that point on."

"Alright," said Blair. "But you did speak to her from time to time."

"I did, yes."

"Okay. And you were specifically, I think, asked by Agent Godbout, who took your statement I think on the twenty-fifth of April, about whether you knew of any problems in their relationship, and specifically I think you were asked to address whether she had problems with him. Do you recall that?"

"I do recall that, yes." *Here we go.*

"Okay. And you told him that as far as you knew they never had any big fights." He put on his glasses and quoted from my statement. "'I never saw any marks on her as if he'd beaten her, nor did she ever hint that it was an abusive relationship.'"

He looked at me over the rim of his glasses. "And that was indeed your best recollection and best information you could give Agent Godbout at that time."

"That's right." I wanted to say more—I wanted to qualify it—but I barely had time to gather my thoughts. Blair was on to the next question.

"You also told the court how Lucy spoke to you about having anxiety attacks and panic attacks."

"That's correct." Was I going to spend the whole session agreeing with his statements? I seemed to have no choice. I didn't dare look at Deanne.

"And at times couldn't leave her home."

"Well, she told me she would sometimes *be* out and have to come home."

"And you say that she went for massage, and … reiki, is that it?"

"Yes."

"Do you know if the massage and reiki treatments were related to the anxiety attacks and panic attacks?"

"I think she would have—I'm speculating here—I think she would have had the massage and reiki treatments as a healing treatment." I wasn't speculating. But I couldn't reveal that I knew.

"Was she someone who seemed to have a lot of complaints about life and about things, her state of health and so forth?"

I had not been expecting these questions about Lucy. It hit me with a jolt of realization: Lucy was on trial too. But who was representing her? The answer hit me with another jolt.

"Well, about her state of health, yes," I said. "I wouldn't say she had a lot of complaints about life, because I saw her as somebody who felt that this was just all part of it and tried to tackle her problems." I had not known this with such certainty until this moment.

"Did she tend to perhaps dwell on physical ailments, physical problems a bit?"

"No, I don't think so."

"In the sense of being maybe somewhat of a neurotic?"

"No."

"Hypochondriac?"

"No."

"Or anything like that?"

"No, not in that way, no."

"You didn't feel that."

"No." It was another unknown truth coming out of my mouth .

"You told the court that in late fall of ninety-four, I think you said, you decided to shut down your friendship with her because she had got mad at you for being happy—something to that effect."

"Yes."

"Can you expand on what you meant?"

"She was angry with me because I told her I was doing fine. And she said something like 'Well, I don't know how you've managed to escape it. Everyone I know is going through something right now.'"

"Okay. She seemed to be, then, sort of genuinely of the view that it was some kind of bad time, that everybody should be having a bad time."

"Yes—I don't know for sure, but she may well have thought there was something in the air that was causing people to go through a bad time.

Everyone who was sensitive to it," I added.

"Does that not suggest that perhaps she was a little neurotic about things?"

"No, I don't think so." I considered. "Neurotic. Can you define neurotic for me?"

Blair shrugged. "Someone who sees a lot of problems where there may not necessarily be problems. That's not a clinical definition, but…."

I nodded. "No, I don't think with that definition that I would describe her as neurotic."

"Okay." He sounded mildly impatient. "Is there *any* definition of the word that you understand that might fit her?"

Lucy Stockman, neurotic. Did she invent problems where there were none? Were her ailments all in her head? I looked straight at Mr. Blair. "I would not describe Lucy as neurotic."

Mr. Blair changed tactics. "To return to your statement you made to Agent Godbout. You stated that Lucy told you that she thought Mr. Brennan was a very gentle soul."

"That's right."

"In fact, you related to this court that that was what you saw too—when Lucy showed you a picture of Mr. Brennan in her kitchen."

"Well, I wouldn't have used the term 'gentle soul' myself."

"But you saw kindness, gentleness…."

"Yes, I did. It changed after—"

"Well, I'm sure it changed after you had begun to have *hallucinations*."

My stomach knotted. "It changed after I saw—"

Blair didn't give me a chance to finish. "Now I just want to go through with you what happened—"

The Assistant Crown stood up. "I wonder if my friend would let the witness continue her answer."

Mr. Blair made a gesture of acquiescence.

"It changed…." My mind went blank. "I didn't see it the night we found the car," I finished. It wasn't what I wanted to say.

"Well, we'll get into that," said Blair. "I just want to go through the events you related to us with respect to the scene when the Suzuki was recovered. You've told us you had to very carefully give Mr. Brennan directions, because you understood that he had a bad sense of direction, you'd been told that by Lucy before."

One by one, Mr. Blair took me through all the 'odd things' that Deanne Fortier had asked me about. The questions droned on and on. There seemed to be no point in them. No obvious winner, no obvious loser in each exchange. I couldn't figure out where he was trying to go, what he was trying to get me to say. The effort of listening to his words, and weighing mine, was exhausting. But it was a relief to be staying on the track of the 'odd things.'

"You told the court that after you invited Mr. Brennan back to your house, on the way back it suddenly crossed your mind that 'This man has killed somebody before and am I being stupid inviting him back to my house'—that sort of thing."

"Yes."

"But all the time Tim was with you—at the site, in your house, you described to us how shaky and teary he was—genuinely upset."

"He *seemed* upset," I said.

"Yes, you say that now. But it didn't occur to you at the time that it was anything but genuine. In fact, in a conversation with your friend that evening you say to her—" He glanced at his notes and quoted my words: "'Either he's innocent or my world has turned upside down and I can't trust my judgement anymore.' Is that correct?"

"That's correct."

"Your judgement at that time, from everything you had observed, what you had seen, how he had reacted, how he had conducted himself in your presence up to the late hours of the evening of the twenty-fourth when you called your friend, your judgement told you that he was innocent."

I stared at him.

"Clearly, what you were telling your friend was that your judgement told you from everything you had observed about him, how he had reacted, his demeanour, everything else, what he said, what he did, told you that, 'No matter what he might have done before, I don't believe he had anything to do with Lucy's disappearance.' That is what you were saying, isn't it?"

This time his words shocked me into speaking. "No, that is not what I was saying. I was saying that my world could very well have turned upside down."

"Well, of course. But your judgement that you're referring to—'either I can't trust my judgement or he's innocent.'"

"That's right."

"So your judgement was telling you that he's innocent. Isn't that what you're saying?"

"My judgement was telling me that I'd picked up nothing from him indicating that he was guilty."

"Ms. McGinn, your recollection of your words to your friend is very precise. And most important, you spoke these words before you had your dream, whatever you're calling it, about Lucy."

My stomach muscles tightened again. "Yes, I was speaking to her before that happened."

"You seem like a person who has good judgement; you trust your own judgement. In your estimation, Mr. Brennan was innocent."

"I didn't say that I was judging him innocent." Suddenly, I was angry. "I said *either* he's innocent *or* my world has turned upside down." I looked straight at Mr. Blair. "I was quite prepared for the fact that my world might have turned *completely* upside down."

There was a silence in the courtroom.

Mr. Blair put on his glasses to consult his notes. He took them off and looked up at me. "These dreams you had—although a couple of them were actually, you said, hallucinations of some kind. Can you describe exactly what happens to you when you have these hallucinations?"

The anger was gathering force. "First of·all, I object to you calling them hallucinations. It makes it sound as though I am on some kind of drug or seeing things that aren't there."

"Indeed," said Mr. Blair. "And what would you have us call them?"

"Visions." I spoke the word without hesitation, or embarrassment.

"And tell us what you understand the difference to be between a vision and a hallucination."

"Technically, I don't know if there is a difference. I just know the connotation attached to each and the disparaging tone in your voice when you say the word 'hallucination.'" I didn't hide the anger in my voice. It wasn't a defensive, explosive anger. It was *right*—righteous anger—even if I was going to get cited for contempt of court.

"Very well, Ms. McGinn," said Blair in a cold voice. "Please explain, then, what happens to you when you have a *vision*." His intonation of the word was no less disparaging. But I ignored the bait.

I took a breath. "It usually happens—not always, but usually—either just before I go to sleep or just as I'm waking up. I am in some kind of altered state—I'm neither asleep nor awake. It's like a waking dream. Except the events are not the fantastical events of dreams that make no rational sense when you wake up. These events are real, logical. I am somewhere else. I am seeing things that are happening to someone else, somewhere else—or that have sometime in the recent past happened to someone. I am watching. An observer of events. A couple of times it's happened when I've been fully awake—I mean in broad daylight, outside. Those times there's no question of it being a dream."

I'd had no idea I could come up with such a rational explanation of my experiences. I felt an odd triumph. It was—I knew—lost on the court. I didn't care. I took a breath and looked straight at Blair. "And then there have been a few times when someone has visited me."

"Like Lucy Stockman."

"Yes. The first time it happened it was more like a dream, but after that it was obviously a visit—she was in the room with me. She was giving me messages."

Mr. Blair looked at me for a moment as if he was going to challenge me, then he looked down at his notes, and back up at me. "And so, on the night of the twenty-sixth, you have a *visit* from Lucy Stockman, who has just gone missing. And she essentially tells you Mr. Brennan had done it, and on the strength of that you went to the police station in the middle of the night. And you spoke to—I think you said it was Sergeant Quinn you saw there."

Mr. Blair looked around as if he were going to have me identify Quinn. He swept his eyes over Counsel and turned back to me.

"Yes," I said of the ghost in the room.

"And I think you said you told Sergeant Quinn that you had a dream, not a vision or a visit. Would you not agree with me that you were reluctant to tell Sergeant Quinn about your—experience—because you were skeptical about what you had seen, and, more importantly, what you had heard?"

"Yes, I admit I was skeptical." It was my first smile of apology.

"And you were skeptical because your experience *before* this—vision—your experience in the first few hours that you had been in Mr. Brennan's presence was that your judgement told you he was innocent."

I was not going to get side-tracked into a discussion of my judgement again. "No, that was not why I was skeptical. I was—"

"You were skeptical because Mr. Brennan had behaved in a way that completely correlated to a man shaken by—"

Deanne stood up again. "Your Honour, again, may I ask my friend to allow the witness to finish her statement."

All eyes were on me.

I breathed in and out deeply. I gave myself time to consider my answer. I said, "I think the more accurate answer is not so much that I was skeptical as that I was frightened. This was the first time this had ever happened to me. I wasn't sure what to make of it."

"Indeed," said Mr. Blair.

"Believe me, I wanted to ignore the whole experience. But I couldn't. I told Sergeant Quinn I had had a dream in which I'd heard an anonymous voice speaking to me because I didn't think he would give any credence to a real visit, especially from Lucy herself. And I really wanted him to believe what he was telling me because—because I thought Lucy was still alive at the time…." My voice broke. "And I … wanted her … *found*."

"Are you okay?" asked Mr Blair. "Do you want to take a break? I only have a few more questions."

I wiped my eyes. "No, I'll be okay."

"I just want to pursue that for a moment, though, if you don't mind, if you want to take a break."

The clerk was suddenly standing before me with a box of tissues and a smile of sympathy. I took a tissue and thanked her. I blew my nose. I looked back at Mr. Blair. "No, it's okay, I'm alright."

It was the truth.

"Okay," said Mr. Blair. "I understand that in your dream or visit from Lucy Stockman, whatever you wish to call it, she more or less told you Mr. Brennan was responsible. Is that it?"

"Yes. I guess what I haven't explained is that it wasn't clear to me whether Lucy was alive or dead—she seemed to be hovering on the brink, but Tim was clearly responsible for the state she was in, and that's why I went down to the police station in the middle of the night. I wasn't really concerned about Tim at the time. I was concerned with finding Lucy and making sure she lived. I wanted Sergeant Quinn to go to this place to look for Lucy."

"Lucy gave you a specific location, then, did she?"

"No, not that specific. It's hard to explain. She indicated a distance to go down Bank Street, down in the Hunt Club area, and said she was in some kind of abandoned outbuilding."

"Some kind of abandoned…?"

"Outbuilding."

"Outbuilding, okay. And did she give you a description of the physical layout of the place or the physical surroundings?"

"Yes, it was supposed to be in a wooded area."

"Okay, thank you. Those are all the questions I have."

I was, in quick succession, surprised, relieved and disappointed.

The judge looked over to Deanne. "Any re-examination?"

Deanne stood up. "Just one question."

She turned to me. "Mr. Blair made reference to a conversation you had with your friend in which you said 'Either he's innocent or my world has been turned upside down and I can't trust my judgement anymore.' And I think you mentioned in reference to that that you had started to change your mind about Tim somewhere along the line. The question is: at which point did you start changing your mind about Tim and why did you change your mind?"

I knew why she was asking this question. She wanted to show that despite any questionable visions, I had already begun to have inner doubts about Tim. I didn't blame her for asking. I responded calmly. "It was that first evening, after I invited him into my home. He had made all these phone calls, and I'd made him tea, and at intervals he would cry and be upset, and at one point when he was crying I had this thought that I wanted him out of my house. It was very fleeting and brief and not like me—I was shocked I would have that thought about someone who was so obviously upset. But when I remembered it later, I wondered if it was a message to me to be careful, that they might be crocodile tears, that he was not all he seemed."

Deanne turned to the judge. "I have no further questions, Your Honour."

The judge turned to me. "Thank you, Ms. McGinn. You are free to go."

I was almost sorry. I had just been getting warmed up.

I was shaking on my way out of Courtroom 32.

Al Lundy was right behind me. "Can I get you a coffee?" he asked.

I laughed. "Coffee! I need a drink!"

Lundy took me down the escalator to the cafeteria in the atrium on the lower level. He led me over to the fridge of juices. He made a sweeping gesture with his hand. "We got the full range of single malts right here."

I picked out a single malt apple. A poor substitute for the real thing.

Lundy found a table away from the others in the cafeteria. "Sorry," he said. "The Crown's got Roach runnin' around and we have to be somewhere in half an hour. Going to have to take a raincheck on that lunch. This is the best I can do."

Under the circumstances, I didn't care. Except the juice wasn't having the desired effect.

Lundy watched me raise the juice bottle to my mouth with both hands wrapped around it. "That bad, eh? Sit tight, I'll be back in two shakes."

Eight minutes later a styrofoam cup was placed on the table in front of me. There was an inch of golden liquid in the bottom of the cup.

I looked up at Lundy. He nodded down at the cup. "Grade A apple juice."

The liquid warmed my throat on its way down and stopped my hands from shaking.

Lundy sat down. "Our Senior Assistant Crown Attorney keeps a stash in his bottom drawer."

"For himself or the witnesses?" The Senior Assistant Crown Attorney didn't strike me as a Marlowe type.

"Let's just say it's communal." Lundy winked. Then his expression changed and he looked at me for a long moment. When he spoke, I had to lean forward to hear. "The only person we don't let into the stash," he said, "is Sergeant Quinn."

I started.

He kept his eyes trained on mine. "It's actually not so much alcohol that was—is—his demon. But an addict will take anything they can get."

"*Addict?*" It didn't come out in the casual tone I was trying for.

"Don't worry, he's fine now. But—" He interrupted himself. "I shouldn't be telling you this, but I think maybe you need to know it more than I shouldn't be telling it to you, so I'm going to tell you." He paused and looked at me.

I met his eyes. Barely breathed.

He sighed. "He got into a bit of trouble a few years back. When he was in the drug unit." He shook his head. "It's like a doctor having access to all those pills. Too tempting. Force turns a blind eye if it can. But Quinn was getting out of hand. Erratic."

I held my breath then.

"His wife threatened to leave him if he didn't get help."

"I assume he did get help?" My voice cracked.

"Yes, into rehab. Thanks to Ellen."

"What d'you mean?" I tried, and failed, to keep the guilt out of my voice.

"Ellen—his wife." He shot me a glance. "I guess he never mentioned the coincidence."

"No." But a fragment of conversation had come back to me. *I've begun to realize not all Ellens are created equal.* And the familiar way he called me "El." I was almost more shaken by this information than the other. Just who had I been for Quinn?

"So, she got him in rehab," I prompted.

"Yeah—couple years back now. He was in for six weeks. Then on leave for a few more months. Then he came back on the force—on limited hours. Beginning of last year. Desk duty." He shook his head again. "That'd be enough to send *me* around the bend. I don't know what he was doing there the night you came in. I didn't think they had him on nights yet."

At one time I would have been surprised to hear he'd been at the station at a time he wasn't supposed to be. Now it was clear we'd had an appointment with destiny. Possibly arranged by Lucy herself.

"You said his wife threatened to leave him. Did she—did they work it out?"

Lundy was watching my face.

And now I saw it. Nothing got past him. He had seen it all: my relief that Quinn wasn't coming today. My reaction about his addiction. My start at the use of my name. My curiosity about his ex-wife. This was why Lundy thought I should know. Not to tell tales on Quinn or to warn me off because my interest in him was out of line. He was concerned. Concerned about *me*.

He heaved a sigh that expanded his belly. "She left him while he was in rehab. But they never got divorced. She came back after a year—after he got clean. That was late last summer. But it's looking rocky again. I'm not sure what's going on right now. Quinn's pretty close-mouthed about it." He paused and spoke in a voice that matched the compassion in his expression. "And you will be too, won't you?"

I nodded and tried to convey my appreciation in my own expression. But my mind was reeling. *They never got divorced. She came back.* That, not just the case, was why he'd stopped seeing me. My brain felt like someone had fired a stun gun at it. I downed the last of the Scotch.

Lundy was looking at me again. A little harder this time. Then he reached into his pocket and pulled out a card. He clicked a ballpoint pen, scrawled a number. Handed it to me. I was having a déjà vu.

"Don't think I ever gave you one of these," he said. "Use it, will you? If you ever need to."

I took the card. Flicked the edge with my finger. "Thanks, I will." I managed a smile. "If I need to."

"That other number's my pager," nodded Lundy.

"Hey, we getting a little personal here? Your pager? What next?"

Sergeant Howard Roach was suddenly standing over us.

Lundy winked at me. "Safer to call me than the Roach. I'm a happily married man."

Sergeant Roach turned a chair around, swung a leg over it and sat down, leaning his arms on the back of it. "You're a son of a bitch with a roving eye. Don't listen to him, Ellen. Whatever he's been tellin' you. He's full of shit." His tone was nothing but pleasant.

"Watch your mouth, Howie. There's a lady present."

"Yeah, and we were supposed to take her to lunch. Sorry, Ellen. Blame the Crown."

"She's okay," said Lundy. "She got the lunch she was after." He nodded at my cup.

Roach peered into it. Sniffed. Smiled. "Crown Royal, we call that. Emphasis on 'Crown.' Glad Big Al's been lookin' after you. But I gotta take him away. Sorry—Crown's orders."

As usual Sergeant Roach was looking everywhere but at me as he spoke. Not much got past him either. Wherever it was happening.

The two men stood up.

"I was just giving Ellen some information I thought it might be good for her to know."

"Something she didn't know?"

"Well, I think she did. I was just giving her the facts."

"What more is there?" Roach's face held a bland, innocent look.

"We'll never know," said Lundy. "They only pay us to deal with facts."

I liked Al Lundy. A lot. I suddenly remembered Quinn telling me to ask them about Bryn. "Someday I'd like to hear the story of how Tim happened to find the body."

"'Happened' is right," said Lundy, making quotation marks in the air. "He was supposedly continuing the search."

"With his new 'bimbo,'" added Roach.

"Except she was working for us," said Lundy.

"She was amazing," said Roach. "The way she got him to take her into his confidence." He shook his head.

"Course, a couple of things helped," said Lundy.

I looked from one to the other. They had their alternating lines down like a comic routine.

"Money for one thing," said Roach.

"A big car," said Lundy.

"And a big set of knockers." Roach held his hands cupped out in front of him. He looked around and put them down. "He thought he had it made. Stupid jerk."

"In the news it said he walked into the police station. Did he give himself up?"

Lundy snorted. "Hardly. He was still playing the innocent boyfriend. But we arrested him immediately. We were counting on him to find the body. In fact that was the only reason we could arrest him."

"Why?"

"If anyone else had found it we wouldn't have a case against him. There's no other solid evidence. But the 'coincidence' of this happening is just a bit too staggering."

"So the argument is that he knew all along where the body was."

"Yup, but he's claiming he was framed. That Bryn was the one who actually spotted the body. That we planted her."

"But she approached Brennan on her own," said Roach. "She'd talked to him before we even hired her. In fact, that's how we found her—we had Lucy's house bugged. We heard her interviewing Brennan. We called her in to see if she wanted to help. She did. She'd become convinced from talking to him that he was guilty."

"He slipped up with her too—the way he did with you." Lundy was nodding at me. "Told her the car had been found 'exactly the way I left it.'" He made quotation marks in the air again. "Then corrected himself to say 'exactly the way she would have left it.'"

This was even more damning than the things he'd said to me. It was good to find out he'd slipped up verbally with other people too. That I hadn't imagined it. And maybe it would lend weight to my evidence at the trial.

"We made sure she was on the level," Roach was saying. "Then we figured out a plan. Told her what to do. What to say." He shook his head. "The balls of that woman."

"I wish I could have been more help." I didn't though. Not in that way. I knew that now.

"Your support of Lucy was the best help we could have had," came the bland reply.

They shook my hand in turn. They thanked me for doing my bit.

"See you at the trial," said Roach. "It'll likely get going in a year or two. We'll be in touch."

I watched them leave. Big slow-walking men with an aptitude for solving murders.

I didn't tell them the trial had just ended.

I was heading for the phone booths in the main entrance when a stocky, freckled woman stopped in front of me. "I'm sorry this is the way we had to meet again."

I stared at her. She wore her hair pulled back. She had puffy eyes, as if from crying, or lack of sleep. It was no one I recognized. "I'm sorry. Do I know you?"

"Marnie Baxter."

I tried to hide my stunned surprise. "You're here to give evidence at the hearing."

She nodded. "This afternoon. Are you done?"

"Yes, just finished. Thank God."

"I've been trying to come to terms with what happened. I can't believe how I gave Tim the benefit of the doubt. Searching with him those first few days." She seemed to shudder.

I looked around the hall. I was probably not supposed to be talking with another witness. "Did you know him well?"

"No, not well. We—Trish and I—we tried to be a friend to both of them. We had a few meals with them. He's a sociopath. He becomes whoever he thinks you want him to be."

I looked at her. *Who did he become for you?*

I chose my next words with care. "There were some of her friends who only saw the innocent soul. The people I spoke to feel he betrayed their trust."

"He did," said Marnie.

I looked into her eyes. Could this woman who knew Lucy be equally responsible for her murder? Had she got caught up in something that had gotten out of control? Something that had made her afraid to come forward because she would be implicated?

It was impossible to believe—despite the contradictions in her partner's words, despite my own psychic experiences. Thank goodness I wasn't being asked to judge.

She was watching me through her troubled puffy eyes. Troubled and, it seemed, wary. "Maybe, after this—maybe we could get together, compare notes."

"Maybe," I said, and left her to take the stand.

I called Angel from a pay phone. I told him I was done and taking the rest of the day off.

He'd already figured as much. He told me to go unwind.

I told him that was exactly what I was planning to do.

25.

KENDRA MACKENZIE WAS AS TALL as I was. Big-boned. She had blonde hair pulled back in a loose ponytail. Clear eyes and a generous smile. And Trish's strong-looking massage-therapist's hands. I liked her instantly.

"I think it's my head that needs to be massaged most," I told her before she started. "I just finished testifying at the hearing for Lucy Stockman, and it won't stop spinning around."

Kendra looked sympathetic. "Curtis told me you were involved in that case. It's been rough on everyone. Don't worry, massaging the rest of you will still your brain. And release some of the tension from the hearing."

I was skeptical. Not only was there all the new information about Quinn, there was also a fresh doubt that I had done anything for Lucy, either in searching or in testifying. And then there was meeting Marnie again. She held no place in the police's theory. Maybe for good reason. Or maybe things were not as simple as they wanted them to be.

I felt Kendra's hands trying to loosen up what Curtis called the "plank" in my back, sure that she wasn't going to succeed. But gradually, in spite of myself, I felt myself relaxing, drifting away. I dozed off and on through much of the hour, waking up briefly when Kendra got me to turn over on my back, and then again when her healing hands had finished their work.

She came back into the room when I'd dressed.

"Thank you. I've just become a convert to massage. I wish I hadn't waited so long to come here."

"I think you came at the right time," she smiled. Then she paused, as if hesitant to say something. "I don't really understand this," she said at last. "But while I was working on you, I kept having this thought go through my head that I think I'm supposed to pass on to you." She smiled at my startled face. "It sometimes happens with clients."

At one time, not that long ago, I would have dismissed her as a flake. I wouldn't have been here at all. But now I looked at her, and for some reason I wanted to cry.

"You know the truth," she said. "That's the message I kept getting. Does that make any sense to you?"

I nodded, and then my eyes did fill with tears.

Traffic was light on the highway through Hull. I took in, and released, large quantities of air. All the way up the rise to the hills and the turn-off at Tulip Valley. I couldn't stop.

The trial *was* over. I could step out of the prisoner's box. The witness had finished testifying. The Crown had rested her case. The jury had reached its verdict. The judge was going home. The judge, in fact, was going to retire. For good.

I was guilty and not guilty.

Which makes me innocent. And in my innocence, protected. I had had nothing to fear from Tim. He had not been going to harm me. Whether he was evil or not. I was not the judge of that. There was only one thing I needed to know: that I could rely on my instincts—on my interior voice, which the trauma of this experience had forced me to start hearing. It was not about losing control. It was, in fact, the very opposite. It had taken the vision in the pine grove to get me to listen to myself. That vision had had immediate verification—and from Quinn himself. My world, as Mr. Blair had reminded me, had been turned completely upside down. But now—now it was inside out.

I made the turn onto the 105, rather than onto River Road for home. I still had time before dark.

Big wet snowflakes began to fall. I watched the snow melt on contact with my windshield, thinking about my visions and the police's theory. The police had the facts, but they didn't have the story between the facts.

What if they had joined up the facts wrong? If you connected the dots in the wrong order, you would get a different picture. The same was true if you were missing some of the dots. You'd get a more straightforward picture. A simpler story than the one in my dreams and visions. The story I had gotten didn't contradict the facts. It was just more complex. So much more complex. The truth often was. And I, apparently, knew the truth. Lucy had been giving it to me all along.

———

THE PHONE WOKE HER UP. It was Curtis, calling to find out if she was coming up the next day.

She hesitated. The volume on the TV upstairs had been abruptly turned down. Was Tim listening? "I'm not sure if it'll work," she said, "though I'd like to. Can I let you know later this evening?"

The cottage loomed a haven in her mind—or a hell if Tim chose to make it one.

Then she saw the time. Shit. It was almost six. The bank would be closing. "Curtis, I'm sorry, I have to go. I have to call the bank. I'll call you later this evening."

She eased her body up the stairs. Tim was sitting at the kitchen table, flipping the pages of the *Sun*.

"Bill wired the money."

Surprise. Suspicion. Hope. Elation. "How do you know?"

"Cuz I talked to him while you were sleeping. He said it will be in your account by Monday."

"Monday," she repeated. "It should be there now. If I phone the bank now, it should be there."

Tim glanced up at the clock. "Bank's closed. He just got there at the end of the day. They said it was too late to process today."

"That's bullshit. You're *lying* to me."

The word infuriated him. He stood up, gripped her cheeks in his hand, squeezed. "I do not lie."

He let go of her face. She swallowed, tasted blood in her mouth. "My bank's open on Saturdays. If Bill got to his bank before it closed, the money will show up in my account tomorrow."

She braced herself for the blow.

But the blow didn't come. Instead, Tim was staring off into the room. It made her uneasy, that vacant stare.

Finally, he focused back on her. She couldn't look into his eyes. They weren't the eyes she knew. Suddenly, she didn't know him anymore. What had happened to them? What had happened to *Tim?*

"Don't you understand? I'm worried about you." His voice was cajoling.

"What are you talking about?"

"Don't you worry?"

"What are you *talking* about?" For a bizarre moment she thought she was talking to Curtis.

"He hurt you before. He might hurt you again."

"*Who?*"

"That weasel. Curtis."

"Curtis! He never hurt me!"

"He did. You told me. He's jealous."

She stared at him.

"He might lose it, Lu. He might hurt you. I'm scared for you. Don't go up there. Please don't go up there."

"I haven't said I'm going up there. And even if I was, you're being ridiculous. Curtis is not going to hurt me. You don't know the first thing about him."

Tim's eyes were suddenly filled with hatred. He spoke in a monotone voice that wasn't his. "I know everything about him. I watch his every move. I know what he's thinking. I know how jealous he is. I know that if you just look at another man, he's going to lose it."

"Oh, for God's sake, Tim. Stop sounding so hysterical." She turned away in disgust.

Tim grabbed her arm, pulled her around to face him.

She yanked her arm so hard it came free. The momentum it gained was the wind up to a pitch; her fist was the ball. It connected with Tim's stomach.

He wasn't prepared. Her fist hit softness. Not the softness of her mother's stomach, but enough to make her step back for one stunned moment, expecting to see her mother's eyes, full of shock and pain and hurt.

Instead she saw rage. Rage and ridicule.

"Go ahead—go ahead and hit me. I deserve it." He grabbed her wrist. He jammed himself in the stomach with her hand, over and over.

She ignored the pain in her hand. She watched it as if it was someone else's hand punching him. She spoke as if the bizarre assault wasn't happening. "If that money isn't in my account by noon tomorrow…."

"What? What will you do? Punch me in the stomach again? Like this?"

"I'll call the police!"

He stopped in mid-punch. Her hand felt like jelly.

"And tell them what?"

"That you've defrauded me out of thousands of dollars. That you've stolen from me, and probably from other people too."

He couldn't hide what was in his eyes. She saw it. Unease. Trepidation. *Guilt.*

She pressed her advantage. "I can't help you anymore. I tried and look what you've done to me. You've lied to me and cheated me and stolen from me."

Tim dropped her hand. He sank down into a kitchen chair.

She kept talking. Maybe if she kept talking, he would surrender, admit defeat. Admit his lies. Admit he needed help.

"I know you can't help it. It's not your fault. I understand why you've been stealing from me. I wanted you to be independent. I guess I wanted it too soon. I shouldn't have cut you off my account. I was naive to think you could cope. It's the only way you know how to survive. But it doesn't work, Tim. You can't keep *taking* from me. Your survival is going to be the death of me."

"No!" He looked up. "I would never do anything to hurt you. You know that, Lu. I love you."

"I can't cope anymore. I don't know how to help you anymore. You need real help. More than I can give you. More than your psychologist can give you." She stopped herself from saying "medical help."

Panic in his eyes. "But you won't leave me? Tell me you won't leave me. Tell me, Lu."

Her voice was gentle. Gentle in its infinite weariness. "I can't do this anymore, Tim. I have nothing left to give. Look at me. I'm spent. Used up. You've got to—"

"But once I'm in my own place...."

She shook her head. "It's over, Tim. I'm sorry, but it's over."

She hadn't meant to say that outright. Not yet. Not until she had confirmed the money was in her account. She braced herself, waiting for the rage and the blows. But Tim started to shake. His eyes glazed over. She watched him as if he were herself, having a panic attack. Confused, shaking, weeping. He sat on the kitchen floor, hugging himself, rocking. "Help me, Lu. Help me."

She knelt down beside him. She held him. Stroked his face. Crooned to him. "It's okay. It's okay. I'm here. I'm here."

He continued to tremble, to rock himself. What should she do? Should she take him to the hospital? The Royal Ottawa? Was he having a nervous breakdown?

But at the word "hospital," Tim's shaking increased. "I'm too scared to go there. Don't make me go, Lu. Don't leave me. Please."

She was becoming more agitated. What did she do when she was overwhelmed? "Let's go see Trish. Maybe she can help."

Tim was nodding. She eased herself out of his clinging arms. She dialled Trish's number.

There was no answer. She left a message.

She made Tim a cup of hot milk. They sat on the couch. She held him, rocked him.

Half an hour later, Trish called back. Tim took the phone. She listened to him telling Trish how terrible he felt, how confused and upset. How afraid. Then, like a little boy, he handed her back the phone without saying good-bye.

She could hear Trish's voice saying "Hello? Hello?" clearly wondering where Tim had gone. "Hi, it's me," she said. "I know it's short notice. But—do you think you could see us?"

There was a pause. "I can see you, but I need my dinner first. And if you can get Tim to eat something that would be good too. Soup, or something soothing. Call me back after dinner."

She leaned against the wall when she'd hung up the phone. Could she become any more exhausted?

"It's good you're going."

She turned around. Stared at Tim. He was nodding, talking almost to himself. "She'll talk you out of it. You'll listen to her."

"Talk me out of what?"

"Going up there."

"Going up *where?*"

"To Curtis's."

"You were *eavesdropping.*"

But Tim was talking as if he hadn't heard her. "Promise me you won't go."

She sighed. "I'm not going."

"Call him. Tell him you're not coming."

"I'll call him. But after dinner." She sagged. "Let's eat something. Then we'll call Trish too."

The food seemed to revive Tim, turn him back into himself. He began to ramble on about his new place. He could handle being on his own, he said. He was looking forward to it. He understood she couldn't be there for him anymore. He just wanted her to be happy, to feel better again.

She forced herself to eat. It was a wonder the soup went down. There was a huge knot in her chest. Beyond the sternum injury. An obstruction in her digestive tract. The soup had to slide around it. She swallowed gingerly. She barely listened to Tim. She was relieved he was calm.

"We should call Trish," she said, when they were doing the dishes.

Tim was giving her a blank look. "Trish?" he repeated.

Did he not remember his anxiety attack? She bit back an impatient reply. She knew all too well how out of it a panic attack could make you. "Trish," she repeated. "We called her earlier. She's going to see us tonight."

Tim shrugged. "I don't need to talk to her. I feel fine."

She was relieved. It wasn't fair to subject Trish to his erratic behaviour. Every minute he was a different person. "We have to call her though.

She's expecting our call. You have to talk to her, tell her you're feeling better."

"Sure, okay." He shrugged again.

She dialled the number. Handed the phone to Tim when it was ringing. Got on the phone after he'd spoken. At the sound of Trish's calm, kind voice, she was suddenly overwhelmed with gratitude. Gratitude for all that Trish had done for her all these years. She opened her mouth and heard her gratitude come spilling out. Gratitude she had never taken the time to express before. "I appreciate your having been there. Not just today. But all the times you've been there for me, all your kindness. Thank you, Trish."

On the other end of the phone, Trish sounded mystified but touched. They said good-bye.

She waited until Tim was ensconced in front of the TV, then went downstairs to call Curtis to tell him she wasn't coming. She was bursting with gratitude for him too, but kept the conversation neutral. She had a feeling Tim was on the upstairs extension. It didn't matter if he was. It didn't matter at all.

After she ended the call, she curled up under the covers. She was more exhausted than she had ever been in her life. Weary. Sore. Beaten up. Beaten. No, not beaten. Never beaten.

She lay listening. The house was silent. For once the TV was not blaring at full volume. Tim was up there. She could feel him up there. Maybe he was learning to enjoy the silence. Maybe he was finally accepting that it was over.

The quiet was not just outside. Something inside, too, was now silent. Some voice, some agitated ticking or vibration that had been so pervasive throughout her life she had barely noticed it. It was only now that it was gone that she noticed its absence. Was it merely the fight gone out of her? *No.*

It wasn't defeat. It was admitting the truth: she had failed. *They* had failed—as a couple.

It wasn't her fault. Or his. The circumstances were too much for them. Had she really been so naive to think they could overcome the odds?

She listened to her breathing—careful and shallow from the injuries. She let it lull her to sleep. Sleep was what she needed most. She would spend the summer restoring her health. She could already see herself in a small cottage on the Gatineau River. She could go for long walks. Maybe Ellen would lend her one of their canoes. God knows, they had enough of them. And she would sleep. Sleep in the silence of the country. Deep, restorative sleep....

There is money in the bank—more than promised. There is enough to buy a house on the river. A log house almost identical to Ellen's. She invites Ellen over and shows her all the rooms. "See, look, the layout is identical." Ellen is as amazed as she is.

The house is big, but she isn't lonely by herself. She walks through the rooms, savouring their emptiness. Planning how she will furnish them. She walks out of the house and up to where the railway tracks intersect with the road. She looks up the tracks. Overhanging branches on either side wave in the breeze, welcoming her. There is no one in sight. The sun is shining. She could walk along the tracks and not be scared.

She steps from tie to tie—small steps, like a little girl. She counts the ties. Something breathes behind her. The hairs of her neck stand on end—just before the hands reach out. The same hands, always the same hands, choking off her air....

Gasping, sobbing, panting, she pulls at the hands. She tries to scream. Nothing comes out. She keeps pulling at them, and suddenly they give way. And the scream comes out. Ear piercing. Strong enough to wake the dead.

And herself, out of sleep. She sat up in bed, gasping and panting, drenched in a cold sweat. Tim's arms were around her. They were holding her too tight. She pulled at his hands, loosened their hold. They were the same hands.

She screamed again, and freed herself from Tim's grasp.

She ran upstairs, blind in the blackness.

She came up short against the kitchen counter. Through her panicked gasps for air, she could hear him on the stairs.

Hide. She had to hide.

She ran into the bathroom. Climbed into the bathtub, pulled the shower curtain across. Shaking. Wishing she was still dreaming. Not in the middle of this nightmare.

The bathroom light was suddenly flicked on.

She pressed herself against the cold tile, eyes wide in the too-bright light. Unseeing.

Steps sounded on the linoleum. The curtain yanked back so hard it tore.

She covered her head, the tap was digging into her ribs. She heard a voice talking, felt hands grip her shoulders.

She couldn't hear the words. But the tone penetrated. It was gentle. Not angry, not threatening.

She let herself be pulled to her feet, pulled out of the tub. She let Tim take her into the sitting room. She let him hold her, rub her back.

She tried to make her body register the message that the action was soothing, that it could relax. But her body stayed rigid. Shaking.

There was only one message that registered, that kept repeating in her brain: it's the same hands.

Her brain would not register that those hands were comforting her. Even as they were.

Her choking spasm gradually ebbed. Her breathing slowed. But her body stayed rigid. Her neck ached.

Tim's words finally filtered through. He sounded as if he were speaking more to himself than to her. "It's alright. I'm here. I won't let him kill you. I won't let him kill you. You can sleep now."

She didn't move. As long as they stayed frozen in this position, she would be okay.

Hours seemed to pass.

"Come on, baby," Tim said finally. "Let's go back to bed. You're okay now." She felt him pulling her up.

"If you make me move, I'll scream again." She spoke quietly, but meant it. Her voice frightened even herself.

Tim's hands dropped. "Well, are you just going to sit there all night?"

"Yes."

He yawned. "Well, I'm going back to bed."

She watched him disappear into the kitchen. Heard his footsteps on the stairs.

She sat until dawn, not moving. Not thinking. Except for two thoughts: in the morning she would call Lakshmi upstairs to apologize for the screaming, to assure her there was nothing to worry about. And then she would call the bank. One last time.

On the phone in the morning, Lakshmi sounded preoccupied. "Oh, I didn't hear a thing. But I need to get my car out. I'm driving to Montreal for the weekend. Can you or Tim move your cars?"

"Oh! Yes. Of course."

While Tim was moving the cars, she called the bank. There was no reason to be put on hold first thing on a Saturday morning.

"Nothing has come in, Ms. Stockman," Claire said for the thirtieth time in five days. How could she speak so patiently? "But it's still early," she continued. "You might try again in an hour."

The money was still not there at ten-thirty. Or eleven.

Her agitation was increasing by the minute.

She confronted Tim. "You have one more hour. Then I'm calling the police. So call your friend Mr. Torrence and find out what's going on."

Terror in Tim's eyes. "I *can't*. He's doing me a favour—he said it would be there. I can't keep bugging him—"

"Then I will."

"No."

"Why not? Because if I call, I'll find out there is no money? That there never was?"

"No!"

"Then why did you cross out his phone number in your address book?"

"I didn't!"

"Don't lie to me! I'm sick of your lies!"

She raced down the stairs, as fast as her bruises would let her. She had to get out before she exploded. She needed a break. Just for the day. One day to forget about her massive debt. To forget about the mess of her life. She would go to Curtis's after all. To hell with Tim.

She scribbled a list of chores for him. Something to keep him occupied.

She found him on the couch, as usual, TV light flickering on his face. She held out the piece of paper and made her voice calm, relaxed. "I'm just going over to Bank Street to pick up a few things. A new shower curtain, some food. I made you a list of chores to do this morning."

Tim's look at her was suspicious. "You'll be back soon? You're not going anywheres else?"

She took a breath. "No. I'll be back for lunch. I'll bring us back something to eat."

Tim's face seemed to relax. He nodded and glanced down at the list. "Okay. I'll get this stuff done while you're gone. I should stay here anyway. Marnie said she might drop off some information on hunting clubs this morning."

He got up to see her to the door.

She made herself move calmly under his eye. Reached for her handbag in the closet. Said good-bye. Closed the front door behind her. Got in her car.

At the corner, she didn't hesitate. If Tim intended to follow her, if he thought she was going to Curtis's, he would go up the canal, heading north.

She turned south. The Saturday traffic on Bank Street swallowed her up. She would pick up a few things—food to take up to Curtis's. She had a cheque to deposit—a cheque she'd kept hidden from Tim. She would deposit it and check on the mythical wire transfer.

There was a metered parking spot on the other side of the street from the Fresh Fruit Company. She zipped into the spot before anyone else could claim it. She turned off the ignition and leaned back against the headrest. Exhausted. She didn't know why she was keeping up the charade. It had become an automatic reflex: pick up the phone every two hours, speak to Claire at the bank. Something to distract her from facing the truth. The truth was: no money was coming, no money ever had been coming. She let that fact sink in. She looked squarely at her line of credit. At the twenty-two thousand she owed. She made herself breathe. It wasn't the end of the world. She could re-mortgage the house if necessary. Sell, even. People went into debt every day. Much worse than she was. They survived. She would too.

She closed her eyes and repeated the words like a new mantra. *It's only money. I will survive. It's only money.*

Something unclenched. Some choke hold. She got calmly out of the car and locked the door behind her.

A car suddenly jerked to a stop beside her. The passenger door opened, and Tim was in front of her.

There was no time to react. She was grabbed, shoved into the back seat, Tim right behind her, his hand over her mouth. He yanked the door shut.

"Thank God we found her so fast." He was speaking to the driver. The driver's head was craned around, her mouth open in surprise. "She shouldn't be driving," he added. "She's having a panic attack. Drive us to your place, Marnie. She needs somewhere quiet to calm down. I'll come back for her car. I can't take her home. She's been crazy at our house. She thinks someone's going to hurt her. We need to take her someplace she'll calm down."

Unbelievably, Marnie was driving on. From the back, she could see wide, concerned eyes in the rear-view mirror. She tried to yell through Tim's hand. Tried to bite it.

"I brought her pills," Tim was saying. "She'll calm down in a minute."

The next instant her mouth was being forced open, pills shoved in. Her jaw was clamped shut, as if she were a dog. Her nose pinched hard.

"Swallow!"

She couldn't breathe. She was going to be smothered. She swallowed. Tim released her nose, but kept a hand over her mouth. She sucked in air through her nose. She could barely get enough.

Tim was still talking to Marnie, his tone calm, relaxed. "She's been talking crazy. Saying she's leaving me. She'll be better when she wakes up, she'll...."

The words faded out. Darkness crowded in at the edges....

She came to. Bleary-eyed, dazed. Trying to figure out where she was.

She was lying on a couch. Not her own. Someone was leaning over her. Tim.

His mouth was moving. The words began to register. "You're not going to leave me, are you Lu? You're going to come home so we can have lunch? So we can be together?"

She found her memory of the events. And her voice. "What the fuck do you think you're doing! How dare you—"

A hand was clamped over her mouth again. Something forced in. More of those goddamn pills. Her pills. Her nose was pinched shut. She tried to fake the swallow but Tim kept holding her nose. She was going to suffocate. She had to swallow.

In the background she could hear a voice. Female. Agitated. Marnie's. "What are you doing? You can't give her more of those. She'll O.D."

"She's not going to O.D. I just want to calm her down, get her to see sense. To say she's not leaving me."

But I am. She couldn't get the words out.

She lost track of the number of times she came to. The number of times she screamed her outrage at him. The number of times he forced more pills down her throat. Each time the scenario got hazier and hazier, her voice weaker and weaker. A videotaped scene replaying over and over, the quality getting worse with each repetition. It was the darkness that got more vivid. The darkness lulled her into a deep sleep.

Not the one she wanted. Not the one she wanted at all.

26.

I FOUND IRWIN ROAD AND cruised in second gear, looking for the narrow dirt road. When I found it, I turned left and bumped my way down the lane to the large white pine in the middle of the circle. I rounded the loop to the side where the path was supposed to begin.

The snow had stopped. I got out of the car. The relief from finally giving my testimony and the relaxation and peace Kendra had instilled into me changed to a sombreness that matched the late afternoon sky. But the sun was finding cracks in the clouds, putting a diffuse glow on the trees.

I found myself staring at the path, surprised at how visible it was. The deciduous trees on either side of it arced toward each other, making and marking a natural entrance to the grove within. From there, on either side of the path, the trees were lined along the side of the road, obscuring the pine grove beyond them. It was a row of trees whose new leaves shimmered innocently in the warm spring sunlight.

These were the trees you would see first if you came along this road looking for a woman whose body might have been pulled out of the river and discarded here. These were the trees that would invite you to go through their arch, into the hidden shrine beyond.

They were poplar trees.

I entered below their bowing branches into the soft silence of the grove.

I had not had a chance to really see it before. It was serene, beautiful even, with thin streamers of light filtering through the canopy of pine branches. The police tape was still wrapped around the trunk of the pine. It would, I thought, be there forever.

I sat down cross-legged, leaning back against the tree trunk. I closed my eyes and let my thoughts return to Lucy. She had come to me smiling in peace. It hadn't seemed like the ethereal peace of the dead. She had found that peace—somehow, in the midst of the nightmare—before she had been killed. Despite the harrowing last days of her life. It was something deeper than accepting her failure and her debt. Trish had said that despite her physical energy being depleted, there was something calm inside her. Where had she found that calm? When?

I kept my eyes closed, my breathing relaxed, my mind open. I asked Lucy herself.

And her answer came. She took me back to her bedroom, doped up on painkillers on Easter Saturday night, keening long, drawn-out sobs of despair.

SHE HAD HEARD THESE SOUNDS before—these long, low cries of grief. She reached inside her memory, back to her childhood home, up to the third floor. The drugs made it vivid, immediate.

She is six? Seven? She is playing in the attic room. It is a hospital room. Her dolly is in her own old crib. She has removed the sheet for the dust and put Dolly in. It has high bars to keep her from climbing out.

Dolly is naked under the doll's blanket. Burning up with fever. Soaking wet from the cold water she has poured over her to cool her down.

She is wearing her mother's white cardigan backwards. Over her face she has tied a tea towel, so that only her eyes show. It's hard to breathe through the linen, but she keeps it on. She can't be a nurse without the mask. Nurses don't have faces.

She tells Dolly she has to stay in the crib. That she is sick, sick, sick. "Your mother doesn't want to see you. You are too sick. You can't climb out. You can't get up. You have to stay here. By yourself."

The words give her satisfaction. Dolly's suffering gives her satisfaction.

Dolly begins to cry. She is surprised. Dolly has never cried before, except when she makes the sounds for her. She is not making the sounds.

They are not the same kinds of cries she would make. They are not the kind of cries she makes even when she's not pretending. These are long, low, sobbing sounds. Scary sounds.

They are coming from somewhere else in the room. Somewhere near the stairway.

She goes over to the top of the narrow stairs, cocks her head. She pulls the towel off her face so she can hear better. The cries are coming from the bottom of the stairs.

The stairs are narrow and dark. They are not supposed to be dark. Someone has closed the door at the bottom of the stairs. The cries are coming from behind the door.

Her breathing gets faster. She is beginning to shake and sweat. She can't go down the stairs in the dark.

She runs back to Dolly's bed.

Dolly is still crying, but not as loudly as before. She wants to hit her.

She can't stay here. Dolly is sick. Dolly has to stay by herself.

She goes back to the top of the stairs. She makes herself stand at the top and stare into the darkness of the stairway. If she stares long enough she'll be able to see better, the way she does in her bed at night. She just has to make herself stay there long enough.

The cries from down below continue—long, drawn-out cries. Like the dog down the street when it gets left outside at night. She feels the hairs rise on her arms and the back of her neck.

Gradually the outline of the steps comes into view. If she takes one step at a time, just slowly, she won't trip. There is nothing between her and the door at the bottom of the stairs. Nothing can get her. She hopes that's true.

The railing is her friend in the dark. She feels all its smooth bumps. She doesn't let go all the way down the stairs.

She is on the last step. Her heart has moved up into her throat. It's pounding away. It's loud in her ears. Blocking out the crying. Almost.

Behind the door at the bottom of the stairs, there is the sound of another door slamming in the distance. The cries abruptly stop.

She opened her eyes. Her head was heavy, foggy, from the drugs. Had she heard the front door? She strained her ears for the sound of footsteps.

Nothing.

Tim must have gone out. Thank God.

Daylight had come. Easter Sunday. She ached all over.

She rubbed her hands over her face. Winced as the motion of raising her arms hurt her sternum. She was spent, her face puffy.

Her mother had cried this way too. Why? What had she lost?

She eased herself out of bed and made her way gingerly up the stairs. She felt like an old woman. In the bathroom, she splashed water on her face. She expected to see despair in the face in the mirror. It wasn't there. There was something else. Something she barely recognized. Was this, could this possibly be, the semblance of peace?

How could she be at peace? Nothing had changed—everything was getting worse. Worse than anything she had ever imagined. Her bank account was draining away, dollar by dollar, even as she stood here. She was alone, cut off from friends, family. Her body had taken more abuse than should have been possible. But it was going to end. Soon. She was going to start over. In a new way.

Her mother had never had that chance.

Had she wanted it? She had done what was expected of her. She'd married a successful man. Produced children. Created a beautiful home. Looked after everyone's needs except her own.

No. That was where she had drawn the line. She'd taken care of her husband's needs. Only his. And sometimes Anna's. And even that had proven too much. She'd been meant to be a poet, not a wife and mother. She'd made do with writing in notebooks that she'd burned when she got too sick to write in them anymore. Just because her mother had always been hard at it didn't mean she'd found it fulfilling. Like herself, writing for the government. Fulfillment was a joke. Where had she thought she'd got this need to write? Where had she thought she'd got her need for solitude and space?

Her mother had claimed hers.

And she, Lucy, had suffered as a result. It wasn't personal. It wasn't meant to hurt her.

And so then, what had her mother lost?

Everything else.

Lucy stared at herself in the mirror for a long time. She breathed in a deep, painful breath. With the exhalation came forgiveness. The beginnings.

27.

....

I T WAS ALMOST DUSK BY the time I got home. I had less than half
an hour before the sun set. I changed into my jeans and a warmer
jacket and took myself down to the point. The river was the pale
blue water of evening, tinged with black moon-shaped shadows where
the breeze still riffled it into gentle waves.

I stood for a long time at the edge of the water, feeling my face illuminated, even slightly warmed in the April air. And then I retrieved the
lawn chair from its shelter in the bushes, opened it up, and sat down,
facing the sinking sun. Absorbing all the things Lundy had told me
today. Lundy and Kendra—and Lucy.

Had she ignored her intuition, too?

I thought back to the way she had talked about Tim before he'd
been released. There had been nothing but excitement and enthusiasm
emanating from her. It hadn't felt like she'd been hiding any doubts,
even from herself. But maybe things had been different while he was
in prison.

The sun was sinking lower. As it sank, the light became more intense.
It would only last moments. The revelations had to come now, in that
intensified light, or they would not come. I didn't care that it was an
irrational thought. Some truths, I was learning, were irrational.

But the truth about Tim wasn't irrational. Things *had* been different
in prison. In prison, he could be whoever she wanted him to be. He
had spent most of his adult life in one. There was nothing there to help
him define himself. No occupation, no interests—beyond what prison
offered—no relationship. He wasn't free to grow the way normal people

did. So he had become what Lucy wanted him to be. He could be a perfect mirror.

He becomes whoever he thinks you want him to be. Marnie's words.

He had been a mirror for all of us. Whatever we had expected Tim to be, he had become. I had been upset and shaking the night I found Lucy's car, and so had he. His reactions had mirrored mine. Who knew if it had even been conscious on his part.

There had been no premeditated plan to con Lucy. It was a certainty. The police had it wrong. A woman begins to write him, she offers him a glimpse of her own life, and then an invitation into her life—and into her heart. How could he, a man without a life, refuse that opportunity? He had taken on her life in the absence of his own, and Lucy had thought she'd met her soulmate. His capability for violence had come out even while she visited him in prison, but then, Lucy had a violent nature of her own. It had possibly, sadly, been the only genuine similarity between them.

He definitely had capabilities. Maybe he had *in*capabilities too. An inability to love. In prison he had offered Lucy unconditional love. But probably only after she had presented the idea to him. I doubted Tim Brennan knew anything about unconditional love. I doubted Tim knew anything about love at all. Lack of love in his life was probably the root of all his crimes. Certainly there had been no one to love him in prison. Probably not even himself. But he had a need to be loved, like everyone else. And Lucy had come along, and he'd sucked her love into him, with his insatiable need. And when he'd got out, he'd gone further—tried to choke off her will. To take over her life. Because he had none of his own.

I shivered. The sun had abruptly taken back its warmth. It was slipping behind the hills. Had I been heading down the same dark road? I thought about Quinn. This was not a man with no life or identity. Because he had these things, he had not, thank God, been simply a mirror for me. He'd tried to mirror me, that was obvious now. But the mirror had cracks, and if I had trusted my inner voice sooner, I would have seen them. He wasn't as perfect a mirror because he wasn't as "empty" as Tim.

But *something* was missing from his life. Maybe a sense of being truly in control. For reasons I couldn't begin to guess at. Drugs would have been a means both of trying to regain control and ultimately of losing it. So—what? He had turned outward to the women in his life to assure himself he still had power? To cover up his own insecurities?

Had everything been a lie between us? Maybe not. From what Lundy had said, it was true that when he'd first told me about his marital situation, his wife had left him. In light of the circumstances, he had probably not expected her to come back. He might even have been expecting to be divorced by the time the trial was over. But Quinn had likely not been thinking about the long term at all. He had, it seemed clear now, been trying to fill a void in his life *then*. He'd wanted to claim me, *secure* me, by telling me things he thought I would want to hear. And I had oh so willingly allowed myself to be secured. Because his controlling behaviour had come across as concern. Caring. And that was something I had been missing. Or thought I had.

Maybe I wasn't being entirely fair—to either of us. There was no denying the physical attraction. That went both ways. And he had clearly enjoyed playing the protective cop to the witness in distress. And the witness had enjoyed his protectiveness, even his possessiveness and authoritarian manner. I could forgive myself for that; I *had* been in distress.

I wondered about the other Ellen in his life. His wife. How far had she sacrificed her own autonomy before she'd seen the truth? Had Quinn been violent with her? I hoped he hadn't gone that far. If he had, I hoped she had been able to pick up the pieces and go on.

As Lucy had been intending to do.

As I was going to. Thanks to Lucy.

I watched the twilight gather the hills to itself and then felt my way back up the familiar path to the house.

The sun streaming in my bedroom window woke me minutes before the alarm. I dressed and carried my knapsack down to the point: a sole pallbearer. When I emerged through the narrow pathway opening onto the point, I caught a glimpse of red by the water. A familiar kevlar canoe was pulled up on shore, its paint gleaming in the early morning light. Marc sat beside it, his wrists leaning loosely on his knees, his face turned to the bare rock of the cliffs across the river. Beside him, Beau lay companionably. The sun behind them caught the honey gold of Marc's hair, Beau's fur, and the paddles lying beside them and seemed to be making an artistic statement about symmetry.

Marc turned at the sound of the rustling bushes and gave me a quizzical look. "Did you sleep well? You didn't get eaten alive yesterday?"

Beau got up to greet me, tail wagging. I leaned down to give him a hug. "Just little bites taken out of me. Nothing that won't heal." I set down my knapsack with its precious cargo and joined Marc on the rock. Beau settled back down on my other side. "How was the trip up?"

Marc's arm was around me. He pulled me in close. "I had to chop my way out of the bay, but it's a beautiful morning for a paddle." He looked at me. "I wish you had let me come."

"I know. But I didn't want you to hear it there."

"Where will I hear it?"

I nodded at the canoe. "That seems like a good place. Let's go do this thing." I patted the knapsack beside me.

Marc stood up and reached a hand down to me. He didn't let go. We faced each other. His expression was solemn but tender. "This is a big step for you, Ellen McGinn. Are you sure you want to get back into a canoe with me? I wasn't very patient with you in the past." His tone was rueful.

I gave him a teasing smile. "I will, if you promise not to dump me."

Marc kept his face solemn, but warm humour glinted in his eyes. "*Plus jamais, ma chère.*"

We headed downstream, passing the occasional drifting ice flow. Behind me I could feel Marc powering the canoe with strong, competent strokes.

We paddled to where the river widened and the current slowed, and then we stopped. I turned around in my seat to face Marc and unzipped the knapsack, lifting out the metal urn. Neither of us spoke. Beau's watchful eyes from the centre of the boat seemed to know. I took the lid off and let the memories of Belle come. Then I tipped the urn over the side of the boat.

The ashes pouring out made a rustling grainy sound—like sand and bits of gravel. It wasn't the sound I was expecting. I was expecting the whisper of dust.

It seemed to take a long time to pour Belle's ashes into the river. They clung to the surface only for a moment before disappearing below. I had thought they would get picked up into the breeze, or stay on the surface, not sink so decidedly.

The water was clear. An unusual phenomenon in spring. I watched the ashes make their way down into the depths beyond the light. I kept peering over the side of the boat until I couldn't see them anymore.

Then I looked up to find Marc waiting to hear my story.

Afterword

I had the dream the night after I spotted Louise Ellis's car. It was parked on the shoulder of River Road in Chelsea, Quebec, not many kilometres from my house. I didn't know for sure, then, that the car *was* Louise's. I knew her from Canada Post. We had both been contracted to work on the annual *Souvenir Collection*, she as the writer, I as the editor. We had become friends.

Two hours after I saw the car, I received a phone call from her partner, Brett Morgan: Louise was missing.

I drove back to River Road, confirmed the plate number, and called Brett and the police. Eventually they both arrived at the site.

That night, I didn't sleep well. I was worried, not only about Louise, but also about Brett. He was an ex-convict, with a manslaughter conviction behind him—a man whose release from prison Louise had successfully advocated for just the year before. Tossing in bed, I went over all the things he'd said and done that evening. They didn't add up.

It was when I finally slept that the dream came. My old school friend Joanna was sitting on the bed. Her mouth was moving, her lips still closed, as if she were trying to find the right words to speak. As if she weren't used to speaking at all. Or as if she were trying to translate into words a message that was coming to her in some other language or form I couldn't begin to guess at. The language of the other side.

When she finally spoke, it was three short sentences I have never forgotten:

Look in the 'opler grove. Write it in a book. Tell Mary she's safe.

An image came to me of poplars or aspens. I had no idea who Mary was. And then I woke up.

I had never had a dream like this before. It was more of a visitation. But why Joanna? I hadn't seen her in years. But she had always struck me as someone with integrity. Someone you could trust. Now she was telling me to search, to reassure Mary (I remembered she was Louise's sister.) And to write it in a book.

I immediately got up and recorded in my journal everything from the evening before.

I spent ten weeks searching for Louise, aided by information from a deep-trance psychic.

All during my search, and in the months afterward, waiting for the trial and then giving my testimony, I thought about Joanna's admonition in that dream. *Write it in a book.* I had written in my journal, but my journal is also a source of material for my creative endeavours. And if my own search would make a powerful story, it had been made possible by Louise's even more profound experience. I had to tell both. In fact, I made a commitment to Louise to tell her story.

After testifying, I obtained permission to attend the rest of the trial. I spoke with Louise's other friends and colleagues. I visited the prisons she had visited. I read two of her journals that had been used as trial evidence. There was a stereotype she seemed to fit: a woman taken in by a convict and con artist, trying to "rescue" him. Louise had not been trying to rescue Brett. I knew she had been on a specific journey of her own. But I didn't understand it. And I wanted to understand. I wanted to tell her story with empathy. To do that, I had to get into her head and her heart—into her soul.

It wasn't easy. We had been friends, but not close friends. And her growing negativity the previous fall had put me off. I had shut down the personal side of our working relationship. So I didn't know what had been going on in her life the previous year. But through the research and the writing, through the continuing dreams and encouragement I felt were coming from Louise herself, understanding and empathy gradually came. I was ready for the telling.

My first attempt was to write a true crime story. But even after all my research, I didn't have the full story on Louise. No one did. A more serious stumbling block was that my own story came out sounding so self-conscious it fell flat on its face.

Then I tried fiction—wholly fiction. But the things I did know about Louise, her circumstances and her character, and even the setting and so much about my own search were too compelling to fictionalize. After many false starts, I simply allowed to come through my pen whatever and whoever wanted to be in the story, whether factual or not.

The character of Lucy Stockman remains close to my experience and research of Louise Ellis. I did give myself creative licence with her background and upbringing. I invented Brett's background and the content of his letters to Louise, except for the note that appears on page 264, which Louise had copied into her journal. I kept the facts of their meeting and developing relationship, but the details and the dialogue are my own. I also kept the facts of Brett's previous convictions, and the Supreme Court examination is straight out of the official transcript. The wording of the "Missing Person" poster on page 56 is an exact duplicate of the wording on the poster distributed for Louise.

Ellen McGinn's character, circumstances, and relationships are entirely fictional. She slipped surprisingly well into the facts of my search. Her dreams and visions are similar to some of my own dreams but are derived mostly from the psychic assistance I enlisted. Her eulogy at Lucy's memorial service is cribbed from the one I gave at the service for Louise.

Detective Sergeant Steve Quinn is a creation of my imagination. The Ottawa-Carleton Regional Police were unfailingly professional throughout the investigation.

The remaining characters are either fictional or composite.

Louise did give me a copy of the *Tao Te Ching* for my birthday, with the same inscription that Lucy writes to Ellen. I never read the little book—or understood it—until I started the writing.

In all of the liberties I have taken with our respective stories, Louise's and mine, my intention has been not to hide the truth but to reveal it.

In this blend of fact and fiction, I found the freedom to do that.

A Few Last Words

On March 5, 1998, after a trial in an Ontario court of law that lasted six months and saw more than ninety Crown witnesses testify on entirely circumstantial but compelling evidence, Brett Morgan was convicted of first-degree murder in the death of Louise Ellis. He was sentenced to twenty-five years in prison without chance of parole.

On June 23, 1998, on the day Louise would have turned fifty, her sister Mary gave birth to a beautiful baby girl.

And on April 24, 2002, seven years to the day that he reported Louise Ellis missing, Brett Morgan died in hospital after a battle with Hepatitis C.

Acknowledgements

As a work of fiction based on a true story, *Tell Anna She's Safe* relied on conversations and interviews with innumerable people—family and friends of Louise Ellis, police involved in her search, and officials at the prisons where Brett Morgan served time. My appreciation goes first and foremost to Louise's family, and especially to her sister, Mary Ellis, for giving me her blessing to tell this painful story, for understanding my intention to tell it from a sympathetic, not sensationalist, perspective, and for allowing me access to Louise's two journals that were used as evidence in court.

My research really began the night after Louise was reported missing, when I enlisted the assistance of a deep-trance psychic to help me try to find her. My thanks go to Don Daughtry and the late Jean Daughtry of Myndstream for their assistance in getting answers to my many questions.

I am deeply indebted to Asante Penny for being with me on this journey from that first traumatic night, through all my struggles to understand Louise's interior journey, to rejoicing with me in the acceptance of the novel for publication.

Norm Barton set aside his understandable concern that I not have anything to do with Brett Morgan to help with part of my search and was a rock of support at Louise's memorial service. John Maisonneuve spent hours with me recounting his relationship with Louise and filling in many gaps in my knowledge of her. I know I raised some painful memories but hope that all the time we spent talking was in some way also cathartic. Miriam Russell generously answered all my questions about her close friend. I also appreciate the conversations I had with many of Louise's other friends and colleagues who shared their memories with me before I spoke at the memorial service. My thanks go to Peter Gallinger, Iain Baines, Heather Quipp, Brenda Wagman, Ron Pouliotte, Audrey Kaplan, and Tracy Westdale, and my apologies to anyone I've forgotten.

The trial was another avenue of research. I'm grateful to Ottawa Assistant Crown Attorneys Malcolm (Mac) Lindsay and Louise Dupont and defence lawyer Patrick McCann for granting me permission to sit in on the rest of the trial after I gave my own evidence: I filled seven notebooks with material. I'm also grateful for the support and information on police procedure I received from Staff/Sergeant Bob Pulfer (now retired) and Detective Sergeant John Savage (now deceased) of the then Ottawa-Carleton Regional Police Service.

As part of my research, I visited the prisons where Louise had visited Brett Morgan. My thanks go to all those at Correctional Services Canada who assisted me: Chris Stafford for providing me with contacts at both Warkworth and Pittsburgh institutions; John Odie, who allowed me to persuade him to give me permission to visit Warkworth; and Dave Phair at Warkworth and Donna Shetler and Mike King at Pittsburgh, who showed me around the respective visiting facilities and answered all my questions on visiting protocols. Any errors in police procedure or prison protocol are entirely my own.

I could not have completed this work without the support of my own family and friends. To my Mom and my late father, my gratitude for giving me the opportunities, especially a love of books and a literary education, that set me on the path. To my sisters, Nancy Beverly, Kathryn Missen, and Lynne Jolly, for never doubting my writing aspirations, and especially Lynne, for reading the first, long draft and showing me how to cut half of it out, and for buoying me up when the long process of submitting a manuscript for publication got me down. Special thanks go to my niece Meaghan Beverly for her eagle eyes on the galleys and all the "good catches."

And then there were my readers: Darrell Neufeld read every chapter (at least twice) with gratifying enthusiasm and egged me on; Akka

Janssen, David Black, and Vince Chetcuti gave me invaluable comments, edits and critiques; and Sandy Thomson helped me rework the climax and injected me with renewed enthusiasm and optimism when she declared that the most recent draft be "recommended for immediate publication."

Jim MacTavish provided me with medical and forensic information. Susan Towndrow kindly identified and spelled out the names of the Hungarian dishes mentioned in Chapter 18. And *merci* to Linda Landry for correcting all my French. If there are still errors, she's not to blame.

Excerpts from the Drowning Accident Rescue Team (DART) website (www.dartsac.org) are used with permission, including the change of pronoun from the masculine to the feminine.

It may seem odd to acknowledge a provincial park, but given the difficult subject matter I was tackling, I have a great appreciation for the serene lakes and warm Canadian Shield rocks of Algonquin Park, where on my canoe trips I found exactly the environment I needed—beautiful but also isolating!—to pull much of the first draft out of me.

My heartfelt thanks go to my fellow book club members, who graciously agreed to read the manuscript as a book club choice and offered valuable feedback; and most especially to member Luciana Ricciutelli, who happens to be Editor-in-Chief at Inanna Publications: she came to the meeting with something I was not expecting but will always be grateful for—an offer to publish. Lu's sensitive and incisive editing has given the book a polish that even a writer who is also an editor could not achieve. Thank you, Lu, for believing in the novel and in me and for conspiring with the other two Lu's—Louise Ellis and Lucy Stockman—to bring it to the world.

Finally, I want to acknowledge and thank Louise herself. In life, she challenged me; in death, she came in dreams to encourage me and, I swear, charged me with the telling of her story. Louise, I'm sure it took far longer than you were expecting, but I hope I got it right.

Photo: Darrell Neufeld

Brenda Missen's short fiction has been published in the crime anthology *Cottage Country Killers* and in the *Algonquin Roundtable Review*. Her fiction was awarded second prize in the Ottawa Independent Writers' short story contest in 1996. Her work has also been published in *Canadian Wildlife, Canoeroots, Kanawa,* and her local newspaper, *Barry's Bay This Week*. Born, raised, and educated in Toronto, Brenda Missen now lives on the Madawaska River in rural Ontario with her dog, Maddy.